CHALLENGES OF TAWA

THE SKY ELDERS

CHALLENGES OF TAWA

R.J. YOUNG

4 Horsemen
Publications, Inc.

DEDICATION

To my brother Ray. You gave me a place to stay when I needed it. You lent me money when I was broke. And you gave me the beatings I deserved when I was a bratty kid. Thanks for everything.

TABLE OF CONTENTS

CHALLENGES OF TAWA

HISTORICAL MAP REFERENCES

Big Sand: The Basin Salt Flats in Death Valley, CA
Blue Patowa'Kacha: The Ocean
Canyon of Legend: The Black Canyon, site of Hoover Dam
Crystal Cave of the Spider Women: The Cave of the Winds in Colorado
Earth Lodge: The Keweenaw Peninsula in Michigan
Endless River Agazzi: The Mississippi River
Gitche Gumee: Lake Superior
Kolhu: Chaco Canyon, New Mexico
Land of Everlasting Summer: The Four Corners region of CO, UT, AZ, NM

Manitou's Rise: Manitou Incline in Manitou Springs, CO
Norumbega: The Great Lakes Region
Pisas Vaya River: The Colorado River
The Demon Undercaves: Okawville, IL
Red Sky Forest: San Bernardino National Forest, CA
Shining Rock Mountains: The Rocky Mountains
Shipapa-Lina: Mesa Verde in Colorado
Shouting Mountains: The Coso Mountains Range of Eastern California
Spirit Fire Hill: Coso Volcanic Range in CA.
Swimming Bear and Night Way River: Mancos River and San Juan River
Tai-May Valley: San Luis Valley, Colorado
Ulah-Nane: North America
Wala-Wa: Concho, AZ near the St. John's River

PREFACE

This book is a metaphor for what happens to indigenous cultures when colonizers arrive. The eponymous Sky Elders are powerful ancient beings who represent powerful empires who arrive with their own agendas. The tribal community depicted in this book is fictional but loosely based on the lost pre-Columbian Pueblo people of the American southwest.

This novel calls upon the rich mythology of the indigenous people of the Americas. This meaningful folklore has never been appreciated the way other cultural legends have.

For the name of the tribe depicted here, I use the Hopi word Itiwana, which means "Middle." This represents how the tribe becomes unwillingly caught in the middle of a civil war between elder gods.

The story will also have an aspect of historical fiction because it will offer a fictional reason for the mysterious disappearance of the pre-Columbian Pueblo people. It will also proffer an explanation for the creation of the cliff dwellings in Mesa Verde, and why they were inexplicably abandoned. It will further incorporate the presence of Viking invaders as well as a reason for the Medieval Warm Period.

Relax, read, and enjoy.

R.J. YOUNG

CHAPTER ONE

*1228 AD: The Strong Debi-Kway Season of the
Great Turtle's Trek*

No living person had ever seen a beast as terrifying as the one Tawa encountered that morning.

The intrepid son of the tribal chieftain spotted the flying monster some time after he had ventured out of the Itiwana village. Tawa was not timid, but he still shuddered at the sight of the airborne nightmare.

He had wandered farther from home than most Itiwana were normally comfortable journeying. It was before dawn when he left his village, looking for prey to bring home and feed his people. He could surely impress his father if he were to return with some much-needed food.

He first saw the silhouetted, winged creature swoop out of the sky as he crept through some thick shrubbery. He ducked behind a tree and watched the flying nightmare use its large claws to snatch up a grown deer. The deer bucked and tried to defend itself with its long antlers, but the monstrosity lifted the animal as if it were weightless. Tawa could only watch in stunned amazement as the gigantic avian soared over the mountains with its struggling prey.

Unnerved by the sighting, Tawa abruptly decided to return to the familiar lands of his home in Shipapa-Lina. It was an exceedingly long walk back to the mesa. He was fit and trim but often lacked patience. Every step of the trip seemed to take an agonizingly long time, as if the day were deliberately slowing down just to irritate him. Exasperated, he blew his shoulder-length hair out of his youthful but striking face and trudged through the summer heat. He looked warily to the sky for a sign of the flying beast as he sought out the higher altitude of his home on the mesa, sauntering with his spear sloped over his shoulder.

He found himself in familiar country eventually. Tawa passed many of the small farmsteads scattered outside the main villages of Shipapa-Lina and Kolhu. His trek became easier when he reached the roads which the Itiwana of the twin settlements had built throughout the Land of Endless Summer. After a half day's travel, he could see where the gentle slopes of the mesa rose to a cliff over a steep escarpment, with a cantilevered rock overhang.

Tawa spotted the reassuring and familiar shape of the sun temple silhouetted against the dimming sky over the mesa.

The temple walls were constructed from stone, shaped like a half-moon, with a wooden timber roof sheltering it. Inside the main section were two large, round pit rooms called kivas. A walled-off section contained several rectangular and circular chambers.

The sun temple had been designed by the legendary Morning Star, founder of the Itiwana as a celestial shrine to the sun, moon, and stars. The original purpose for this celestial observatory had been lost to time, but it was still maintained and utilized today, used to monitor the movements of heavenly bodies. Pekwin the sun priest, who was Tawa's great uncle, preserved it well and watched the stars each night. Pekwin claimed to have recently spotted a blue star, which was a portent of something important to come.

Once safely at home, Tawa boasted about his adventure to the village healer T'Soona, but his story was dismissed. The healer assumed the size of the respective beasts Tawa described had been exaggerated by the active imagination of youth. Tawa was only sixteen summers old and eager to prove his mettle, which made it easy to dismiss such a spectacular claim.

"It was beyond belief," Tawa said with animated hand gestures.

"Indeed it is," T'Soona replied sardonically. "I suggest you spend less time staring at the skies and more with a fine girl your own age."

Despite his young age of merely twenty-five summers, T'Soona was the tribe's healer. This was because he was the son of Hano, the late medicine man. Slim of build and angular faced, he had a sarcastic way of speaking which could be very irritating. Doubly so since the healer did not seem to care that Tawa was the chief's son. Tawa's father respected T'Soona's honesty, despite his stinging tongue.

Tawa began to doubt himself, given that whatever he had seen was silhouetted against the sun and quite far away. Perhaps the poor animal grabbed by the flying beast was not actually a grown deer. Maybe it was only a fawn. Had he fooled himself into thinking he had seen a flying monster?

Tawa watched T'Soona build a strange device which was a combination of a sundial and a record of the seasons passing. He used the ways of the Before-Age, brought here by the revered Morning Star, harkening back to the day the Great Turtle left. By this measure, it was now the Strong Debi-Kway Season of the Great Turtle's Trek. T'Soona was clever with his hands as well as with his words.

As young Tawa walked away irritated, his eyes strayed to the Great Lodge, which stood on the edge of the mesa's hanging cliff. It was from there, just above the escarpment, that his father Yana-Luha presided as ruler of the Itiwana people. Young Tawa was the only son of Yana-Luha, the tribal high chieftain and hereditary patriarch of the Star Clan. It was his father who had ordered him not to stray too far from Shipapa-Lina.

The youth worshipped his father, but was angry about being condescended to as if he were just a typical child. He was the future leader of the Star Clan and might possibly be high chieftain of the tribe someday. He felt he should be allowed to prove his worth.

Tawa strolled into his clan longhouse and paced, musing over the day. *If only someone else had seen it, then I could be sure. But I doubt that anyone else will ever encounter it.*

The arrow pierced the heart of the pheasant and the bird dropped onto a prickly cactus. Pogum crossed the field to fetch his prize. He yanked out the arrow and placed the fallen bird into the basket with the rest of his prey. He had slain a half dozen pheasants and now scanned the sky for more.

In recent days, Pogum had spent considerable time hunting alone. The dearth of large game had become such a problem for the Itiwana, Pogum set his mind on bringing home alternate sources of food. He had already successfully caught some fish earlier in the day and was now bringing home a basket full of pheasants. It would not be enough to feed the whole tribe, but at least the children would not go hungry.

Pogum was a lean, sinewy man of twenty-nine summers. He had a streak of white in his dark hair. There was a slight scar on his cheek and several more on his body, from battles he had fought when other tribes had tried to raid their corn crop. He was once captured and brutalized, leading to numerous more small scars on his arms and torso.

Pogum was extremely self-conscious of what he deemed to be a damaged, disfigured body. He always felt people were seeing horribly mutilated skin. Even though they frequently told him his slightly defaced skin was not as bad as he felt it to be, and described his physical damage as mere blemishes, Pogum did not believe them. He was convinced that he was hideous, which was part of the reason he often preferred to be alone.

He hiked with patient determination through the arid valley under the mesa's escarpment, smelling the columbines and looking upward at the reddening sun. Pogum drew back his bow and shot down another pheasant with impeccable aim. This was a very minor challenge for such a consummate bowman. The basket was nearly full, and daylight was waning.

Perhaps just one more bird and I'll return home.

He paused when he heard the sound of someone or something treading on grass. Pogum nocked another arrow in his bow and spun around while drawing back the bow string in one deft movement. He targeted the sound, which came from behind some leafy bushes.

"You'd be wise to step out where I can see you," Pogum shouted.

A stranger staggered into view. He was a bearded man, wearing a jaguar skin adorned with eagle feathers and cactus spikes. He held what appeared to be a wooden sword. The most startling thing about the man was how his body was marred all over with tiny punctures.

"I ... found it," he muttered weakly, then dropped his wooden sword and collapsed onto some wildflowers. Pogum rushed to examine him. The marks all over the man were thousands of bee stings. Pogum checked the man's breathing and felt for a heartbeat. He detected neither.

He has gone from this world, Pogum thought. *Who could he be? What did he find?*

Pogum buried the man under a shady tree with a pile of stones, dirt, and muddy leaves. He said a quick prayer to Awona'Wilona the mighty creator. *Rest well, stranger.*

Pogum found he had lost his desire to kill anything else. Night had fallen and it was time to go home. With a sad glance at the pile of stones, he picked up the basket and began his trip back to Shipapa-Lina. He thought about the dead man, feeling regretful that the last thing this man saw was his scarred frame. He wondered if he should tell the chieftain about this stranger but thought better of it.

Yana-Luha has much to contend with now, due to the food shortage, he thought. *I won't bother him with this vexing mystery. I will return here in time with T'Soona, the healer, after we have dealt with the more immediate situation. It's probably not an imminent problem.*

CHAPTER TWO

The Kiva in the Sun Temple was unoccupied at the time; even Grey Pekwin the sun priest was still asleep. The main ceremonial kiva was often used for religious rites or important ceremonies. It was built partly into the ground, with a small ladder to climb inside. There were benches of clay and stone against the circular walls, with a raised bench for the chieftain. An adobe fire pit sat in the center of the circle. Ventilation shafts in the walls and ceilings vented the smoke.

Between the chieftain's raised bench and the fire pit was a deep cavity covered by a wooden board with a hole in its center. The board was painted with religious imagery. Periodically, the board was replaced for a new generation. The hole, called a *sipapu*, was said to be a portal to another realm. Grey Pekwin frequently prayed over the *sipapu*.

In the silence of dawn, fire and smoke abruptly shot up from the *sipapu*. It formed the Cosmic Pillar, which nearly reached the ceiling of the temple. The fiery pillar gave off no heat but emitted otherworldly energy. From out of the Cosmic Pillar came numerous black orbs, which swirled like insects for a time and then floated out of the temple through the ventilation openings.

Once outside, the multitude of black orbs immediately flew off in various directions, at unbelievable speed. The objects dotted the early morning sky. Within moments, they were all gone from sight.

Except for one. A single orb transformed into a golden eagle, with dark brown plumage, grey underwings, and a golden crown. The bird circled over the temple and flew loops in the air. This eagle was the current physical form of the Sky Elder known in legend as Manabazo, the changing one.

Manabazo had not been to this mortal world in so many years and gleefully savored the feel of the arid air. He happily took in the view of the Land of Everlasting Summer. Despite the dire reasons for his return, he found great pleasure in rediscovering these endless golden plains. He had never stopped loving this land during his long absence. He had missed every cactus, tree, fish, and butterfly. Despite being tasked with saving the Tree of Life, this was his moment of joy.

Below him was the mesa that housed the village called Shipapa-Lina, home of the Itiwana. Manabazo glided, watching the Itiwana for most of the midday hours. He did not want them to know he was there. Not yet.

He had no need to hide. There was not a single living person among the Itiwana who had walked this land when Manabazo had last been here. That was many generations ago, in the age of legends. The age of Morning Star, the bow priest. There was no chance anyone would recognize him, especially in this current avian form. They would surely know his name but only from the old stories. The Itiwana had no hint the exalted Sky Elders walked the world again.

As Manabazo watched the Itiwana from above, he was impressed with the progress they had made. The mortals had greatly expanded Shipapa-Lina from what was once but a small village on the mesa into what now appeared to be a thriving civilization.

The Itiwana had built a sizable irrigation system with water from the Deep Well and reservoir. They had constructed pit houses in the ground, protected them against the weather by timber and clay roofs. They appeared supported by wooden posts, with ladders for entry. There were also above-ground homes made of timber and tree bark, braced with wood poles, lined with straw, and sealed with mud. Their field of corn crop took up much of the mesa.

The Sun Temple designed by Morning Star three centuries ago—with some help from Manabazo—appeared complete and stood proudly among the smaller structures of the Itiwana village. He was glad to see they still had a place of worship for their gods.

The chief's longhouse, a single-family dwelling built for members of the Star Clan, stood near the Sun Temple at the center of the village. The longhouse was made of wood posts and bark, its arched timber roof lined with leaves and grass, and waterproofed with sap. The other dwellings surrounded the longhouse in a symmetrical pattern. The Great Lodge, where the chieftain's Shakowin council met, was near the edge of the cliff overhang.

The Itiwana village was now spread out far enough that there were multiple dirt roads running throughout the Land of Everlasting Summer, leading out of the valley. Many of them led to the Itiwana twin city of Kolhu. Small clan camps and farms were situated between the villages.

While the Itiwana grew their own corn, the men still formed hunting parties to provide game meat while the women farmed and the children gathered berries in the nearby woods. Manabazo could see some women weaving baskets to carry food and making pottery jars to store water.

The men wore a deerskin breechcloth around the waist. The women wore a woven rectangular cloth garment wrapped around the body and fastened over the shoulder, with a belt wrapped several times around the waist. On chilly winter nights, they would wear robes with fur and feathers. They generally wore footwear made from plant fiber or animal hide, such as moccasins or sandals. The tribe had farming tools made from stone and wood and bone. Their weapons mostly consisted of spears, stone tomahawks, and the bow & arrow.

Manabazo felt a sense of pride at how far the Itiwana had come from being the rag-tag group of water-dwelling refugees Morning Star had forged into a tribe so many generations ago. He would have to help their current leader if the Itiwana were to survive the trials to come, just as he and Kokopelli had helped Morning Star three centuries ago.

It was the Kisose, or Harvest Time, for the Itiwana. The people of Shipapa-Lina were quite busy this particular morning, since the corn crop was ready to be harvested. The women of the tribe were gathered to collect the maize. It was the most important time for the tribe. Every seventy-five days, the harvest became the priority.

The Itiwana were led by Yana-Luha, the *kikmongwi*, meaning high chieftain of the tribe. Muscular and square-jawed, with a prominent nose and a mane of wavey hair, Yana-Luha was a powerful man of thirty-one summers. As he ambled through the cornfield, he watched with pride how efficiently the women of the tribe handled the farming chores. His wife Atira had helped to organize the system and methods they used, and the women worked cooperatively to perform their tasks. The crops were more important than ever, considering the troubling food situation.

He smiled and gave some encouraging affirmations to the women as he passed through the corn field, before returning to the chief's longhouse. He had a substantial problem to address.

The children of Shipapa-Lina also participated in these duties. The little ones who were too young to farm or forage, however, were currently sitting on the grass near the Speaking Mound and listening to Hani the teacher. The children shouted enthusiastic greetings at Yana-Luha as he passed.

"Good morning, young ones," Yana-Luha said. "Learn your lessons well."

After he passed, Hani once more called the children to attention and recited the story of the early days of the Itiwana tribe.

"This is the way it began..."

"War!" *the deep, thunderous voice boomed, alarming the Dwellers-on-the-Water.*

The islanders of idyllic Tokapela panicked as the entire landmass shifted and began to move. Every structure on the island began to crack and crumble, while the water level abruptly rose. Yet even that did not scare the islanders as much as the magnificently deep and loud voice which again roared the word "War" in the gravest intonation.

The voice came from the tip of Tokapela, at the base of the speckled green protruding formation called Skull Mound, where their most sacred ceremonies were performed. This day, it proved to be more than a mere sacred site. The mound rose, revealing large eyes and a larger mouth. The face of a mountainous Turtle tasted oxygen for the first time in untold ages. The Turtle's flippers extended from the shell, which was concealed under the soil. It was the first time those titanic flippers had left the shell in eons. The Dwellers-on-the-Water had thought the openings to be shallow caves. Once those mighty flippers were out, the Turtle started paddling.

Over many generations, the inhabitants of the island had stopped believing what previous generations once suspected: The city of Tokapela was built on the back of a colossal turtle.

It was long ago when the Spider Mother descended from the Skyland on a web line and set down on the back of the Great Turtle, who had risen from the deepest canyons beneath the Blue Patowa'Kacha, the Great Water. She placed a tiny bit of seed on the Turtle's shell. It began to rapidly expand, flowering and developing, growing larger until it became the tropical utopia of Tokapela, the Turtle Island. Paradise on a Turtle's back.

They were friends until the Great Turtle fell into a long sleep and Spider Mother became lonely. She sailed away on two giant bamboo reeds. In her wake, she left a rainbow-colored web bridge behind her. This rainbow web bridge would connect Tokapela to the northern mainland. In this far-off domain, a group of unusual travelers had appeared out of a cavern from the Hollow Earth. They found an inhospitable world awaiting them.

Over time, these wanderers began seeking ways to escape drought, enemies, and predators. Fortunately, they found the rainbow web bridge and came to the island with their cattle. Eventually the web path vanished and the new arrivals, cut off from the rest of the world, became the-Dwellers-On-the-Water tribe. They lived in their private nirvana for centuries. Those who suspected they resided on a living creature eventually died and their progeny forgot the theory. This day, the truth exploded into their peaceful world, changing everything.

It was only the night before that the Blue Star appeared in the sky. Following that, the Islanders observed the distant, fiery pillar come down like lightning, vanishing beyond the horizon. The star and this "cosmic pillar" were the talk of the island all day. Many on the island worried, seeing this as a portent of danger.

They were right.

"War!" the Turtle bellowed again as it paddled furiously.

The little huts and cottages, which were made of horizontal logs lined with mud and mortar, containing central fireplaces, started shattering due to the tremors. The people were rocked by the sudden convulsions of the island. Panic ensued and they ran for their fishing rafts.

That panic increased when Unktehi appeared. The titanic, horned sea serpent broke the surface of the Great Water. The fearsome beast rose in front of the Great Turtle, casting a shadow over it. The snake-like monster emitted a loud, echoing hiss, and bared its giant fangs. Unktehi reared for an attack as the Dwellers-on-the-Water screamed in terror.

Unktehi lashed out, but the Great Turtle pivoted quicker than expected; the serpent's teeth connected only with the Turtle's impervious shell. Unable to pierce the shell, it pulled back, allowing the Turtle to attack. The titans wrestled in the vast waters, creating massive waves.

The islanders were thrown around as if by a powerful earthquake. Huge tidal waves washed over Tokapela, dragging them into the Great Water. The ones who reached the rafts were overcome by the large waves, which capsized the crafts. The women, men, and children of the island were helpless in the mighty current. They were drowning.

The horned serpent tried biting the Great Turtle on the throat, but the Turtle pulled its head and neck deeper into the shell, protecting its throat from the lethal poisoned fangs. Abruptly changing strategy, the Great Turtle quickly thrust its head outward. Opening its massive maw, the Turtle locked its strong, snapping jaws around the serpent. Unktehi hissed in agony as those majestic jaws closed around it. The snake writhed, unable to free itself.

Blood spurted in all directions as the Great Turtle snapped the Horned Sea Serpent in half. The split remains of Unktehi sank into the blue water. As for the Turtle itself, it resumed swimming, dropping below the surface, not to be seen again.

The survivors of the cataclysmic battle grabbed desperately at the damaged rafts and the driftwood that remained of their once tranquil city. Fearful and traumatized, they floated in the blood-red waters, seeing no hope of rescue or survival. Parents tried to reassure their terrified children that the turtle would return, as they silently prayed for some miraculous salvation.

Before nightfall, they spotted the ship. It was a wooden, double outrigger sailing ship, although they had no idea what to call it. They were not familiar with ships, yet they cried out for help. They need not have yelled. The ship was heading straight for them.

Aboard the craft were two brothers who called themselves the bow priests. Their names were Morning Star and Evening Star. They had been sent there from a faraway place by the Spider Mother, who had sensed what would happen and dispatched the formidable pair of warrior-heroes to save the people who lived on the island which was once her home.

Rescuing the Dwellers-on-the-Water, the brothers fed the survivors with their stored supplies. Changing direction, they headed for the nearest shore. Days later, they reached the coast of a lush green land. Morning Star chose to stay and safeguard the survivors while Evening Star took the ship and returned to the service of the Spider Mother.

Soon after they disembarked, the siren call of the most beautiful flute music called to the group. The mysterious tune invited them further inland. Morning Star led them, slaying bears and wolves to protect his new friends on their long journey together. The music led them to a semi-arid land, vastly different from the water world they came from. This would become their new home. Once the Tree of Life was planted, it led to the long summer, which has lasted till this day.

This new home would have a difficult infancy, however. The Great Turtle had warned them about war, and yet the erstwhile Dwellers-on-the-Water had no idea that it had but barely begun – and would soon threaten them all!

Hani concluded her story. "That was how the legendary Morning Star, ancestor of Yana-Luha, first created Shipapa-Lina. Tomorrow I will tell you about the war of the Sky Elders, and of how Morning Star slew evil Shakok. You can go play now. And remember, the Sky Elders are always watching us!"

CHAPTER THREE

"Nothing," Grim Hobomok grumbled. A failed hunt. Again.

Hobomok was the best tracker among the Itiwana and had long been hailed as the most successful hunter in Shipapa-Lina. He was the man they had always counted on to bring back the food. It had long been a source of pride and even conceit, knowing he was the tribe's greatest provider of meat.

That morning he had failed and not for the first time. In recent days, he had returned empty handed on three occasions. It seemed as if all large game had vanished from the Land of Everlasting Summer. Where were all the elk and buffalo and deer? After days of searching, he could not find a single fresh track.

I must find some large game, he thought angrily.

Hobomok was one of the tallest people in the tribe, as well as the most stoic. He rarely smiled and did not appreciate frivolous humor. His hairline was receding and tied in a long ponytail. He had wide eyes and a missing tooth due to a tournament fight with Yana-Luha when they were younger men.

He led seven hunters of the Moon Clan who had fallen into the habit of following Hobomok since his unerring instincts rarely failed to lead them to a large animal.

The clan men said nothing but were clearly surprised to learn that even Hobomok was unable to find food.

Hobomok's concern was not solely motivated by the idea of children going hungry. It was also about pride. As chief of the Moon Clan, his reputation was built on the fact he was a great hunter. He constantly bragged to anyone with ears how he was the superior tracker, and only Pogum could match his skill with a spear. He feared that he would become dishonored if he could no longer successfully do what had always brought him glory.

"Curse the gods for this," he hissed, forced to tell his fellow Moon Clan hunters they must return to Shipapa-Lina with nothing but the small rabbit one of them caught.

Tawa was sitting on a bear skin in the Star Clan longhouse, leaning against a wooden support pillar. He was meant to be studying the clay tablet records of the tribal history but was not at all interested in that topic at present. He was still thinking of monsters. His parents had not believed him either. No one who had heard his tale could believe it. His mother ordered him to devote his morning to knowledge and not tall tales.

She had a point. He was probably going to be the Chief one day; he was obliged to familiarize himself with the sacred writings. Just then, though, the concept bored him. Who cared about ancient clay tablets when he'd just seen a giant monster bird? How could a stale old legend compare to that?

He was aware his revered descendant Morning Star had guided the naïve Dwellers-on-the-Water to safety here on land after the Great Turtle had awoken. Morning Star followed the music and led them to the land where they organized the building of the twin villages of Shipapa-Lina and Kolhu. The Dwellers-on-the-Water became known as the Itiwana.

Morning Star led the Itiwana during the first great war of the Sky Elders. When the war began, the tribe stood against the intimidating Shakok, a Winter Wind Kachina who commanded his army of fierce Kiwaksa Two-Faces. Morning Star was the father of the Star Clan and named as the first high chieftain of the tribe.

Kokopelli, the nomadic flute playing avatar of the Sky Elders, recruited and trained Morning Star to serve Awona'Wilona the Great Spirit. Awona'Wilona was the *Ibo-Fanga*, ruler over the Sky Gods of summer. He was known as "The Unseen in Charge of all Life" and the "Earth Maker." The shape-shifter Manabazo joined Morning Star and Kokopelli as they opposed Malsumis, named as the God of Infinite Menace in the sacred clay tablets.

Malsumis was a Winter God who desired to destroy Yaxche, the tree of life, which held the *Oki* or Life Force that created the bond between man and nature. The Oki was also responsible for sustaining the long summer. Destroying Yaxche would bring on an age of winter. Malsumis' plan came to be called the "Enemy Way" by the Itiwana. Great Awona'Wilona's philosophy was called the "Blessing Way" because he believed there should be a spiritual union between all things, men, animals, plants, insects and fish, all swathed in an endless summer.

The Sky Elders were divided against one another in a long war. Summer fought winter in endless conflict—with the Itiwana people caught in the middle. This was where the tribe got its name. Itiwana meant "middle" in the speech of the Before Age. They became pawns fighting the Kiwaksa Two-Faces in an area of Ulah-Nane, now called the Land of Everlasting Summer.

Morning Star finally killed Shakok with an enchanted stone tomahawk and golden arrow. His Itiwana people helped the summer Sky Elders of the Blessing Way defeat Malsumis' Enemy Way of winter. Afterward, Malsumis was imprisoned by Awona'Wilona. The war was over, although many Itiwana lost their lives in a conflict they never wanted.

As the unwilling wife of the slain Shakok, Asdazza the Kachina nature spirit also thanked Morning Star for freeing her from the bondage of her cruel husband. As a reward, she lay with him for one night before returning to her realm of the Kachina. A season later, she returned to bring him his newborn twin sons, Sapling and Flint. She proclaimed that their progeny—with the mixed blood of mortal and Kachina, known as Mastop-Kachina—would be great chieftains and guardians of the mortals of Ulah-Nane. Sapling grew to become the first ruler of Kolhu, while Flint succeeded his father as the chieftain of Shipapa-Lina.

The respected Star Clan of the Itiwana line still contained the blood of Mastop-Kachinas, which had continued unbroken for countless seasons and generations. Tawa was the newest and youngest of that proud family line.

An irritated Tawa paced his clan longhouse, lost in his distracted thoughts. He contemplated the frightening creature he had seen, uninterested in the Sky Elders. It just did not seem important to learn about them for now.

Manabazo was still in his eagle form, flying in circles and looking down at Shipapa-Lina. The Sky Elder was enjoying being back in the mortal world, but decided it was now time to get on with the business at hand.

He swooped low, heading toward an opening in the chieftain's longhouse. He finally set his talons down on the edge of the smoke opening of the longhouse. Manabazo observed the Shakowin meeting, which had just begun.

CHAPTER FOUR

The women were still quite busy seeing to a healthy corn harvest, while the children and elderly were leaving the village to collect nuts and berries. The young male hunters were not having the success the harvesters were experiencing. They returned once again with no food, except some small game. Only Pogum could claim a good day's catch.

When more hunters returned with another disappointingly small prize, Yana-Luha began to fear the supply of large game prey was running so low in the Land of Everlasting Summer, he would no longer be able to feed his people.

Yana-Luha gathered his Shakowin council, which consisted of four important voices. Grim

Hobomok, the head of the Moon clan, sat fuming with bitter frustration at his failure to provide meat. He tightly squeezed a wooden stick used for beating birds out of bushes. Beside him was T'Soona, the healer, now representing the Sky Clan, since the death of old Hano. On his left was Grey Pekwin, the village elder, head priest and uncle to Yana-Luha. Lastly there was the chieftain's beloved wife, Atira the flute woman, born of the Sun Clan. It was her opinion he valued above all others.

They met in the chieftain's longhouse, sitting in a circle on the floor, to discuss the growing dilemma. None of them paid any attention to the big eagle perched on the ledge of the smoke opening, except for Grey Pekwin, who could not seem to take his eyes off it. Pekwin, a squat little man with a weathered and wrinkled face, gazed at the bird with deep-set eyes that seemed to have seen far too much of the world.

Yana-Luha was a charismatic presence and had been the leader of his people for several seasons, following the death of his mother, who had led the tribe for many summers. The head of his Star Clan had traditionally held the position of *kik-mongwi*. He peeked out of the entrance to the longhouse and glimpsed yet another hunting party, this one led by his cousin Aholi, returning without anything to show for their efforts.

He shook his head sadly. "I miss the days when I would look off the Hanging Cliff and see herds of elks and deer crossing the horizon. I miss the creatures the Great Spirit sent to us. My wise mother often said we would be punished for abusing the gifts of nature."

T'Soona tried brightening his chieftain's mood. He was a mirthful man and always tended to be humorous. "We should fish more often. The Pisas Vaya River is not too distant. I adore fishing. It's a wonderful time for contemplation and meditation. I often advise those I've healed to take some time relaxing on the banks of the river. And of course, we can use the fish."

"We do not need to fish," Hobomok the huntsman snapped defensively. His pride was hurt because his reputation as a great hunter was suffering. He was the age of thirty summers, but his hunting skills surpassed even the elder hunters of the tribe.

"The herds have simply moved to evade the hunt," he said. "Animals can be surprisingly cunning that way. But they are still out there somewhere. I will bring back meat, even if I have to stray beyond the familiar fields of the Land of Everlasting Summer. I promise this."

"You may very well be correct, Hobomok," Yana-Luha said. "However, it does not seem to matter. Whether the herds have indeed fled the Land of Everlasting Summer or if we have hunted them to oblivion, the answer is the same. We no longer have enough game near Shipapa-Lina to sustain us. That means hunting expeditions may take weeks to return with food for the children.

The Sky Gods are angry with us. This situation reeks of imminent peril."

Grey Pekwin was not looking at the others and barely seemed to be listening. He was consumed by the sight of the bird at the smoke opening. Pekwin was almost hypnotized with fascination, apparently seeing something no one else did.

"The corn crop is good this season," Atira said. The wife of the chieftain was the age of thirty-two summers. She was a tall woman of regal beauty, with ebony tresses reaching below her knees. "And we've gathered many types of berries," she said. "The children won't starve."

"The children need more than corn and berries," the chieftain replied. "I think we should begin raising turkeys as they do in Kolhu."

"Don't forget fish," T'Soona added, to alleviate the tension. "Fishing is good."

"Enough about the fish," Hobomok snapped, annoyed. He did not have much of a sense of humor, especially when his pride was bruised. He tightly squeezed the stick, as he tried controlling his mounting fury.

"It's a worthy idea," Atira said. "Perhaps the women could begin to sew fishing nets as well as baskets for the corn."

Hobomok was becoming angrier and angrier with each mention of fishing. He considered the idea of replacing hunting with fishing as a slap to his face. They were disrespecting him.

"Are you saying you have no faith in my ability to find prey?" he snapped. "You are only a woman and you do not understand these things. I note that your precious flute has not lured the herds back to us."

"Perhaps I should come along on the next hunt," she said. "You could use my help. Me and my flute."

Hobomok was so angry he almost snapped his stick in half. "I need no one's help on the hunt. A woman has no more place in a hunting party than she does in a Shakowin. You should be seeing to the corn with the other women."

"The corn is being tended to, Hobomok," Atira answered. "Unlike the meat you promised to supply."

Hobomok lost the last of his self-control and jumped to his feet. "No one speaks to me that way! No man and certainly no woman."

Yana-Luha immediately leaped to his wife's defense, standing protectively between her and Hobomok.

"Step back, Hobomok. I won't say it again."

Hobomok knew from painful experience he was no match for Yana-Luha in battle. The chieftain was a Mastop-Kachina, possessing the ancient strength. Despite each generation being less powerful than the previous one, the chieftain was still a mighty fighter. The two had fought in tournaments. Yana-Luha was undefeated and seemingly unbeatable. Although slightly taller than Yana-Luha, Hobomok was less muscular and far less formidable.

Aside from that, Yana-Luha was the *kik-mongwi* of the Itiwana, which meant that everyone in Shipapa-Lina was obliged to obey him. Hobomok attempted to hide any hint of the intimidation he felt as he stepped back.

"As you wish, *kik-mongwi*," he said, forcing the bitter words out of his mouth.

Yana-Luha scowled sternly at Hobomok. "I allow a certain amount of rebelliousness from my people because I am not a deity, and I know the present situation is very tense, but I warn you never to speak to my wife that way again, or we will fight and I will kill you."

Hobomok trembled with anger and a touch of fear, but common sense allowed him to hold his tongue. He gave a respectful bow to his *kik-mongwi* and backed away a few steps.

T'Soona tried again to keep emotions from escalating. "I love these free exchanges of ideas. It's a wonderful thing for everyone to share their thoughts and feelings, don't you think?"

Yana-Luha put the distasteful incident behind him and focused on the real crisis. "I fear the choice I may have to make soon. However, if all the big game has indeed vanished from the Land of Everlasting Summer, we may need to vacate Shipapa-Lina."

Atira was stunned. "Leave Shipapa-Lina? Live somewhere beyond the Land of Everlasting Summer? After so many generations here?"

Young T'Soona was equally taken aback. "This is a very serious suggestion, *kik-mongwi*. I hear your esteemed ancestor Morning Star screaming in protest from the afterlife."

"No one hates the idea of dishonoring my family line of great chieftains more than I, good T'Soona," Yana-Luha answered glumly as he strode with measured steps through the longhouse. "But I have a greater responsibility than preserving my family legacy. The needs of my people come before my honor. If we must abandon Shipapa-Lina to find a home where the game roams freely, we will do so."

Hobomok was pushed beyond the limits of his patience. He spit on the longhouse floor and marched quickly to the entranceway, without saying a word. His abrupt attempt to slip out without permission failed.

"Hobomok!" Yana-Luha yelled, his voice filled with the power of a hurricane. "Where do you think you are going? I have not dismissed the Shakowin."

Hobomok stopped and looked back, not hiding his disapproval for the *kik-mongwi*'s decision. "Before we admit defeat and leave the home of our ancestors, I intend to prove I can provide for the Itiwana, even if you cannot."

T'Soona and Atira both cringed, knowing what was coming next. They watched as Yana-Luha crossed the room, his face as dark as storm clouds.

"You spoke moments ago of your anger that others doubted your ability," Yana-Luha said with a low, menacing voice. "And now you openly doubt my abilities as leader? Are you disrespecting me, Hobomok? Are you challenging me?"

Hobomok was scared but stood his ground. "I want what's best for the Itiwana."

"As do I," Yana-Luha said. "And it is my judgment that prevails. If I decide we will leave the land of Everlasting Summer, then we will. Am I in any way unclear in this matter, Hobomok?"

Hobomok offered an insincere bow that reeked with disrespect. "Of course, *kik-mongwi*."

The smoldering impudence was abundantly clear to Yana-Luha, but he chose not to settle the matter now. This was not the time to discipline the rebellious leader of the Moon Clan.

"You may go now," Yana-Luha said.

Without another word, Hobomok stomped out of the longhouse. The rest of the Shakowin were disturbed by his blatant rebelliousness, anticipating troubles to come.

"Disrespectful boar," T'Soona said. "Stupidity follows him around like a duckling."

"Forget Hobomok," Yana-Luha said. "There are more dire matters to contemplate."

Despite his dismissal of the issue, Yana-Luha had the feeling Hobomok was going to cause trouble. In the meantime, he had a greater problem. He turned authoritatively toward Atira, T'Soona and Grey Pekwin.

"I need to be alone," he said. "I must ponder these things. Please leave me."

T'Soona gave a respectful bow to Yana-Luha. "Of course. And if you need a place to think privately, I recommend going fishing."

"Thank you, T'Soona."

T'Soona exited the dwelling. Pekwin was still looking at the eagle. He glanced at Yana-Luha and pointed to the avian, then left without a word. Yana-Luha glanced at the bird but did not understand what Grey Pekwin was indicating.

Once he and his wife were alone, Atira put her arms around her husband, and he embraced her tightly. No matter how bad things were, the world seemed better when she was there.

"What will you do, beloved?" Atira asked.

"I don't know, my dearest one," Yana-Luha said. "It's the gravest of problems. I need to think. Please allow me solitude for communion with my thoughts."

Atira kissed her mate three times. "As you wish, my chieftain. My husband. My love."

Atira left her distraught husband to the solitude of the chieftain's longhouse. He hated the idea of leaving Shipapa-Lina. His descendants had led this tribe for so many generations. His mother had presided here very well for most of her long life. How many winters and summers had passed while the Itiwana lived and prospered here? Yana-Luha felt like a failure for even considering the idea of leaving. Yet what choice did he have? If the food was no longer there, they had to go where the food was.

A voice broke the silence, saying, "The *kik-mongwi* has a momentous decision to make. It's the sort of choice that causes a lesser man to break."

Yana-Luha looked to the smoke opening, startled by the unexpected voice. He spied only the eagle. He stuck his head out the smoke opening to see who was there, but no one was in sight. Where had that voice come from?

The eagle spread its wings, looking right at Yana-Luha. "I'm here. Do not fear."

Yana-Luha jumped back, startled by the words. These utterances were not like a regular voice. They seemed to be audible whispers echoing inside the bird's caws. The way the bird was staring at him, it was obviously more than a normal avian.

"Can you speak?" Yana-Luha asked the bird.

"Do not be fooled by the beak. I can do considerably more than just speak," the bird said, in its strange way. "Now don't just stand there with a hanging jaw. You're the *kik-mongwi*, the keeper of the law. You have the blood of the gods inside. Show some Star family pride."

Yana-Luha forced himself to regain his composure. "You know of the Sky Gods?"

"I surely do, I cannot deny. Seeing as I am one of those who live in the sky," the eagle said. "I am the avatar of the Sky Elders, Manabazo by name. Perhaps you've heard of me since your legends have given me fame."

Yana-Luha was struggling to retain his façade of calmness. "Manabazo? The Sky Elder who helped my ancestor to fight Shakok?"

"Indeed so, and he fought well. I was there when vile Shakok fell," Manabazo told him. "I once helped your ancestor and now I will help you. Focus your mind since there is much to do."

"Much to do?" asked the still overwhelmed Yana-Luha. "What must I do?"

"I am just the first; there will me more. We Sky Elders are getting set for a terrible war," Manabazo said.

"Against who?"

"Against others of our kind," Manabazo explained. "We are not all of the same mind. Our foes are called the Enemy Way. They will be arriving any day. You know the legends; they fought us back then. Now they are preparing to fight us again."

"But why?" Yana-Luha asked. "What do they want?"

"To destroy the Yaxche," Manabazo said. "But we must preserve the Tree of Life."

"Tell me more," Yana-Luha said. "I need more information."

"Complete information will come in time," Manabazo said. "To waste precious moments now would be a great crime. We should not delay by talking. Deadly foes are stalking."

"This is tragic news, I cannot deny," Yana-Luha said. "But what do you need of us? We are just men."

Manabazo replied, "You are men caught in the middle. Your desire for peace now matters little. You cannot avoid this fate. You must prepare for this before it's too late."

Yana-Luha was unsure how he should react to this. The ancient gods had returned and were dragging the Itiwana into an unwanted war. "But how can we fight against Sky Elders?"

"My evil brethren will not come to you themselves, my friend. They have servants who they will surely send. In the last war they used the Kiwaksa Two-Faces. Now, they will use other fearsome races. Our foes have many adherents in this land. Those followers will come here with weapons in hand."

A distraught Yana-Luha was at a loss about how to get his people out of this. "We can barely feed ourselves right now. Getting into a war..."

"I will show you where you can find animal prey. You will not have to move away," Manabazo told him.

"That, at least, is good to hear, great elder," Yana-Luha said, with mixed feelings.

Manabazo fluttered his wings. "Not all will be good, I must say. There will be danger on the way. You will meet a great foe while you hunt your prey. If you are not careful, tomorrow will be your final living day."

"What danger?" Yana-Luha asked.

"You hunters will be hunted, by a beast from the skies. A fearsome winged creature with demonic red eyes," said Manabazo. "It rules the air above where you must go. It is powerful and deadly beyond anything you know. The beast A'Chiyala has returned to this land. To find the food you need, you must take a stand. This monster you must find a way to kill. If you succeed, you will be able to eat your fill."

"I know the legends of the monster A'Chiyala," Yana-Luha said. "I thought it was gone from the world forever. I seem to owe my son an apology. He saw it and no one believed him. I must admit, we thought you Sky Gods were no longer among us. No one has seen you for so many generations."

"We were gone, but we are once again here. As is the beast A'Chiyala who all should fear," Manabazo said. "The reason for our war, you will soon learn. You may rue the day we made our return."

"I wish to know it all," Yana-Luha said. "Yet my priority is food for my people. Tell me where we must hunt and how to kill the mighty A'Chiyala."

Manabazo shook his white, feathered head. "As far as killing A'Chiyala, I sadly cannot say. There is no known mortal way. If there was such a method, I would know. No human can slay this horrid foe."

Yana-Luha was becoming frustrated. "Can you help us defeat it?"

"I am forbidden to fight in this war, by the will of the Great Spirit. I must not battle these enemies unless Awona'Wilona commands, and I hear it."

Yana-Luha tossed up his arms in disappointment and annoyance. "You've come to tell me it's hopeless, then?"

The bird flapped its wings. "Nothing is hopeless, as your ancestor did prove. Just believe me when I say your tribe need not move. There are ways you can win the day. Awona'Wilona is with you, so be sure to pray. Meet me at the Deep Well in the early morning light. Prepare yourself for a momentous fight. And there is one more thing you must also do. Be sure to bring your wife and son with you."

"Atira and Tawa?" Yana-Luha asked. "Why would I risk harm to my wife? And Tawa is barely the age of manhood. How can he help against this beast?"

The eagle turned from Yana-Luha and spread its wings wide. "Do not ask why it must be so. Just trust me that he must go. Until the dawn, I say goodbye. Now, I surely must fly."

The bird flew off, swooping through the skies, enjoying the feel of the wind and the sun. Manabazo felt a deep sense of guilt for dragging the peaceful tribe into a war with forces they could not understand, but he had to obey his Ibu-Fanga Awona'Wilona.

Meanwhile, Yana-Luha stood looking out the smoke opening of the chieftain's longhouse. So much had happened in the last few minutes. The Sky Gods had returned. But why? What was this war about? Why were the Itiwana involved? Manabazo had intimated the reason for the return of the Sky Gods would be bad for the Itiwana. And what did his wife and son have to do with any of this?

So many questions swam in his brain. Firstly, however, he needed to prepare for the hunt tomorrow, as well as for a battle with a flying beast which cannot be destroyed. He had to prepare his people for a war.

The Great Spirit is surely angry with me, Yana-Luha thought. *I am being tested. I pray to Awona'Wilona I will meet the challenge, and that my family will not meet any harm.*

Yana-Luha marched outside and found his cousin Aholi, the son of Pekwin. "Spread the word to everyone in the village, and to the outer farms. Tomorrow at dawn, I will address the tribe at the Speaking Mound."

"Yes, my *kik-mongwi.*"

Atira was nearby and noticed her mate's distressed body language. "What has occurred since I left you, dearest?"

"Come speak with me," he said. "We should bring my Uncle Pekwin, too. I have so much to tell you that will make you doubt my sanity. In a way, I hope I am insane, because the alternative will be an abomination for our future."

CHAPTER FIVE

Yana-Luha did not sleep well in the long-house that night, after his encounter with Manabazo. His people were soon to be dragged into a war of gods in order to protect the Life Tree Yaxche. More immediately, he worried about his imminent encounter with the legendary beast A'Chiyala. How do you fight a beast no mortal can kill?

Worse still, his wife and son Tawa would be with him. Yana-Luha could not stand the thought that his beloved mate and child might be murdered by this creature. He used to tell Tawa stories about A'Chiyala when Tawa was a small boy and now the youth was likely to confront the monster whose very name once terrified him.

A'Chiyala was not actually one of the Sky Gods but rather a Poshayanki. The Poshayanki were savage battle beasts who served the high-level Sky Gods, such as Awona'Wilona and Malsumis. They were the attack dogs of the Sky Elders. There was no way to reason with them.

Yana-Luha was in the longhouse of his clan. Among those in the longhouse were his wife, his son, his uncle Pekwin the Grey, and his cousin Aholi who lay next to his wife Evaki. The chieftain fidgeted and sighed as he lay in his bed, which was a mat of woven grass, straw and skins, surrounded by a wooden frame. The distraught chieftain was so fitful as he lay next to his wife that he woke her up. She knew her husband well and it was obvious he was deeply troubled.

"Is there more you need to tell me?" she asked.

"You should go back to sleep," he replied. "Sadly, there's nothing you can do."

"I can listen."

Yana-Luha sat up, reluctant to tell her their son was soon to face the greatest danger the Itiwana had known in generations. "What I have to say, you most certainly do not want to hear. Keep a brave heart, my love."

Yana-Luha related the parts of the story he had neglected to inform her of earlier. He told her Tawa had to come with them. Atira lay silently, staring into the darkness, taking in every word. Yana-Luha had always admired her ability to stay calm during a crisis. Seeing as their son was in jeopardy now, he admired her strength even more.

"Our son must be kept safe," she said firmly. "He has lived only sixteen summers, and I will not see him sacrificed to a monster, even if the Sky Gods demand it. I'll defy Awona'Wilona himself and let the Life Tree die, in order to protect my child."

"I understand your feelings," Yana-Luha said. "But there is more to think of in this matter. We must feed our people and Manabazo is the one who can lead us to where we'll find new game. His condition for this service is that our son come along. As the leader of the Itiwana, I cannot ignore anything that will save our people. Consider also that Tawa will likely be the leader of the Itiwana one day and he should learn now that a leader must risk himself or even his own flesh-and-blood for the good of the people of Shipapa-Lina."

Atira stared at the ceiling as if she were making eye contact with the Sky Elders. "I have been the wife of the *kik-mongwi* too long. I understand the duty of our family. But I will be there too, and I will die defending my son against anyone or anything who would harm him."

The following morning, Yana-Luha stood on the Speaking Mound in a clearing on the mesa, at the part of the village furthest from the cliff. The entire village, as well as the local farmers, all waited for the chieftain to speak. Women, men, and children were curious to know what important information their leader wished to share.

Yana Luha appeared wearing the headdress of the chieftain, as was traditional. The Itiwana chieftain's bonnet was made of long eagle feathers, connected to a buckskin band, with a long train hanging down his back. He was led to the mound by Pogum, brother to Atira.

The Shakowin and Pogum stood behind Yana-Luha as he stepped up on the mound. The chattering crowd instantly went silent. The chieftain was at his most magnetic and commanding. He got directly to the point.

"The Sky Gods have returned," he announced.

The entire Itiwana tribe stood confused. The unexpected statement left them all dumbfounded. What did the chieftain mean?

"I have a story to tell you," Yana-Luha said. "You will find it hard to accept. I won't condemn you if you doubt, but I ask you to trust me. We have difficult days ahead."

Yana-Luha told his story and his people listened. What he described was so fantastic, they would not have believed it had it come from anyone else. But the trust they had in Yana-Luha allowed them to leap beyond logic and accept his tale on faith.

"I believe you," Grey Pekwin said. "I have always known they would return one day."

"Thank you, wise one," Yana-Luha said.

The crowd was silent, until a lad named Yoki blurted out, "Why do the Sky Gods want us to go to war? How can we protect the Yaxche if they can't? How can we survive such a war?"

"I understand your fear," the chieftain said. "I can't answer your questions, but I can take you to someone who can. Come with me."

When they all reached the Deep Well and reservoir, no one was there to greet them. Only a deer stood nearby, sipping from the water. Yana-Luha looked around, trying to spot an eagle. *Where is he?* Yana-Luha wondered.

The Itiwana were beginning to have doubts when they reached the location where their leader had promised them answers, but no one was there. Was Yana-Luha going mad?

Surprisingly, the deer lifted its head and looked over the group. "You've arrived on time, and I give you praise. We must begin at once since this journey may take days."

Everyone stared in stunned shock at the talking deer. Some of those present had only half believed their leader when he said the Sky Gods were back. Now there was no denying it. This talking deer could only mean the Sky Elders had returned.

"Manabazo?" Yana-Luha asked.

"Of course, it's me. Observe and see," Manabazo said. "I told you I would be here. Or do you know any other talking deer?"

"None that I recall," Yana-Luha replied. "The deer I've met tend to be tacit."

Manabazo raised his head, proudly displaying his antlers. "The gift of silence is a grand thing, but a deer will never know what it's like to sing."

Yana-Luha grinned. Despite his strangeness, there was something likable about this Manabazo. "Speaking of singing, you were a bird yesterday."

Manabazo reared up on his hind legs. "I can be a bird and I can be a deer. Who can say what I'll be when the morrow is here?"

The entire Itiwana village gazed in awestruck silence. None among them ever expected to be in the presence of one of the mighty Sky Elders. Everything Yana-Luha said was true. The Sky Gods were back, and a war was imminent.

"Remarkable," Atira whispered in awe.

Grey Pekwin stepped to the fore, savoring the honor of meeting one of those he had long worshipped. He folded his hands in a respectful gesture, bowing to the ancient Sky Gods.

His hoarse voice said, "You honor us. We worship Great Awona'Wilona."

Young Tawa neared Manabazo and examined him in fascination. The boy circled the deer, smiling excitedly. He had the blood of the Kachina inside him but never imagined he would ever actually meet a being even higher than a Kachina.

Manabazo was amused by his youthful enthusiasm. "Like what you see? Why not carve a bust of me?"

This was the most exciting moment of Tawa's life, and he felt vindicated. "I told everyone of the flying monster, but no one believed me. I am not afraid to face it again."

"Pekwin, take the tribe back to the village," Yana-Luha ordered. "I leave the Itiwana in your hands while I am away. I need to select those who will come with me because we require food for our tribe and monsters are waiting to attack us."

Manabazo trotted at a steady pace to the north, in the direction of the Shining Rock Mountains. "You speak true. There is much to do. Sunlight goes to waste. We must be in haste."

Yana-Luha pointed, indicating the people he had chosen to follow Manabazo. "It begins now, my brave ones. Expect this to be a most memorable day."

The still confused group gathered their wits and obeyed their *kik-mongwi*. They followed the strange, prancing deer northward, feeling a mix of wonderment and terror. Yana-Luha was accompanied by his wife Atira; her younger brother Pogum, who was a good hunter, as well as the best swimmer and fisherman among the Itiwana; the proud and arrogant Hobomok; Aholi, cousin of Yana-Luha; and young Tawa.

Along with these five tribal luminaries were a dozen fellow Itiwana hunters who volunteered for the dangerous and possibly suicidal journey. All twelve were fiercely loyal to Yana-Luha. If their chieftain was riding off to face a monster, his bravest men vowed to be at his side. Young

Yoki of the Moon clan was sent to collect spears and arrows for the trip, although they all feared such weapons would not be adequate.

Yana-Luha pulled Aholi aside. "I find it prudent to be prepared, good cousin. I suspect we may need more force than we currently possess. I wish you to visit with my sister and entreat the aid of Kolhu. Our predicament necessitates the special gifts my sister is blessed with."

Aholi, at the age of thirty summers, was the roadman of the Itiwana and usually entrusted with such missions. Aside from that, he was cousin to Molowia, the Casique Shaman Chief of Kolhu. He was aware she had a fondness for him. He was, after all, a naturally cheerful and likable fellow, with a pleasant and round face under the narrow strip of upright hair that ran from the crown of his skull to his forehead. Everyone liked Aholi.

"Of course, *kik-mongwi*," Aholi said. "A wise decision. I leave at once."

"A more trusted roadman there is none," Yana-Luha said. "Go with fortune. I must begin my own long journey."

Yana-Luha and his braves made the trip on foot because they had no mountable animals. The Itiwana had once attempted to train moose and elks to be ridden. Their ill-fated efforts were quickly abandoned. The contribution of these animals was limited to meat from that time onward. The Itiwana had become accustomed to walking wherever they needed to go.

Young Tawa was energized. He rarely got the opportunity to participate in hunts. The ruling family did not ordinarily bother with such things. Tawa spent much of his time studying his lessons and training to fight. Now he would be in the thick of an adventure. *I will show everyone I am a man now and can do whatever the warriors do.*

His mother, however, was concerned for him, wondering what part Manabazo expected him to play in this strange adventure. Yana-Luha gave her a reassuring nod to show he was not worried. In reality, he was hiding his own anxiety about the boy's safety.

Grey Pekwin watched the group of braves leaving. Ever since he had been told about Manabazo's arrival, the old sun priest had longed for a chance to speak with a real Sky God but today was not the time for such indulgences. He had been asked by Yana-Luha to rule Shipapa-Lina in his absence. He was the oldest man in the Land of Everlasting Summer and had been a close advisor to Yana-Luha's mother, the former high chieftain. He was one of the few to whom Yana-Luha would trust the care of his people.

As Grey Pekwin walked with a meditative pace, intending to check on the progress of the corn harvest, he peered up at the clouds and wondered whether the Sky Elders were looking down on them. If so, what were they planning? Grey Pekwin had a feeling of dread. He sensed the return of the Sky Gods would lead to nothing but suffering for the Itiwana.

CHAPTER SIX

Yana-Luha's party had walked for an entire day, trekking over many green fields and hills. When the group camped for the night, most were unable to sleep because they imagined a giant bird-like monster devouring them in their sleep. Atira played her flute, which helped keep the others calm and even allowed a few nervous Itiwana to doze off.

Sitting beside his wife as she played, Yana-Luha scrutinized the area, attempting to spot Manabazo in the darkness but the Elder was nowhere to be found. He hoped the shape-shifting Sky God had not abandoned them. Yana-Luha detected something moving in a tree. He spotted the shiny eyes of an owl looking down at him. The owl stared with the same intensity as the eagle had done yesterday.

"Manabazo?"

The owl fluttered its wings and spoke. "Sleep, good Chief. The night is brief."

"In this case, I fear dawn will come all too soon," Yana-Luha said quietly as he lay down to get some sleep. He felt more secure knowing Manabazo was keeping watch over them.

Aholi the roadman walked along one of the newly created roads made of packed earth, leading from Shipapa-Lina to Kolhu. He had walked every path in the Land of Everlasting Summer. Normally, he did so alone. On this occasion, he had some company.

His spouse Evaki joined him for this trip. This was somewhat unusual but not unheard of. It was useful when danger was anticipated, because a second person would be there to carry the message if Aholi was to fall.

Evaki would not have been Yana-Luha's choice if he had known about it. The woman was known to the tribe as "Woeful Evaki" because of her gloomy, pessimistic tendencies. This made her a poor representative of her people. However, with many of the tribespeople away on their trek with Yana-Luha, Aholi had to pick a replacement and he enjoyed his wife's company.

It was a mystery to the tribe how the upbeat and optimistic Aholi could co-exist, let alone love the eternally depressing Evaki. She was not only discouraging, but her long face with the prominent cheeks and jaw, along with her large teeth, caused some children to call her "Lady moose face." None of this mattered to Aholi, however. He loved her.

He was not blind to her downbeat nature. "Be sure to let me do the talking, sweet one."

"She probably won't help us anyway," Evaki said in her deadpan way. "This is a fool's journey."

"Just leave matters to me, cherry blossom," he replied.

They came to a creek where a log was used as a bridge. Aholi slowed down. "This is the spot I told you about. Stay calm and follow my lead. Everything will be fine."

"It will probably kill us," she stated.

He signaled for her to stop. "I've done this many times. Just trust me and do as I do."

"Very well. Let's get this over with."

Aholi took a few steps closer to the creek and the log bridge began moving. It abruptly bounced into the air and a furry head appeared from under it. Despite having seen this many times, Aholi was nervous. The normally dispassionate Evaki backed up several steps.

Wishpoosh the Beaver Spirit emerged from the water. Wishpoosh was a Poshayanki, one of the battle beasts left over from the previous Sky Elder war. Large as a Mastodon, the huge creature's flat tail was rowed with sharp, boney spikes. It had taken up residence in the creek and over time had bonded with the people of Kolhu, thanks to the special abilities of their shaman chief Molowia, a Mastop-Kachina. It now acted as a guardian on the main road to Kolhu.

Aholi stood calmly as possible, having been through this repeatedly. As the massive Beaver approached him, he showed no outward fear. The creature could sense courage, as well as the person's honor and integrity.

Wishpoosh plodded toward Aholi, looking down at the Itiwana roadman. The Beaver pressed a big snout against Aholi, sniffing him vigorously.

"You remember me, don't you, Wishpoosh?" Aholi said. "I'm a friend."

It's going to kill him, Evaki thought fearfully.

After a few tense moments, Wishpoosh moved away and returned to the creek, vanishing under the water's surface. Aholi let out a relieved breath, then regained his composure.

"You see, all is well," he said, holding out his hand. "Come along now."

She took his hand. "It'll probably kill us on the way back."

He chuckled. "Why do I love you so much, my apple blossom?"

"It must be my natural beauty and charm," she replied. "Of course, I'll be old someday."

He led her by the hand as they continued down the road. "And remember to let me do the talking."

Yana-Luha and his Itiwana group had resumed walking just after dawn the second day and continued without a break for several hours. They crossed over many more hills and waded through a shallow stream. It concerned them how there were no large game animals to be found. It seemed Manabazo was their only hope for finding food.

Manabazo resumed his deer form and led the band of braves to the outer fringes of the Land of Everlasting Summer. By mid-day, Hobomok the hunter was becoming impatient, tired of this endless walking. When was he going to get to hunt something? If there was a beast needing to be slain, Hobomok was determined he be the one to do it. He loved to outshine Yana-Luha.

Hobomok hated the tradition inferring those with the bloodline of Morning Star were to always be voted leader. Hobomok felt the best hunter should be the ruler of the Itiwana, and that would be him, not Yana-Luha.

Atira worried about her reckless son. She dreaded what was awaiting them. Young Tawa, on the other hand, was savoring every minute of the trip. He loved being on an adventure. Deep down, he was afraid of meeting the flying monster again but the thrill of seeing new lands and proving his worth to his father overcame his fear.

At the hottest part of the day, the Itiwana group came across the torn and half-devoured remains of three elk. Something had savagely slain and eaten the animals. Everyone present was chilled by the sight of the dead elk.

"I think we now know what happened to all the large game in the area," Yana-Luha said. "They were either killed or chased away by this beast A'Chiyala."

Before anyone could respond, the moment they all feared finally occurred. A loud, frightening shriek came from above, sounding like the fusion of the caw of a bird of prey and the wail of a banshee. A shadow passed over the group. Alarmed, they all looked up and froze, staring in terrified awe at what they saw. A'Chiyala, had arrived.

A'Chiyala was a fearsome looking beast. It had the appearance of a vulture but was larger than a moose, with a wingspread three-times that long. A'Chiyala had three legs, each one having six razor-sharp clawed talons. Its eyes were blood-red. Whenever it shrieked, it sounded as if the bird-beast was saying "Die."

A'Chiyala swooped low toward the hunting party with astonishing speed. Yana-Luha was the first of the men to gather his wits while the rest were still staring in fixated horror. He took command of the situation.

"Spread out and stay low," he commanded.

His authoritative voice shook the rest of the party from their transfixed state. They scattered, keeping low to the ground. A'Chiyala homed-in on one of the hunters and raked the man's back with talons that could cut through stone. The man screamed as his back and spine were sliced open.

A'Chiyala grabbed his victim, carried him up hundreds of yards into the air and then dropped him. The hunter's body shattered on impact.

As A'Chiyala dived for a second attack, Yana-Luha cried "Weapons! Attack!"

All the members of the party except for Atira and Manabazo focused their weapons on the approaching beast. Arrows and spears struck A'Chiyala but did not stop the aerial monster. A'Chiyala kept coming, and this time was focused on Tawa.

Tawa realized the flying nightmare A'Chiyala was heading straight for him. Filled with the foolish bravery of youth and unwilling to appear fearful in front of his father, Tawa stood his ground, firing an arrow. He aimed for A'Chiyala's scarlet, unblinking eyes. The shot was well aimed and missed the beast's eye by less than an inch. There was no time for a second shot.

Atira was horrified as the monster quickly closed in on her son. She was not a warrior and had no weapons, but she did have her flute. With no other recourse, she lifted the flute to her lips and began to blow. The sound did not have the tranquilizing effect on A'Chiyala that it had on other beasts but did distract the air monster, making it take its eyes off the boy for a moment.

Yana-Luha leaped to his son's defense, tackling the boy to the ground and protecting the lad with his own body. Since A'Chiyala had been distracted by the music, it was unaware its victim had been shoved to the ground. Too late to change its trajectory, A'Chiyala stretched out its claws, slicing several gashes in Yana-Luha's shoulder. The wounds weren't deep, but they were painful. Still, it was worth it to the chieftain to see his son safe. At least, for the moment.

A'Chiyala circled once more and made another dive, this time heading directly for Atira. She froze as the shadow of the hideous Poshayanki fell over her. Its "Die" scream terrified her. Pogum raced to defend his sister but feared he was not going to make it in time. Yana-Luha also realized in horror he was too far away to save his wife.

"No!" he screamed, as those terrible talons were poised to rip apart the woman he loved.

CHAPTER SEVEN

The fierce A'Chiyala swooped with savage fury toward Atira, eager to rip her to pieces. None of the other Itiwana were close enough to help her. Yana-Luha was horrified that he would not be able to save his wife.

Just as the creature's talons were inches away from its prey, the aerial beast was butted off course by the antlers of Manabazo in his deer form. Although Manabazo was less powerful than A'Chiyala and had been instructed by Awona'Wilona not to engage any followers of Malsumis in battle, he could not stand by and watch Atira be mauled by the savage A'Chiyala.

Manabazo knocked A'Chiyala slightly off course, just enough that the monster missed its mark. The flying terror was not harmed by the impact but was enraged someone had come between itself and its prey.

A'Chiyala hovered, locking eyes furiously with Manabazo. A'Chiyala was not known for being intelligent. Its purpose was simply to attack. However, A'Chiyala did recognize a Sky Elder when it saw one. The creature was confused. A'Chiyala was a Poshayanki, war beasts that served the Sky Elders. A'Chiyala was loyal to Malsumis, and it was also dimly aware that some of the lesser Sky Elders opposed mighty Malsumis. However, A'Chiyala was not the smartest of the Poshayanki, and sometimes got confused about who was on whose side in the war of the Sky Gods. Should it kill Manabazo? Would Malsumis be angry if it did?

The powerful but simple beast made the only decision it could. It retreated to ask for new orders. A'Chiyala needed to confirm whether or not Manabazo was one of Awona'Wilona's followers before killing him. The sky monster ascended and soared away over the mountains.

Manabazo himself was relieved he did not have to fight A'Chiyala. Aside from the fact Manabazo had been instructed to limit his participation to being an advisor, he was well aware that A'Chiyala was beyond the power of a lower god to defeat. The creature would surely kill him next time. This was merely a temporary reprieve and the monster would surely be back.

The hunting party watched A'Chiyala fly away. After taking a moment to feel the relief that they had survived, they took stock of their situation. One man was dead. Atira rushed to Yana-Luha and Tawa.

"Are you hurt?" she asked them.

Tawa rose undaunted, roughly wiping the dirt off himself and glaring hatefully at the departing A'Chiyala. He was embarrassed at having needed to be saved from this ugly monster.

"I am unhurt, mother," he said.

The relieved Atira turned her attention to her husband, who was bleeding from his shoulder. "You foolishly brave and exhilaratingly magnificent man. Is it very painful?"

"Only in an extremely agonizing way, but I've had worse," he said, then patted his son on the back. "You were very brave, son, and that arrow shot was nearly perfect. The beast almost ended up with one eye to balance out its three claws. Quite impressive, considering the circumstances. I'm a proud father at this moment."

"I'll make you prouder next time," Tawa responded.

Atira did not want to hear that. "Next time you'll let your father and the older hunters handle things," she snapped at him.

While she scolded her son, she was removing some of the healer cloths from the medicine kit T'Soona had given her. She wrapped the cloths around Yana-Luha's bleeding shoulder.

"Don't chastise the boy, my love," Yana-Luha told her. "He did well. Did you not see that arrow shot? He was wonderfully calm in the face of horror. He'll need that courage again soon, because I don't think the beast will be satisfied with just one victim."

"It's true. The danger is not past," Ancient Manabazo said. "Of the monster A'Chiyala, we have not seen the last."

Once Atira finished tending to his shoulder, Yana-Luha joined the rest of the party who were gathered around the ravaged body of the slain hunter. The chieftain kneeled beside the body and closed the victim's eyes. Yana-Luha felt great guilt for bringing the man on this quest.

"We need to bury him," the chieftain ordered.

The slain hunter was covered with a pile of rocks and stones. A traditional ceremony for the dead was performed. The ceremony concluded with a mass, simultaneous cry toward the heavens to announce that an Itiwana was ascending. A moment of silence followed the ceremony.

"You will not be forgotten," Yana-Luha said quietly.

When the ceremony was over, it was time to move on. Yana-Luha looked to Manabazo to lead the way. "We should resume our trip now. I want to be away from this place. And I also want to thank you for saving the woman I love."

"I was outmatched, I confess," Manabazo responded, "but I could do no less. However, there is no time to talk. We must resume our long, long walk."

The hunting party recommenced its trek along the foothills of the Shining Rock Mountains. The copper color of the stone seemed to shine in the blistering sun. They walked until the early evening hours. The group continued watching the skies, dreading the sight of A'Chiyala swooping through the clouds or the sound of that terrible cry.

Manabazo galloped near to Yana-Luha to advise him. "In a short time, A'Chiyala will return. His primal rage will quake and burn. His masters will command him to slay. This will be a very bloody day."

"Who precisely are his masters?" Yana-Luha asked. "Does he take his commands directly from Malsumis or are there other Sky Gods in between who the monster answers to? Are we being watched? Is the enemy close? What is this foe planning?"

Manabazo flicked his tail. "I cannot be sure. I wish I knew more. There are things my senses cannot see. Something is blocking me. I wish I could travel to investigate with my own sharp eye. However, the enemy would know if I were nearby. Malsumis may still be locked away. Sadly, I cannot truly say. He has servants who are working to set him free. You do not want that to happen—trust me."

"Then perhaps we should find out for certain," Yana-Luha suggested. "Information is power. Do you know where Malsumis was imprisoned?"

"From the fiery peaks of Spirit Fire Hill, he waits at rest. He was trapped by Awona'Wilona in the Shouting Mountains of the West."

Yana-Luha looked over his men, searching for a certain face. "Pogum, come here."

Pogum quickly responded to his chieftain's summons. The formidable Pogum had proven his unshakeable devotion to his chieftain on many occasions. When he was caught and tortured and scarred, he was rescued by Yana-Luha. This traumatic experience made him extremely loyal to his leader, even before the chieftain's marriage to Atira merged their clans.

"Yes, my *kik-mongwi*?" he asked, always ready to be of service.

"I need you to perform a very important errand for me, my friend," Yana-Luha informed the devoted Pogum. "You will not enjoy this trip, but someone must go and I've chosen you."

"My curiosity is aroused," Pogum replied.

"I need someone to make the long journey to the Shouting Mountains," Yana-Luha announced. "There seem to be events taking place there which will affect the Sky Elders, the Itiwana, and perhaps all of Ulah-Nane."

"These are intelligences unknown to me, fascinating as they seem," Pogum said.

"They won't be unknown to you for long," Yana-Luha answered. "Manabazo and I need to know if Malsumis's servants have freed him yet. You're the fastest runner, the best climber, the finest swimmer, and the most skilled in canoeing.

You can cover the distance faster than anyone. I now charge you to make the trip as quickly as possible and return to us. You will tell us what in Awona'Wilona's name is happening there."

Pogum bowed his head respectfully. "I am honored you've chosen me for this. I will make you and my clan proud. Tell no man that Pogum hesitated in his duty. I leave at once and I will not return until I know all that can be known."

"You are a good man, Pogum," Yana-Luha said. "May Awona'Wilona protect you."

Pogum said goodbye to his sister Atira and his nephew Tawa. It would be weeks or even months before he returned. He did not mind traveling alone for so long because no one would have to see the scars he found so hideous. Pogum hoped the information he would eventually bring home would not come too late.

Aholi and Evaki reached the Itiwana community of Kolhu. Surveying the area, Aholi was surprised by how much Kolhu had grown since he was last here. They had expanded, not only in size but also in the development of the dwellings. This was not a village. It was a city.

The people of Kolhu had built many large dwellings called great houses. They were constructed from adobe bricks, made of earth, sand, clay and dung. Several levels tall, the structures were designed with hundreds of spacious rooms and kivas, surrounding a central plaza. The dwellings had grain storage spaces. Each great house was like its own small village.

There was an elegant and geometric design to the city, which may have been oriented to the moon and sun. Aholi regarded their sophisticated irrigation systems, as well as the farming area, which included a wild turkey enclosure.

Near the canyon wall called Threatening Rock was the grandest of the great houses, known as the Sun Dagger House. Covering several acres, the four-level, nine-hundred-room structure was semicircular with thirty-two smaller kivas and three great kivas. It was the center of religion and government for the Itiwana of Kolhu.

"Magnificent," Aholi said.

Even woeful Evaki could not think of anything negative to say about the amazingly modern city, and so remained silent. They were greeted by their fellow Itiwana brothers and sisters, who had not seen him in quite a long while. Most of them were unfamiliar with his wife and she did not exactly endear herself, due to her dour attitude. Still, they offered to show her around while Aholi was ushered to meet their leader Molowia.

Inside the Casique's chamber on the ground level of the Sun Dagger House, Molowia sat cross-legged on a bale of straw, eyes closed, facing a small fire. She was a short, pudgy woman, with rubicund skin and frizzy hair. Her hands were outstretched forward toward the flames, and she whispered an almost inaudible chant. Aholi remained silent, not wanting to be disrespectful by disturbing her.

"Welcome, cousin Aholi," Molowia said, eyes still closed.

"Hello, Molowia. It has been some considerable time. It's good to be with you again."

Molowia opened her eyes. "Sit, please."

Aholi sat upon a second bale of straw. Molowia somehow rotated towards him without using her hands. She did not smile. Aholi noticed she was unusually grim. Did she know what he was going to ask? She did possess inexplicable abilities.

"Cousin, we have a grave problem," Aholi said. "You will be amazed to know..."

"...That the Sky Gods have returned?" Molowia said. "I am aware. Horribly aware. I have had portentous dreams, which compelled me to perform a vision quest. And what I saw frightened me. It would terrify any sane mind. Yes, I know about this horrid war and want no part in it. Do not ask."

Aholi was surprised by the suddenness of her rebuke. "Cousin, your brother needs your help. The Itiwana need your help. Your abilities will..."

She held up a finger to silence him. "Perhaps I should speak louder. Did you not hear when I said not to ask me this? Look around you, cousin. Look at the beauty of Kolhu. We have built something here. This city is the most modern in all Ulah-Nane. We live in peace, and we eat well, and my people are happy. Why in the name of sanity would I drag them into a war we have no part of?"

"But we need you," Aholi said. "Your brother..."

"My brother is an obsolete fool," she said. "He stubbornly listens to old Pekwin, who still worships these beings who have never done anything for us. Generations ago they involved us in their wars and when they were done with us, they abandoned us to survive on our own. They did it before and they are doing it once again. Don't help them. Do not become savages in the service of savage gods. We will be all the worse for it."

Aholi was becoming agitated. "We may have no choice. Malsumis and the Enemy Way have mortal servants who will be coming for us. We need to protect ourselves. You can help us."

The glow of the fire flickered over her face, and Aholi could now see how sad she was. She clearly did not like refusing but showed no sign of relenting.

"I cannot," she sternly stated. "I am sorry for you. For all of you. So very sorry. Perhaps if my brother made it clear to them that Shipapa-Lina would not participate in this farce, these foes you speak of will not attack."

"And then?" Aholi asked, fidgeting anxiously. "Even if we should refuse to fight, these savages will come to the Land of Everlasting Summer and take what their masters want. We can't just assume they'll leave us in peace. We need to prepare."

"Do as you will," she said. "My brother is endlessly stubborn and will act as he thinks he must. Please tell him I wish him well. I wish you all well, but I will not allow Kolhu to participate."

"I cannot accept this," Aholi cried angrily. "You sit here safely, protected by Wishpoosh, but we..."

"Enough," she said, louder than Aholi had ever heard her speak. "You act as a child. My word is final. Kolhu wants no part of your war. All I can send with you is my hope. You may stay to rest and eat as long as you desire. Please leave me now. Goodbye, cousin."

Aholi accepted he was beaten. Despondent, he rose. "You disappoint me in the most colossal way. Your brother will be sad. If Shipapa-Lina falls, I hope your conscience survives. I will leave immediately. I find I do not desire the hospitality of Kolhu any longer. Farewell, cousin. Enjoy your safety."

Aholi stomped angrily out of the Sun Dagger House, leaving the remorseful Molowia alone with her doubts and guilt. She could sense the fury and disappointment emanating from him. *I so wish I hadn't been forced to do that.*

Aholi marched past the people of Kolhu, not acknowledging any of them. He found his wife standing with a woman who seemed to be looking for an excuse to get away from her.

"She said no, didn't she?" Evaki asked.

"Let's take our leave of this place," he said, with disgust in his voice.

"I knew she'd refuse," Evaki said. "Pompous shaman."

"Come along."

Aholi ignored the well-intentioned farewell wishes of the Kolhu people. Evanki, however, was not as diplomatic.

"It was no great pleasure to be here," she chided. "I suppose you don't need courage or loyalty when you can hide behind a giant beaver."

The pair disgustedly made their way back home. Aholi hated having to bring this news back to his chieftain. *I really didn't believe she'd turn me down*, he thought.

While this was happening, an unfamiliar woman appeared in Kolhu. Hers was a name out of ancient legend and the Itiwana of Kolhu had once worshipped her as their patron Sky Elder. She had a young face but ancient eyes. Two tufts of hairs stuck out and upward on either side of her head, like little horns. On her forearm was a discolored blotch of skin shaped like a bison. Her garments were made of bison skins.

This was the first time she had set foot in Ulah-Nane in centuries. She had long hoped that the next time she trod upon this fertile soil, it would be for a more pleasant reason. However, the brewing war among the Sky Gods did not permit her the luxury of waiting for a more auspicious moment. She had returned to Ulah-Nane on a mission.

None of the population was aware she was among them. Soon enough, she would announce her presence. For the time being, she had business elsewhere with their sister-tribe. She got down on her hands and knees to transform herself. Within moments, she had morphed into a large, white bison. The albino animal trotted out of the valley.

It was just before nightfall when Yana-Luha's hunting party arrived at their destination. It was a place the Itiwana knew as the Tai-May Valley. As they reached the top of a grassy hill, the group looked down and spotted the answer to their prayers... bison.

The largest herd of bison any of them had ever seen wandered slowly across a vast field. There were thousands of them. The herd stretched as far as the Itiwana could see. Best of all, these were particularly large bison, considerably bigger than the biggest bison the Itiwana had seen before. The males stood almost seven feet high at the shoulder hump. They were wide and solidly dense with muscle. The animals also had sharp, curved horns. Deep footprints indicated their three-thousand-pound weight, yet they moved with surprising grace. The females were somewhat smaller than the males but were still of imposing size. The herd was uniformly huge, almost majestic. Any one of them could feed a whole clan. This was better than Yana-Luha had hoped for.

"Spectacular," he said.

"Indeed," Atira responded, impressed.

"I've never seen such colossal bison," Tawa observed. "I'm seeing so many new things on this trip."

"These bison are specially birthed," Manabazo told the others. "They are the largest bison on Earth. It was arranged that way, you know. The White Buffalo Woman has made it so."

"Who's the White Buffalo Woman?" Tawa asked.

"You'll meet her one day, this I vow," Manabazo answered. "In the meantime, she's left this gift for all of you, here and now."

Proud Hobomok the hunter moved toward the herd, spear raised. He finally had the chance to remind the others that he was the greatest hunter of all. "Come. Follow me. Let us bring home some meat."

"Throw no spear," Manabazo cried angrily. "This is not why I brought you here."

"What do you mean?" the annoyed Hobomok asked, eager to kill some prey.

Atira understood immediately. "This is a gift to us from the gods. We're supposed to bring them back to Shipapa-Lina, so we can feed off them for years."

Yana-Luha nodded. "And we can use their hides for clothes and bones for tools. They will be invaluable to us."

Hobomok only wanted to do what he did best. "And how do you expect to get all these beasts back to Shipapa-Lina?"

Atira raised her flute. "I suspect I can handle that."

She blew a tune on her flute. It was soft and tranquil at first, although it grew louder and more hypnotic as it progressed. For the first few minutes, nothing seemed to happen. Then, however, the bison moved in her direction. Just a few moved toward her at first but soon more and more began to respond to the mesmerizing music. Atira walked for a bit, and the bison followed her. The animals were entranced by the sound and would follow her anywhere.

"It's working," Yana-Luha said. "They're trailing you."

Atira stopped playing. "I can do it. I can get them all to follow."

"Excellent," Yana-Luha told her. "It's almost nightfall, so we'll camp here. Come the morning, we'll start the trip back to Shipapa-Lina. Soon, we'll have more than enough food for the children. We just need to survive this night."

As if on cue, the fearsome "Die" shriek of the monstrous A'Chiyala echoed. Everyone recoiled, weapons raised, as the beast emerged from behind the Shining Rock Mountains. It sailed the dimming skies like a hell-sent demon.

"It's back!" Tawa cried.

This time, the flying monster dived straight for ancient Manabazo. The creature grabbed Manabazo by the scruff of the neck with its large, pointed beak and yanked the shape-shifting Sky Elder off the ground. Manabazo let out a cry of pain. A'Chiyala jerked its head back-and-forth and swung Manabazo around, like a leaf shaking on a branch in the wind. The beast released the Sky Elder and tossed him across the field. Manabazo crashed to the ground and lay there, unmoving.

A'Chiyala quickly forgot about him and circled for its next attack. The Itiwana gasped in stunned shock. Not even the legendary Manabazo could stop the flying nightmare.

A'Chiyala had been given new instructions by its masters and this time it was not going to let Manabazo or anyone else stop it. The beast had been commanded to destroy all the Itiwana, especially Yana-Luha and his family. A'Chiyala was single-mindedly determined to let none of the Itiwana survive. "Die," it screeched, "Die!"

CHAPTER EIGHT

The Itiwana scrambled in every direction as the monstrous flying beast A'Chiyala swooped down at them, cawing "Die! *Die!*" in its horrific way. Some of the men made fruitless attempts to slay the creature with their spears but the rest wisely ran for cover. A'Chiyala was beyond their ability to harm.

A'Chiyala aimed for Yana-Luha and his family. All three legs and all eighteen claws were out-stretched, ready to rend its intended prey into tiny fragments. Yana-Luha stood his ground. It was surely suicide, but he hoped this sacrifice would allow his wife and son to escape.

Fortunately, Yana-Luha had loyal tribesman who would die for their leader. And that's exactly what they did. Two of them valiantly placed themselves between A'Chiyala and their leader, becoming human shields. A'Chiyala grabbed the two men around their heads with its huge claws and lifted them both off the ground. As A'Chiyala carried them higher into the sky, it squeezed the skulls of the struggling men tighter and tighter until they cracked like nutshells. Once the creature was high enough, it dropped the men to the ground, shattering their bodies.

Yana-Luha felt terrible that two men had just died for him, but he had no time to dwell on it because the beast was circling to attack once again. Looking around for some defensible cover, he recalled the bison herd. Surprisingly, the herd had not fled when A'Chiyala appeared. They seemed agitated, but the animals held their ground. Although this was strange, it gave the Itiwana a place to hide.

"Take shelter among the herd," Yana-Luha cried. "Lose yourselves among the animals."

The Itiwana instantly fled into the herd, staying low to the ground, desperately attempting to use the sizable bison as shields against the nightmare from above. As Yana-Luha sprinted into the herd, he saw a woman standing on a hill overlooking the field. No one else seemed to notice her, not even A'Chiyala. She was too far away for him to see clearly, but he could tell she was making some sort of hand gestures, and the bison seemed to be responding to her signals.

A'Chiyala made a strafing dive for Tawa and Atira, who were huddled together among the herd. The aerial beast almost got its claws on the pair when suddenly, two of the huge bison moved nearer to the mother and son, in order to shield them. At the same time, two more of the bison lurched upward on their hind legs, their horns reaching high in the air. They gored the bestial A'Chiyala's underbelly with those dangerous horns. The monster squealed in pain.

Yana-Luha was incredibly surprised to see that the wounds inflicted by the bison horns had actually drawn some blood from the beast. The horned animals did more damage than all the Itiwana spears or arrows had managed.

A'Chiyala cawed in anger and made its ascent, moving out of range of the bison horns. The monster circled for a few minutes, as if debating whether or not to attack again. The presence of the bison seemed to give A'Chiyala pause. After straining its simple mind to make a decision, A'Chiyala chose to wait for a better opportunity to carry out its orders. It veered away from the herd and vanished over the nearby mountains.

Yana-Luha was relieved to see it go. The Itiwana chieftain turned his attention back to the woman on the hill, but she was no longer there. Where had she gone? Who was she? Why had she helped them?

He checked on the two victims of A'Chiyala, who were dead. He had expected they would be. Yana-Luha wished they had not had to sacrifice themselves for him. As he kneeled beside their bodies, he spotted something moving to his left. Manabazo was alive and well.

Still in his deer form, the shape-shifting Sky Elder rose unsteadily to his four hooves and shook the grogginess out of his antlered head. Regaining his composure, the ancient being trotted to Yana-Luha.

"I grieve the loss of men so brave," Manabazo said. "I lament their lives could not be saved."

Yana-Luha glared hatefully at the mountain A'Chiyala had vanished behind. "They will be avenged. Somehow, I will kill that monstrosity."

"This you must indeed do. Because A'Chiyala will not stop hunting you."

Yana-Luha pointed to the hill where he had spotted the woman. "Did you see anyone over there?"

Manabazo shook his head. "I was in no position, being in an unconscious condition."

Yana-Luha looked over the bison with great interest. "You said these bison were specially birthed. They are certainly most unusual. Their horns hurt A'Chiyala more than our weapons did. An unexpected benefit."

"Very fortunate, I must say," the deer said. "It's likely the White Buffalo Woman planned it that way."

Yana-Luha moved closer to a bison, studying it intently. "So, we have not only found a source of food, clothes, tools and labor, we may also have found some weapons. I must thank this White Buffalo Woman one day."

Manabazo's eyes twinkled slyly. "One day, you may."

Night fell over the field and brave men were buried. The specter of A'Chiyala hung over the encampment and no one slept.

Pogum had walked all night at a brisk pace, covering quite a distance in a short time. As dawn rose, he stopped briefly for a rest. He picked some fruit for his morning meal and then resumed his trip. He found the old goat herd trail, which he was familiar with because he had been this way several times on fishing trips. As he had done in the past, he followed the goat herd trail to the Swimming Bear River.

Pogum walked the familiar creek bed until he reached a spot he had not visited in quite some time. It had been several summers since he had seen the Emerald Overlook. It was still just the way he remembered it. There was a moss-covered tree house atop a blue spruce, just beyond the creek bed. Several canoes floated in the creek, tied to the tree.

As Pogum got closer, he noticed the child sitting on the grass at the base of the tree, surrounded by a collection of clam shells. The boy had been collecting them during every visit he and his father took to the Blue Patowa'Kacha

Great Water. The boy had them arranged in some sort of symbol or mandala. Pogum had no clue what the arrangement of shells symbolized but the boy obviously did. The child did not acknowledge his arrival.

"Fine morning, isn't it my young friend?" Pogum said. "And a fine collection of shells you have there. You've grown since last I set eyes on you. Is it possible you remember me?"

The boy raised his eyes to Pogum for a moment and then returned his gaze to the shells.

"I thought not," Pogum said. "Is your father about?"

The boy yelled, "Father," without taking his eyes off his shell mandala.

Moments later, a man stuck his head out of the tree house, holding a bow and arrow. He was a lanky, bald man with a huge nose and sleepy eyes. He was known to everyone simply as Long Nose. He did not seem to recognize Pogum at first, but then a memory clicked in his head.

"The Itiwana fisherman," Long Nose said.

"I'm happy that you remember me," Pogum said, even though he assumed Long Nose remembered him only for his scars. "Old friends reunite, eh? It's been too many summers since we fished together."

Long Nose lowered his arrow and bow. "You've come to fish?"

Pogum smiled a charming smile. "As an honest, honorable friend, I cannot honestly say so. In truth, I came for one of your canoes. I need to borrow it. I must reach the Pisas Vaya River by nightfall. It may be several weeks before I can return the canoe to you, but you know I am true to my word of honor."

Long Nose's expression did not change at all. "My price is still the same."

"Corn, of course," Pogum said amiably. "We have a good crop this season. Tell me how much you want and when I get back, you'll have it. And as for the boy, I'll bring him some clamshells from my journey."

"As much maize as two men can carry. If you agree, take the canoe." Without another word, he ducked back into the tree house.

Pogum chuckled at the man's eccentricities. "Most grateful."

As Pogum untied the boat, the Clamshell Boy said, "Get me good shells."

"I promise."

Pogum hopped into the boat and paddled. His canoe moved quickly up Swimming Bear River, toward the Night Way River, and eventually to the Pisas Vaya River.

Yana-Luha led his Itiwana braves back to Shipapa-Lina. He grinned as he watched his wife Atira playing her flute and leading the bison herd. The sound of the flute music echoed through the valley and entranced thousands of the huge animals. The creatures seemed docile, content to follow the soothing sound. Due to their size and the way they had charged at A'Chiyala, Tawa named them Eyota Tamma Waneta, which meant "Great Thunder Chargers."

Occasionally, Yana-Luha thought he spied the figure of that mysterious woman again, standing in the distance and beckoning the bison to follow the Itiwana. Every time Yana-Luha attempted to get close enough to have a better look or communicate with her, she seemed to vanish. No one else spotted her.

He wished he could ask Manabazo about her. *Did the Sky Elder seen her?* he wondered. Unfortunately, Manabazo was nowhere to be found. When they awoke, the deer was gone. Still, there were birds in the sky and other small animals lurking around. Yana-Luha assumed one of them must be Manabazo but was unable to deduce which it might be. He occasionally spotted a white buffalo moving through the herd and wondered if, perhaps, it was Manabazo's latest form.

Everyone was watchful and wary of A'Chiyala. They kept their eyes on the skies. Many times the travelers were startled by normal birds who they mistook for A'Chiyala at a far distance. There was every reason to assume the monster from the sky was not done with them yet. All the tribespeople secretly wondered which of them would be the next to die if the flying horror returned.

Only young Tawa seemed free of fear. The boy was so laden with enthusiasm and enlivened by the many new things he was seeing, he pushed

A'Chiyala out of his mind. Tawa was fascinated by the bison. He had never before seen one so large. He wondered what it would be like to ride one of these beasts. Being young and impetuous, he took a running start and leaped onto the back of the closest animal. The bison bucked and jumped, attempting to dislodge the unwelcome human sitting on its back.

The Itiwana welcomed the diversion and loudly cheered the chieftain's son. Tawa was thrown from the bison and crashed to the dirt. The men laughed and howled their appreciation of his efforts. Atira stopped blowing her flute for a moment, concerned her son was hurt, but the youngster quickly pulled himself off the ground, exaggeratedly wiping the dirt off with a smile. When she confirmed he was unharmed, she resumed playing her magical tune.

The overzealous Tawa was undeterred and ran to another bison, jumping on its back. The men again cheered him on. Yana-Luha smiled, proud of his foolishly brave son. The boy certainly did not easily accept defeat. He would need that quality if he became the next *kik-mongwi*. Also, his efforts were lightening the mood of the men.

Amazingly, after several attempts and many bruises, Tawa managed to remain atop one of the bison. He waved his fist triumphantly in the air as the Itiwana chanted his name, "Tawa. Tawa." Even Yana-Luha joined the chant, beaming with pride.

To pass the time, the men made a contest of seeing who else could ride a bison. Most of them got bucked off, but some stayed on for a considerable time. Tawa was the only one who managed to break his mount and remain atop the beast. Tawa had always been good with animals.

So, this was why Manabazo wanted Tawa to come along. Clever old Sky Gods, Yana-Luha thought.

Yana-Luha was quite pleased with this development. He was not sure if it had anything to do with his wife's flute playing, but regardless, Tawa had proven that these animals could be broken and used as mounts. This was wonderful news for several reasons. Firstly, it would compensate for the shortage of large beasts in the Land of Everlasting Summer. Secondly, if these animals could be ridden, they could become formidable weapons.

Warriors riding atop huge bison, the chieftain of the Itiwana mused. *That will be an imposing sight which should intimidate any foe. This herd is a many splendored gift indeed. Thank you, White Buffalo Woman, wherever you're hiding.*

Pogum awoke in a glade of tall grass beside the Pisas Vaya River. His canoe was tied to a log several feet from where he slept. He had paddled vigorously throughout the previous day. He had gone two nights and a day without sleep when exhaustion finally overcame him, and he stopped for some well-earned rest.

After making breakfast of some fish he speared in the river and getting a drink of water from a spring he found nearby, it was time to resume the trip.

After several more hours of paddling down the Pisas Vaya River, Pogum finally spotted the Canyon of Legend. He marveled at the majestic beauty of the large valley. Pogum recalled the legend stating the exalted Morning Star had originally met the Sky Elders on this very spot.

I have reached sacred ground, he thought.

He paddled to the land, and tossed his paddle aside, stretching his arms. He had made exceptionally good time because the current was with him. As much as he enjoyed canoeing, his arms were sore and tired. He would welcome the opportunity to walk.

When he set foot on the shore of the river, he dragged the canoe out of the water and hid it among some bushes, hoping no one would find it. He would need it to return to the Land of Everlasting Summer and knew Long Nose would be unhappy if he lost it.

Pogum took several minutes to rest before continuing on his long trip. Looking around at the lovely, peaceful canyon, he allowed himself to soak up the essence of historic importance.

This area was often called the First of Sitting Places. The legends explained how Morning Star had heard the flute music of the blessed avatar of the Cloud Elders named Kokopelli. He directed the survivors to the Land of Everlasting Summer, where Shipapa-Lina was built.

Pogum got to his feet, prepared to travel west, fully aware he still had a long way to go before he reached the Shouting Mountains. Pogum planned to approach one of the local tribes and bargain for the use of provisions. He carried nothing but his spear in his travels.

Before taking a step, Pogum believed he detected flute music. For a few moments, he assumed it was all in his mind, but before he could get very far, the melodious sound got louder. He stopped, realizing it was not just his imagination.

Where is that coming from?

Using his tracking skills and sharp hearing, he homed in on the sound. Holding up his spear defensively, with trepidation about what possible unseen menace could be lurking nearby. He stepped through a thick cluster of bushes, ready for danger. Once he spotted the source of the music, he froze. He deduced who it was, despite never having seen this being before.

The being he found was sitting on a stone playing a long, golden flute. The man was small, stocky and hunchbacked. This being had a rooster-like quality, with a long, sharp proboscis, and a coxcomb on his head. His eyes were quite large, his skin was made up of multi-colored patches and he had six fingers on each hand.

Pogum dropped to his knees, in awe. "Kokopelli."

The bird-like being fixed his overly large eyes on Pogum. Kokopelli continued playing his instrument, but to Pogum's amazement, the music became words. The utterances were somewhat musical but clearly words.

"I am he who you say I am," Kokopelli's flute pronounced. "I am he who you need."

"I... I thank you," Pogum said. "I am most grateful for any help the mighty Sky Gods can provide."

"I am he who is honored by your respect. I am he who brings you a gift."

"A gift?"

Out of his flute came a bubble. It was opaque and floated to Pogum. It popped near the Itiwana, and revealed a beaded bracelet, which fell to the ground. Pogum picked it up and examined it with confused interest.

Kokopelli continued playing words. "I am he who wants you to put it on. I am he who tells you to make a fist."

Pogum obediently put the bracelet on his wrist and made a fist. When he did, sharp thorns popped out of the bracelet. When he unclenched, the thorns vanished. Pogum gave Kokopelli a puzzled look. "What do I do with..."

"I am he who advises you to be patient and trust. I am he who cannot directly intervene but wants you to succeed. I am he who now supplies you with a method of faster travel."

"You will?"

Kokopelli resumed his music playing. The song was beautiful. Before long, something came trotting out of the woods. It was a white stallion, but the oddest thing about it was that it was glowing. To make it even more unnerving, it was an ugly horse, skinny with crooked legs and a matted coat.

Kokopelli played, "I am he who introduces you to the Ghost Stallion. I am he who instructs you to climb on its back. I am he who tells you it will take you to the Shouting Mountains."

Dumbfounded by what he saw, the befuddled Pogum crept nervously toward the animal. He had never seen a horse, and this creature was a physical wreck. It inspired no confidence in Pogum.

"I'll do as you say, great one," Pogum said uncertainly. "I trust the Sky Elders."

He touched it and it was surprisingly cold. He gently mounted the horse. "I thank you both for..."

He never got the chance to finish his sentence. The Ghost Stallion abruptly lurched forward and Pogum had to grab hold of the beast to keep from falling off. The horse moved with uncanny speed as it sailed across the grass. Pogum lost sight of Kokopelli and the valley. Moving at this speed, Pogum predicted he would be in the Shouting Mountains by morning.

What will I have to contend with when I arrive?

The spirited riding contest with the bison lasted throughout the entire day. The Itiwana men chose to distract themselves from the threat of A'Chiyala, while Atira continued to lead the herd toward Shipapa-Lina.

No attacks had come from A'Chiyala since the bison had driven him away. Yana-Luha was not letting his guard down. If they could get through the coming night, they would be back at Shipapa-Lina by the next afternoon.

The only thing worrying him was the possibility this horrid air beast might follow them back to Shipapa-Lina, where it could prey on the children of the Itiwana. He prayed to Awona'Wilona this would not happen, but feared in his heart that it might already be too late.

Pogum had ridden the Ghost Stallion into the night when the horse slowed and stopped at the edge of an arid valley, on a hill with a panoramic view. Pogum looked over the strange terrain. It was difficult to see in the darkness, with only the dim light of the crescent moon.

"Is this where we need to go?" he asked. "And why am I asking you? You don't speak. Or do you?"

The Ghost Stallion said nothing. If the creature could communicate, it showed no interest in doing so. It did not even look in Pogum's direction.

"I thought not," Pogum said, climbing off the horse. He crouched on the edge of a hill, trying to examine the valley in the moonlight. When he turned around, the Ghost Stallion had vanished. Pogum was not surprised.

"Thank you for the trip," he said." I hope you'll be back again."

Pogum walked briskly, descending into the salt-crusted valley. As the sun came up, the scorching hot temperature assailed the pinkish-colored salt flats. He had never felt such heat. Pogum deduced he was in the Big Sand. Travelers had told him about it, but he never appreciated how angry the sun could be.

I've never been so far from Shipapa-Lina, he thought.

He spotted two people in the distance. At first it was only curiosity that made him look their way but he then heard the sound of a woman screaming. The sound made him examine the scene more closely. On second look, it appeared the two figures were struggling.

"Cease in the name of Awona'Wilona," Pogum shouted as he ran toward the two strangers. "I will see an end to this."

The victimized woman and her attacker turned to look at Pogum. The pretty young woman was kneeling on the ground, struggling against the two withered, claw-like hands that clutched at her throat. Those hands belonged to a grey-haired hag in a raggedy black robe. The old crone sneered at Pogum, and he saw her eyes and skin were as grey as her hair.

"No further," the hag demanded, as she gestured with one hand for Pogum to stop, while the other hand still choked her gasping victim. "This is not a matter to concern you."

Pogum stopped several feet away from the two women. He held his spear threateningly but hesitated to act. He had never killed an old woman before, not even a frightening looking crone like this one.

"You may be correct that this is no concern of mine," Pogum said. "But I would dishonor myself and every Itiwana if I were to walk away from this scene of cruelty. Release the girl or you force me to intervene. It would pain me to slay a woman, especially one of your years."

The old hag pointed at Pogum. "You are a long way from home, Itiwana. You do not understand what strange occurrences befall the world beyond the Land of Everlasting Summer now that the Sky Gods have returned."

"The Sky Gods?" Pogum asked, wondering what she knew about the Sky Elders. Perhaps she possessed the information Yana-Luha needed.

"Yes, I know of those who come from the skies and take Earthly form," The hag said, still throttling the other girl. "I know far more than you do, man of the Itiwana. Return to where you came from and hope that you survive the coming storm."

Pogum poked the old crone lightly with his spear. "We will discuss the Sky Gods and coming storms after you have released that girl. This you must do."

"I release her from this life," the hag said, tightening her grip. "She dies here on this spot."

"Then you compel me to act," Pogum replied.

"Do not be foolish," the old hag said with a raised voice. "You understand nothing. Go from here and do not meddle."

Pogum frowned. "I regret this."

Reluctantly, Pogum stepped forward with the intention of forcibly separating the two women. To his astonishment, when the old woman touched his chest, a spark flashed, and he felt a painful impact, as if something had exploded against his body, adding a new burn to his scarred frame. The impact tossed him backward, and he crashed onto the sand.

He was momentarily dazed. Shaking his head to focus his thoughts, he wondered what sort of being this old lady was. The old hag tossed the pretty, young woman aside and stalked toward Pogum. He had dropped his spear and felt too dizzy from whatever the old crone had done to him to stand upright. He crawled backward, leery of the hag's power.

The hag shouted something in a language Pogum was not familiar with. Her wrinkled fist crackled with some unearthly, eldritch energy. "You made a mistake, Itiwana. You should not have interfered!"

CHAPTER NINE

Still stunned from the power of the old hag's attack, Pogum struggled to regain his footing. A dizziness made it difficult to stand. The sneering hag waved a withered fist, which glowed like a small star.

"Run away," the old woman ordered, sneering at him with yellow teeth. "Flee and be glad you survived this encounter. I could easily destroy you. This is no place for one such as you. I will let no one interfere in this matter."

While the hag's attention was firmly on Pogum, the young woman who Pogum had tried rescuing saw an opportunity. She snatched up Pogum's fallen spear and hobbled to her feet. She thrust the spear hatefully into the old hag's back. The hag screamed as the spear pierced her heart. She collapsed to the ground, cursing in an ancient, unknown language.

Her last understandable words were, "Fool. You Itiwana fool."

The old woman cursed Pogum till the end, even as she turned into a pile of salt. A timely wind blew and dispersed her remains. It took only moments for the last remains of the old woman to fade from sight.

Pogum studied the pretty young girl. She was a lovely female, with dark skin and strange tattoo marks on her arms. These may have been religious symbols. She smiled at him and Pogum felt a wave of desire, but then glanced with shame down at his scarred body. He assumed she was disgusted by his facial scar.

"Thank you, brave warrior. I am grateful for your arrival," she said, holding out the spear. "Yours, I believe."

Pogum back took the weapon. "I will likely be needing that. I am Pogum of the Itiwana."

The girl put her hands on her hips and looked Pogum up and down. "You're a fine figure of a man. I am Yee-Na-Doshi, the Priestess of the Evening Star. The spirits sent you in my time of need."

"And that old crone?" Pogum asked, looking for traces of the hag.

"That was the Salt Witch," the priestess said.

"One of the Sky Gods?" he asked.

"No, she is as mortal as we," Yee-Na-Doshi answered. "But she has been taught the eldritch powers of the ancient guardians. She serves Malsumis. There is a war coming between the great Sky Elders."

"I know of this," Pogum said, kicking the salty remains of the witch. "It's the reason I have come so far from the Land of Everlasting Summer. If you have any information that can assist me..."

"I know a few things," the girl said. "Come with me to my village. We will speak of many strange things."

Yana-Luha and his Itiwana hunting party were nearly back at Shipapa-Lina. They recognized the increasingly familiar landscape and were beginning to dare believe they would actually make it home without being ripped apart by A'Chiyala. Atira led the way, still playing her flute and enticing the bison to follow her. Tawa continued riding proudly atop the lead bison, showing off his knack for mastering beasts.

The mood changed instantly when the spine chilling "Die" shriek came from the sky. They looked up and witnessed the hideous A'Chiyala circling high above them. The Itiwana stared fearfully upwards, awaiting an attack. The sky monster continued to circle the area but did not dive. It seemed to be waiting for something.

"What is it doing?" Tawa wondered aloud.

"It appears to be playing with us," Hobomok answered.

"No," Yana-Luha countered. "It's looking for an opportunity. We're all too close to the bison. It doesn't like them. They can hurt it. As soon as one of us gets far enough from the herd, our flying foe will find its courage again. It's a disgustingly patient beast."

Yana-Luha was very worried. His biggest fear was that the monster A'Chiyala would follow them back to Shipapa-Lina where it would prey on women and children of the tribe. That fear seemed to be coming true. They were very close to home and the creature still stalked them. The bison were not going to provide sufficient protection once they got back home. His people did not live in bison pens. He refused to bring this horrible danger to his people. He had to solve this problem now.

"We will pause here," he told the group. "Rest yourselves. Be sure to stay close to the herd or you'll never get the chance to taste the bison meat we traveled so far to get."

Atira ceased blowing her flute and the bison herd stopped. Some of the animals began grazing, while others were agitated by the close presence of A'Chiyala. The Itiwana were fearful of A'Chiyala and made certain they kept close to the big animals.

Yana-Luha paced the grass, wondering what to do about A'Chiyala. As his eyes scanned the herd, he glimpsed that strange white bison again. White bison were considered good omens and Yana-Luha decided to get closer, hoping that saying a prayer in the proximity of the lucky animal could help him reach an epiphany.

He moved through the herd. The bison were all so huge that he quickly lost sight of the rest of his hunting party. He had also lost track of the white bison and walked through the grazing herd, trying to find it again.

After searching for several minutes through an endless mass of bison, he suddenly found himself face-to-face with a smiling woman in a bison skin.

"Have you been looking for me, Yana-Luha?" she asked. "What can I do for the *kik-mongwi* of the Itiwana?"

"It's you," Yana-Luha said. "Finally, you've overcome your shyness. It's good to see you more closely."

"Do I disappoint?"

"Not at all," Yana-Luha replied. "You're a vision. And you do not look at all like a buffalo. I assume you're the White Buffalo Woman that Manabazo has been praising."

"Is that who you think I am?" the woman said, petting a bison. "Would you care to know my true name?"

"I would indeed," he said.

"Why?" she queried. "If I tell you my name is Tesen-Wi, how does that help you? Is that what you truly wish to ask? What do you really desire of me?"

"I want to thank you for the bison herd you so kindly provided" he said. "Such generosity doesn't come along each morning. Your gift could be the salvation of the Itiwana. On behalf of my people, I am grateful."

"It's wise on our part, isn't it?" she asked. "Don't you think we want you and your people to thrive? Have you forgotten we need your help? Why would we not help you find food?"

"Very good points," Yana-Luha said. "Still, I wanted to thank you personally."

"Is that all you wanted of me?"

Yana-Luha had the feeling she already knew what he wanted. She seemed to be way ahead of him. "No. There's something else. You're most astute. I was planning to ask this of Manabazo, but he seems to have vanished again. Apparently, it's a habit of his."

"What did you wish to ask?"

"I need a way to fight A'Chiyala. The beast has followed us for the entire journey home and shows no sign of giving up the pursuit. It will continue the chase until we reach Shipapa-Lina, where all my people will be endangered. I keep envisioning dead children. Dead women. Death from the skies. I cannot let that beast wreak havoc upon my Itiwana. There must be a way to stop it."

"And if I intimated there was one, what would that mean to you?" she asked.

Yana-Luha knelt on one knee in front of her. "Please, if you know, you must tell me. I have to know."

Tesen-Wi folded her arms and gracefully moved nearer to Yana-Luha, giving him a very stern look. "What are you willing to risk? What are you willing to sacrifice?"

"Anything. I will risk anything for my people," he said. "Task me and I shall prevail."

"Are you certain?"

Yana-Luha stood tall, looking her directly in the eye. "I have no doubt. No hesitation. I am unwavering in my course, like an arrow from a bow. I will do what needs to be done."

She put a gentle hand on his shoulder. "Will you change your mind if I tell you that this will be the end of your life as you know it? Will it deter you if I say that you will never see Shipapa-Lina or your family again?"

Yana-Luha remained calm on the surface. He had feared that protecting his people would be a task that could only be accomplished at the cost of his life and now it seemed this was to be his fate. Yet what else could he do? He had to protect his people, just as he had always done. If it was the last thing he would do in his life, then it was a good way to die.

"I will do what must be done," Yana-Luha bravely said. "I swear to Awona'Wilona, I will perish in flames to save Shipapa-Lina."

Tesen-Wi tilted her head and folded her hands. "What else is there to say? Why hesitate? Are you ready?"

"Let's begin."

She gestured for him to accompany her. Yana-Luha bravely followed, knowing his hours in this world were coming to an end.

Pogum and Yee-Na-Doshi reached an area called the Sand Altar. Pogum looked around, observing that the area was full of desert wildflowers and desert marigolds. There was a small encampment with a bonfire at the center. Wigwams made of bark and animal skins were spread out across the field. Numerous men were present, either milling about or quietly chanting some incomprehensible mantra.

"This is where I live," Yee-Na-Doshi announced, with a dramatic, sweeping hand gesture.

Pogum found this very strange. It did not look like an established village where someone might live and farm. It appeared to be a makeshift camp used only for a single night.

"It is quite ... uncluttered," Pogum said.

"We live simply," she replied.

Pogum took in all there was to see. "There seems to be a noticeable absence of other women."

"They're out foraging. They'll return shortly," she said and gestured to summon her fellow villagers. "Meet my people."

Pogum's instincts were buzzing with apprehension. Something was amiss here; not the least of which was the fact that the women were supposedly out foraging when there were no forests nearby. It was a desert. He decided to remain calm and see how things played out.

"I shall be honored to do so," he said. "Now that we have reached your village, such as it is, you can begin imparting intelligences to me about the war of the Sky Gods."

"Ah yes, the Sky Gods," she said. "In that regard, I do have something to tell you."

All the people of the Sand Altar suddenly converged on Pogum, surrounding him. Pogum noticed with trepidation that they were carrying sticks and clubs. His sense of impending danger was screaming in his head.

Yee-Na-Doshi smiled. "Perhaps I should have mentioned that we serve the mighty Malsumis, who you call the Dark God of Infinite Lament. Praise his name."

The people of the Sand Altar all lifted their clubs and sticks, brandishing them menacingly. Pogum was completely surrounded. He lifted his spear defensively, aware there was no way to win this fight. The odds were too great. Still, he was determined to fall in battle, rather than submitting to the inevitable.

"I should have trusted the stink in my nose when I first set foot upon this wretched excuse for a village," he said. "You reek of foulness. My single regret in life is that I shall have died a fool for saving you, woman."

"Yes, it was indeed most kind of you to rescue me from the Priestess of the Evening Star," she said. "If you hadn't arrived, I would be dead now instead of she."

Pogum realized how blind he had been. "She was the priestess? Then you are the Salt Witch."

"I see the slow fire of intelligence starting to glow in your eyes," she said. "But your wits have sparked to life too late."

"But I saw her turn to salt. How...?"

"Questions, questions," she sang musically. "I am not here to supply you with information. We only want your blood. Friends... make this Itiwana feel unwelcome."

Pogum crouched into a defensive posture, holding his spear tightly. "Let no man here say Pogum did not bring honor to the Itiwana when he fell."

The mob of mysterious men set upon Pogum like a pack of wolves. Pogum made a valiant effort and managed to stab two of his attackers, but he faced insurmountable odds.

Yana-Luha followed Tesen-Wi the White Buffalo Woman to a cluster of tall trees which formed a circle. She signaled him to stand in the center and he did so. He tried controlling the feeling of fear making his heart pound. Was this where his life would end?

"Do you know how old these trees are?" she asked. "Have you any idea how many rituals the Sky Gods performed here in the ancient past?"

"I've no inkling what the answers to those questions are," Yana-Luha responded. "Nor have I any great curiosity about them. Unless it is relevant to killing A'Chiyala, I would prefer not to know."

"Are you feeling nervous, *kik-mongwi* of the Itiwana? Will you avail yourself of a last chance to change your mind?"

"I have foresworn myself," he said. "Let it be done."

Tesen-Wi grinned. "Do you not realize you have already begun? Have you any idea that you have four of the five things you need to succeed?"

Yana-Luha was getting impatient. "I don't know what you mean. What four things?"

"Do you not have the blood of the Kachina within you? Do you not have the courage and nobility to willingly sacrifice yourself for your people? Have you not been marked by the talons of a Poshayanki in battle? Are you not standing in an ancient, sacred circle?"

Yana-Luha was still confused. "I suppose this is all true. And the fifth thing?"

The White Buffalo Woman held out her hand and revealed a large red-and-green leaf. "Do you know what this is? Have you ever seen a Yaxche leaf?"

Yana-Luha took the leaf from her. "Is this a leaf from the great Tree of Life?"

"What do you think?"

Yana-Luha studied the leaf. "This is what I need to defeat A'Chiyala? I can't say it meets my expectations."

"Have you ever swallowed a leaf? Can you picture yourself doing it now? What are you waiting for? Why haven't you swallowed it yet?"

"Swallow it?" Yana-Luha asked, warily. "And this will kill me?"

"Who said you will die?" she asked.

Yana-Luha was baffled. "But didn't you say... No, say nothing else. Every answer confuses me more."

He shoved the leaf into his mouth and swallowed it. It tasted very strange, but it did little more than make his body tingle. He was filled with an unfamiliar energy.

I can only ride out the tide of events, he thought.

Tesen-We smirked with satisfaction. "Do you know the spirit dance? Can you do it for me now?"

Yana-Luha was far too confused to do anything but comply. He initiated the ancient ceremonial spirit dance. As he did so, his body began to feel odd. He became both energized and feverish. Something was happening to him.

"Who can say what change will come?" Tesen-Wi announced. "What will the *kik-mongwi* become?"

Yana-Luha did not realize at first that as he danced, his body was beginning to change. There was a sharp pain for a moment and then a chill. Next came a feeling of static shock. His whole body was afire with some uncanny energy. Yana-Luha was evolving. The man he had been was being replaced by the entity he was becoming. His metamorphosis had begun.

CHAPTER TEN

Yana-Luha was mutating into something new. Slowly, a set of wings grew out from his back. The nails on his fingers grew and extended until they became rock-hard claws. His senses expanded and he could now see and hear in ways he had never imagined before. He felt stronger than ever. He felt invincible.

He was now a completely different being than he had been only minutes before. Yana-Luha had transformed into something utterly new. He was instinctively aware he was no longer human.

"What am I?" he asked.

"Have you heard of the Great Thunderbird?" Tesen-Wi asked. "Do you know that the Sky Gods use nature guardians to defend against

Poshayanki like A'Chiyala? Did you suspect that we needed someone like you to volunteer for this duty? Is this not clearly a trade? Can you accept this is part of our price? Are you ready to do so?"

"I am firm in my course," the newly empowered Yana-Luha said as he practiced flapping his new wings. "So this is what you meant when you told me my life as I knew it would end. I am no longer what I was. I am the Thunderbird."

"Are you ready to face your arduous task?" she asked.

"I am ready," he said. "Do I have time to say goodbye to my family?"

"Do you wish to?"

"Of course," he said.

"Then why should I stop you?"

Spreading his wings, Yana-Luha the Thunderbird leaped into the air and kept rising. His new wings flapped in the wind, and he experienced the glory of flight. It was exhilarating. The freedom of flight was as intoxicating as his new, powerful form. His old life was truly gone.

Tawa and the rest of the hunting party were wondering where Yana-Luha had gone. He had wandered off into the herd some time ago and they had lost track of him. Tawa had looked around for his father, but the chieftain was nowhere to be seen. Where had he wandered off to?

Tawa returned to his mother to admit he had failed at locating his father. Yet before he could say a word, something extraordinary happened. The members of the hunting party spotted something large flying through the air. They immediately assumed vile A'Chiyala had returned. Fearfully, they moved quickly into the herd for protection. The group raised their weapons instinctively, despite knowing they were useless against the monster.

The Itiwana soon realized this was not A'Chiyala approaching. It was something else. It appeared to be a man-like form, sailing gently through the air in a less aggressive posture than the beast A'Chiyala had used. The assembled group watched with cautious curiosity as the flying being came closer and closer. It was not until the winged figure was mere yards from the ground that the Itiwana recognized who it was.

"Father?" Tawa gasped.

"Beloved?" Atira whispered in amazement.

The Itiwana gazed in awed silence as their chieftain stood among them, with wings and clawed fingers. What had happened to Yana-Luha? Hobomok felt a wave of fear at the sight of the transformed *kik-mongwi* and threw his spear. Yana-Luha swatted it away with ease. Everyone present stood still, uncomprehending what they were seeing.

Yana-Luha smiled at them. "Do I shock you, my love? I know this is unprecedented in our lifetime. Not since the Sky Gods last walked the Earth have we seen such strange goings on. I am an example of that. I have traded myself for their aid and now I have changed. I am of the sky. I walk among you one last time to say farewell to you all."

"Farewell?" Atira asked worriedly, moving toward him. "What do you mean?"

"I mean I have sacrificed the life I so dearly love in exchange for this new form," Yana-Luha said to his wife. "This is the God's price. My time in Shipapa-Lina is over. The mortal world no longer has a place for me. I go to fight A'Chiyala."

Atira reached for her husband but hesitated to touch him, not knowing what to make of his transformation. "I don't understand. What has happened?"

Yana-Luha gave her a reassuring smile and put his hands on her shoulders. "Change, my love, and just in time to save our people. We cannot let A'Chiyala follow us to Shipapa-Lina. I met the White Buffalo Woman, and I have been reborn as the only weapon that can battle the monster. And since the creature is all but unkillable, I expect our fight to rage for a very long time. Yet win or lose, I cannot return to Shipapa-Lina. I am no longer one of you. I live in the skies now. I must guard those below from terrors above. This is the last time you will see me."

"No," Atira said, throwing her arms around him. "You can't leave us. You can't leave me."

"I wish I did not need to," he said to her, tenderly. "You were always the best part of me, my love. But this cannot be undone. My destiny lies above. This world is finished with me."

Tawa kneeled to his sire and chief. "Father? Must you go?"

Yana-Luha put a hand on Tawa's shoulder. "Ah, my son. My wonderful son. You've made me so proud. I'll miss all the things we did together and all the things we shall never do. I regret not being able to see the man you will become. I am sorry to leave you all the responsibility for our people in such a perilous time. But what's done must remain."

"But…" Tawa began

Hush," Yana-Luha said. "You look so sad, but do not despair. You are the leader of the Star Clan now. It is my final wish that the tribe make you my successor as *kik-mongwi*. When they do, guide our people well and do honor to our clan. Listen to your mother's advice, as I always did. She gives the wisest council. Trust her and trust yourself. These are the last words of advice I give you, my son."

"I will do honor to you, Father," Tawa said, his voice cracking. He suppressed a sob, not wanting to be remembered as a crying child. "Will we never see you again?"

"No, my son," Yana-Luha said. "Our time together is over. Just carry the memories of what I taught you all the days of your life. Remember that you come from a proud heritage. The strength of our forefathers is your strength. Be strong and proud and wise, because the responsibilities of the father now become those of the son. I know you'll be magnificent. Prove to the world that I am not mistaken."

Atira was crying and Tawa was trying not to. Yana-Luha embraced them both in a loving hug. "I am leaving so much behind. I'll miss everything. Everything in the world. Most of all, you two."

"My heart will be empty without you," Atira tearfully said.

The poignant moment was broken by the horrible sound of A'Chiyala's caw in the distance, shrieking "Die, Die." The sky monster came into view, diving toward the Itiwana.

Yana-Luha stepped away from his family and his people, to spread his wings. "It's time to live up to my bargain. My old life ends, and my battle begins. Live well, all of you. Atira and Tawa... My love I leave with you. Farewell."

Yana-Luha took to the skies, fiercely determined to defend his people. Atira wiped her eyes as she watched the great love of her life shrink in the distance.

Farewell, my dearest love, she thought. *I'll never love anyone else.*

"Goodbye Father," Tawa whispered, trying to be strong. "I will always honor you."

A'Chiyala slowed, confused by what it saw. It hovered, baffled by this flying man. The newly empowered Yana-Luha took advantage of the beast's confusion. Utilizing surprising speed, he raked his new claws across the monster's stomach area, tearing several gashes in the creature. A'Chiyala screamed in anger and pain.

The enraged beast retaliated. They rammed into each other and began to battle in earnest. They tumbled through the sky, spinning head-over-heels, slashing each other. They wildly zigzagged across the sky until A'Chiyala had had enough of the conflict and chose to retreat. The beast darted away to the North Mountains, pursued by Yana-Luha, who vowed to remain eternally on guard, protecting the skies above the Land of Everlasting Summer. The being once known as Yana-Luha, now called the Thunderbird, vanished into the skies and into legend.

Pogum awoke, unsure of where he was. After the followers of the Enemy Way fell upon him, he had not expected to ever awaken again. Why was he alive? They had beaten him rather thoroughly and he was covered in bruises and contusions. His head ached where someone had clubbed him across the temple. He was bleeding from a cut on his forehead. Pogum focused his concentration on his current situation. Where was he?

Pogum was seated on the ground, with his back resting against a post. His hands were tied behind the post and his ankles were bound tightly together. He tried wriggling free but realized it was useless. He had been too well-secured by his foes.

He saw Yee-Na-Doshi and the followers of the Enemy Way gathered around a large bonfire. The sun had gone down while he was unconscious, and the fire lit the encampment. The men all wore animal pelts of wolves and cougars over their heads and shoulders, as they danced a strange ritual dance Pogum had never seen before. Yee-Na-Doshi stood nearby on a raised sand dune, chanting with her arms raised.

What are they doing? Pogum wondered.

After her chanting, Yee-Na-Doshi shouted to the night skies, "Oh great and terrible Malsumis, rightful lord over all things. We of the Antejini call upon you and the Sky Elders who follow you to grant us the power to serve you as your earthly warriors. We offer you the sacrifice of this follower of Awona'Wilona in return for the honor of serving you."

Sacrifice? Pogum thought. *That would be me. So, this is why they kept me alive. But that privilege will not last much longer if I do not get free.*

Pogum struggled to get loose as they danced a ceremonial dance to appease Malsumis. He was not the only sacrifice, as there was also a wild mountain lion tethered to a wooden stake. It had some welts and cuts, obviously having been mistreated when being prepared for sacrifice. Pogum did not want to join the cat in dying to appease Malsumis. He sought a means to escape and spotted his spear lying nearby just out of reach.

He then remembered about the beaded bracelet Kokopeli had given him. He clenched his fists and the sharp thorns protruded. He used them to cut his bonds. He was now loose and able to fight. As the two Antejini men bent over to untie him,

Pogum swung his arm and used the thorns to cut the throat of one of the men. The other opened his mouth to yell, but Pogum reached up and grabbed him by the throat, preventing him from shouting. They scuffled until Pogum killed the second man by slicing the artery in his neck.

Pogum grabbed his spear and took a knife off one of the fallen men. He sprinted toward the nearest hill, under cover of darkness. As he passed the mountain lion, he swung his spear and cut the ropes, freeing the animal.

Yee-Na-Doshi turned and spotted the escaping Itiwana. "He's free! Stop him!"

A half-dozen of the Antejini ran in pursuit of Pogum, who had fled to the hill. The mountain lion watched the running men and followed.

The angry Yee-Na-Doshi glared ragefully, unable to deliver the promised tribute to Malsumis. Her eyes were drawn to the closest of her men, and she abruptly stunned him with a bolt of energy.

"Burn the new sacrifice," she commanded.

Other followers of the Enemy Way carried him to the bonfire and tossed the unconscious man into the flames. Yee-Na-Doshi raised her arms to complete the ritual.

"And now, mighty Malsumis, give us the power."

A few hundred yards away, Pogum dashed frantically up the hill, scared for his life. He was aware the Antejini would be mere moments behind him.

When he passed over the hill, he took advantage of the darkness to hide himself behind a desert tree, scant seconds before his enemies arrived. He peeked from hiding while the silhouetted figures searched the dark night for him. Two of the Antejini men were skulking close by, searching every brittlebush and shadow for Pogum. One of them wore a cougar pelt and the other a wolf pelt.

As the two men searched, they abruptly stopped in their tracks. The men began to tremble, quaking in violent spasms. Pogum watched as the men jerked wildly in paroxysms of pain. Next, to Pogum's astonishment, they began to transform. Their bodies became distorted and slowly took the shape of something more animal-like.

The man with the wolf pelt morphed into a hybrid wolf-man, while the one with the cougar pelt transformed into a human cougar. They were a horrifying mix of man and beast. They stood on two legs, but their heads were fully animal-like. Both the frightening hybrids howled savagely at the moon, reveling in their new power.

Merciful Awona'Wilona, Pogum thought fearfully.

The two beasts began sniffing the air. They turned in Pogum's direction, as if they had picked up his scent. Growling ferociously, they stalked toward Pogum with murderous intentions.

CHAPTER ELEVEN

Pogum crouched behind the desert tree, spear held defensively in his hand, ready to fight. The pair of hybrid animal-men had sniffed out his hiding place and were creeping menacingly toward him with the intention of mauling him savagely. Pogum's heart thumped explosively inside him. The man-beasts were seconds away from finding him.

The mountain lion unexpectedly popped out of the brittlebush. It hissed vengefully, tearing at the wolf-like man. The other hybrid creature turned its attention to the newly arrived cat. The moment the creature's focus was diverted, Pogum popped out of his hiding place and threw his stolen knife at the cougar-man. The hybrid being roared in dire pain as the knife pierced its back. Injured, the creature staggered away, raging with primal anger.

Left alone, the wolf-man snarled, injured by the mountain lion, which was still attacking it. Pogum brandished his spear threateningly at the beast man. Some human aspect of the monster realized that his chances were very bad and decided to back off. Both of the beast-men slipped away into the night.

Pogum bowed gratefully at the mountain lion. "Thank you, my friend."

The mountain lion sniffed him before trotting off into the dark. Pogum hid behind a rock as an army of animalistic bipeds ran past in pursuit. They tracked the sound of the mountain lion and followed it. Once they were out of sight, Pogum ran north. He ran until daylight.

In the morning, Pogum finally stopped to rest. He sat near a desert oasis, hidden among some bushes. He tried not to nod off, leery of the possibility that his pursuers might have tracked him. He felt wretched. After being beaten up and running all night, he just longed to sleep but did not dare. As he rested, curled up with his spear, he tried making sense of what he had seen the night before.

"What were those animal things?" he muttered aloud.

"They are called Skinwalkers," a voice said. "Vile things."

"Who...?" Pogum cried, leaping to his feet and holding his spear in a threatening manner.

A human form materialized in front of him. Pogum was flabbergasted to see the transparent spirit form of Molowia appear.

"I'm pleased you've come to no harm," Molowia said. "The mountain lion made a convenient tool."

Pogum's jaw slacked agape. "Molowia? I am as glad to see you as I am confused by this."

"This is the spirit form of my vision quest," she said. "Despite myself, I've been watching what has occurred. I am gratified you've not fallen to a monster or an evil spell."

"I've been ill-used but I am unbroken in bone and spirit," Pogum said. "Thank you for your concern. Were you controlling that mountain lion?"

"Influencing," she replied. "It needed very little incentive to attack."

"I imagine not," Pogum said. "Did you say those beasts were called Skinwalkers?"

"That is their name. They are soldiers for the Enemy Way," Molowia said. "The Antejini have gained power by breaking taboos. They are Clitz-Yati, which means they are pure evil. They become the embodiment of the pelt they wear."

"And that woman? The Salt Witch. And what of the Priestess of the Evening Star."

"Yee-Na-Doshi is the Salt Witch," Molowia said. "She has learned how to master body switching. She was taught by Dagwona, a dark Katchina. Dagwona is called the witch of the whirlwinds. They are both more powerful than even I."

"Ill news," Pogum said.

"Indeed," Molowia replied. "The Priestess of the Evening Star follows the Blessing Way. She went to confront the Salt Witch yesterday. The Salt Witch is old, while the Priestess was young and her magic strong. The priestess would have killed her yesterday, but the Salt Witch stole her young form. Still, the priestess was strong and would have won. Sadly, you stumbled upon the fray at the worst time."

Pogum bowed his head sadly. He realized what a tragic error he had made. "I am to blame. I am an utter fool. I cannot bring the priestess back to life, but I can make the Salt Witch pay. There will be blood and there will be reckoning. I so vow. It is a matter of honor. The Salt Witch must die."

"You have a man's job ahead of you," Molowia said. "I thus offer advice about what you should do next. You need someone to help you. I cannot, since I am not really here. This is an astral image. But I can show you the best way. Go where I tell you and you'll find help. You must locate the Wood Men."

"Who in Awona'Wilona's name are the Wood Men?"

The Itiwana hunting party returned to Shipapa-Lina. Atira led the way. She focused on playing her flute, hoping to distract herself from the fact that her lover was gone forever. Not far behind her,

Tawa was riding along, still atop his bison. He had wanted a triumphant return atop his Eyota Tamma Waneta. Instead, he was part of a sad procession of warriors who had lost their leader, as well as three other lives.

As the depressed hunting party led the massive herd of bison into Shipapa-Lina, only Hobomok felt positive. He had never liked Yana-Luha. It had long angered him that Yana-Luha became the *kik-mongwi*. Now that the old chieftain was gone, Hobomok perceived an opportunity. The Itiwana would need a strong leader now that this war of the Sky Gods was upon them. Tawa was only a boy. The Itiwana needed a man.

The entire population of Shipapa-Lina turned out to greet the returning heroes. Grey Pekwin had arranged a grand welcome. The tribe was thrilled to see the bison herd because it meant the food shortage was over. The Itiwana people cheered their saviors with happy cries, vociferous chants, and festive dancing. For just a few minutes, this was a joyful moment among the Itiwana of Shipapa-Lina.

The mood swiftly began to change. Grey Pekwin was the first to deduce something had gone terribly wrong. The crowd of onlookers noticed the frowning faces of the returning warriors and realized the *kik-mongwi* was nowhere to be seen. Atira lowered her flute and walked like a zombie back to the chieftain's longhouse. She did not acknowledge anyone who spoke with her. A sense of dread was growing among the inhabitants of Shipapa-Lina. Something was definitely wrong. Where was their leader?

Tawa stepped onto the Speaking Mound near the chieftain's longhouse, where the *kik-mongwi* would often address the crowd. Everyone gathered around, alarmed by the fact that Tawa, and not his father, was preparing to speak to them. Tawa raised his hand to indicate quiet, just as he had seen his father do many, many times. The nervous crowd was silent, hoping that their fears would not be realized.

"Loyal people of Shipapa-Lina," Tawa said loudly, with a voice that was simultaneously sad and surprisingly authoritative. "It is with a heavy heart that I speak to you now, to tell you a tale of sacrifice and heroism that will live on in our legends forever. I must tell you all about the last days of the bravest and noblest man to ever grace Ulah-Nane. I shall forever honor him as the greatest Itiwana of all."

His voice began to crack. He turned his back on his people so they would not see him cry.

Pogum had left the sweltering Big Sand behind. He was making good time. By the following morning he had reached the Red Sky Forests where the tall pines rose to the sky, rising through a layer of mist. The leaves and needles of the huge trees covered the forest floor. Sunbeams pierced the forest canopy in thin strands of sunlight. It seemed so peaceful there; Pogum fervently hoped the Skinwalkers were not tracking him because he would hate to bring such evil to a place of beauty.

Molowia had given him thorough directions. Pogum was unsure what precisely he was supposed to do when he reached his goal. He was unfamiliar with the legends of the Wood Men before. There was apparently a caste of the Cheenook Giants called the Urayuli who once served the Sky Gods. They were known for their power but not their intelligence. From what Molowia had told him, Pogum presumed today would be another unusual day.

Pogum found a fallen, hollowed-out tree on the ground. As Molowia instructed, he grabbed a rock and pounded it against the hollow tree. The sound echoed for miles through the silent forest. Pogum waited with nervous anticipation for the Wood Men to show up. He hoped this meeting would go better than the previous encounters he had experienced on this trip.

Pogum detected someone or something moving among the foliage. Whatever they were, these new arrivals were large. They stomped and crashed clumsily through the greenery. Pogum gathered his courage, hoping he was not going to regret coming here.

The Wood Men came into view. A dozen members of the Urayuli tribe had come in response to the drumming. Pogum had never seen their like. Most stood seven-foot high and had so much thick body hair, it seemed almost like fur. The hair on their heads hung down to their waists and their beards reached to their abdomen. Their foreheads were heavy and almost Neanderthal-like. The strangest thing about them was that their arms were extremely long; their fingers almost reaching their ankles. When they walked, they hunched over slightly, and their knuckles dragged on the ground.

The twelve Wood Men surrounded Pogum, staring at him with their yellow eyes, full of curiosity. They did not know what to make of him. Pogum was relieved they were not attacking but they did not seem overly friendly either. They were interested in him but clearly had not made any decisions yet, assuming they were capable of making a well-reasoned decision.

"Um, greetings," he said timidly. "I am Pogum of the Itiwana of Shipapa-Lina in the Land of Everlasting Summer. I come as a friend. I stand alone before you. May I have an audience with your leader?"

The Wood Men looked around at each other and then back at Pogum in dull confusion. Pogum doubted they understood him. He wondered if they spoke a different language or perhaps had no spoken language at all. He wished Molowia had warned him about the language problem. He spoke in the ancient tongue which all Itiwana knew. It had been passed down through the generations from Morning Star.

"Do you understand me?" he asked. "Can you speak?"

One of the Wood Men said "Guk," and that was the only response Pogum got.

"Guk?" Pogum repeated. "I assume that doesn't mean anything and you're just grunting."

A noise high in the tree indicated someone was moving around up there. He spotted someone leaping across the branches. Whoever it might be, he or she was small and moving fast. This was obviously no Wood Man.

A young girl dropped out of the trees, landing gracefully in front of Pogum. She was roughly the age of fifteen summers. She was extremely thin with wavy brown hair. She smiled a disarming smile at Pogum, making him less self-conscious about his scars.

"Hello Pogum of the Itiwana of Shipapa-Lina," she said. "I am Nulia Juk of the Juk clan. I speak for the Wood Men. I have been expecting you."

"Have you?"

"We have," she chirped. "The spirit of wise Molowia contacted us. She is a sorcerer well known to us. She told me you were coming and what you need."

Pogum realized he had wronged Molowia in thinking she had sent him into the situation blindly. Pogum wondered about this girl. "Are you part of this tribe, Nulia?"

"My family—the Juk clan—have lived in this forest for generations," she said. "We perform the Naukin Dance for the Kachina nature spirits, to help grow berries and other fruits. We Juks have become closely bonded to the Wood Men who dwell here. We understand them."

"Then they do have a language?"

"Of a sort," she said. "They speak with their movements. Their language is mostly visual, with a few grunts. The tone of the grunts is pivotal to communicating. We have learned it."

Pogum was glad for the convenience of a translator. "Did Molowia tell you what I need from your hairy friends?"

"She did," Nulia responded, no longer smiling. "But I am reluctant to ask my friends to fight. We have lived in peace and harmony within the Red Sky Forest for generations. Should I ask them to go to war?"

Before Pogum could answer, the sound of roaring and growling came echoing from all around. Something else was moving in the forest and it was not the Wood Men. Pogum had a horrible thought. *What if they tracked me? Have they followed me this far?*

His dire thoughts were realized when ten Skinwalkers leaped out of the foliage. They charged not only at Pogum but at Nulia who was standing near him. Wolf-men, cougar-men, jaguar-men, and all manner of animal hybrids converged savagely on the scene. Nulia froze as the Skinwalkers lunged at her.

A Skinwalker was only inches from Nulia when one of the Wood Men grabbed it by the scruff of the neck, lifted it ten feet in the air and slammed it to the ground with enough force to snap its spine.

The Wood Man stomped the Skinwalker to death under a large heel.

The twelve Wood Men howled primal cries of anger as they lashed out at the intruders who had attacked their friend and dared invade their forest. Pogum joined them in defending their land against the nine remaining Skinwalkers. For the first time in three hundred years, there was violence in the Red Sky Forest.

The battle was ferocious and bloody. Both sides were caught up in a primal lust for battle. The size and strength of the Wood Men, aided by the skill of Pogum, clashed with the speed, fangs, and claws of the Skinwalkers.

Nulia breathed deep as she summoned her wavering courage, watching two fierce armies war against each other. She did not want to step into this chaos but could not stand idly by. She fought off her fear and grabbed a rock to throw but became distracted by a noise behind her.

When she turned, her fear changed to delight. She saw someone she loved. It was Isara-Itatsok Juk, the Priestess of the Evening Star.

"Sister," Nulia cried, elated.

In the body of the priestess, Yee-Na-Doshi the Salt Witch smiled at the girl who believed she was seeing her sister. The witch often took advantage of her foe's naivety.

"Hello dear one," Yee-Na-Doshi said, feigning affection.

Nulia ran to the woman who looked like her sister, embracing her. Nulia had not seen her sister since Yee-Na-Doshi had gone away to become a novice priestess, studying with the same Shaman who had trained Molowia.

"Thank Awona'Wilona you've arrived," Nulia said. "We are under siege. Your shamanic powers can save us."

The disguised Salt Witch put a gentle hand on Nulia's head and stroked her hair. "I could, dearest heart. But the fact is, I prefer to do... this."

Dark, unearthly energy crackled from Yee-Na-Doshi's hand and Nulia screamed in tortured agony. She fell to the ground, unconscious, while the Witch laughed.

CHAPTER TWELVE

Yee-Na-Doshi very much enjoyed inflicting pain. She stood over the fallen Nulia for a few moments, smiling broadly. She savored the pained and confused look on the young girl's face. Yee-Na-Doshi then turned her attention back to the wild battle between the Skinwalkers and the Wood Men. It was not proceeding as well for her animalistic minions as she had hoped. She came up with an idea to use the Nulia as a pawn. She dragged the unconscious girl into the open, where all the Wood Men could clearly see her.

"Stop it, you hairy buffoons," Yee-Na-Doshi shouted. "Stop fighting or I'll kill your little friend!"

The Wood Men did not hear Yee-Na-Doshi over the ruckus of battle, since they were too focused on their life-and-death struggle to pay attention to that slight voice in the background. They were single-minded at the best of times and could not process words while they were in a self-defense mindset. Also, they did not understand the language the Witch spoke, so Yee-Na-Doshi's threats were wasted.

Only Pogum took notice of Nulia's predicament but was occupied fighting off one of the Skinwalkers. The creature was trying to rip out his throat, so he could not come to her aid. He hoped Yee-Na-Doshi would not kill Nulia before he reached her.

Pogum received some welcome assistance when one of the Wood Men yanked the Skinwalker away from him and slammed it into a tree with such great force, the impact shattered its bones. This freed Pogum to help Nulia.

While Yee-Na-Doshi was focused on the overall conflict, yelling in vain to get the attention of the Wood Men, Pogum was able to slip stealthily out of the battle zone and into the surrounding foliage. He crept stealthily around behind Yee-Na-Doshi. He was preparing to skewer her in the back with his spear when she suddenly turned around, as if she had sensed his approach.

"It's not so easy to sneak up on a witch," Yee-Na-Doshi said, grinning smugly.

"You may be mistaken in that belief," Pogum said.

While Yee-Na-Doshi was focused on Pogum, one of the Wood Men tossed a defeated Skinwalker in her direction. Both Nulia and Yee-Na-Doshi were knocked to the ground as it smashed into them. Pogum quickly grabbed Nulia, yanking her clear of danger.

He stood protectively between her and Yee-Na-Doshi. As the Salt Witch regained her feet, she found herself caught between Pogum's spear on one side and the huge Wood Man on the other. Still stunned from the impact of the collision, it was hard to summon her magic. To make things worse for the Witch, her Skinwalkers were clearly losing the fight against the Wood Men. She decided that it was prudent to retreat.

"A wise woman knows when the day is lost," she said to Pogum. "There will be a reckoning between we two, Itiwana."

"Indeed there will, Witch," he answered.

Yee-Na-Doshi waved her hands and was encircled with a cloud of dust. When the dust cleared, Yee-Na-Doshi was gone. The Wood Man stared in uncomprehending confusion. Pogum merely sneered at her escape from justice.

The Skinwalkers were being overpowered by the superior strength and numbers of the Wood Men. Only four remained and their leader had fled. Once they witnessed Yee-Na-Doshi vanish, the remaining Skinwalkers retreated to the Big Sand. The Wood Men grunted "Gug, Gug," as the intruders escaped.

Pogum kneeled to attend Nulia. "Are you harmed badly?"

"I am unhurt but confused," she said. "Why did my sister…"

"That was not your sister," Pogum interrupted. "That was Yee-Na-Doshi the Salt Witch. She has stolen your sister's body. I fear your sister is dead."

Nulia buried her face in her hands and cried for several minutes. Finally, she spoke with a soft, sobbing voice. "My sister left the Juk clan several years ago when the Chepi nature spirits summoned her to train with the great shaman to become a priestess. I haven't seen her since."

Finally, she raised her head. Her face had no expression on it. "The wretched thing that killed my sister has escaped. I will convince my friends to help you. The accursed witch Yee-Na-Doshi must be punished."

A mourning period was being observed in Shipapa-Lina. The Itiwana honored the memory of those who had been lost to them. Most of all, they mourned the loss of their beloved *kik-mongwi*. The spirit dance was done in homage to the great leader who had given up his home and family to protect his people.

Atira spent much of the first day alone. She sat near a lily pond and stared into the water. Sometimes she cried and sometimes she was a mask of resolute calmness. T'Soona watched her from afar and longed to comfort her but respected her desire to be alone. He was aware she would have some difficult days ahead of her and vowed to be there for her.

Not everyone was idle in mourning. Some Itiwana were busy working. The cobblers were occupied building a wide fence in order to prevent the bison from wandering away. Yana-Luha had given up everything to bring meat to his people, thus Grey Pekwin gave orders to cage the beasts.

Aholi informed Pekwin that Molowia refused to aid Shipapa-Lina in the upcoming war. Pekwin was not overly surprised but felt disappointed, regardless. Still, he had faith that the mighty Sky Elders would see them through, despite the dangers.

Tawa tried hard to focus on his people instead of his feelings. He planned to teach the other Itiwana to ride the creatures, just as he had done. These beasts could be useful in the upcoming war against the servants of the Enemy Way.

For the time being, Grey Pekwin remained the acting leader of the tribe until the Life Long Ceremony could be performed and confirm the new ruler. Pekwin, like everyone else, presumed it would be Tawa. It was not an auspicious time for the youth to take over as leader of the tribe, but the great Sky Elders had set events in motion, and nothing could stop them.

Young Tawa, who was now chief of the Star Clan, sat cross-legged upon the Hanging Cliff which cast its shadow upon the valley below. He glanced behind him at the village where he might soon be leader, and then gazed down at the little farms in the valley below, which would also be his responsibility.

The youth had much to deal with and was quite overwhelmed. While grieving the death of his beloved father, he would likely become chieftain and be charged with preparing the Itiwana for a war they did not understand. This was no small feat for someone who had yet to see his seventeenth summer.

Tawa looked up at the clouds and wondered if his father was there, locked in eternal battle with A'Chiyala. "Can you see me, Father? Can you hear me? I wish I could hear your voice. I wish you could guide me. Yesterday I thought I could do anything, but now I'm scared. The Itiwana need you but all they have is me, and Awona'Wilona help me, I don't know if I'm worthy of this. It should be you leading us through this peril, with me at your side. Yana-Luha and Tawa, fighting the greatest of wars together. But this will not be. The sky has taken you and I fight alone."

Tawa stood up and looked over the Land of Everlasting Summer, wondering if he could save it. "Yana-Luha and Tawa and the days together that never came. I will try to make you proud, Father. I will become greater than myself."

Tawa put on his bravest face as he returned to his people. He would not let the Itiwana see fear or sadness or doubt in his eyes. He needed to inspire them now.

Later, when Manabazo returned to Shipapa-Lina, flying overhead in his eagle form, he detected the somber mood from high above. He deduced something had gone wrong. What had happened, he wondered. Manabazo landed on the smoke opening edge of the chieftain's longhouse. He saw Tawa, Pekwin, Atira and T'Soona inside, all seated on the ground. Each one of them radiated degrees of depressed pessimism.

Taking the form of an Ocelot, Manabazo leapt from the ledge into the middle of the room, making his presence known. "It seems I've missed a cruel twist of fate. My return has come too late. There has been ill news, I fear. And why is the *kik-mongwi* not here?"

After Tawa despondently described his father's noble sacrifice, Manabazo lowered his head. "I wish I had not gone away. Perhaps I could have changed this sad day. But fate has spoken, and the day is done. Responsibility is passed from father to son."

"Yes, this is true," Atira said. "The bones are cast. My husband is gone and now I wish my son to rule, as he was always fated to do. It was my husband's last wish."

Grey Pekwin agreed. "Yes, it would be an injustice to hesitate. We must immediately make the claim to have young Tawa declared the one, true *kik-mongwi* of Shipapa-Lina and the holy chieftain of the Land of Everlasting Summer."

"Don't be in haste," a voice said. It was the familiar voice of Hobomok. The hunter strutted into the longhouse like a cock of the walk. "Your memories are a bit defective. You've forgotten that I am a member of the Shakowin, too."

"This isn't an official Shakowin," Pekwin said. "We were merely discussing the great Yana-Luha and plans to appoint his son as the next *kik-mongwi*."

"I must protest that," Hobomok said. "There is a war coming and the Itiwana do not need a child leading them. This dangerous situation calls for experience, wisdom and maturity. I hereby declare myself as the best man here to become *kik-mongwi*."

Atira jumped to her full height. "Your impudence is astonishing. Must you ever play the fool? This is no time for infighting among the tribe. We must align ourselves behind Tawa."

Tawa boldly stepped forward to face Hobomok. "I am now Chief of the Star Clan. It is tradition that my clan's chief and a descendant of Morning Star become tribal chieftain."

Hobomok puffed out his chest. "That is not a law, and traditions must change over time. I represent the largest clan among the Itiwana. I should be *kik-mongwi*."

"I will not step aside for you," Tawa replied defiantly. "Fear is not in me."

"Then I challenge you by rite of combat," Hobomok declared.

"We don't do that anymore," Atira cried. "We haven't chosen a leader by combat since before I was born."

"If you like tradition so much, respect this one," Hobomok replied. "I insist on the combat. To the winner goes the headdress of the chieftain."

Pogum hiked north, leaving the Red Sky Forest far behind. He never for a moment forgot the urgency of his mission. His people were counting on him. He marched briskly uphill, glad he was no longer alone. Nulia had insisted on accompanying him, along with two of her Wood Men friends.

Pogum was concerned about bringing a girl of fifteen with him on such a dangerous mission, but she was necessary to communicate with the Wood Men. Pogum needed the help of the two powerful, hirsute beings and he could not speak the Urayuli language. They seemed to have only one word in their vocabulary and that was "Gug", which meant nothing to Pogum, yet Nulia seemed to have no trouble understanding and speaking to them. Therefore, he had to bring her along. She told him the names of these two particular Wood Men were Ko-Ko and Faw-Faw.

At first, Pogum feared she would not be able to keep up with him, but the young girl had a lot of energy, as well as a grim determination to locate the Salt Witch, so she kept a brisk pace. Sometimes the big Wood Men fell behind, forcing Pogum and Nulia to wait for them. Pogum was glad for their help but hoped Ko-Ko and Faw-Faw would not delay him too much.

The group had crossed some mountains, which was exhausting. They now passed over the flats, surrounded by cactus and low desert shrubs. Pogum and Nulia were thirsty, although the two Wood Men showed no sign of thirst. Pogum dug a hole and struck water. He and Nulia used a reed she had brought with them to sip the refreshing liquid. Despite the heat, they had to continue because time was precious.

They spotted something that appeared to be a wandering group. A few makeshift teepees were set up. The people who were camped seemingly used bighorn sheep as pack animals, but the sheep were dead. These people were clearly on their way somewhere, crossing the desert. Pogum wondered who they were.

Pogum caught sight of someone lying on the sand. Alarmed, he rushed to see if the person was alive. As they came closer, they noticed more bodies scattered around; dozens of them. They were all female and had been sliced open at either the stomach or the throat. Blood was sprayed across the sand. Horrified, Nulia turned away and almost vomited. It was a gruesome scene. Even Pogum was struggling to remain calm on the surface.

"So terrible," Nulia gasped. "Who would commit such a massacre?"

Pogum studied their garb. They wore dyed deerskin robes with rabbit-fur trimmings, each of a different color, which told him who these unfortunate people were. "These women were of the Corn Maidens."

"Who?"

Pogum looked sadly at the bodies. "They are harvest shamans. They're a traveling sisterhood devoted to seeing that the crops of Ulah-Nane grow. When a tribe has trouble with its crops, they can call upon the Corn Maidens who utilize their special touch and save the harvest. They are led by Iyatiki the Corn Mother. The Itiwana have called upon their services in the past."

"Why should anyone want to kill them?" Nulia asked.

"I don't know. It makes no sense. I..."

Faw-Faw interrupted with a "Gug" sound and gestured toward something unseen. Pogum and Nulia looked in the direction indicated. Faw-Faw was fixated by one of the bodies.

"What's wrong with him?" Pogum asked.

Nulia spoke to the Wood Man in that strange way they communicated and asked him what the matter was. Nulia reacted with obvious surprise and knelt beside one of the bodies.

"He says she moved," Nulia told him. "She might be alive."

Nulia touched the unmoving woman, who suddenly turned over and screamed in terror, "No, stay back! Don't touch me!"

The woman flailed defensively, dreading what these new arrivals might do to her. She was clearly fear-stricken. Her horrific ordeal had left her traumatized.

"Don't hurt me!" she cried.

"Hush, no one wants to hurt you," Nulia said soothingly. "We just want to help."

"We're friends," Pogum said, kneeling beside her. "Are you hurt?"

The woman, still trembling, was unsure whether or not to trust these people. "I... I'm not physically harmed."

"I am Pogum. This is Nulia. What should we call you?"

"I... I'm Bluebird, the Blue Corn Maiden."

"What happened here, Bluebird?" Pogum asked.

"We were attacked," Bluebird cried, sitting up. "We received a request for help with a corn maize. We left our temple in Kelcoquin and they ambushed us here. They slew many of us. The Corn Mother is dead. The rest of us ran. We were trying to reach the safety of the underground caves when they caught up with us here. During the massacre, my sister Corn Maidens were running in a panic. I threw myself to the ground and played dead by putting myself in a meditative trance. It must have worked because they overlooked me."

"How long have you been here?" Pogum asked.

"I'm not sure," she said, with a tremulous voice. "I only awoke from the trance-state moments ago."

Pogum examined the other women. "They're cold. They've been dead for hours. Why would someone do this?"

"And who?" Nulia added.

Bluebird hugged herself, as the shock of the tragic event sent a chill through her slender body. Was this a nightmare?

"They called themselves the Tunerak Destroyers," she said softly. "I don't know what they wanted. All they said was 'No survivors.' They stayed true to that agenda. Mercy was not in the plan. For all that I know; I may be the last of the Corn Maidens."

"We can't leave her like this," Nulia said. "Not after such a tragedy."

"I don't want to leave her," Pogum replied. "But where we are heading may do nothing to improve her humor."

"Faw-Faw and Ko-Ko will look after her," Nulia said, gesturing toward her two large friends.

Bluebird first noticed the Wood Men. "I've never seen those creatures outside the Red Sky Forest."

"They're needed now," Nulia said. "They're my friends."

Bluebird closed her eyes to shut out the world. "We all need allies now, don't we? And I... I don't want to be alone at present. I need some friends just now. May I come? Please. Perhaps I can help."

Pogum thought about it and gently touched her shoulder. "Perhaps you can."

The entire Itiwana tribe had gathered outside the Sun Temple in Shipapa-Lina because a fight was about to begin. Before they had a chance to properly mourn the passing of the great Yana-Luha, the Itiwana congregated to watch his son Tawa fight to earn his position as tribal leader.

Surrounded by all the people his father had watched over for so long, Tawa stood prepared to defend the family legacy and his own right to be the *kik-mongwi*. His father had entrusted the good of the Itiwana to him and he would not surrender three hundred years of his clan's rule without fighting like a demon for it. Despite his growing doubts, he was determined.

Hobomok facing his young opponent, filled with confidence. He was larger, stronger and a far more experienced fighter than Tawa. He had no doubt he could defeat this unworthy youth and finally claim leadership of the Itiwana, as he had always dreamed of doing.

Manabazo had not left the Land of Everlasting Summer. The last time he took his leave of them, they had lost Yana-Luha. Now he was staying close to the new leader. Manabazo was in his bird form, watching from atop the chieftain's longhouse.

Grey Pekwin ordered the commencement of the drum ceremony that would begin the fight. He saw the potential in young Tawa to be a great ruler and an asset to the Blessing Way. He hoped the Star Clan chief would meet this first challenge to his reign and continue the legacy of his bloodline.

Atira and T'Soona the healer stood near Tawa. Atira stared with loathing at the man who was trying to usurp her son's position. She had never liked Hobomok and feared he might win the fight and become her new chieftain. She did not want to serve him. Atira was convinced Hobomok would make a poor leader for the people of Shipapa-Lina.

Hobomok noticed her glaring at him and threw her a pompous grin. "You can still be the wife of the *kik-mongwi*, fair Atira."

"Only if I were struck in the head so hard that I lost all reason," she snapped back contemptuously. "Otherwise, I'd prefer to be stung to death by the largest, ugliest scorpion in Ulah-Nane."

T'Soona smirked. "I believe she just said no."

"Silence yourself, T'Soona." Hobomok said. "I shall be your new leader momentarily. Don't irritate me more than usual."

"You may be surprised what the boy is capable of," T'Soona replied.

Hobomok waved off the comment. "The only skill young Tawa will have the opportunity to display is an ability to heal quickly from a brutal beating."

Tawa stood uncertain but defiant of his larger opponent. "Did you ask me here for a talking contest, Hobomok? Let us see who will gain honor and who will lose blood."

"With infinite pleasure, boy," Hobomok said. "I've waited too long for this day."

The drumbeat ended and Grey Pekwin announced, "Let it begin."

The crowd fell silent as the two rivals clashed in battle.

CHAPTER THIRTEEN

As the battle began, Tawa and Hobomok circled each other, each sizing up their opponent. Hobomok displayed a self-assured smile, knowing he had height, weight, and experience on his side. Tawa seemed at a disadvantage, but he was a Mastop-Kachina, with a grim determination that he would not let centuries of leadership by his clan come to an end.

Hobomok made the first move, lunging at his smaller opponent. Tawa deftly sidestepped the attack. The young clan chief moved quickly, dancing in circles around grim Hobomok, with lightweight footwork. Hobomok was annoyed the boy would not lock-up with him in a test of strength. Tawa was clearly quicker than he.

He pursued his younger opponent, confident that if he could get his hands on Tawa, he would end this quickly. Tawa, however, would not give him the satisfaction. The younger man backpedaled and blocked Hobomok's blows. He continued ducking and dodging, bobbing and weaving. Tawa's clear objective was to wear the big hunter down.

Atira was so worried, she clutched tightly against T'Soona's bicep. T'Soona found he liked the feel of her hand squeezing his arm. Above them, Manabazo watched the battle in his bird form, not interfering or commenting.

The blood of the Mastop Kachina gave young Tawa reserves of energy and resilience Hobomok could not match. After several minutes of utilizing an agile hit-and-run strategy, Tawa surprised Hobomok by suddenly switching his tactics. He kicked out with his right foot, connecting with Hobomok's stomach. Hobomok doubled over as the kick knocked the air out of him. Tawa took advantage of his foe's momentary vulnerability and threw himself at Hobomok with wild abandon, flailing with all the power of a Mastop Kachina. Hobomok was surprised by the ferocity of Tawa's sudden assault.

Despite the pounding Tawa gave him, Hobomok refused to fall. He managed to compose himself and rally with a counterattack. He replied with clubbing blows that pushed Tawa back. The younger man was now on the defensive.

Hobomok had regained the advantage and was madder than ever. He wanted to end this now. He kept punching with every ounce of muscle. Tawa was surprisingly resistant. Still, Hobomok felt it was only a matter of minutes before the smaller, less experienced youth fell, allowing Hobomok to claim his victory.

Tawa escaped the ruthless assault by doing a backflip that created distance. He landed gracefully on his feet and started circling again. The two opponents paused, as if taking the measure of the other.

Just then, both fighters and the crowd were distracted by the sound of heavy hooves charging toward them. The onlookers quickly parted, as a huge white bison stormed through Shipapa-Lina. Everyone watched as the big animal headed directly for the two combatants.

"Bison amok," T'Soona yelled.

Atira took out her flute to tranquilize the animal with the sound, although she did not recall seeing any white bison among the herd she had brought there. Other members of the tribe grabbed nets and spears to drive the beast back to the pens built for the Eyota Tamma Waneta.

Every Itiwana was transfixed when the bison began to transform. Its body shrank and morphed into a human form. Before the astounded eyes of the Itiwana stood Tesen-Wi, the White Buffalo Woman. The tribe gawked with mouths agape.

Only Manabazo was unfazed by her arrival. Resuming his ocelot form, he leaped from the top of the chieftain's longhouse to the ground in front of his fellow Sky God.

"Ah, Tesen-Wi is here. How are you, my dear?" Manabazo said.

Tesen-Wi smiled at him. "Have you missed me, Manabazo?"

"I've been starved for your loveliness, I must say. You have returned on a most pivotal day."

Old Pekwin stepped forward. Someone had to speak for the Itiwana and everyone else seemed too befuddled by these strange beings. "Holy Manabazo, is this the White Buffalo Woman who provided us with the herd?"

"Why ask him?" Tesen-Wi commented. "Why not ask me?"

"We wish to thank you for your generous gift," Pekwin said. "You saved our tribe. We are in your debt."

"Do you truly feel indebted?" Tesen-Wi asked. "Will you listen to my words?"

"We will," Pekwin said.

Tesen-Wi gestured toward Tawa and Hobomok. "Why do you fight? What will this resolve? Are you squabbling children?"

It was Manabazo who answered. "They fight to see which of them rules. Aren't mortals such childish fools?"

Tesen-Wi narrowed her dark eyes. "Why do you disappoint the gods? Do you think we came here to watch you turn against each other? Can't you realize the peril we all face? Don't you want to hear about a better means of choosing your leader?"

Atira was eager to learn about another method of choosing the new chieftain because she feared Tawa would lose this fight. "We do. Tell us."

"May I suggest your potential leaders go on a quest instead?" Tesen-Wi said.

"A quest for what and when?" Tawa asked. "Speak the words."

Tesen-Wi walked through the assembled Itiwana. The crowd parted for her. Grey Pekwin folded his hands and bowed. Hobomok was visibly unhappy with the interference but feared to dispute a Sky Goddess.

Tesen-Wi spoke. "Do you not know that great Pautiwa once tended the ancient tree Yaxche, known as the Tree of Life, which contains the Oki Life Force of the Earth? Are you aware that Pautiwa told no mortal where the tree Yaxche stands? Are you aware that as long as the Yaxche tree lives and grows, the indigenous tribes of Ulah-Nane will thrive?"

"We know the legends quite well," Pekwin answered.

"Will you take my suggestion that he who first finds the location of Yaxche the Tree of Life will be the *kik-mongwi*?" Tesen-Wi said.

"A test from the Sky Gods?" Tawa said. "What better method could we ask for?"

"Do you accept the challenge?" Tesen-Wi asked.

"Oh yes," Tawa said, glad he did not have to fight Hobomok. "This is good."

Hobomok was disappointed. He would rather simply fight Tawa and get this over with. Now he would have to go on some vague quest in order to become the *kik-mongwi*. He wished Tesen-Wi had not come along when she did. However, the deed was done and Hobomok could not bow out gracefully. How could he refuse one of the Sky Elders?

"I'll meet this challenge with great pleasure," Hobomok said boldly.

"Are you so confident?" Tesen-Wi asked. "Are you so naïve?"

Manabazo chuckled. "Mortals often have little sense. They can be rash and dense. Yet they can rise to great deeds. They will accomplish what we need. A leader is due. The choice is between two. The challenge is done. Soon, there will be only one."

Pogum and his companions resumed walking early, after a good night's rest at an oasis. The pair of large Wood Men slept soundly and would not be roused, so Pogum, Nulia and Bluebird took turns keeping watch. Faw-Faw awoke and immediately snatched some fish from the water with his hands. After the group all shared a fish breakfast, it was time to get moving again.

Bluebird was a woman of twenty-two summers, with hair dyed blue by plant extracts. As she walked, the young corn maiden warmed up to Pogum and talked more freely with him. They conversed through the day and Bluebird even managed a smile. Pogum liked her smile but was self-conscious about his facial scar.

Nulia found herself feeling left out. As the hours passed, she felt something more intense than just the irritation of being ignored. Seeing Pogum offer his hand to Bluebird to help her up a steep incline, Nulia felt jealousy. She liked Pogum very much and was frustrated by the fact this other woman was getting all his attention. Nulia chided herself for her immaturity and lack of priorities. She forced herself to focus on their objective, which was to find the witch who had slain her sister.

After a trek in the heat that seemed to take an eternity, they finally reached Spirit Fire Hill. The eerie mound rumbled, sounding like an angry god was inside. It occurred to Pogum that may very well be true. They saw smoke spitting out of Spirit Fire Hill, turning the sky grey. Pogum and his group approached cautiously.

"At last," Pogum said, relieved he had managed to reach his objective.

"And now?" Nulia asked.

Before Pogum could decide his next move, Ko-Ko—who was much taller than Pogum and could see over obstacles the humans could not—gestured and muttered "Gug."

"He sees something," Nulia informed the others.

Pogum climbed up onto a large rock, where he had a better view of the base of the fiery hill. He spotted a large group of men below, practicing some sort of mass drill. The plain around the volcano was replete with those strange men. Pogum recognized the attire as identical to the bee-stung man he had buried. The men wore jaguar skins and eagle feathers. Their upper bodies were protected by a type of padded vest with cactus bristles. All the headdresses were adorned with shiny stones that offered a certain degree of protection. They were training with wooden shields and a type of oak sword called a *macuahuitl*, studded with tiny stones and shards of volcanic glass.

Bluebird climbed up beside Pogum and gasped when she spotted the men. "That's them. Those are the Tunerak Destroyers. They killed my sisters."

"I need to get closer," Pogum answered. "The rest of you stay here. This is my obligation, and I am honor bound to complete the task."

"Be careful," Bluebird said, gently touching his arm.

Nulia gritted her teeth, finding this very annoying. She tried pushing such thoughts out of young her mind.

Pogum chortled at Bluebird. "A warrior does not win honor by being careful. Courage is a man's gift, and I will not waste the bravery that Great Awona'Wilona has given me."

Without another word, Pogum leaped down from the big bolder, determined to learn anything and everything possible and bring that news back to his leader. The women watched him go, impressed by his fearlessness.

"Astounding valor," Bluebird said.

"Indeed," Nulia agreed, staring at Pogum until he vanished from sight.

The Itiwana gathered at the Deep Well and reservoir to give a proper send off to the two men who were competing for leadership of the tribe. Tawa and Hobomok stood next to each other, facing their people. Tawa had his father's bow and arrows, while Hobomok held a long spear. Both looked highly determined and confident, although in reality, neither had any inkling where to look for Yaxche, the Tree of Life.

Tesen-Wi had vanished overnight, but Manabazo still remained, having grown rather attached to the Itiwana. In his turtle form, the ancient Sky God rested on the edge of the reservoir, watching the proceedings. If the stakes had not been so high, he would have been amused by it all.

Atira and T'Soona agreed that Grey Pekwin should remain as acting chieftain of Shipapa-Lina until the victor of the competition returned and took his place as leader. Assuming, of course, either one of them ever returned. Atira wished she could do something to help her son but was aware Tawa had to do this entirely alone, or he would prove unworthy to rule. She worried Hobomok might try something devious to eliminate the competition.

T'Soona could see how worried Atira was about her son. He wanted very badly to console her and tell her he would always be there for her, but that would not be proper. She had just lost her husband and now her son was in danger, so this was not the time to try winning her affections.

Manabazo began the event. "Let the quest begin. And may the deserving man win."

Tawa and Hobomok raised their respective weapons and let out spirited howls, defying anyone or anything to try stopping them. The tribe members responded with cheers and howls of their own, encouraging the rivals onward to glory. After the cheers died down, Tawa and Hobomok faced each other and gave faux-respectful nods to their rival. They were both aware this cordiality would only last until they left Shipapa-Lina.

"Start. Depart," Manabazo directed.

The two men marched off to begin their search. Tawa glanced back toward his mother, who mouthed the words "Bless you." He smiled reassuringly and trekked onward, determined to find the Tree of Life and continue his clan's legacy of rule over the Itiwana. He feared what he would encounter along the way. Something told him this would not be easy.

CHAPTER FOURTEEN

Tawa spent the entire day wandering across the Land of Everlasting Summer in a futile attempt to find Yaxche, the tree of life. He was not confident he would find it. The Itiwana had been living in the Land of Everlasting Summer for so many generations and no one had ever seen the Tree of Life. Clearly, it was extremely well hidden. How could he find it? His doubts about himself were growing. Would he fail his father so soon?

His only consolation was that Hobomok would have just as much trouble finding it as he would. Of course, this meant the two of them could spend months or years wandering around Ulah-Nane. That would not benefit anyone.

He could not help thinking that Tesen-Wi the White Buffalo Woman would not have sent them on a hopeless quest. She must realize the need for strong leadership over the tribe in the days to come, considering the imminent war. She would surely want this matter of leadership resolved as quickly as possible, would she not? She must have had a reason for choosing this means to settle the issue. *What is her true plan?*

As Tawa walked, he remained uneasy and alert for a possible ambush by Hobomok. Hobomok wanted so badly to be the new *kik-mongwi*, Tawa could easily imagine the arrogant hunter making an attempt to eliminate the competition. Every noise made Tawa crouch apprehensively into a defensive posture. He expected to see a spear come out of the greenery, heading directly for him. Tawa kept an arrow in his bow constantly, expecting he would need to defend himself at any moment.

Tawa stopped at a brook and kneeled to get a drink. He continued watching behind him, worried he might be attacked from the rear while he was in a vulnerable position. He almost jumped out of his skin when a crow landed on a log next to him. He laughed at his own nervousness.

"Brave heart, Tawa," he told himself.

The bird seemed to be watching him fixedly as he drank. "Is that you, Manabazo?"

The bird did not react. "No, I suppose it isn't. Well, greetings to you, black crow. I don't suppose you know where the Tree of Life is. No? Pity."

As Tawa glanced down to look at a small fish in the brook, wondering if it was big enough to be worth catching for lunch, the crow abruptly took flight and snatched the red headband Tawa always wore off his head. "What in Awona'Wilona's name...?"

The bird took to the sky with the headband. Tawa was upset, since that headband had been sewn by his grandmother, the former chieftain, and marked him as both a descendant of Morning Star and a member of the Star Clan. He was loath to lose it.

He considered shooting the bird out of the air, but it just wasn't in his heart to kill the beautiful avian. He attempted following the bird as far as possible. Since he had no idea which way to go anyway, the chase was not diverting him from any planned course. The bird made several short flights, frequently landing on low tree branches, as if it were waiting for Tawa to catch up with it. Tawa kept wondering if this secretly was one of Manabazo's games. Manabazo was the puckish sort.

After chasing the crow for a while, Tawa was drawn to a noise in a nearby glen. He recognized it as a human voice crying out but detected something else, as well. There was another sound, which could have been people humming. He became fearful, wondering if danger was near. Arrow at the ready, Tawa crept closer, to see what was happening. Crouching low, he peeked through the bushes. His eyes widened with stunned surprise at what he witnessed.

He spotted his rival, Hobomok the Hunter, being dragged along the ground by seven masked men with painted skin. Two of them had a firm grip on Hobomok's ankles, pulling him along the grass, while the other five walked in tight formation around him. One of the men was carrying Hobomok's spear.

Grey Pekwin had told him stories about the seven Koyamishi Mudheads ever since Tawa was a small child, which allowed him to recognize them immediately. Each wore an earth-colored cotton mask. The masks had black rings around the eyeholes and every mask depicted a different expression: Happiness, sadness, anger, fear, confusion, amazement and contemplation. The Mudheads were naked, and their bodies painted pink, red, and yellow. They each carried a pack of seeds by a string around their necks. The Mudheads all hummed in unison.

"What do you want of me?" Hobomok cried in panicked distress, as they easily dragged him over grass and rocks. "I am the leader of the Itiwana, and I demand you release me."

Even when he's terrified, his conceit is still mountain sized, Tawa thought.

He wondered what the Koyamishi Mudheads would want with Hobomok. Legend had it that they served the Sky Gods, but whose side were they on? Appearances would indicate they served the Enemy Way. If so, he had to do something to help Hobomok. Although Hobomok was his rival and it would be easier for Tawa to allow the Enemy Way to eliminate him, Tawa could not do it. His father would not approve of this. If he was to be leader of the Itiwana, he could not simply walk away while one of his people was in danger. Not even Hobomok. *I fear I will greatly regret this foolishness if I live.*

Despite his fear, Tawa followed behind the Koyamishi Mudheads, trying to formulate a plan. He was unsure about the precise nature of the Mudheads powers, but legend said they could manipulate emotions. The strange beings had clearly overpowered the fierce Hobomok without a wound among them. Tawa had to be cautious with these masked Mudheads.

The Koyamishi Mudheads reached a clearing and released Hobomok's ankles. They stood in a circle around him, still humming. Hobomok was on his knees, looking up fearfully at the strange beings who surrounded him.

"What is it you want?" he shouted, confused and desperate.

The one with the Fear-mask came close to Hobomok and looked him in the face. As he did so, Hobomok was instantly filled with the most horrible, overwhelming fear he had ever felt. He threw himself to the ground, cowering, screaming, and begging in abject terror. Tawa watched from his hiding place. He wasn't sure what they were doing to Hobomok, but he was appalled by this cruel treatment of one of his Itiwana. He had to do something.

The Mudhead with the Sadness-mask took over from the one with the Fear-mask. He stared at Hobomok and turned the Itiwana hunter into a sobbing mass of disconsolate misery and woe. Hobomok groveled, crying like an infant. He could not fight the Mudhead's emotion-manipulating powers.

Tawa fired an arrow at the Mudhead with the sad mask on. Before it could reach its mark, the arrow was snatched out of the air by the Mudhead in the Amazement-mask. The Mudhead in the Anger-mask opened his little bag of seeds, swallowed one and immediately vanished. While the shocked Tawa attempted to figure out what had just happened, his instincts told him someone was behind him. He spun around to see the Mudhead in the Anger-mask staring at him.

The Mudhead in the Anger-mask tossed a seed at Tawa. The young Itiwana swatted it away with his bow, but when the bow made contact, the seed exploded. The concussion of the blast knocked Tawa off his feet. He crashed to the grass, dazed. The Mudhead in the Anger-mask grabbed Tawa's wrist and dragged the dazed Itiwana Clan Chief to the clearing with the others.

Hobomok was curled up on the ground in the fetal position. When the Mudheads stopped torturing him, Hobomok looked up and realized they were distracted. They were all focused on some new victim who was being dragged closer. Hobomok saw it was Tawa. He hoped they would be satisfied with torturing the young Star Clan Chief and forget about himself. The frightened hunter dashed for freedom, but two of the Mudheads grabbed him with extraordinary strength and tossed him back into the circle.

By the time Tawa cleared his head and regained his senses, he was already in the circle with Hobomok. He was frightened but determined to control his fear.

"Hello again, Hobomok. Fine company you've been keeping," Tawa said.

"Stop playing the fool, whelp!" Hobomok shouted. "We're going to die."

Tawa stood and faced the Koyamishi Mudheads, putting on his bravest face to hide his terror. "My father once said the man who hides his face is hiding his own shame. Before I ask what you're ashamed of, will you tell me what you want with us?"

The Mudhead in the Contemplation-mask said, "Go can one. Stay will one. Choose must you."

Tawa got the gist of the backwards message. "So, one of us may walk away and it's ours to say which."

"It must be me," Hobomok shouted frantically. "I must live. The Sky Elders would approve. I must take the Itiwana by the reins and lead them. Do with the boy as you will."

Tawa grimaced. "Every word proves you less worthy to lead the Itiwana. But if there's a sacrifice to be made, it seems it must be mine. Like my father before me, I must walk the noble road, as befits the *kik-mongwi* of Shipapa-Lina. Make it so, you masked mystery men. Release my tremulous friend and contend with me."

"Yes, I should be the one to survive," Hobomok yelled. "I must rule."

The Mudhead in the confusion masked stepped aside. "Go will who?"

Tawa gestured for Hobomok to go. "I leave the future to you, Hobomok. And remember, the enemies you must overcome are not always from the clouds or the forests. There is a more tangled forest inside the mind, where demons dwell. Learn a lesson from my father and I. Put others first. I hope you can rise above yourself. Farewell."

Without a word, Hobomok ran as rapidly as he could. He ran for miles until he could not run any more, looking over his shoulder the whole time. Mixed with his fear was the satisfaction that his competition for the leadership of the Itiwana was gone.

Tawa remained in the clearing, encircled by the menacing Koyamishi Mudheads. He was terrified but determined to do his father proud by dying defiantly.

"Go on, then," he said. "Make your lord Malsumis proud. Be done with it. Be quick."

The Mudhead in the Fear-mask stared at Tawa. Just as had happened with Hobomok, Tawa felt a wave of blind terror filling his mind. He had never been so scared. His heart pounded, and it was all he could do not to scream. Unlike Hobomok however, he did not cower or beg. He remained on his feet, enduring the feeling of unbridled horror. He refused to allow the servants of the Enemy Way to see how deeply terrified he was. His father would not have succumbed to terror, and neither would he. *I am my father's son!*

"N...No fear," he blurted out.

After a full minute of torment, the mental assault stopped. The Mudhead in the Fear-mask moved away. Tawa took a deep breath, trying to compose himself after the torturous experience. Then the Mudhead with the Happy-mask stepped forward and put his hands on Tawa's shoulders. "Passed have you."

"Passed?" Tawa asked, befuddled.

"Tesen-Wi by sent were we," the Mudhead said. "Tests our passed have you."

"Tesen-Wi? So, she's the mind behind all this."

The Mudhead in the Amazement-mask held out his arm. The same black crow that had led Tawa to this spot landed and perched on the Mudhead's arm. It was still holding Tawa's red headband. The Mudhead handed the band back to Tawa.

"Thank you," the young Itiwana said.

The Mudhead with the Happy-mask pointed at the bird and said, "Follow must you. Goal your reach will you."

Tawa struggled to understand the backwards dialogue. "Are you saying this bird will lead me to the Tree of Life?"

"Quite not," the Mudhead answered. "Know who others find will you."

"I did not quite understand that," Tawa remarked. "But I understand you're on my side, so I'll follow the crow. Thank you."

The bird took to the air and the Mudheads all pointed, indicating Tawa should follow it. Tawa bowed respectfully and left the Koyamishi Mudheads behind. He hoped this bird would lead him to the Tree of Life.

Pogum moved with nimble stealth, hoping to get a closer look at the Tunerak Destroyers. He had been entrusted with a vital task by his *kikmongwi* and would rather die than fail. He vowed to let nothing stop him from learning all there was to learn.

Being a hunter, Pogum was accustomed to moving covertly. He covered himself in dust to better blend with his surroundings. He crouched low and moved through some tall desert weeds. Sulphuric smoke from the hill seemed to form into a skull-like shape. The volcanic gases smelt like rotting eggs.

He finally reached a location close enough to observe what was happening at the base of the hill. He dared not get any closer. Pogum observed that the Tunerak Destroyers had stopped their seemingly relentless training and were now involved in some sort of ritual. They were all kneeling, facing the base of Spirit Fire Hill. He spotted the Salt Witch Yee-Na-Doshi, who had somehow beaten them there using her mystic powers, still possessing the body of Nulia's sister. She stood at the forefront of the group and chanted in an ancient language, waving her arms in a very animated manner.

What in Awona'Wilona's name is that witch planning now? Pogum wondered.

Pogum observed the ritual, speculating this was some attempt to raise Malsumis from his eternal prison. *I sense ill fortune on the horizon,* he thought.

Pogum watched as a small section of the hill's base broke off from the rest of Spirit Fire Hill. The piece was roughly man-sized and seemed to be moving by itself. Then, to his disbelief, he noticed it had arms and legs and the ability to walk.

"Rise Stone Coat," the Salt Witch yelled. "Rise and serve mighty Malsumis."

It's a man of stone, Pogum thought, alarmed. *By all the Great Spirits. The Witch has conjured a warrior made of stone.*

CHAPTER FIFTEEN

The Salt Witch finished her incantation and laughed as the fearsome result of her handiwork took its first sluggish, lumbering steps forward. Its stone feet sunk deep into the sandy ground as it stomped along.

"You are more magnificent and frightening than I had dared imagine," the Salt Witch said, giddy with success. "Come Stone Coat. Come forward to serve your masters, the Sky Elders of Winter."

Pogum watched from his hiding spot as the large, stomping rock monster walked slowly toward the Salt Witch. Even the assembled legions of the Tunerak Destroyers gaped nervously, with jaws hanging open. No one had ever seen any-thing like Stone Coat.

The Salt Witch cackled at the intimidated Tunerak Destroyers. "Behold how true power allows nightmares to walk the Earth. Great Malsumis has offered up a small portion of his limitless power to give us this weapon, which we will use in his name. If the mortals dare to send any champions against us—such as they did gen-erations ago when the accursed Morning Star slew Shakok—the cretin will have to face Stone Coat, who feels no pain, knows no fear and cannot be beaten."

The Tunerak Destroyers were so roused by the Salt Witch's speech, they forgot their terror and let out a supportive cheer. This proved they were justified in their worship of Malsumis.

"Great Malsumis has spoken to my mentor Dagwana," the Witch continued, "and she has passed the secret on to me of the three signs. When these three sacred omens occur, majestic Malsumis will rise again to lead us against the forces of hated Awona'Wilona. Until then, we will ensure that the three sacred signs occur, and we will find Yaxche the Tree of Life and destroy it. And When Malsumis rises, he will reward us with wonders that mortals cannot conceive of. Hail Malsumis, the true master of all life!"

While the Tunerak Destroyers cheered and the Witch laughed, Pogum decided he had seen more than enough. His *kik-mongwi* would want to know all he had learned. He must report about the Skin Walkers and the Tunerak Destroyers and the Salt Witch and Stone Coat, and—most importantly—that Malsumis was not yet free but awaiting three omens. Pogum slipped away unseen. It was time to head back home.

Pogum returned to his four companions, only to find a fifth person there. One of the Tunerak Destroyers was present, but he was not doing any destroying. His wooden *macuahuitl* sword lay broken on the ground. Ko-Ko was holding him upside down by the ankle while Faw-Faw was crushing the wooden shield in his oversized hands.

"He's one of those who murdered my tribe," Bluebird shouted with hateful venom. "Have your huge friends kill the vermin."

"We should wait until Pogum returns," Nulia said. "He may want the swine alive."

Pogum stepped out of the shadows and made his presence known. "You are wise beyond your years, young Nulia. I do want this cretin breathing. Well done, all. We have a captive now."

"But his kind destroyed my sisters and Corn Mother," Bluebird cried. "The Corn Maidens are no more and it's due to the likes of him. Let the hairy ones crush the life from his worthless body."

Pogum held out his palm to silence her. "Not yet. This snake may have information that can help save my people and end the threat of the Enemy Way forever. He may know about the three omens."

"What three omens?" Nulia asked.

"I'll explain it all later," Pogum said. "We must begin our trip back. There is a beast down in that encampment that even your two massive friends dare not confront. Have the large ones carry this villain back with us, so the chieftain of the Itiwana can wrest the necessary information from him. Bluebird, be patient. What he tells us will help defeat the Tunerak Destroyers and avenge your sisters."

Bluebird sneered hatefully at the Tunerak Destroyer but could do nothing else at the moment. "Very well. I will do as you say. I have little choice."

"Come then," Pogum said. "There's so far to go and so many things that will try to stop us from getting there."

Tawa strained his young body to keep up with the black crow and not lose sight of it. The bird flew low and stopped frequently, allowing Tawa to catch up. Tawa had no clue how long or far he had jogged. He was tired and simply wanted to rest. He wondered if endurance was a part of the tests he had to pass.

I hope this bird truly has some notion where it's going. I'd despair of chasing it across Ulah-Nane if the reward is just some eggs and a worm.

Finally, the bird led him down an incline into a canyon. Tawa sighed as he scrambled down the hill after it. *It's found a new direction to lead me now.*

He saw the bird land on a stone on a dirt mount, by the western wall of the canyon. Tawa scrambled down the hill, worried he might lose track of the crow. When he reached it, he was surprised the bird did not fly away. What was it waiting for?

Tawa took note of a large, limestone archway that led to a cave in the canyon wall. Was this what the bird had been directing him toward? Was he meant to go in there? Since the bird was not moving, he did not see any other options.

"Now a new mystery must be explored," he muttered in trepidation. "Be brave, Tawa."

He stepped through the archway and found himself in a dark tunnel. As he moved uneasily through the blackness, he felt a breeze blowing through the tunnel.

A tunnel of winds? he thought. *Strange.*

He continued along the dark passageway until he spied a light further down the tunnel. He crept cautiously until he emerged in a large chamber. The chamber was replete with crystal formations. The crystals seemed to glow with a natural iridescence, and outcroppings of stalactites and stalagmites extended from the cave walls in every direction, defying natural laws. Tawa was overcome by the beauty of this hidden place.

He perceived the slight sound of something moving. Bow and arrow in hand, he scanned the area cautiously. Tawa deduced the sound was coming from a big pit. It was a skittering sound. He pointed his arrow toward the pit and waited to see what would emerge.

Moments later, three female heads arose from the pit. Tawa's eyes widened in confusion. Who were these women and what were they doing in a pit in this cave? The women rose out of the pit without using their hands, as if they were floating upward. One of the women was old and grey haired; the second was younger and pretty, while the third was barely out of her childhood years.

Who are they? Tawa wondered.

Before he could think of anything to say to them, his surprise turned to horrified astonishment. As the women climbed out of the pit, Tawa jumped backwards upon seeing what was below their normal-looking arms. The women had six long spider-like legs coming from their rib area. The legs had eight-sections and were covered with tiny hairs. Equally bizarre was that they had arachnid-shaped abdomens below the waist.

Spider-Women! Tawa thought aghast, ready to fire his bow. *They're loathsome.*

The three Spider-Women skittered nearer to Tawa, studying him with bemused curiosity. He was horror stricken but fought to hide this fact. With tremulous hands, he aimed his arrow at the oldest one, who was leading the other two.

"No farther," he yelled. "If you understand me, stay where you are. I am not in a peaceful vein this day."

The Spider-Women stopped. The eldest smiled, seeming rather amused by the threat. "Unleash your shaft if you wish, young Tawa of the Itiwana. You cannot..."

"...injure us," the youngest one continued. "But there is no need to fear. We..."

"...wish no harm to you," the third one said. "We are not your..."

"...enemies," the eldest finished.

Tawa was mystified at the way they finished each other's sentences. *Look at them. So repulsive. So monstrous, and yet, all my instincts tell me they are sincere.*

Tawa hoped these unnatural things were allies of Tesen-Wi. Heart-pounding, he lowered his arrow. "It seems I do not need to introduce myself. Good. And once you have told me who you ... ladies are, the pleasantries can be dispensed with."

"We are The Na-Ash-Jai Spider Women," the eldest said. "I am Oona. These are my..."

"...sisters," the youngest said. "I am Abit and..."

"...I am Echigas," the middle sister said. "We are the Eyes of Tomorrow."

Tawa was getting accustomed to being baffled. "You are of the Sky Gods, no doubt?"

"We are children of the Spider Mother," Oona said. "But we do not..."

"...live in the clouds," Echigas, continued. "Mother gave up the sky in favor of..."

"...the deep earth," Abit added. "We prefer the serene darkness. We are..."

"...peaceful creatures," Oona said. "We want no part of the war between Awona'Wilona and Malsumis. This is why..."

"...we live here in seclusion," Echigas stated. "Our knowledge of the future..."

"...can be useful to both sides," Abit told him. "And we wish to remain neutral."

Tawa was beginning to worry that these women were not going to help him. Apparently, they had special knowledge but no intention of sharing it.

"Then there is nothing here for one such as me, it seems," Tawa said. "I've come a long way to ask a question because I was told someone here could answer it, but that seems foolish now. Have I failed my people?"

"Matters can be altered to your liking, young one," Oona announced. "You are of the blood of Morning Star, who our mother so dearly favored. Thus, if you are willing..."

"...to bargain," Abit said. "We will do something for you, if you..."

"...do something for us," Echigas concluded.

Tawa was leery about making a deal, but he was in a weak position. "What would you ask of me?"

Oona smiled an ominous smile. "Nothing today, boy. You will do us a service..."

"...at another time," Echigas proclaimed. "At a time of our choosing..."

"...you will repay your debt," Abit told him.

Tawa hated the idea of making a blind agreement with a group of strange spider-women, but the Na-Ash-Jai had the information he wanted, so what else could he do?

"I so vow," he said.

Oona pointed at him. "Say it..."

"...again," Abit cried. "Swear that the issue of this day shall stand..."

"...as your bond," Echigas added.

Tawa got down on one knee. "By the blood of Morning Star, in the memory of my father, and on my honor as the rightful ruler of my clan, I swear that when you have a need, this debt shall be paid, or I will die trying."

"Well Spoken," Oona said. "You have the spirit of Morning Star in you. Our..."

"...mother so loved Morning Star," Echigas said. "Ask your question..."

"...and we shall answer truly," Abit stated.

"Tell me where to find Yaxche, the Tree of life," Tawa asked.

Oona laughed. "Easily done. But before you take directions, heed..."

"...our warnings," Abit said. "Yaxche is guarded. To reach it..."

"...you must break the beast Mapingwari and ride it," Echigas said.

"The beast?" Tawa asked. "There's a beast called Mapingwari? Is nothing ever easy?"

"Listen now, young one," Oona said. "We will now..."

"...tell you what you wish..."

"...to know."

Tawa listened carefully to the instructions that would lead him to his goal. When the Na-Ash-Jai Spider-Women finished, Tawa thanked them and quickly rushed out, glad to be away from these monstrosities. The Spider-Women laughed, as if they knew something he did not. Tawa hoped he would not someday regret this promise.

Tawa walked quickly through the tunnel of winds, glad to see the sunlight. *Those women were terribly eerie,* he thought, feeling calmer now.

As he took a deep breath of fresh air, he saw the black crow still standing on the mound, as if it were waiting for him. Amused, Tawa held out his arm and the crow fluttered its wings and popped up, perching on Tawa's upper arm.

"It seems I have a new friend," Tawa said to the bird. "You never can predict when you'll meet one. And especially not one so sleek and quick and useful. You could be a help to me if I can count upon your continued loyalty. Come then, Black Crow. Somewhere adventure is waiting; the Tree of Life is growing; a beast is lurking; and I'm getting hungry. Let's see what happens next."

CHAPTER SIXTEEN

Pogum and his four allies had been walking for two days. They had not rested much because Pogum wished to reach Shipapa-Lina as quickly as possible, in order to relate the information he had gathered. However, the Wood Men enjoyed sleeping quite a lot, and Pogum was forced to grudgingly accommodate them. It was not easy to argue with two giants who were cranky from lack of sleep. Finding water was a problem until they got out of the desert.

Their captive Tunerak Destroyer was regularly tied to a desert tree while the others rested. Pogum, Nulia and Bluebird would take turns staying awake to watch him and ensure he did not escape. The Tunerak Destroyer, whose name was Xolotl, felt humiliated and enraged by his capture and was constantly watching and waiting for an opportunity to escape. However, he was more than a little intimidated by the Wood Men and became a cooperative captive when they were close at hand.

Eventually, the travelers spotted the giant red trees, giving evidence they had reached the Red Sky Woods. Nulia was glad to see the familiar terrain of home and it seemed to Pogum that the Wood Men were excited to be back as well. Pogum was sorry to be losing two such powerful allies but hoped he would not be needing them anymore.

Once nestled in the relative safety of the Red Sky Woods, Ko-Ko banged on a hollow log to summon his fellow Wood Men. The entire Urayuli tribe arrived quickly. Pogum counted forty-two of them, and some appeared to be female, although he was not completely sure. The apparent females did not have those long beards, although they did have stubble. The hirsute tribe engaged in some sort of strange head-butting greeting to welcome Ko-Ko and Faw-Faw back. They lifted Nulia in their huge hands and gave her a gentle tap on the forehead, too.

Pogum tied Xolotl to a tree. He and Bluebird took the opportunity to sit and rest for a few minutes. The Wood Men offered them some berries and nuts to eat, which they gratefully gobbled down.

Bluebird placed an affectionate hand on Pogum's knee. "I thank Awona'Wilona you came along when you did. You are an impressive man, Pogum of the Itiwana. Can it be only a coincidence that such a man appeared in my time of distress?"

Pogum turned his head to hide his facial scar. "There are no coincidences, Bluebird."

"I fully agree," she replied. "We were fated to meet, I think. Some destinies intertwine beyond all untying. Perhaps Awona'Wilona himself wants us to be together."

"Are you saying you want to come with me?" Pogum asked, pleased but amazed this lovely woman would want to spend time with a scarred mess such as himself.

"I do," Bluebird said. "My sisters of the Blue Corn Maiden tribe and I were pastoralist nomads, who travelled from place to place. We had no permanent home. Now, I may very well be the last of my sisterhood, so I have nowhere to claim as my own. I am alone. I have been to the Land of Everlasting Summer before, and I like the region and the people. I would know you better, brave Pogum. I think our story is just beginning."

Pogum could not admit out loud how much he liked the idea of Bluebird coming back to Shipapa-Lina with him. He was too afraid. Could she ever love someone so gruesomely scarred?

"I suppose honor demands I comply," he said. "It would be an injustice to abandon you here without a home. I invite you to Shipapa-Lina."

Bluebird touched Pogum's hair in a flirtatious way. "I knew you were not a man who would abandon me. I know a good man when I see one.

Those are not the eyes of a man who refuses to offer succor to one who needs it. I see a great man and more of your company do I desire in the future. I knew the day I met you, as I know today, you would change my life. I thrill at the thought of what we'll do tomorrow."

"Suddenly tomorrow seems very ... pleasant," Pogum responded, blushing slightly. "I am not a man for words, but..."

"Then let's have no more words," she said, throwing her arms around him and pressing her lips against his. Pogum was not sure how to react at first but soon found himself becoming lost in the moment. He allowed himself to accept that, despite his ugly scars, she wanted him.

Nearby, while watching the man she had become enamored with kissing another woman, Nulia's initial reaction was anger, followed by sadness. She had suspected Pogum dismissed her for being a child and would never return her affections. Since Bluebird came along, she feared Pogum would prefer the corn maiden, and now that fear had come true. Nulia turned away, unable to watch any longer, wiping tears off her cheeks. Whatever she had hoped would happen between herself and Pogum, it was over before it began.

Soon afterward, Pogum announced it was time to go. The Itiwana needed to learn what he had discovered. He told Nulia he was leaving with Bluebird.

"Too much needs doing to tarry here any longer, enchanting as your forest is," he said.

Nulia wanted to say she was coming with him, partly because she needed his help to get revenge against the Salt Witch but also because she hated the idea of being apart from him. Yet she was aware his attentions were reserved for another woman.

"I can't go with you," she said. "My family needs to be informed that my sister has gone to join our ancestors."

"Of course," Pogum said. "They've lost one daughter and the other should be with them."

Nulia did her best to hide her distress. She hated the idea of Pogum and Bluebird going away together but knew when she was defeated. She forced a smile onto her face.

"When will you be leaving?" she asked.

"Upon the now," Pogum said. "There is no time to dawdle. We have a very long way to go. I admit that I'll miss having your powerful friends to carry our captive."

"Is that all you'll miss, good Pogum?" Nulia wondered.

Pogum smiled warmly at her. "You, most of all, will be missed, sweet Nulia. You have been a dear friend and staunch ally and I will remember you fondly. I hope we meet again."

Pogum noticed a tear slide down Nulia's tanned cheek and wiped it off with his finger. "As a fisherman, I see enough salty water. I don't wish to see it in your eyes. Never let that starry twinkle be dimmed by sprinkles of sadness. Do not be moved to tears by goodbyes. In time we'll say hello again."

Nulia wiped her eyes. She wanted to do something to ensure her place in Pogum's memory, so he would think of her fondly. She did not want him to ever forget her.

"Wait here," she said and slipped away to talk with Faw-Faw. She returned to Pogum with good news.

"Faw-Faw has grown fond of you during our trip," she told Pogum. "And I think he enjoyed his time in new lands. He seems to like traveling. So I have convinced him to accompany you back to the Land of Everlasting Summer. He appears quite excited by the idea."

"He will be most welcome," Pogum said. "I can surely use his assistance."

"I know," Nulia replied. "Just remember what I told you about communicating with the Wood Men. Faw-Faw will understand your hand gestures and tone. He may not know the words, but you should be able to let him know where you want to go."

"I expect we will get along splendidly," Pogum told her. "Thank you again for all you've done, dear Nulia. May Awona'Wilona smile upon you."

"And you, brave Pogum," she said, kissing him on the cheek. "I am certain we will meet again. You can always count on my aid, and the help of the Wood Men. May Awona'Wilona guard you on your trip."

"Now let me see you walk through the trees once more, before I go," Pogum asked her.

"I'll run through the trees for you, Pogum," she said. "Watch me run."

Nulia scrambled up a tree like a squirrel and ran from branch to branch, from tree to tree, as if she had been born among the treetops instead of on the grass.

Pogum smiled. "Run, little one. I hope you never stop."

He announced it was time to go. Faw-Faw picked up the captive Tunerak Destroyer, who was not inclined to resist the giant. With Xolotl draped over his shoulder, Faw-Faw followed Pogum and Bluebird as they began the journey. Watching from high in the tree, Nulia felt her heart sink as Pogum walked away. *The one thing I will never do is forget you, Pogum.*

After days of walking, following the path the Na-Ash-Jai spider-women had indicated, Tawa reached his destination. On top of an extremely steep incline which the spider-women called Manitou's Rise (named for one of the Sky Elders) was the tree Tawa had sought for so many days.

"At last," he said, still puffing from climbing the slantwise slope.

The tree was positioned exactly at the highest point. It was tall but not the tallest Tawa had ever seen. Not tall enough to seem unusual. It seemed so normal in fact, he wondered for a minute whether he had the right tree or not. The only odd thing about it was that the wide canopy of branches stretched out unusually far in every direction. He could not remember ever having seen branches this long on a tree of this type. It was as if the tree was trying to reach around the world. Otherwise, the tree was unremarkable. How many people might have seen this tree and thought nothing of it?

With Black Crow on his shoulder, he cautiously walked closer to the dark brown tree with the deep groves. He stepped over the thick roots which protruded from the earth like veins bulging through skin. The large dark green leaves had serrated edges.

Remembering the spider-women's forewarning about a beast called Mapingwari, Tawa was on guard, fretfully anticipating danger. He was not even certain how to ensure if this was the correct tree.

When he was nearly close enough to touch it, he overheard a loud buzzing and halted anxiously. "Be alert, my feathered friend. I have a foreboding sense that menace is afoot."

He spotted what appeared to be a huge shadow moving in his direction. Uneasy, he put an arrow in his bow and pointed it at the object. Upon closer look, he realized it was not a shadow or single object. It was a swarm of bees.

"I don't believe this arrow is going to do much good, Black Crow," Tawa mumbled. "It would be prudent to retreat, I think."

Tawa ran from the tree, wisely getting some distance from the swarm. He noticed the bees were not following him, so he stopped to observe them. He watched the insect swarm circle the tree, where they created a ten-foot-high living fence. Tawa was not anxious to attempt piercing the protective circle because his instincts told him he would be quickly stung to death should he try. It was a vexing problem that could not be solved with either an arrow or a helpful crow.

"There's always something cleverer than ourselves, Black Crow," Tawa said. "This will take some thought, it seems."

As Tawa paced, he noticed an immense footprint on the ground. He was unsure what kind of creature could have left such a print but whatever it might be, it was apparently large and heavy, with sharp claws on its forepaws. Could this be Mapingwari?

Tawa timidly followed the prints to a nearby thicket of tall shrubs. As he got closer, he smelled the scent of a living creature. He recognized an animal smell when he detected one. There was something hiding behind the bushes. *Brave heart, Tawa.*

He could make out a shape through the thicket. Whatever it was, it appeared to be big and hairy. Tawa could hear heavy breathing. Had he found the beast Mapingwari? He was not sure what would happen when he met this mystery monster, but he hardened his rapidly beating heart to confront the tremendous creature beyond. If there was a beast here, he had no choice but to face it. Taking a deep breath, he reluctantly stepped through the thicket, arrow at the ready, prepared to defend himself against whatever terror awaited him.

CHAPTER SEVENTEEN

Trembling, Tawa crossed to the other side of the thicket. There he encountered his beast, but it was not exactly what he had expected. He found himself facing a giant sloth, which was dozing peacefully in the afternoon sun.

Tawa lowered his bow, not sensing any menace from the oversized creature. Certainly, it was a gigantic beast. It was at least an eight-thousand-pound, twenty-five-feet-long and ten-feet-high animal. It had curved, slicing, six-inch claws on its front feet. Yet despite its intimidating mass, it did not seem hostile.

"Is this really Mapingwari?" Tawa wondered aloud. "I am both relieved and disappointed."

Mapingwari opened its eyes halfway and looked at Tawa for a moment, with very little interest and then went back to sleep. Clearly this human was not worth losing any sleep over.

"And now?" Tawa said to Black Crow, as if he were expecting an answer. "Gratified as I am not to be fighting a monster, I'm unsure how this sleepy thing can help me against a swarm of angry bees. The Spider-Women spoke about riding a beast. Do they mean this lazy monstrosity? I cannot picture myself charging into battle atop this indolent brute."

Impulsively, Tawa decided to climb onto the sloth's back. He stepped up on the creature, which opened its sleepy eyes. Tawa wondered if this would stir Mapingwari to some sort of action. Instead, the animal merely lifted its head slowly and studied the little human. Tawa detected a hint of annoyance in Mapingwari's attitude but nothing threatening. He continued his climb until he seated himself upon the animal's back, near its front legs.

"All right, Mapingwari. Let's see your spirit," Tawa yelled, nudging Mapingwari with his feet. "Ho there, sleepy giant. Let's away."

Mapingwari twisted its neck around to glare indifferently at the strange little being who was bouncing on its back and making noises. Boring quickly of this, Mapingwari lowered its head and went back to sleep.

"Oh, by Awona'Wilona's grace," Tawa snapped. "This is preposterous."

Tawa continued to dig his heels into Mapingwari, hoping for a reaction. He tried hard to instigate some sort of response but all he received as a reward was the sound of snoring. Tawa frowned in exasperation.

"What a tragedy you are," he said, irritated.

Tawa sat impatiently, wondering what use he could make of this slumbering sloth. He remembered the Spider-Women mentioning he would have to "break the beast." Tawa had always had a knack for breaking his mounts, just as he had done with the bison. If he could do it with them, he could surely do so with this creature. This one was just larger and lazier. It would be a challenge, for certain.

Tawa began to pet Mapingwari and speak to him softly. What he said did not matter because Mapingwari did not understand a word. He mostly rambled, speaking in the soft tones which animals found soothing and appealing. His touch was gentle, with a repetitive motion. He continued this technique for a long time until Mapingwari finally raised its head. The giant sloth looked at Tawa again but without the annoyance it had displayed in its eyes earlier.

"Ah, good, good," Tawa said. "Let's be friends, you and I."

Minutes later, Tawa was delighted when Mapingwari finally stood up. The beast yawned and stretched, now roused from its habitual lethargy. Tawa patted Mapingwari lightly on its massive back.

"That's it, my fine friend," Tawa said. "Wonderful. I had faith we could work together. Now, great Mapingwari, let's walk our way to the Tree of Life and see if bees are a match for such a beast. Ho, Mapingwari."

He lightly nudged the giant forward. After a bit of hesitation, Mapingwari slowly made his way forward, trampling over the thicket and inching toward the tree. The creature moved very, very leisurely, and Tawa tried his best to maintain his patience because the short trip seemed to be taking an eternity. Gradually, the tree loomed larger as Mapingwari casually lumbered nearer to it.

Tawa wondered about the bees. What would happen when they tried passing through the swarm? Maybe Mapingwari would find them only a minor annoyance, but Tawa would not be so blasé about it. He imagined thousands of little stings all over his body. *This seems unwise.*

He noticed, however, that the bees seemed to be reacting to Mapingwari's approach. Their buzzing became louder, and they flew more erratically, as if they were agitated, or maybe even scared. If bees could panic, this is what it would look like.

Tawa raised his eyebrows in bemused surprise when Mapingwari's long tongue whipped out and snatched a dozen of the bees out of the air, swallowing them with a loud gulp sound. The rest of the swarm immediately reacted to the danger that the Sloth posed and retreated, either fleeing to the far side of the tree or to the safety of the higher branches. They fled from a predator. The path was now clear.

Tawa smiled, patting Mapingwari affectionately. "Ha. You are the king of beasts and bees, Mapingwari, my friend. The little buzzing pests were faint of heart. I thank you, large one. I owe you. Whatever it is you eat, I'll bring you scores of it."

Mapingwari got close enough to Yaxche that he was able to lick the bark. Apparently, he liked the taste. Tawa slid off Mapingwari's wide back and stood before the legendary tree. At close range, it radiated a sense of majesty. He could smell the centuries it had seen.

The instant he touched it, he felt a tingle of energy, which then burst across his body as a feeling of indescribable power. His mind became filled with a sense of well-being and clarity that the young Itiwana had never experienced or even imagined. New thoughts entered his head. Great thoughts. When he lowered his hand, he was a new man.

"So, this is truly Yaxche," Tawa whispered, calmly. "Grown by Morning Star and Pautiwa at the bidding of Awona'Wilona, back when Shipapa-Lina was young. It has stood here, holding back the winter for centuries. This tree is the bringer of the endless summer."

Tawa took several moments to drink in the glory of the Tree of Life, before beginning his triumphant return to Shipapa-Lina as the unchallenged *kik-mongwi* of the Itiwana.

Pogum and Bluebird trekked across a field, followed by Faw-Faw the Wood Man, who was carrying the bound Tunerak Destroyer known as Xolotl. It had been a full day since they had left the Red Sky Forest behind. Faw-Faw looked around like a curious and excited child, experiencing all the new sights, sounds and smells. These recent excursions out of the forest were a treat for Faw-Faw, who had never strayed far from home before. His innocent fascination with everything he witnessed caused him to frequently stop and stare, which slowed down the group's progress. Wood Men moved slowly enough, even at the best of times.

Pogum was becoming a bit annoyed that Faw-Faw was repeatedly hindering his progress, but he realized he had to tolerate it because the big Wood Man was a valuable asset to him. He would surely need the huge man's aid.

Xolotl was still intimidated by the frightening power of the Wood Man, who carried him around as if he were as light as a twig. He remained alert for a chance to flee. The Wood Man was slow and stupid, while the other two tended to walk far ahead, lost in their deep, amorous conversations. Xolotl hoped the proper opportunity would present itself and he could escape before they reached the Land of Everlasting Summer.

Although Bluebird was still distraught from the recent deaths of her sister Corn Maidens, she brightened a bit and became less despondent due to her association with Pogum. She had come to trust him as an ally and protector, as well as finding herself very attracted to him. She conversed with him as if she had known him for years.

Pogum was enjoying Bluebird's company and trying hard not to let himself be distracted by his interest in her. He would have loved to lay down in the grass with her and love her with total abandon. She was not put off by his scarring and actually considered him a desirable man. He wished he could take her at this very moment.

But this was not the time for such selfish pleasures. He had an assignment and was honor bound to bring his information and his captive back to Shipapa-Lina before he indulged his own urges. He would not split himself between duty and desire.

Pogum stopped when saw the desert sands in the distance. "This is the part I have been dreading most. The Big Sand ahead is the den of the Skinwalkers. I imagine we may find the Salt Witch there as well. She seems to travel swiftly."

"We need to cross this region?" Bluebird asked.

"I fear so," Pogum told her. "I need to reach a certain hill. Then we can travel by an usual method to the Pisas Vaya River, which leads back to the Land of Everlasting Summer."

Xolotl took the opportunity to unsettle his captors. "You won't make it. The Salt Witch told us the Skinwalkers are hunting for you. You are about to step into a hornet's nest full of horrific predators who savor a good kill and who live to serve mighty Malsumis. Once they are done rending your body to tiny fragments, Great Malsumis will claim your pitiful soul and torment you for eternity and beyond."

Pogum slapped the portentous words out of Xolotl's mouth with the back of his hand. Bluebird went pale, horrified by the thought of being ripped apart at the hands of some beast-men. And could Malsumis really claim her soul? Eternal torture was a horrifying idea.

Pogum, on the other hand, was obdurate in his intention. No threats or Skinwalkers or witches or even Malsumis himself would keep loyal Pogum from reaching Shipapa-Lina and doing his duty to Yana-Luha.

"Even if I am doomed to failure, my soul would not be worthy to join great Awona'Wilona if I did not try. I have foresworn myself to finding a way to prevail. I'll look for a different route and if there is none, I'll fight legions of monsters for each tiny step forward."

"Wait," Bluebird said, having had a timely and fortunate recollection. "There is another way."

"Where?"

"Not far from here, to the east," Bluebird said, pointing. "There are forgotten caverns and tunnels which our ancestors called the Nadir. Mother Corn told us about them. She said her foremothers once used them to avoid the desert heat while traveling. They have not been used in ages because Mother Corn and Grandmother Corn before her, were panicked by closed-in places."

"Can you lead me there?" Pogum asked.

"I can, brave Pogum," she answered. "Most surely. Mother Corn used to point out the entrances to the Nadir whenever we passed one. I made a map in my mind of each one, in the event I ever needed to go there myself. It seems that time has come. Follow me, noble Pogum, and trust me."

"I do," Pogum said. "Lead the way, my lovely Bluebird. By Awona'Wilona, we'll prevail by the end of this day. We will crush the prophecy of this Tunerak swine with our clenched fists and force him to swallow it."

Hobomok the Hunter was wandering through the forest on the outskirts of the Land of Everlasting Summer. He had run in a panic, fleeing from the Koyamishi Mudheads and became so frightened, he had gotten lost. Fortunately, he was a hunter and tracker, and was therefore able to make his way back to the Land of Everlasting Summer.

The landscape was again familiar, telling him he was close to Shipapa-Lina. He was returning home to become the new *kik-mongwi*. True, he failed to find the Tree of Life but he was now the only survivor of the quest, since Tawa was certainly dead. Hobomok wondered what he should say, now that he was almost home. How should he describe what had happened? He did not want to tell the other Itiwana that he ran away and left young Tawa to die. How should he explain Tawa's death without making himself seem cowardly?

He was aware the rest of the Shakowin were against him. They would certainly use any possible shadow of dishonor to make the argument Hobomok was unworthy to be the *kik-mongwi*. He had already failed to find Yaxche, so any other defeat might give Pekwin, Atira and T'Soona the leverage they needed to thwart his plans.

He strode slowly back to Shipapa-Lina, working out exactly how to tell the Itiwana the last descendent of Morning Star's lineage was gone for good and the reign of Hobomok of the Moon Clan had begun.

Bluebird led Pogum and Faw-Faw to the stump of a desert tree, near a moss-covered boulder. In between the stump and the boulder was an oval hole, big enough for a person to crawl through. It was partially obscured by some bushy shrubs. Bluebird pushed the vegetation aside.

"There it is," she said. "Our path to the underworld."

Pogum fought off a sense of nervous trepidation, vowing nothing would deter him. "It would be craven to falter," he said.

Pogum took two sticks from the tree and spent a few minutes rubbing them together, making a pair of torches, one of which he gave to Bluebird.

"Follow after me. I can only hope our gargantuan friend Faw-Faw will fit inside. I'm not certain what we should do with our despicable captive, however."

"I have a good idea," Bluebird said, with a sly, almost sadistic grin.

With some prompting from Bluebird, Faw-Faw tossed the bound Xolotl into the hole. The Tunerak Destroyer screamed as he vanished into the subterranean darkness. Bluebird chuckled at his fear.

"If there is any danger at the bottom of this pit, let him face it first," she said.

"Ruthlessly efficient," Pogum said. "Well thought. I'll go next."

Pogum crawled nervously into the hole, dreading what dangers awaited in the darkness at the bottom.

CHAPTER EIGHTEEN

Pogum crawled into the hole. It was not a straight drop. The shaft was diagonal. There were roots sticking out from the inside of the shaft that he could grab onto, slowing his slide to the bottom. It was pitch dark, and he hoped nothing exceptionally large and hungry was waiting at the bottom.

Pogum slid to the bottom of the pit and held up his torch, illuminating an underground tunnel. Next to him lay Xolotl, who was grumbling after hitting the ground rather hard, still trying to get free from his bonds.

Pogum took note of the size of tunnel's size. There was ample room to stand and move around. He hoped the roof of the tunnel was high enough for big Faw-Faw. Roots from surface trees protruded from the cave roof and hung down like stalactites. The walls were greenish-brown, and the place had a damp smell.

Bluebird slid down behind Pogum, landing on her posterior with an "Ow." Pogum offered a hand to help her up. She raised her torch to inspect the ominous underworld.

"What a horridly dreary place," she said.

"What expectations did you have of an underground tunnel?" Pogum asked. "Did Mother Corn describe something more fanciful?"

"She described nothing," Bluebird answered. "But I have heard about this hidden place for so long, I imagined more grandeur. This does not fulfill my expectations."

A grunting sound came from the diagonal shaft. Pogum peered up the shaft and saw two large feet. Faw-Faw made a panicky "Gug, Gug" sound from inside the shaft. He was not accustomed to closed-in spaces.

"I think our hairy friend is stuck," Pogum said. "Calmly, calmly large one. We have you."

Pogum and Bluebird grabbed Faw-Faw's ankles and yanked very hard. Faw-Faw dropped from the shaft, crashing to the ground with a "Gug." He studied the cave, befuddled.

"What he lacks in grace, he compensates for with loyalty," Pogum said, helping the Wood Man to his feet. "Stand tall, my large friend."

Faw-Faw rose to his full height but were it not for his natural slump, his head would have hit the cave roof. As it was, he had barely an inch clearance. Pogum pointed to the trussed up Xolotl and made a lifting gesture. Faw-Faw got the gist of it. He tried slinging Xolotl over his shoulder as he had done earlier, but there was no room for that in the shallow cave. Faw-Faw instead dragged Xolotl behind them.

"Ow," Xolotl squealed. "Ouch. Ow, stop that! This hurts. Ouch."

The small group walked through the tunnel, with Pogum leading the way and Bluebird close behind. Faw-Faw did not understand why they were there and was uncomfortable being in a confined space, but he would not leave his new friends. He followed and hoped they would lead him to the open air again, dragging his complaining captive.

As they walked, the tunnel expanded higher and wider, which made Faw-Faw a bit more comfortable. Pogum hoped they were going in the right direction. It was difficult to get his bearings without celestial navigation.

The tunnel finally led to a wide, open cavern. The trio surveyed the surprisingly large space. Hundreds of bats hung from the cave roof. There were numerous little holes or small burrows all along the cave floor. The abundant holes led to an ant colony-like series of interconnected tunnels and chambers, each designed for a different purpose.

Pogum, Bluebird, and Faw-Faw were all focused on one object, which stood in the middle of the large cavern. It was a stone statue, as tall as a tree, surrounded by a deep, round trench. It depicted an angry-looking man with ice for a beard and flames surrounding his feet. It appeared to be a totem of worship.

"Who is that? And who built it?" Bluebird asked.

"I cannot begin to speculate who the makers were," Pogum said, "But I think the image it represents is Malsumis. He is a Winter God. The flames might be meant to signify the flames of Spirit Fire Hill where Malsumis is imprisoned."

"That would mean followers of his once used this deep domain as a place of worship," Bluebird said.

Pogum spotted several burnt torches on an altar at the foot of the statue. Looking around warily, he felt extremely exposed and vulnerable in this dark place.

"And it's very possible they still do," he said. "We must be away with all speed."

Faw-Faw suddenly roared, as if he were in pain. He lifted his arm and Pogum spied what looked like a needle sticking out of the Wood Man's bicep. Just then, another needle flew passed Pogum's face, missing by a fraction of an inch.

"They're definitely still here," Pogum said.

Out from those little tunnels came the Yehasuri. Deceptively fierce, the Yehasuri were tiny men and women, ranging from twelve-eighteen inches tall. They wore skins from moles and bats. The small beings had diminutive bows made from twigs. The miniscule wooden needles served as arrows for them. They began firing at the intruders.

Pogum felt a dozen needles piercing his skin at numerous points over his body. Bluebird cried out in panic as she was jabbed multiple times, across her legs and waist.

"Pogum, do something," she shouted.

Pogum was at a loss. There were hundreds of the miniscule Yehasuri surrounding them. He could possibly pick off one or two with his spear if his aim was good but what would be the point? There were too many to fight in such a fashion. He tried shielding Bluebird with his own body, but the needles were coming from every direction.

"We have to get out of here now," he shouted.

Grabbing Bluebird by the hand, he tried ushering them back to the tunnel they had entered from. Faw-Faw dropped Xolotl and followed after them. Pogum and Bluebird had barely taken a dozen steps when a wave of dizziness overwhelmed them. The cavern seemed to become distorted, and it was impossible to tell up from down.

Poison, Pogum thought. *Poisoned needles.*

Bluebird collapsed. Pogum attempted to lift and carry her, but he was too weak. He collapsed as well. He fought hard to remain conscious, but his mind slipped into a dark, dreamless sleep. Faw-Faw realized his friends were in danger and lifted them up under each of his arms, carrying them. The needles were stinging him painfully, but the poison was not having the same effect on the big Wood Man that it had on Pogum and Bluebird.

Faw-Faw reached the shaft to the surface but was so big he couldn't squeeze through it without getting stuck. He had needed help getting through the first time. There was no possibility he could make it while carrying his unconscious friends. The simple-minded Wood Man was stymied with indecision. What should he do?

Confounded by the situation, Faw-Faw placed his friends gently on the ground and started digging around the shaft, hoping to widen it. While trying to expand the shaft, he only weakened it. His frantic efforts caused the shaft to collapse. The roof fell in on him. With a panicky roar, Faw-Faw vanished under a pile of dirt and stone.

The Yehasuri warily approached the remains of the shaft. They gathered around the unconscious Pogum and Bluebird. The Yehasuri studied the collapsed shaft to be certain that the giant was not coming out. After waiting to make sure the colossal Wood Man was no longer a threat, they bound the sleeping pair with snakeskins. The tiny beings now had two sacrifices to offer Malsumis.

When Hobomok returned to Shipapa-Lina, a crowd gathered around him. Every man and woman among the Itiwana wondered if he had found the tree Yaxche. They also speculated regarding where Tawa might be. Hobomok was coy about dispensing information, telling everyone to gather at the Speaking Mound near the chieftain's longhouse. Word swiftly spread across Shipapa-Lina, and soon all the Itiwana waited near the mound to hear what had happened.

Atira had been playing her flute by the lily pond when T'Soona came to tell her Hobomok had returned but Tawa had not. Atira gasped, fearing the worst.

"Do you think...?" she began.

"Think nothing," T'Soona advised. "We shall listen first and then think. We need information before we act."

The nervous mother rose to her feet. "T'Soona, I don't know what I'd do if I didn't have you by my side when things go askew."

She gave T'Soona a warm hug, and he closed his eyes, savoring the feel of her body pressed against his. *If only...* he thought.

"Come," she said, grabbing him by the arm, dragging him to the Speaking Mound.

Minutes later, Atira and T'Soona joined Grey Pekwin and the rest of the tribe at the Speaking Mound to hear what Hobomok had to say. Manabazo was still in Shipapa-Lina, having decided to remain for a time to watch over the Itiwana. He had once again taken his eagle form and observed from atop the longhouse.

Hobomok stood upon the Speaking Mound, attempting to look sad when he informed the crowd of the bad news about their almost-leader

Tawa. Atira tightly held T'Soona's hand, which T'Soona enjoyed.

"My friends. My people," Hobomok said loudly. "I stand before you today to say…"

Before Hobomok could utter another syllable, T'Soona spotted something high above.

"Look," he yelled, pointing. "Smoke signals."

Everyone turned to see whiffs of smoke in the distant sky. The alternating combination of small puffs and long columns of smoke told of victory.

Atira yelled excitedly, "It's Tawa."

Impossible, thought Hobomok. *It can't be from him. He must be dead by now.*

Everyone cheered the evidence of the young man's success. Atira hugged the smiling T'Soona, who took the opportunity to embrace her in return. Grey Pekwin allowed a reserved smile to slip onto his weathered face. Even Manabazo flapped his wings in celebration. Only Hobomok remained silent and unsmiling.

The gleeful Atira said a thankful prayer while T'Soona took the opportunity to annoy Hobomok once again. "What were you going to say, oh mighty hunter?"

Hobomok clenched his fists, concealing his rage. "It … is not imperative. It can wait until tonight. By then, we'll all be certain whether or not it was truly Tawa sending that message."

"I warned you not to underestimate the boy's capabilities," T'Soona commented merrily. "Another lesson learned, eh?"

As the crowd laughed, Hobomok narrowed his dark eyes. "One day, T'Soona, I will flay you, chew you up like a wolf devouring a rabbit and spew you from my mouth."

Hobomok stomped away and T'Soona chuckled. "By Awona'Wilona, the pleasure I get from goading him."

Atira read the smoke signals again, savoring the victory sign. "If Hobomok is upset now, wait until my son gets back and we make him the new *kik-mongwi*."

Deep in the underworld, Pogum awoke. His mind slowly cleared, and his blurry vision focused. He realized he was still in the Nadir cavern. Those torches he had seen on the altar were now lit and illuminated the area. He was still bound and could see Bluebird lying next to him, tied up and unconscious. There was no sign of Faw-Faw.

Pogum and Bluebird were at the edge of the deep, circular trench that surrounded the statue. Flames spit out of the pit and Pogum could feel the searing heat. He had an unpleasant premonition regarding what—or who—was to be tossed into that fire pit. He struggled to extricate himself from his bonds, but the knots were expertly tied.

The Yehasuri were in a crescent moon formation, facing both captives and the statue. Standing with them was Xolotl, who the little beings had untied. Pogum deduced they had recognized

Xolotl's attire and identified him as a follower of the Enemy Way. That, along with the fact he was a captive of the people who had intruded upon their territory, convinced the tiny terrors they shared a mutual enemy. Whatever the reasoning, Xolotl was free and among allies.

"Awake, are you?" Xolotl asked. "Matters have changed a bit, haven't they, Itiwana?"

"Not so very much," Pogum answered. "You are still a dishonorable coward and no doubt of it. Your existence will never be worth the pain of the mother who bore you. That will never change."

Xolotl kicked Pogum soundly in the ribs. "I'll cut out your contemptuous tongue."

Pogum gritted his teeth, unwilling to reveal that the kick hurt. "My words are proven. A coward to the last. Whether it's against unarmed women or bound men, you disgrace yourself with your lack of courage or honor."

"Silence!" Xolotl yelled, kicking Pogum a second time. "I will not be lectured by the likes of you. No corn growing Itiwana questions the bravery of a Tunerak Destroyer. For those ignoble words, you will be the first one sacrificed to mighty Malsumis."

Xolotl rammed his foot into Pogum's chest, pushing the bound Itiwana to the very edge of the trench, trying to force him into the blazing inferno.

CHAPTER NINETEEN

Pogum squirmed, desperately trying to keep himself away from the flames. Bluebird awoke and saw was happening. Realizing Pogum was in danger, she kicked Xolotl, distracting him. He angrily kicked her back. Pogum took the opportunity to swing his feet around and trip Xolotl.

As Xolotl fell, an angry howl echoed through the cavern. Xolotl and the Yehasuri looked around to find the source of the roar. Out from the tunnel came an angry Faw-Faw, who had amazingly survived the cave-in of the shaft. He had powered his way to freedom and come back, looking for his friends. He was covered in scratches and dirt from the cave-in, but his wild spirit was undiminished.

Faw-Faw charged toward the pit. The little Yehasuri scattered, fearing the giant would trample them. They fired their needle-arrows at him again, but as before, the poison had no effect and the sting of the needles simply made Faw-Faw angrier.

Xolotl backed away from the angry giant but could retreat no further due to the flames rising from the pit. He tried using speed to evade Faw-Faw, but the huge Wood Man had a long reach. The big man grabbed the Tunerak Destroyer with unexpected quickness. Xolotl screamed in complete horror as Faw-Faw lifted him high in the air and threw him into the inferno.

The Yehasuri continued to attack Faw-Faw with their tiny weapons. They feared the giant since no one had ever shrugged off their poison needles before. Faw-Faw grabbed two stones and threw them at the miniature warriors, crushing some of the Yehasuri. The tiny tribe had never seen the like of the Wood Man before and scrambled in a panic, trying to find a strategy to deal with his size and power.

While the Yehasuri were focused on Faw-Faw's rampage, Pogum rolled nearer to Bluebird. "Get closer. Get back-to-back. Let me untie you."

Obeying Pogum's suggestion, she wriggled until her shoulder blades were pressed against his. Pogum was able to free her hands with his thorn bracelet, despite being unable to see what he was doing. Once her hands were free, Bluebird took the bracelet and cut Pogum loose.

"Fine work," Pogum said, stretching his arms out. "Now we must get out of this cave of chaos."

"Tell me you have an idea," Bluebird insisted. "Speak comfort to me. Say you know what to do."

Pogum looked up at the tall statue and noticed there was one large, excavated hole in the upper wall of the cavern, slightly above the statue's head. The other holes and burrows went downward in the manner that ants would build a colony. This single hole was larger and in an unusual location, away from the rest. What could it be for? Pogum observed a small plank leading from the top of the statue to the hole. Was it a way out?

Pogum grabbed Bluebird by the hand, pulling her to the edge of the flame trench.

"Jump," he ordered.

"What?" Bluebird cried, looking at the flames. "Did the poison make you lose your senses?"

"Jump over it," Pogum insisted. "We need to reach the other side."

Bluebird looked down into the fire pit. "But ... should we fall..."

"We won't," he said. "I give my word upon that."

Bluebird reluctantly agreed. Hand-in-hand, they leaped over the circular trench of fire and came down at the foot of the statue, aside the wooden altar. Faw-Faw still battled the tiny Yehasuri. Pogum could not leave the loyal Wood Man behind.

"Faw-Faw. Here. Come."

Pogum's cry drew not only the attention of Faw-Faw but of the Yehasuri as well. They had been so fixated on Faw-Faw's ruckus that Pogum and Bluebird's escape had gone unnoticed. Now aware of the pair's escape, they moved to a closer spot, where their little needle-arrows could hit the two targets.

Pogum quickly grabbed the wooden alter and held it defensively in front of himself and Bluebird, protecting them from the needles. At the same time, Faw-Faw leaped over the circular fire trench and joined his friends at the base of the statue. Faw-Faw used his own body to block the needles from reaching his companions.

Pogum pointed upwards. "We have to go up there, Faw-Faw. Do you understand? Up."

Faw-Faw looked above with puzzlement, not comprehending what Pogum was saying. All he really understood at this moment was how much those needles hurt him. He just desired to get back to the surface.

"He doesn't understand," Bluebird said, wincing as a needle missed her ear by inches.

"We just have to begin scaling this hideous statue and hope he follows," Pogum said. "Go. Start climbing. We'll defend your rear."

Bluebird began her ascent, using whatever handholds and footholds she could find to scale the statue. Pogum held the wooden altar higher, leaving himself vulnerable below the chest. Faw-Faw gallantly stepped in front of him and bore the brunt of the needle assault. Pogum took advantage of Faw-Faw's immense height and commenced climbing the statue behind

Faw-Faw's back. Faw-Faw looked up, confused. Pogum gestured for the Wood Man to follow him. Faw-Faw hesitated but finally got the clue and began to climb.

The trio reached a point high enough on the statue where the tiny arrows of the little Yehasuri could not reach them. They were out of range but not yet safe.

Pogum was the first to reach the top and the other two arrived seconds later. The Yehasuri watched furiously from the ground. A group of them carried timber beams, with which they could cross the trench. They first poured water into the pit, to smother the flames.

Pogum examined the wooden plank that connected the head of the statue to the large hole in the rear wall. The plank was narrow but seemed sturdy enough. He was not sure if it would support Faw-Faw's weight, but it seemed safe for Bluebird and himself. He hoped.

"Follow me, Bluebird," he said.

Balancing himself, one foot in front of the other, he slowly crossed the plank. Below him, the Yehasuri were dowsing the fire in the circular pit. He focused only on the plank and the hole in the wall. He reached his goal and stepped into the holed-out tunnel, which he hoped led to safety. It was too dark in the tunnel to determine where it actually led. Looking down, he realized the Yehasuri were shimmying up the wall like insects, closing in on Pogum and his allies.

"Come Bluebird, hurry!" he said.

Bluebird nervously stepped onto the plank and tip-toed across, trying not to think of either the inferno below or the diminutive enemies scampering up the wall with cruel intentions.

"Give me your hand," Pogum shouted.

Bluebird held out her trembling hand. Pogum grabbed it, yanking her to the relative safety of the hole. She wrapped her hands around his neck, feeling more secure that way.

Pogum gave her a hug. "You're safe, sweet maiden. Breathe easy."

Faw-Faw followed his two friends but as he crossed the plank, it snapped in half under his weight. Faw-Faw fell, to the horror of his friends. Luckily, the Wood Man had exceptionally long arms and managed to grab the edge of the hole in time. Pogum helped him pull his considerable bulk up. The huge man seemed relieved. Bluebird glanced down and saw the Yehasuri still quickly climbing the wall. They had almost reached the hole.

"We should make haste," Bluebird said, wary of the coming danger.

"Yes, follow me into the dark," Pogum said. "Don't misstep. Be on watch."

Crawling into the shadowy, mysterious tunnel, Pogum prayed it would lead to freedom. Faw-Faw's head repeatedly hit the tunnel roof. Bluebird could not determine if it was her imagination, but thought she heard tiny footsteps closely pursuing them.

The little hole finally led to another but smaller cavern. Shining through the darkness from the far end of the cavern was a circle of sunlight, indicating an exit from the perilous underworld.

"I think we've found the path out," Pogum said, extending his hand to Bluebird. "Come, my lovely. Follow me."

"Anywhere," she answered.

Followed by Faw-Faw, they tip-toed cautiously through the dismal cave, excited by the feel of heat and the sound of howling wind. *We're near the surface.*

As the trio got closer to freedom, they found that the cavern was partially flooded from an underground stream. Ankle deep at first, the water was up to their knees by the time they reached the center of the cave. The sunlight from the opening warmed Bluebird's skin.

"Thank Awona'Wilona," she said. "We made it."

Just as the sunlight touched her round face, she heard a wail that sounded like a baby crying. She stopped, looking back into the darkness of the cave.

"What's wrong?" Pogum asked.

"Don't you hear that?" she asked. "It's a child. There's an infant in there."

"It must be a trick," Pogum said. "Let's flee this place."

Something moved in the darkness. Bluebird pointed. "Look."

A toddler came into view, splashing through the shallower level of water. It let loose with a high-pitched, mournful cry, stretching out a tiny hand in an apparent appeal for help. Bluebird rushed forward to save the child.

"Stay calm. I'm coming," she said.

Pogum grabbed her arm. "No! It's a trick. We must go."

She yanked her arm free of him and rushed to the small child. She reached out to lift the toddler in her arms. "Come with me. You'll be safe."

As she picked it up, the child's face immediately transformed into a horrific dwarf with a large mouth and jagged fangs. It howled and attempted to bite her neck. She screamed and struggled with the little beast.

A Water Baby, Pogum realized with alarm, rushing to her assistance.

As he splashed across the flooded cave floor, more of those little needle-arrows flew near him, coming from the dark, proving the Yehasuri were still persistently following them. *Curse them!*

The Yehasuri, however, did not reckon with the power of Faw-Faw. The huge Wood Man lifted a bolder and tossed it. Some of the Yehasuri were squashed by the stone and others were knocked down by the splash. The rest retreated, having had enough of this giant.

"Splendidly done, my furry friend," Pogum said, as he thrust his spear into the Water Baby. It squealed as the weapon pierced its heart. Bluebird threw it back into the water.

"What in the name of..." she cried, horrified.

"I've heard of the Water Babies," Pogum said. "I had no idea how revolting they were."

"Water Babies?" she asked. "You were right. It was a trick. I feel so foolish."

"Don't chastise yourself," Pogum said. "You're a compassionate-hearted beauty. Now let us leave this place."

Pogum led Bluebird and Faw-Faw through the cave opening, and they found themselves in the sunlight once more. They could now relax, feeling safe back in their own bright, warm world. Faw-Faw was especially happy to feel non-claustrophobic.

Pogum looked out at the vast plain of sand and hills. "We've made it. I believe we should be close to my transport."

They did not have far to walk before Pogum spotted the hill where he had last seen his mysterious horse. As they ascended the hill, he realized he did not know how to summon the creature.

"Where is this transportation?" Bluebird asked.

Pogum did not have an answer for that. He looked around and shouted, "I am here. Kokopelli wishes you to give me transport. Where are you?"

Nulia and Faw-Faw watched in extreme confusion as Pogum continued crying out to the sky. Nulia wondered for a moment if his mind had been broken by the incident in the Nadir. She learned how wrong she was when the eldritch Ghost Stallion suddenly reappeared. It looked over the trio with cold eyes. Bluebird jumped backward, frightened by the homely beast, while Faw-Faw roared a challenge at it.

"Calm, calm," Pogum said to Faw-Faw. "It won't hurt you. It will take us to the Pisas Vaya River, which leads to my home."

Bluebird pointed fearfully. "We are going to ride on that thing?"

"You and I will," Pogum said. "I'm not sure about our friend Faw-Faw."

Seeming to understand his words, the wretched looking skinny horse abruptly morphed and transformed into a huge, beautiful stallion, big enough for all three of them.

"Amazing," Pogum said in awe.

"I can't understand this," Bluebird said. "Are you sure this is safe?"

Pogum patted the horse gently. "Don't worry. I think it likes you."

Grey Pekwin had arranged a reception for the returning Tawa. Dancers and musicians were ready to perform. Decorative arrows and spears were arranged in a pattern on the ground as a tribute to the warrior returning victoriously. A bison was being cooked for a feast. A small, symbolic basket of food was placed on the ground as a gift to a hero returning in triumph.

Atira was at the forefront of the crowd, pacing with nervous anticipation at her son's imminent arrival. She would not relax until she saw him set foot safely on the grounds of Shipapa-Lina. T'Soona stood near, glad to see her looking livelier and more energetic than she had in days. He was aware how anxious she was to see her son. Above them all, Manabazo circled Shipapa-Lina in his eagle form.

Only Hobomok was unhappy. He stood apart from the rest of the tribe, disgusted at their blind, obsequious devotion to a child. What did it matter if he was the son of Yana-Luha or the descendent of Morning Star? Tawa was a mere boy and Hobomok passionately believed the youth would not make as effective or efficient a leader as he himself. Couldn't the rest of these fools see it?

Hobomok also feared Tawa would reveal the cowardly way Hobomok had run from the Mudheads. He could only hope the smoke signal message was a fake or that some unpleasantness befell Tawa during his trip back.

Hobomok's vindictive prayers were not answered. His hopes shattered when someone in the crowd shouted, "Look." He turned, as did everyone else. Hobomok felt a sickness in his stomach when he observed the returning Star Clan chief.

He was only a speck in the distance at first, but it soon became clear this was truly the son of Yana-Luha approaching. The crowd unleashed enormous cheers. The drum and flute music commenced playing, and the dancers started dancing. It was the most festive mood imaginable that Tawa returned home to.

Atira longed to run and greet him but forced herself to retain the poise that the mother of a *kik-mongwi*—as well as the wife of a former *kik-mongwi*—should always maintain.

"I wish every day had moments such as this," she said.

Tawa remained aloof amid the shouted praise of the tribe. Black Crow sat on his shoulder, like a loyal friend. Tawa picked up the basket which had been left for him. He then produced a large leaf from the Tree of Life, held it high so everyone could see it, placed the leaf in the basket and raised the basket over his head. The tribe cheered again.

"Congratulations, my son," Atira said, after the cheers died down. "I so much wish your father were here to witness your success. He wasn't an effusive man, but he would have been misty with pride."

"I wish he were here, as well," Tawa replied. "I always sought to show my quality to him. He will be with us in spirit when I lead you to the Tree of Life."

Hobomok shoved his way through the crowd and elbowed T'Soona out of his way. He circled around Atira and confronted Tawa with a disrespectful, disdainful sneer.

"So, the child-chieftain has returned to us," Hobomok said. "Go on, then. Say what you plan to say. Tell everyone."

"What is he referring to?" T'Soona asked. "Is this something that will humiliate Hobomok? If so, I heartily encourage you to tell everyone and send up smoke signals so all of Ulah-Nane will know."

"One day, T'Soona..." Hobomok grumbled, as he waited for Tawa to expose his craven retreat.

Tawa raised a hand to quiet everyone. Atira noticed how everyone instantly became silent. Only Yana-Luha had ever controlled the crowd this way. Something had changed in her son.

"No humiliations or disparagements," Tawa commanded. "Hobomok and I have both walked our way through paths of mystery and danger that were not meant for timid hearts. It is ours alone to know the perils we faced. But now, what's past is gone and so we start again. All Itiwana, united together in Awona'Wilona's cause, as my father would have wanted."

Hobomok was both relieved and infuriated. On one hand, he was glad the tribe would never learn he had been so cowardly. However, he did not like being in debt to Tawa. He hated that Tawa's generosity had saved his honor. He did not want to be the recipient of any condescending munificence, especially not from Tawa.

"I would speak with you alone, Tawa," Hobomok hissed through gnashing teeth.

Tawa nodded and gestured toward the chieftain's longhouse. "It seems unavoidable."

Grey Pekwin ordered the music and dancing be stopped, but Tawa gestured for it to continue. He stepped into the long house with the highly emotional Hobomok. Tawa's stride was flowing with confidence.

Something is very different about him, Atira thought.

"What game is this, boy?" Hobomok snapped, when they were alone. "I am a warrior, and I am not to be mocked. Do not think I will be trod upon like a worm in the grass. Say what you plan to say. Don't taunt me."

Tawa folded his arms and leaned calmly against the side wall, in an exceedingly relaxed fashion. "Hobomok, my rash friend. You are wrong in more ways than a spider has legs. What occurred on that day was an unfortunate event that can now be forgotten, for the good of all. There is nothing that I blame you for, and I have no desire to dishonor you. We will not speak of it again."

Hobomok abruptly spit on Tawa's feet. "I throw your pity back in your face. I am not your friend, and I will not serve you. You are a runt wolf's cub who is unworthy to rule the Itiwana."

"Sadly for you, it is not your decision," Tawa responded, walking casually around the long-house. "I will lead the Shakowin and other members of the tribe to the Tree of Life tomorrow and then I will be made the *kik-mongwi*. You are welcome to remain a member of my Shakowin, but I don't believe you'll accept that offer."

Hobomok glared at the younger man. "They say fathers can be seen in their sons. It seems this is true. I look at you and I see Yana-Luha. He was as pompous and arrogant as you are. He thought his blood gave him the right to be the *kik-Mongwi.* It was no truer for him than it is for you. But at least your father was a true warrior. The worst thrashings I ever received I took at his hands. I hated him, but he was still a great warrior. You, however, are a tadpole. A stripling who thinks he's a chieftain. I should be laughing at your foolishness but instead I weep for the Itiwana. With you as chieftain, they will never be what they once were. I will not remain to see our people fall to dust under your childish rule."

"If you leave us in our time of trial, you will not be welcome back, Hobomok."

"I will not come back, child," Hobomok snapped. "Not to any tribe ruled by you. As long as you live, I would rather remain a nomad. We cannot share anything—not even a tribe. This is my home no longer. While the Itiwana follow you, I curse them all as fools. Farewell, child. I wish you a plague."

Tawa watched silently as Hobomok stormed out of the longhouse. He shook his head, disappointed, but not surprised. "He has a rare contempt in him."

Outside the longhouse, people watched as Hobomok marched wordlessly across Shipapa-Lina. He did not look directly at anyone. He would not even address his own Moon Clan. He grabbed his spear and stormed away, fuming with rage and hate. He inwardly vowed to destroy Tawa one day. The Itiwana would also need to be punished for their support of the upstart.

Tawa emerged from the chieftain's longhouse and the people looked to him for answers. "Where is Hobomok going?" asked young Yoki of the Moon Clan.

"Sadly, Hobomok has chosen to leave us," Tawa said. "His mind is firm in this. We can only wish him luck on his journey. But enough of good-byes. We have to think of the future."

Manabazo had resumed his deer form and cantered to where Tawa stood. "You know now, don't you? Tawa has seen what is true."

"Yes," Tawa answered. "I have. When I touched Yaxche, it all became clear. It was as if many thoughts were planted in my mind like seeds and immediately grew into a vast garden of knowledge."

"You say it best. Now say it to the rest."

Tawa stood upon the Speaking Mound and addressed the Itiwana. "Listen well, good friends. Hear what I now know.

"Long ago, when the land was lush and great beasts walked the world, Ulah-Nane was ruled by the First Gods. Huit'zilo'pochtl ruled them all. But then the Frost God Itztala'Coliuqui and the feathered wind serpent Quetzal'coatl overthrew him and instigated the unending Age of Ice. The old gods vanished from our realm. After so many generations, the Age of Ice ended.

Then, in the days of the Great Turtle, new gods came to Ulah-Nane, including Awona'Wilona and Spider-Mother. When Malsumis the Winter Spirit planned to bring another Age of Ice upon us, Awona'Wilona had Morning Star and Pautiwa plant Yaxche to prevent this. It grew quickly, creating the Oki. This is the Eternal Life Force which binds man and nature and gods. It is the source of the long summer."

Manabazo said, "The Oki is pure, and the Oki is all. Without the Oki, we all must fall."

Tawa continued, "The Tree of Life allowed the tribes of Ulah-Nane to thrive, and it made the Summer Spirits such as Awona'Wilona stronger. Awona'Wilona became the most powerful of the young Sky Gods and has overseen Ulah-Nane ever since. Malsumis and the other Winter Spirits resent that summer has remained dominant in Ulah-Nane for so many generations."

Manabazo interrupted. "True, you said it well. Malsumis wants a winter eternal."

"So he does," Tawa continued. "And he therefore wants to destroy Yaxche, the Tree of Life. If he does so, a long winter will return. Awona'Wilona will be weakened, and the Winter Gods will become stronger, allowing them to free Malsumis. With him leading their Winter army, at a time when the summer gods are diminished, they will usurp Awona'Wilona."

"We understand," Atira said. "If the Tree is destroyed, the new age of cold will allow Malsumis to become strong enough to be the new Ibo-Fanga of the Sky Gods, and we'll all be at his mercy."

"The Tree's caretaker, though, he was wise," Manabazo added. "He shielded Yaxche from enemy eyes."

"Yes, he did," Tawa said. "Only Awona'Wilona and the tree's caretaker Pautiwa knew where Yaxche was. But they knew Malsumis and the Winter spirits of the Enemy Way would search unceasingly for the Tree, just to destroy it. Therefore, when Pautiwa sacrificed himself in the first war, his last act was to use his blood to cast a curse which shielded the tree from Sky Gods eyes. No Sky Elders can see Yaxche, not even if it is directly in front of them."

"It is completely invisible to them?" Aholi asked. "They can't see it at all?"

"No, and neither can they touch it," Tawa said. "Yet us mortal-born beings can both see it and touch it. Therefore, the followers of the Enemy Way—both mortal and monster—are searching for the Tree to destroy it. They tried centuries ago when the tree was young, but my ancestor Morning Star stopped them. Now the search has begun again, even as we speak."

"This warning must be heeded," Manabazo said. "Strong protection is needed."

"This was the purpose of Tesen-Wi's test," Tawa said. "To determine if the ancestors of Morning Star were as worthy as he had been, to stand as the defenders of the tree. We have passed their test, and now they've tasked us to protect Yaxche. Only we know where it is. If we fail in this undertaking, every person from every tribe in Ulah-Nane will be subject to the whims of Malsumis and his Enemy Way in an unending winter."

Tawa observed how the mood of his people shifted with his last statement and quickly sought to reassure them.

"We will not fail because we are the Itiwana. The darkness is all around us and the grip of Malsumis is closing tighter, but we are the greatest of all tribes. We will stand against the monsters and ancient enemies and winter itself. There are threats gathering to freeze the soul and test the courage of even the bravest of braves. But I know that the stout hearts before me will not shrink from the hazards of the days to come. We will not doom future generations to endless winter and the servitude of abhorrent Malsumis. We will stand unyielding and strong and fearless. It will be a great mistake by the followers of Malsumis if they choose to make the Itiwana their enemy."

Seeing how well his speech was working, he continued to inspire his people. "The long summer will continue, and your grandchildren's grandchildren will tell stories of how we stood unconquered against great enemies. We are Itiwana ... and we will stand triumphant when tomorrow comes!"

The assembled Itiwana howled heartily to show their pride and dedication. Their dynamism demonstrated to their leader how willing they were to fight at his side, even if they had to face Malsumis himself.

Tawa next addressed his Shakowin, who were fully attentive to his word. "We have much to prepare and the days to do so are few. We may face an attack here in our home and we must rethink our defenses. I have a plan to change Shipapa-Lina and make it more defensible. Come, let us talk."

Manabazo was content with what he saw. Although he had expected Yana-Luha to be the one who would lead the Itiwana against the Enemy Way, it was obvious his son would do his lineage proud. Manabazo was confident that if any Earthbound followers of Malsumis tried reaching the tree of Life, the villains would have a difficult fight on their hands.

CHAPTER TWENTY

The Ghost Stallion did as it had been instructed to do and deposited Pogum, Bluebird and Faw-Faw at the Valley of Legend. It then vanished into the ether. The sacred valley was a welcome sight to Pogum. Kokopelli was nowhere to be seen. This disappointed Pogum because he wished to thank the Sky Elder.

"I feel we can, at last, relax our guard," Pogum said.

"Despite the obstacles that impeded us, we evaded the Witch, and now we've arrived safely," Bluebird said. "Even in the most frightening moments, I knew we would."

"So we did," Pogum said. "Awona'Wilona was with us."

"We make a superb team," Bluebird said. "Let's savor this moment."

Bluebird impulsively kissed Pogum. He allowed himself an unrestrained moment of passion, cherishing the feel of her. Pogum wondered how she could be attracted to a scarred grotesque like him. He wished he could stop time and exist forever in this moment.

The Wood Man scratched his head and sat down to observe the human mating ritual with amused curiosity. Pogum and Bluebird noticed they were being watched.

"Uh, perhaps we should … speak later," Pogum said. "For now, let's find my boat. It shouldn't be too far from here. And I must find some clam shells for a certain child."

Pogum located his canoe, just where he had left it. It was a relief that the last leg of his long journey had come. He was almost home. Yana-Luha needed to know what he had learned.

Pogum's next problem was what to do about Faw-Faw. There was no room in the canoe for the giant Wood Man and he was not needed any longer. The danger was passed and there was no one to carry.

Pogum was reluctant to simply abandon the big fellow alone in this valley, so many miles from his home, after he had saved their lives. The Wood Man was sticking close, like a loyal pet.

Bluebird had the same thought. "What about him?" she asked.

"That's the matter I was pondering," Pogum said. "I don't speak his language, so I don't know how we can explain to him why he isn't needed any longer. I don't wish to injure his sensitivities because he's been an ally second to none."

"He does seem to have expectations of accompanying us," Bluebird said. "Rude as it would be, perhaps we should send him on his way."

"I don't believe he wishes to go home yet," Pogum answered. "And I must admit I've developed a strident affection for the big brute. Aside from that, I'm reticent to send him off alone with so many enemies lurking. In truth, we are indebted to him for our lives."

"This is truth," she agreed.

"We'll bring him along, then," Pogum stated.

"How?" Bluebird asked. "He'll not fit in the canoe."

"Inspired fancy of the mind is required," Pogum said.

Pogum spent the next hour constructing a raft from logs and driftwood. Tying the raft to the back of the canoe, Pogum began paddling down the Pisas Vaya River, with Bluebird seated behind him and big Faw-Faw sitting on the raft. Faw-Faw looked around with energized excitement, taking in every new sight on the trip.

Pogum rowed to the riverbank occasionally whenever he spotted some shells on the shore for the Clamshell Boy. Faw-Faw emulated his actions by finding a seashell of his own. He swallowed one but was unimpressed by the taste.

Night had fallen and the world now seemed oddly quiet, except for crickets and the occasional bird cry. Pogum paddled, strangely content while he gazed at the star-filled firmament.

"I believe there are more stars in the sky tonight than ever before," Pogum said. "Have some new ones been created by Awona'Wilona to celebrate our safe return?"

Bluebird also looked upward. "Perhaps there are, dear Pogum. Mother Corn used to say the spirits of the virtuous become stars in the sky. One day, perhaps we'll be guiding travelers like ourselves on some sacred mission."

Pogum smiled. "Such a sublime thought."

They continued to drift peacefully down the Pisas Vaya River. The danger seemed years behind them, and it was as clement a night as any of them could remember.

It took Tawa nearly an entire day to lead his mother, T'Soona, Manabazo and representatives of the Itiwana clans to the site of Yaxche. When they arrived, the group beheld massive Mapingwari, exactly as Tawa had described him. The creature awoke just long enough to look the new arrivals over and immediately went back to sleep.

"Uncanny," T'Soona murmured in awe, never having imagined such creatures still existed.

Tawa pointed to Yaxche. "There it lies. The heart of it all. The Tree of Life."

Atira was a bit disappointed by its unexceptional appearance. Only the branches were slightly unusual. "This is the one?"

Manabazo, still in Deer form, trotted around. "It must be the tree because I cannot see. I find I am blind to a tree of this kind."

"If Manabazo can't see it, then it must be the right tree," T'Soona said. "The giant sloth was enough to convince me, however."

"If you require still more evidence, try touching it," Tawa said.

T'Soona and two fellow Itiwana walked toward the tree, only to be driven off by the enormous bee swarm. The insects again formed a protective wall around Yaxche. Everyone backed far away from the tree, except for Tawa who remained perilously close to the swarm.

"So, it is the right one," Atira stated, happily.

"You have discovered the tree," Manabazo said. "A great victory."

"The first of many," Tawa said.

All of Shipapa-Lina and the outer farms gathered for the Life-Long Ceremony which would pronounce Tawa the new *kik-mongwi* of the Itiwana tribe. It was a festive day that raised the spirits of a people who had been through a great deal of turmoil in recent weeks.

Tawa sat upon his new bison steed, who he named Mountain Fury. The tribe assembled on the top of the Hanging Cliff and lined up along a dirt path. They sat cross-legged while bison and rider trotted down the trail, which was lined with stones. The Shakowin council stood at the end of the path waiting for Tawa. A steady drumbeat played, as tradition demanded.

Tawa climbed down from Mountain Fury and approached the Shakowin, which currently consisted of Grey Pekwin, Atira, and T'Soona, with Manabazo—still in deer form—acting as a special advisor. Tawa knelt before them. Pekwin carried the ceremonial headdress of great chieftains. After chanting an ancient refrain, he held the headdress above Tawa.

"By right of blood and by virtue of heroic deeds worthy of a great leader, we of the Itiwana place our trust and future in the one named Tawa. Do you accept this honor?"

"Upon my soul and my honor, I do," Tawa answered, removing the red headband that had long marked him as the son of a chief.

Grey Pekwin placed the headdress on Tawa. "By the glory of Awona'Wilona, it is done. The Itiwana have a new *kik-mongwi*."

Atira handed him his father's spear. Tawa stood tall, bowed his head slightly to the Shakowin, then turned to face the tribe. He raised the spear above his head. The Itiwana unleashed a vociferous cheer to honor their new leader. The reign of Tawa had begun.

Tawa climbed onto Mountain Fury and rode the animal back down the road through the center of Shipapa-Lina. The rest of the tribe followed him, moving in formation. The drummer trailed along, keeping the steady beat. Never so proud before, Atira was impressed with how noble Tawa looked leading the procession.

As the parade of tribespeople circled Shipapa-Lina, the group became aware that someone special had arrived. To everyone's delight, Pogum had returned. The long-absent traveler stood near the chieftain's longhouse, waiting for the crowd to pass by. Bluebird was by his side. Atira was particularly thrilled to see her brother safely home.

Another chant arose, sounding the tribe's joy at Pogum's safe return. Atira broke ranks with the rest of the Shakowin and dashed to embrace her brother, hugging him warmly.

"Of all the things in Shipapa-Lina I've missed, my sister was the utmost among those," Pogum said. "Your voice is a most welcome sound."

"I feared I would not see you among us again, dearest brother," Atira said.

The tribe gathered around the sunburned Pogum and the equally bronzed Bluebird. They wondered who this pretty new arrival was. Tawa stepped to the forefront, greeting his uncle.

"I knew from the moment you left, you would be standing here amongst us again," Tawa said. "Your tenacity made it inevitable. I welcome you back, Uncle."

"It feels good to have the grass of Shipapa-Lina under my feet," Pogum said. "I am pleased to see you again. This is Bluebird the Blue Corn Maid, who shared strange adventures with me."

"Greetings, Bluebird," Tawa said. "Welcome to Shipapa-Lina."

Pogum noted the headdress Tawa wore. "But why are you wearing the mantle of chieftains? Where is Yana-Luha?"

"We should speak in private, Uncle," Tawa stated. "So much has transpired. T'Soona will see to the Blue Corn Maid's comfort."

Tawa, Pekwin, and Atira led Pogum to the chieftain's longhouse. Sitting on the floor, they told Pogum the sad story of the sacrifice Yana-Luha had made, as well as the many other things which had occurred while Pogum was away, culminating in Tawa becoming the new chieftain. Pogum listened to every word with melancholy resignation.

"He was always a brave and noble leader," Pogum said. "Yana-Luha was a man second to none. I owed him my life. Never again will we behold his ilk. I wish I had been given the opportunity to bid him farewell. All I can do now is offer my allegiance to my nephew, the new *kik-mongwi*. I wish to present you with the intelligences I acquired on my journey."

"Good," Pekwin said. "We have been so distracted here of late, there's hardly been time to even speculate about what you may have discovered. We must know it all."

"I've returned with tales to astonish," Pogum said. "I have collected information I hope will allow us to defeat the Enemy Way. There are fierce enemies out there you could scarcely imagine, but they truly walk the grass of Ulah-Nane. We must prepare swiftly, because nightmarish forces are coming, and we'll have to bleed to survive."

A commotion outside interrupted them. "What in Awona'Wilona's name...?" Atira said.

The foursome stepped out of the longhouse and observed the tribe staring at the huge Wood Man, who was lumbering through the center of Shipapa-Lina. Some among the Itiwana were pointing their arrows at the strange being, while others held spears.

Bluebird ran protectively in front of him, imploring the Itiwana not to shoot. "No! He is not your enemy. Don't harm him, you foolish..."

"Stop!" Pogum yelled, running to intervene before anyone was injured. "He's my friend."

"Friend?" T'Soona asked. "I cannot wait to hear the stories of your adventures."

"Lower your weapons," Tawa ordered, trusting his uncle.

"Ah, a Wood Man is here," wise Manabazo announced. "Be calm. He is nothing to fear."

Faw-Faw became agitated by this unwelcoming reaction. The big man was still on alert for enemies. Pogum and Bluebird calmed him. The tribe relaxed, as well.

"This is Faw-Faw of the Wood Men," Pogum said to the crowd. "He has become my friend and ally. I owe my life to his loyalty. He is powerful and useful to have along. He doesn't speak, but he fights quite well."

"I see," Tawa said. "We'll find somewhere for him to sleep. I suspect you're all hungry. We'll feast and discuss what you've learned."

Manabazo trotted to the center of the crowd. "Indeed, we must plan. We must begin as soon as we can. Much needs to be done. Be prepared, everyone. And most of all the leader of the Star Clan. You must be ready, young man. Your training must start. Be ready in mind and heart."

"I am ready to begin," Tawa said. "I follow your lead, Manabazo. I appoint you my high advisor. The knowledge you give, I will use to prepare for whatever nightmares Malsumis and the Enemy Way may unleash upon us. By Awona'Wilona, I will not fail. I swear it."

The period known as the Great Training Days began. Manabazo proceeded to mentor Tawa in warfare, as well as in logic and strategy, just as Kokopelli had taught Morning Star three centuries earlier. His teachings were intense, but Tawa absorbed them more readily than he had done with the ancient clay tablets.

Tawa and Manabazo instituted a guardian force of bison-riding braves called the Two-Horn Riders. They would be the first line of defense for Shipapa-Lina. All the Itiwana braves began training to master their mounts for the upcoming crisis. Pogum became the "War Chief," the field leader of the Two-Horn Riders.

The Itiwana took their training very seriously. Unimagined dangers were closing in, and the challenge Tawa faced was to be ready for the unknowable.

CHAPTER TWENTY-ONE

The Great Training Days seemed to pass quickly for the Itiwana. They had begun in late summer and continued through the mild Ulah-Nane winter. Fortunately Yaxche, the Tree of Life, kept the winter months moderate and short; the Itiwana were unhindered by bad weather as they mastered their bison mounts and perfected their warrior skills.

When spring rolled around, the women of Shipapa-Lina prepared for the next corn harvest. Some of the women took time out from farming to practice their archery, wanting to help defend the village. Most of the older men, who were no longer of warrior age, contributed to Tawa's idea of a restructured Shipapa-Lina by aiding in the construction of dwellings built into the side of the Hanging Cliff.

Meanwhile, Pogum oversaw the daily drilling of the new bison-mounted Two-Horn Riders. Every bison used as a mount by a warrior was given a name. Pogum's bison was called Walking Storm.

No one among the Itiwana worked any harder during the Great Training Days than their leader. Tawa studied day-and-night under the tutelage of sage Manabazo, who trained Tawa to utilize his mind to outwit his opponents. The shapeshifter taught Tawa to think matters through and not be impulsive. Manabazo counseled patience, deliberation, and research before acting.

Tawa, whose mind had been opened and enhanced by his exposure to the Tree of Life, learned to study his opponents before a fight, to spot any weaknesses. The young chieftain learned from his mentor how out-thinking someone was part of out-fighting them.

Near the Deep Well, Tawa engaged in some archery practice. He shot six stones off a log with six arrows. Manabazo observed from the edge of the reservoir in his tortoise form.

"Well done, Star Clan son. Your aim will bring you fame," Manabazo said.

"Perhaps we can settle this war with an archery contest," Tawa quipped.

"A most interesting thought," Manabazo said. "You're learning that disputes can be settled without battles being fought. Answer me this, too—what would you do if your opponent were weaker than you?"

Tawa was quick to answer. "I would allow him to surrender but would be certain not to let my guard down, in case he tried a surprise attack."

"And if he were stronger than you? What then would you do?"

"Retreat, regroup and rethink my plans," Tawa said.

"And if your foe pursued you? What would you do?"

Tawa paused. "Run faster?"

The tortoise shook his emerald head. "No, no. Not so. You need stealth, not speed. You should vanish into the weeds. When the predator is close behind, you must be impossible to find. Fade into the mist. It should be as if you did not exist."

Tawa got the gist of the lesson. "You're saying if I'm fighting an overwhelming foe, I should have my retreat planned out in advance. I should know the easiest route to flee and the best places to hide."

"And perhaps there should be a surprise; something in store for unsuspecting eyes."

"Ah," Tawa said with a hint of a grin. "If I can't fight them in a frontal assault, I should let them chase and lead them into a trap. Or at least to a new location where the terrain gives me an advantage."

"You learn fast, indeed. Your mind works with clarity and speed," Manabazo said. "The Yaxche has changed you, through and through. Your father would be quite proud of you."

Tawa looked up at the clouds, wondering if his father was up there somewhere, locked in perpetual battle with Achiyala. "I wish he were here. I've been having bad dreams, and I fear we will need all the help we can get."

"Indeed, that's a fact. And so, I will act," Manabazo said. "Tawa, take heed. A mighty weapon is what you need. I will supply you with the ideal one. I will see it done."

Hobomok was hunting in the northern lands of Ulah-Nane. The homeless Itiwana had traveled alone for quite some time. He had not realized how long it had been until the spring came. The hunter had been on his own since the previous summer. He became furious every time he thought about Tawa and the Shakowin. They stole his glory and his honor. All the Itiwana shared the blame for supporting the unworthy child Tawa, even his own Moon Clan.

Hobomok had drifted slowly northward since his self-imposed exile began. Because prey had become so scarce in the Land of Everlasting Summer, he migrated to areas where large game was more plentiful. Over time, he found himself further from Shipapa-Lina than he had ever been.

The northern region of Ulah-Nane was far from Yaxche the Life Tree and chilled by the winds from Wuchowson, the titanic bird. The winter was harsher up north. The previous months had been difficult for one raised in the warmth of the Land of Everlasting Summer. Even the animals hid away in their lairs when the snow fell. Hobomok barely survived the longer, colder winter but somehow, his will to live and desire for revenge allowed him to endure.

The long months of loneliness had begun to affect Hobomok's mind. He had spent so much time dwelling upon the wrongs done to him that there was nothing left in his mind other than the desire for retribution. His only goal was to find a way to destroy Tawa and prove to the rest of the Itiwana they had chosen poorly in supporting the unworthy child. They would die after learning Hobomok was the better man.

The wandering hunter finally spotted a prey worth hunting. It appeared to be a large coyote. It ran quickly across a prairie with great speed. Raising his spear and taking aim, Hobomok threw his spear with all the power of his good right arm. His deadly spear-throwing skill had meant the end of many, many creatures in the past. The spear streaked through the air with unerring aim. It struck the big coyote in the side. The beast squealed and ran out of view, with the spear still imbedded in its side.

Hobomok ran after it, logically assuming the deep wound would bring the animal down before long. He was surprised the beast had not fallen immediately. Hobomok looked for the blood trail which surely must follow the wounded animal. Strangely, he could find none. It baffled him. Such a wound should have left a large splatter of blood. Yet there was no sign of a single drop anywhere. *This is most odd.*

He soon found his spear lying on the ground. It had been dislodged from the coyote's side. When he leaned over to pick it up, he was stunned to discover there was no blood on the tip of the spear. *What insanity is this? I know I hit the beast. How could there be no blood? Is this some bizarre, bloodless monster?*

Before he could grab hold of his spear, he spotted something moving from the corner of his eye. It leaped at him from behind some shrubs. It was the coyote. Hobomok cried out fearfully as the beast lunged at him. Before he could grab the spear, the beast was upon him. It was larger and heavier than any coyote he had seen before. Its momentum, combined with its weight, allowed the animal to tackle Hobomok and pin him to the ground.

Dazed after being pounced upon, Hobomok was petrified when the beast bared its teeth, which were inches from his throat. Hobomok expected to feel the animal's teeth sink into him. What happened next, he did not expect... The coyote spoke.

"Weak, soft, petty thing this is, that wounds Coyote," the creature growled. "It throws a hurting stick at Coyote from far away. A coward it is that attacks Coyote this way. Coyote should kill little, weak coward human."

"No, please, don't," Hobomok cried. "I'll do whatever you want."

"Does weak, soft, scared human want to live?" Coyote asked.

"Y-yes. I'll do whatever you want. Just don't kill me."

Coyote sniffed the trembling human, as if he could smell a liar. After inspecting the frightened man, Coyote decided this mortal was useful.

"The Coyote Spirit is what I am," the creature said. "The Coyote is a hunter. Coyote hunts weak humans. But since the day Coyote renounced Awona'Wilona, Coyote serves Malsumis. Now Mighty Malsumis tells Coyote only to hunt humans who serve Awona'Wilona. Petty, stick-throwing human reeks of being a follower of Awona'Wilona. But Coyote smells something different. Coyote smells anger and hate. Does weak human now hate Awona'Wilona?"

"I do now," Hobomok said with tremulous loathing. "I hate those who follow Awona'Wilona for what they did to me, and I hate Awona'Wilona for allowing them to do what they did in his name. If I flayed each and every one of them, no man or Sky Gods could deny it was justice. I would see them dead and rotting and eaten as carrion."

The beast seemed to smile. "Coyote thinks weak human says it well. Coyote felt the same. Coyote is pleased. The human's flesh is weak, but his hate is strong. Coyote can use that."

"Use?" Hobomok repeated fearfully.

Saliva from the creature's mouth dripped onto the disgusted Hobomok as it spoke in a sinister tone. "Coyote is old. Tired is Coyote. And now Coyote is hurt by petty human's pointy stick. Coyote is not strong now like Coyote once was. But Coyote is clever, and Coyote has a plan. Coyote will get humans to kill each other. But humans fear Coyote. Coyote makes them afraid. So, Coyote needs a disguise. Humans would not fear another weak human. Another soft, weak human can trick them. So, Coyote must become one with a weak human."

"Become one?" Hobomok asked, in breathless dread.

"Coyote will explain the joining to weak human fool. But not with words."

The Coyote Spirit bit down on Hobomok's flesh. Hobomok screamed.

Tawa rode atop his bison Mountain Fury. He followed briskly behind Manabazo, who cantered along in his deer-form. They had been traveling for several hours over grasslands to a destination Manabazo had only hinted at. It was something to do with a weapon.

They reached a valley neighboring the Shell River. Manabazo stopped and gazed at a valley lake, as if he were either reliving a beautiful memory or seeing something amazing that Tawa could not see. Either way, Manabazo seemed to feel something intensely powerful and personal.

"Is this our destination, Manabazo?" Tawa asked.

"This is a special place, there is no doubt. It is a place your legends speak about. This is a place both sublime and austere. In the past, Wala-Wa stood here."

Tawa's jaw sagged. He was familiar with the legend of Wala-Wa. Every child in Ulah-Nane was. It had been the Earthly city where the Sky Gods often dwelled in the period between the end of the Great Winter and the previous Sky Gods war. It had been ruled by Pautiwa, the second most exalted of the Sky Elders.

After the war, Wala-Wa was flooded and sunk by the Sky Gods themselves. No one was sure where the mystic city had stood ... until now. Tawa's eyes searched the lake for a sign of anything unusual or special about this normal-looking body of water but found nothing remarkable at all. It was much like Yaxche. The outward appearance belied its importance.

"I never imagined I'd ever walk in the footsteps of Pautiwa," Tawa said. "Yet so much has happened recently that I never would have dreamed I'd ever see. Life is unpredictable."

Manabazo trotted a few steps closer. "This is the place of my birth. I am one of the few Sky Gods born upon the Earth. I am less powerful than my sky-born peers. Yet I do not regret being born here. In this place, you learn the consequences of what you choose to do. Here one can always find meaning true."

"The true meaning of all things?" Tawa asked.

"Yes, of all things. You could even learn why the bird sings."

"I could learn about my purpose in life?" Tawa asked.

"And the purpose of death ... that final breath," Manabazo answered

"About being a great leader, like my father?"

"And all about trust. For young Tawa to be a leader, that is a must."

"And about war, Manabazo?"

"Hmmm, perhaps so. But if there were a reason for war, would you really want to know?"

"I just know I want this one to be over," Tawa said.

"I agree with what you say. You grow wiser each day," Manabazo replied.

"It's an honor to be in such an exalted place," Tawa said. "Why are we here?"

Manabazo explained, "Before Pautiwa passed on, he left something behind. He left it for future heroes to find. He feared that Malsumis might return, instead of remaining trapped to eternally burn. He assumed if mortals ever again faced the Enemy Way, a mortal like Morning Star might arise to save the day."

Tawa began to comprehend now. "So, he left a weapon behind that we mortals could use against the followers of the Enemy Way. And we're here to find it."

"Found it shall be. But perhaps not so easily," Manabazo said. "As you may have guessed, to prove you are the best, you must pass a test."

Tawa sighed. "I might have known. There's always a test. Very well. Let's face the next challenge. What's another one, more or less?"

Manabazo laughed and trotted down into the valley. Tawa nudged big Mountain Fury and trailed behind his mentor, wondering what to expect.

Hobomok walked briskly across the prairie where he had met the Coyote Spirit. He was full of energy and vigor. He could not recall ever feeling this good ... this powerful. He felt as if the empty void inside him had been filled. Yesterday, he had nothing but a desire for revenge. Now, with Coyote inside him, he had a plan. Hobomok knew where he needed to go. Thoughts were swirling in his brain he never could have conceived of before.

The universe was bigger now. He was grateful to the Enemy Way for sending his salvation. The joining was the best thing that ever happened to him. He marched at a brisk pace, hearing and smelling things he had never detected until his senses were made sharper by the joining. He surveyed the world with the senses of a Coyote.

CHAPTER TWENTY-TWO

Hobomok had built himself a raft and sailed north along the Endless Agazzi River. He smirked as he paddled, anticipating the implementation of his plan. Ever since joining with the Coyote Spirit, his mind had become filled with plans and schemes. He had a plot to destroy the Itiwana and knew who could help him. He affectionately touched the scarred spot where the Coyote's teeth had pierced his flesh.

The Endless Agazzi River connected to the Ice Wolf River. Hobomok knew he had reached the right place when he spotted the long-ships moored to wooden poles. He came ashore in the northern realm called Norumbega, where the many giant lakes, including massive Gitche Gumee, were known to remain icy even in the summer months, due to the Winds of Wuchowson. He was discovering the stories were true because he was cold and dressed for summer. If it had not been for the hot blood of Coyote, he might have succumbed to the chill.

After walking for some time, guided by the Coyote's memories and sense of smell, Hobomok found a colony built on the edge of one of the colossal lakes. It was called Nurumgard. There were several community structures, built from sod placed over wooden frames. He could see people milling about. There were many longships moored in the lake. At the center of the lake was a melting Iceberg, which Hobomok thought was quite beautiful.

As Hobomok approached the colony, he was spotted by the inhabitants. A shout of alarm warned everyone, and they grabbed weapons, quickly lining up in a defensive posture, indicating they were prepared to defend their colony. They did not appear to be the type who played childish games or handled strangers gently.

Hobomok noted that every man among them was quite large, at least a head taller than he. None were scrawny in any way. On the contrary, they were bulky with thick upper arms. Most among them were pale, with red or blonde facial hair. Some wore metal skullcaps, but most wore fur hats. Many of the men were adorned in chain mail, with a leathery breast plate. The big men wore garments made of animal skins and furs.

They had a variety of weapons. Some possessed metal swords, some axes and a few had spears. All of them had large shields.

Hobomok noticed their weapons were not made of wood like the Itiwana's were. The part of him that had the knowledge of the Coyote spirit knew this was important, and it made the northerners highly dangerous. That was exactly what Hobomok wanted.

What are these strangers called? Hobomok thought, trying to sort through all the Coyote's memories. *Ah yes. The Vykans.*

The Coyote part of his mind knew the story of the Vykans. They had come from a cold, harsh land across the sea, looking for new worlds to colonize. The Vykans were the best warriors of their respective home regions, chosen specially by their leaders in the event that they met with unexpected dangers in the new world.

Led by the ruthless Red Lord, they built a small community for themselves in the distant northern lands of Ulah-Nane, which the Vykans called Vineland. The Red Lord ruled from the High Seat in Vineland.

There had long been rumors about them, spread by some local Ulah-Nane tribes with whom the Vykans frequently clashed, and sometimes captured. The Red Lord learned of the perpetual warmth in the southern regions of Ulah-Nane.

He had sent a large party of warriors to explore and map Ulah-Nane. Led by an experienced warrior named Hunwulf, this wandering army of

Vykans faithfully set out to do their duty for their lord. They sailed down the river in their sturdy long-ships, but soon found someone else to worship when Hunwulf and his men came across Giwakna the Ice Wendigo.

The Ice Wendigos were an offshoot of the huge Cheenooks. There were many types of Cheenooks, both in Ulah-Nane and the lands north of it. Some of them were benign, such as the Wood Men. The Ice Wendigo, however, were far from benign.

The Ice Wendigos were a carnivorous variant who lived in the far-off northern, colder climates. While most of them remained secluded in the frozen north, occasionally a rogue creature would make its way down to Ulah-Nane. Giwakna was one of these nomadic Wendigo. He had terrorized the northern Ulah-Nane tribes for years.

When Hunwulf and his men came across the Ice Wendigo, they were in the middle of a battle. The Vykans were fighting a group of Ulah-Nane braves who were hunting Giwakna. When Giwakna appeared, he joined the Vykans in destroying the locals. The Vykans mistook him for the Earthly incarnation of a creature called Ymir the Frost Giant, one of their most famous legends. They abandoned the Red Lord and began their worship of Giwakna.

When the Red Lord came looking for Hunwulf and his deserters, he was stunned to find them in the service of a strange beast. Giwakna led the counterattack and drove the Red Lord away. The Red Lord retreated to Vineland and eventually fled the continent, returning to his homeland across the sea. Hunwulf and his group of Vykans remained to serve Giwakna.

They built the colony Nurumgard in Norumbega near a great lake, not far from the Ice Wolf River, which connected to the Endless Agazzi River. The Vykans would frequently sail down these rivers and perpetuate raids on the indigenous tribes, capturing people to offer as sacrifices for their flesh-eating master.

The Vykans stood in a row, facing the approaching Hobomok. Strangely, he felt no fear. Somewhere inside him, the Coyote reassured him this would work out. Hobomok faced the imposing group of Vykans with a smile.

"Well met to you all," he said, now skilled in the Old Speak. "Do you understand me?"

One of the largest and meanest looking of the Vykans stepped forward. He had a red moustache and stubbly beard. His place of importance was indicated by the ornamental wings on his helmet. He strutted toward Hobomok until the two were eye-to-throat.

"I understand you," the Vykan said, pointing his sword at the newcomer. "I have been taught the Old Speak by the Goddess Pinga. My name is Hunwulf the horrible. I have killed many men and listened to the mournful lamentations of their women. Then I killed the women. You have come to a place where you will find no friends and no pity. Speak your last words before I hack you into tiny sections and feed you to our mighty and terrible master."

Hobomok felt strangely calm. "I greet you, brave Hunwulf. You serve your master well. I have no doubt you could easily chop me to pieces and would most gladly do so. However, if I may be so bold, I request an audience with the terrible Giwakna before you slay me."

"Ha," Hunwulf laughed, encouraging his men to join in the vociferous laughter. "Our fierce master has no use for you except as his afternoon meal. You are an unworthy worm, with barely enough blood in you to spill. If that's all you have to say..."

"Just one last thing," Hobomok said, and suddenly howled a loud, primal howl. It was an inhuman cry. It affected every Vykan, striking a feeling of intense, instinctual dread in all present. Hunwulf back pedaled a step, unnerved by the unnatural howl.

"What in the name of Odin are you?" Hunwulf said, raising his shield.

"I'm an old friend of your master," he said. "Inform him of my arrival."

In the lake, a large being stepped out of a cave in the melting Iceberg, drawn to the sound. The strange being was over eight-feet-tall with albino skin. Its thick body hair was completely white, as were its pupils. Its thin lips could not hide its sizable fangs. The clawed hands and feet were disproportionately large. The shoulders were wide, but the mid-section was so thin, it almost looked like the creature was starving. This was the Ice Wendigo Giwakna.

When the Vykans saw their bestial lord-and-master rise from his cave of solitude, they all kneeled in Giwakna's direction, awaiting his commands. Only Hobomok remained disrespectfully standing.

Hunwulf growled, "Kneel to the Terrible One."

Hobomok complied, with a grin. The Ice Wendigo sniffed the air, trying to detect the scent of his friend the Coyote. His sharp eyes spotted the stranger among the Vykans. Giwakna stepped down onto a long ship which was bound to the iceberg by a hook, imbedded in ice. Giwakna paddled his way to the lake shore.

Stepping on land, the huge Ice Wendigo strode through Nurumgard like a God, which is basically how the Vykans saw him. They feared him as much as they worshipped him. Giwakna approached Hobomok.

"Human does not fear Giwakna?" the Ice Wendigo said. "Human makes noise like Coyote?"

"But I am the Coyote," Hobomok said. "Don't you recognize me, old friend?"

Giwakna sniffed Hobomok. "Giwakna smells Coyote inside human. Coyote is Giwakna's good friend. Why does Coyote live inside human now?"

"I have stories to tell you, my powerful friend," Coyote replied. "And together we have plans to make."

Manabazo led Tawa into the Valley where Wala-Wa once stood. Still atop Mountain Fury, Tawa gazed around at the unremarkable looking valley. He knew this façade of mundane, dreary calm was bound to fade at any moment.

Still in his deer form, Manabazo trotted with purposefulness, leading his young student to the shore of the lake.

"Is this the place?" Tawa asked. "Why are challenges always so inconveniently located?"

Manabazo stopped. "Waiting can be hard. We've traveled far. The challenge is now due. From here, the burden falls on you."

"And what is it I'm supposed to do exactly?" Tawa asked.

"Wait, wait. Wait for fate."

Manabazo tapped his hoof on the shore three times. Moments later came a rumbling sound. The ground lakeside began to shake. A sinkhole opened in front of them. Dirt and dust and grass from the ground fell into it. Tawa felt an eerie chill of imminent danger.

I hate these challenges, he thought. *Why can't I ever prove myself with a foot race?*

Tawa's feeling of foreboding proved justified when a mammoth snake sprang from out of the hole. It reared up, taller than a tree. Its colorful scales glistened in the sunlight. Mountain Fury became agitated. Tawa forced himself to remain calm as the creature glared down at him.

The giant snake hissed menacingly and inched toward Tawa.

CHAPTER TWENTY-THREE

"**I** am Awanyu the Lord of Sssssssnakes," the serpent creature said, looming imposingly over Tawa. "What dost thou wish here, mortal?"

Tawa glanced nervously at Manabazo, who gave him a reassuring nod, encouraging him to continue. Tawa suppressed his fear, addressing the Snake-Lord in his strongest voice.

"I come as the defender of Ulah-Nane," he said. "I claim the sacred weapon of Pautiwa, which I will use in the service of great Awona'Wilona."

The Snake-Lord's tongue flicked forward from its mouth as it spoke. "If thou wouldsssssst claim the sssssssacred weapon, thou mussssssssst passssss the tesssssssst of armsssssssss."

Tawa remained as calm and stoic as possible, under the circumstances. "For my own edification, what will befall me if I should be unsuccessful in the test of arms?"

The colorfully scaled snake lowered its head closer to the young man. "Then thou shalt feel my fangsssss in thy flesh, and my venom shall run through thy veinssssss."

Tawa glared with vexation at Manabazo. "Why do you never warn me about the pitfalls of these tests in advance?"

Manabazo winked at the young *kik-mongwi*. "You must learn to react to surprise. Danger is often hidden from unsuspecting eyes. When peril strikes with surprise; survival requires you to be clever and wise."

"Be cccccccertain," Awanyu warned. "Thou dost gamble with thy very life. I sssssuggesssst thee depart while thee sssssssstill may."

"Your advice is most excellent, great Snake Lord," Tawa replied. "I wish I could follow it. Sadly, I am bound by duty and honor to act foolishly. I need that weapon. Speak the challenge."

Up from the ground came more of the seemingly endless coil of the Snake-Lord. Wrapped tightly in these coils were five weapons: a bow, a club, a spear, a tomahawk, and an arrow. "One choice hast thou. One of thessssssse weaponsssss issssssss the one thou sssssseeketh. Thou hast one guessssss. If thou dost guesssss foolishly, I musssssst ssssssslay thee."

Tawa trembled ever-so-slightly at the mental image of the giant serpent biting him and filling his body with deadly venom. He would not be deterred, however. The war required him to have a powerful weapon, and he had to obtain it.

Tawa looked over the weapons. He dismissed the bow-and-arrow because one is useless without the other. He next ruled out the club because it seemed too crude and graceless a weapon for the ruler of sacred Wala-Wa and the penultimate authority among the Sky Elders. That left only the Spear and the Tomahawk. But which was it?

Tawa recalled something Pekwin had once told him. A spear is symbolic of wit and the ability to look forward toward the future. Similarly, a broken spear indicates peace and an end to the cycle of violence. That certainly sounded like something Pautiwa would have made and carried as a symbol.

"It is the spear," Tawa shouted. "I choose the spear."

The giant snake let out a hiss and reared as if it were about to strike. Tawa winced, raising his arm defensively, bracing himself for a deadly bite, believing he had failed. But the expected bite never came.

"Thou hast done well," Awanyu said.

The snake withdrew into the ground, dragging all the weapons with him, except the spear. The hole in the ground that the serpent had made when it rose now collapsed inward, filling itself with dirt. When the dust cleared, everything was the same as it had been earlier, except for the spear laying on the ground.

"Another fine triumph for you," Manabazo said. "You do your father proud, and your mother, too."

"I hate these tests," Tawa grumbled, climbing down off Mountain Fury. He picked the spear off the grass. It was long and well-made but like everything else he had seen recently; the outward appearance belied the importance of it.

"So, this is the weapon of Pautiwa, is it?" he asked.

"This spear's legend is known low and high," Manabazo said. "It is called the Dragonfly."

"The Dragonfly?" Tawa repeated. "A simple but non-aggressive name. I wonder what power this weapon holds."

Tawa tossed the Dragonfly at a nearby tree. It seemed to leap from his hand as if propelled by unseen forces. Tawa could not believe his eyes as the Dragonfly bored straight through the tree and came out the other side, continuing onward a considerable distance before finally coming to a stop in a second tree.

"By Awona'Wilona's grace," Tawa whispered. "Quite a weapon indeed."

Manabazo nodded. "Indeed, that is true. It will be a great boon to you. It cannot be broken, and flame will not burn through it. Once imbedded, it can only be retrieved by the one who threw it."

"Hopefully, the warriors of the Enemy Way have no weapon such as this," Tawa said. "But hope is not a resource we can count on."

Manabazo trotted to Tawa's side. "Please, no worried faces. Hope appears in the most unexpected of places. Savor the victory won here and now. Hope can always be found, somehow."

"Why is it you're always so much smarter than I am?" Tawa asked. "It's an irritating trait. Ah, no matter. Let me retrieve the Dragonfly so we can return home. I'm sure there will be more lessons on the trip back."

Manabazo chuckled. "Always, my youthful friend. Learning is something without an end."

Hobomok sat on a rock at the edge of the huge lake Gitche Gumee, adjacent to Nurumgard in Norumbega. Giwakna the Ice Wendigo was knee-deep in the cold lake, periodically snatching fish from the water and shoving them into his mouth, chewing with fanged teeth. Hobomok was bemused by the primal display. As a Coyote, he had often done similar things. While Giwakna ate, Hobomok tried convincing him to attack the Itiwana.

"I know you love a good battle, friend Giwakna," Hobomok said. "I can promise you a delightfully fierce battle."

"Giwakna likes to fight," the Ice Wendigo responded. "But Giwakna has lots of fights here. Giwakna can fight Wood Men here. Strong enemies are close. Not worth going far away. Giwakna not like warm places."

Hobomok tried another tactic. "But think of all those tasty Itiwana for you to eat."

Giwakna was not enticed. "Lots of humans closer. Tasty tribes in cold places. Vykans bring them to Giwakna."

This is harder than I thought it would be, Coyote mused. "But they have many large, tasty bison there to eat. Big, delicious bison."

Giwakna swallowed another fish. "Buffalo good to eat, but too far away. Moose closer. Giwakna loves eating moose. Moose live in cold places."

Hobomok's annoyance grew, but he smiled, disguising his impatience. The obvious pattern of Giwakna's refusal gave him an idea. Cold was key to getting his cooperation.

"If you want this place to stay cold, the way you like it, you must help me," Hobomok said. "You know there is a magic tree in the south that makes it warm all the time. If those people win, the tree will get stronger and even the winds from the Wuchowson will not be enough to keep Norumbega cold. Soon, there will be no more cold here for you. Norumbega will become warm and sunny, like the rest of Ulah-Nane. No more nice cold for Giwakna."

Giwakna spit out the fish he was eating and raised his claws, enraged. "No! Not make it warm here. Giwakna hate warm. Giwakna not let it be warm here. Giwakna stop it."

Hobomok was relieved he had finally found the means to manipulate the dense Ice Wendigo. "The only way to stop it is to destroy the Tree of Life."

"Giwakna destroy it!" the Ice Wendigo roared.

"But first we must destroy the Itiwana," Hobomok said. "They protect the tree. We must kill them all and only then can we destroy the tree. Once we do that, it will be nice and cold here in the north forever."

Giwakna loudly splashed his way out of the lake, stomped his wet feet and bared his long fangs. "Giwakna will kill them all! Vykans will help. Vykans obey Giwakna. Coyote show Giwakna where Itiwana are and Giwakna will destroy them."

Hobomok had won his mental victory over the Ice Wendigo. He never doubted that he would. It was now time to plan. The summer was coming and Giwakna would not survive in the south during the warmest months. Hobomok planned to talk Giwakna into letting him lead the Vykans in an attack on Shipapa-Lina, where he could personally eliminate the Itiwana. If he were unable to destroy them, he would need to wait until the winter, when Giwakna would be able to accompany him and the Vykans south.

The winters were mild but cool in the Land of Everlasting Summer. Giwakna would be able to endure it long enough to help defeat the Itiwana. Hobomok was certain the physical power of Giwakna, along with the fear his presence initiated, would be enough to ensure victory over the inexperienced Tawa and his tribe.

I can taste the victory already, Hobomok thought. *I will keep Tawa's scalp as a prize after Giwakna eats his childish brain.*

Pogum rode his bison Walking Storm on a patrol around the perimeter of Shipapa-Lina. He had suggested posting watchmen in specified locations across the mesa. Tawa approved the idea. The people were also in the process of building a perch for a watchman in the highest cedar tree atop the mesa, which had an eagle's-eye view of the valley and surrounding land.

Members of the Two-Horn Riders were assigned specific points around the city to keep a watchful eye out for trouble. In recent days, the Itiwana had spotted members of the Tunerak Destroyers lurking nearby, covertly observing the tribe. These Tunerak Destroyers managed to slip away. Pogum did not want them carrying any more information back to the Salt Witch and the Enemy Way. He also hoped he could make up for losing his former captive Xolotl by apprehending a new enemy to question. As the War Chief of the Two-Horn Riders, he felt obliged to check up on the watchmen.

Atop Walking Storm, Pogum visited most of the guard positions and was heading for the final one. The last watcher was the furthest from Shipapa-Lina, in a wooded area. Trotting at a casual pace, Pogum paused due to a rustle in the bushes. He took an arrow from the saddle where they were fastened and pulled back the bow, aiming toward the sound.

"You have a choice," Pogum said. "You must choose between being hit by this arrow or stepping out of those bushes and showing your face. It shouldn't be an exceptionally difficult decision to make."

Pogum was exceedingly surprised to see Bluebird emerge from the bushes. "I should have known I couldn't sneak up on you, my love."

Pogum lowered the arrow. "You almost found out how good an archer I am. That was foolish. I could have killed you."

"I apologize, dearest," she said. "I just wanted to see you. You spend so much time training the Two-Horn Riders, I rarely get to spend any time with you. I thought perhaps I could join you tonight."

Pogum wanted to be angry, but he could not, offering his hand to help her up onto the bison. "This is not proper, but I'll make an exception just this once. Come."

She took his hand, and he yanked her up onto the back of Walking Storm. She wrapped her arms around him. "Thank you for the ride, dear husband."

"Your company is always a pleasure, sweet wife."

Pogum prodded his mount forward. Walking Storm had only moved a few steps when it bristled at a loud crashing sound in the foliage.

CHAPTER TWENTY-THREE

"Is that an enemy?" Bluebird asked apprehensively.

"No, I do not believe so," Pogum calmly said.

Faw-Faw shambled gracelessly into view as he pushed his way through the bushes. The Wood Man beamed innocently at his two friends.

"Did you follow me, Faw-Faw?" Bluebird chided.

"Gug," Faw-Faw replied.

"It's my fault," Pogum said. "With all these Tunerak Destroyer sightings, I asked him to stick close to you. I guess he may as well join us now. Come along, Faw-Faw."

Bluebird chuckled. "It's like having an immensely large child."

Faw-Faw followed along behind Walking Storm. Bluebird enjoyed being on patrol. It was a nice change from farming. Pogum's eyes darted in all directions, alert for any sign of trouble. He thought he detected a sound and noticed that Faw-Faw was looking off in the distance, focused on something.

"Gug."

"What's wrong?" Bluebird asked.

Pogum spotted the source of the sound. "Trouble."

A half-dozen Tunerak Destroyers leaped out of the greenery, armed with their oak *macuahuitl* swords and shields. This time they were not running away. They had come to fight.

"Death to the enemies of Malsumis!" they yelled as they attacked.

CHAPTER TWENTY-FOUR

The six Tunerak Destroyers waved their studded oak swords and howled some incomprehensible battle cry as they charged from the bushes, intent on killing their prey. Pogum quickly put an arrow in his bow while Faw-Faw raised his large fists defiantly and roared a warning. Bluebird was not a warrior and so slid off the bison, moving away from the battle.

As the Tunerak Destroyers closed in, Pogum eliminated one of them with an arrow. He managed to fire a second shaft, but the Destroyer blocked the arrow with his wooden shield. At the same moment, Faw-Faw grabbed a heavy log off the ground and swung it at one of the Destroyers. The attacker tried blocking the big log with his shield, but the impact was too powerful. The brunt of the blow broke the wooden shield and sent the Destroyer sailing through the air until he smashed into a tree, shattering every bone in his body.

Two of the Destroyers charged at Pogum, who was atop his bison. Walking Storm was startled by the attack and lashed out at one of the men, butting him to the ground and then trampling over him with all its massive weight. His fellow Destroyer paused, frightened at the sight of his partner's fate. Pogum took advantage of the invader's hesitation and dived off his mount, tackling his foe. He slit the man's throat with his thorn bracelet.

The fifth Tunerak Destroyer made the mistake of attacking Faw-Faw. The Wood Man broke his wooden sword and lifted the man in the air, then smashed him down onto the log, breaking his back. Pogum was impressed by the ruthless killing efficiency of such a generally gentle creature when its temper was roused. With five of the Destroyers dealt with, Pogum looked around for the final one.

To Pogum's alarm and great fury, he watched the sixth Tunerak Destroyer grab Bluebird. He had a rigid grip upon her neck.

"Hold fast, Itiwana worm," the Destroyer shouted. "If you dare move toward me or aim that bow at me, I'll snap your woman's pretty neck."

Pogum sneered hatefully at his foe but kept his distance. Faw-Faw stomped forward, but

Pogum held up a hand, gesturing for the Wood Man to stop.

"No, Faw-Faw. Stay," Pogum ordered.

Faw-Faw understood, although he was confused as to why Pogum had stopped him.

The Tunerak Destroyer was satisfied he was in control. "Good. Keep that beast far from me. What I want you to do now is..."

Before he could utter another sound, he was struck by a spear that cut through his neck and completely removed his head from his shoulders. Bluebird cried out as the blood splattered all about. She was simultaneously relieved and repulsed.

Riding into view from behind some trees came Tawa, seated regally atop Mountain Fury. Manabazo trotted along beside him, still in deer form.

"My timing was good. My aim was better," Tawa said, pleased with himself. "You're quite right, Manabazo. Dragonfly seems to aim itself. It flew from my hand as if it knew where it needed to go."

"By your thoughts, Dragonfly was led," Manabazo replied. "Now a Tunerak Destroyer has no head."

"It's very good to see you, *kik-mongwi*," Pogum said to his nephew.

"And you as well, Uncle," Tawa said, trampling the headless enemy while retrieving Dragonfly. "Ah, my friend Faw-Faw is here. Hello large one."

"Gug."

"Are you well, Bluebird?" Pogum asked.

"I'm covered in blood," she lamented, wiping herself off.

"Don't moan," Manabazo said. "Just be glad it isn't your own."

"You should get yourself cleaned up," Tawa told her. "Not that you don't look good in red. Faw-Faw should escort you, in case any other menaces are lurking in the shadows."

"Yes *kik-mongwi*," Bluebird said, still wiping herself. "Come Faw-Faw."

As Bluebird and Faw-Faw departed, Pogum hopped back onto Walking Storm and sidled up to Tawa and Mountain Fury.

"The Tunerak Destroyers are getting bolder," he said.

"So it seems," Tawa agreed. "Their incursions are becoming more frequent and they're getting closer to Shipapa-Lina each time. They are also coming in ever increasing numbers."

"Bad tidings," Pogum replied. "Whatever they are planning, I believe it will be happening very soon. We need to be ready."

Manabazo indicated agreement. "I concur with what you say. Battle may come at any day."

"Then we'll be prepared," Tawa said. "The emissaries of evil think they're hunting us, but they'll soon learn who the real predators are."

Hobomok had been in the Nurumgard community of Norumbega for more than a month. He was eager and ready to lead the Vykans to the Land of Everlasting Summer. Giwakna had given the Vykans orders to assist in the attack on the Itiwana. When Hunwulf suggested they get some extra training by raiding a local village of indigenous Ulah-Nane people, Giwakna agreed.

Hobomok did not like the delay but was overruled and forced to wait. This training exercise would take a full week, at least. After that, it would require several days of sailing the longships down the Endless Agazzi River, followed by two or three days march to reach the mesa. The delay was irritating, but he accepted it as an unavoidable annoyance.

As he patiently waited, he decided to enjoy his free time. He had been spending his idle hours in the company of a slave girl who had been kidnapped by the Vykans. She was one of the lucky ones they chose as a servant instead of a meal for Giwakna. At least, for the time being.

Her face had been painted white before she was captured, as was tradition for the mid-wives of her tribe, and so she was called the Painted White Girl. She continued applying her albino paint after her captivity, making it out of clay and rock powder she got at the water's edge while washing her captor's clothing.

When Hobomok noticed her, he asked Giwakna if he could reserve this girl's favors for himself. The Ice Wendigo agreed, giving her to Hobomok as a gift. Hobomok had not been intimate with a woman for more than a year. Not since before he had left Shipapa-Lina. He now made up for lost time by enjoying the carnal favors of the Painted White Girl as much as possible for human endurance.

The Painted White Girl had become emotionally attached to Hobomok. He had rescued her from the arduous servitude and sexual abuse of the brutish Vykans. She became exclusively his. This eliminated the lingering threat of them making her a meal for the Ice Wendigo. That possibility had horrified her for weeks and she was finally free of the threat.

Hobomok treated her far better than the Vykans and asked for little in return, except sex. He even spoke to her like a human being, which the Vykans had never done. She was glad to have someone to talk to, even if Hobomok did most of the talking. She enjoyed listening to him. She found him interesting and attractive. There was something unusual about him that she had never encountered in any other man.

Hobomok lay next to the Painted White Girl in a small hut. He was talking, and she played with his hair, listening in fascination. She had some news to tell him but waited for Hobomok to finish his musings before she spoke.

"I deserve to rule the Itiwana, you know," he told her, with his eyes closed. "I was their greatest hunter. I provided them food for so many years. Now that they have the bison herds, they don't need me any longer and chose an inexperienced child over me. Foolish choice."

"Yes it was, my dearest," the Painted White Girl said,

Hobomok continued, "The privileged line of Morning Star will finally pay for generations of hubris. Every Itiwana who supported him must suffer as well. By the time I'm done, Tawa, Pekwin, Atira and that insolent T'Soona will all be crushed completely. The rest of the Itiwana will have the choice between serving me or becoming a summer's worth of meals for Giwakna. They'll choose wisely, I think, Once the boy-chieftain is gone, I will savor the moment when I have the headdress of chieftains upon my brow. I live for that moment. My victory will be complete. And you will be there to share it with me, dear girl. I will bring you along. The Itiwana are beneath me now and so you will continue to please me, as you have done. In the future, you will be the consort of the *kik-mongwi* of Shipapa-Lina."

The Painted White Girl smiled adoringly. This was the perfect segue for her news. "You will have not only a consort, my chieftain, but an heir as well. I am carrying your child."

Hobomok opened his eyes and sat up. "You're certain?"

She nodded. "I was a midwife in my former village. I know the signs. I am an expert in this area. I am sure. I carry the heir of Hobomok, future conqueror of Shipapa-Lina."

He rolled over and touched her belly. "Well, well. This is indeed unexpected but happy news. So, I have an heir. The line of Hobomok will go on, ensuring a vassal for the power of Coyote will exist should this body be slain."

The Painted White Girl was confused. "I do not understand."

He chuckled as he rubbed her belly. "You don't have to understand. Just know you are carrying something more than a normal child. He stands to inherit so much. If I succeed, this child will inherit the mantle of ruler of Shipapa-Lina. If I fail and I fall, he will inherit a power that will place him above either Itiwana or Vykan. If he is a boy, I will name him Hayoka, after my father and I bequeath him everything ... as does the Coyote. Therefore, either my legacy or my vengeance will live on after me."

Weeks later, summer came to the Land of Everlasting Summer. Tawa had reached the age of seventeen summers, which would have marked him officially a man among the tribe had he not already become the *kik-mongwi*. Official manhood came with leadership of the tribe. He spent his birth celebration day in an atypical fashion ... in combat.

The Itiwana of Shipapa-Lina had been in several battles with the Tunerak Destroyers during the past weeks. The Destroyers had clearly been observing the Itiwana. Tawa knew they were attempting to determine the numbers and defenses of the tribe. After losing their scouting party to Pogum and the Wood Man, the Tunerak Destroyers had obviously decided it was time to stop planning and start attacking.

The Tunerak Destroyers were surprised at how prepared the Itiwana were. The Itiwana had fortified their defenses with Tawa's new design. New walls and other barriers made it harder for anyone coming up the mesa to reach Shipapa-Lina in wide formation. They would have to cluster, making them more vulnerable.

Aside from that, the Itiwana were meticulously constructing a unique form of cliff housing, built in shallow caves on the canyon walls of the Hanging Cliffs, shielded by the big rock overhang above. A sophisticated series of ladders would allow the Itiwana to reach the higher cliff chambers and balconies. The ladders could be pulled up to keep attackers from climbing to the cliff chambers. When these cliff dwellings were complete, the Itiwana would be extremely difficult to attack. The Destroyers had to hit them now.

Aside from these improvements, there was also improved strategy. Tawa, Manabazo and Grey Pekwin brilliantly anticipated every type of attack the Destroyers attempted. Atop their huge, intimidating bison, the Itiwana formed a defensive line around Shipapa-Lina, determined that no one would pass. They succeeded in that goal. Try as the Tunerak Destroyers might, they could not pierce the protective line the Two-Horn Riders held so valiantly.

While scouting, Pogum discovered the Tunerak Destroyers were massing nearby and readying themselves for the next effort to break through the Itiwana defenses. Tawa and his advisors had deduced that an assault would come in the next few days, and judging by the past attacks, it would probably come early, before the heat of the day rose too high. Therefore, each morning Tawa and his Two-Horn Riders formed a defensive perimeter across the Mesa, ready for an attack. They knew it would come soon.

Molowia was brooding, alone in her chamber in the Sun Dagger House in Kolhu. Guilt was tormenting her. Guilt for not helping her brother and the people of her twin city.

She had been using her Vision Quest astral form to monitor what was happening with the Itiwana of Shipapa-Lina. What she envisioned had horrified her. The violence she had seen and what she knew was yet to come was monstrous. She wanted so much to help them, but the idea that Kolhu might get dragged into the war was anathema to her.

She knew the ramifications of Malsumis and the Enemy Way destroying Yaxche. The cold weather would return, and the Tunerak Destroyers would run wild, rampaging in worse ways than the unfriendly tribes who occasionally attacked the Land of Everlasting Summer. Could even Wishpoosh protect them if the Destroyers were backed by the power of Malsumis? The abilities she possessed were formidable, but could they protect Kolhu against the Salt Witch?

What should I do? Do I dare get involved?

Although Pogum was the War Chief of the Two-Horn Riders, Tawa felt it was his duty to join his fellow Itiwana in combat. His father Yana-Luha would surely have joined the battle and so Tawa could not sit idle, in the safety of his longhouse, while others fought to defend Shipapa-Lina.

Tawa had been well-taught by Manabazo and was prepared to fight. The months of training paid off, and he proved he was a formidable warrior, despite his youth. He had been transformed since the previous summer.

Tawa and Pogum were mounted on their bison, at the forefront of their army. The rest of the Two-Horn Riders, atop their own mounts, were in a row behind their leaders. Faw-Faw was among them, the only one on foot. They waited, knowing the enemy was near.

Grey Pekwin and Atira were left in charge of Shipapa-Lina while Tawa and all the warriors were guarding the Mesa. Thirty women of the tribe were lined up in a row behind a newly built adobe wall. Each was armed with a bow and arrow. They were to be the final line of defense for the village, should the enemy fight their way passed Tawa's warriors. These chosen women were known as the Bow Sisterhood, trained since childhood by Yana-Luha's mother.

The female force stood pensively, hoping their bow skills would not be needed.

Hani the teacher, daughter of the late Medicine Man Hano, paced in a small circle, trying to control her growing sense of dread. She glanced over a Woeful Evanki, who was calmly testing the tensile strength of her bowstring.

"Aren't you going to say something gloomy?" Hani asked. "Perhaps about how the enemy will rape us?"

Evaki produced a small crystal shard, sharpened into a blade. "If those filthy buffoons dare try anything like that with me, I'll slice their tiny tuneraks off."

Hani laughed. "I now understand what Aholi sees in you. You have fire."

"Enough to burn a man," Evaki said. "No one but Aholi touches me."

Evaki abruptly fired her bow, and the arrow sailed across the field, impaling a field mouse. Hani was reminded not only of how much Evaki hated mice but also that she was probably the second-best archer among the Itiwana, bested only by Pogum.

Hani spotted her brother T'Soona walking nearby. T'Soona was a healer, not a warrior and had been left behind in case there should be wounded who needed attention. He escorted the non-warrior class of the tribe to the Sun Temple. Children, the elderly, and the women not trained for battle would all wait there for safety. They did this every day until the attack came.

It was on the evening of Tawa's birth celebration day that the enemy finally attacked. The Tunerak Destroyers came charging toward the tribe, some of them in ram-pulled chariots and the bulk of them on foot. They had studded oak *macuahuitl* swords and shields. The invaders screamed war chants and the praises of Malsumis as they advanced.

Tawa raised Dragonfly over his head. "Warriors. Let us defend our home and families! Ride for glory!"

The Itiwana shouted their war cries. Led by Tawa and his best men Pogum and Aholi, they charged into the fray, meeting the Tunerak Destroyers in a furious clash.

CHAPTER TWENTY-FIVE

The two armies clashed in the hot summer sun. The Itiwana fired their arrows at the incoming force of Tunerak Destroyers, but the invaders had wooden shields. The Destroyers brought all their deadly skill and lethal training to the assault upon the Itiwana of Shipapa-Lina. Tawa and Pogum were at the forefront of the chaos, battling with fierce fervor against the invaders. Riding high atop their bison mounts Mountain Fury and Walking Storm, they were an inspiring example to the rest of the Itiwana Two-Horn Riders.

The Tunerak Destroyers had been training for this war longer than the Itiwana had. With their shields to block the Itiwana arrows, and their heavy *macuahuitls* to strike with, the attackers assumed they would overcome this tribe of corn-growers in a single day, despite being outnumbered.

The Tunerak Destroyers were proven completely mistaken in their appraisal of the Itiwana's strength. Aside from having superior numbers, the Itiwana had been trained far better than the enemy anticipated. With some guidance by Manabazo, their leader Tawa had the Itiwana well prepared to repel anyone.

The most unexpected advantage of the Itiwana were their bison mounts. The Tunerak Destroyers had expected the battle to be strictly on foot. A few of the Tunerak Destroyers had a small force that consisted of chariot-like carts, pulled by a pair of rams. They had been certain their chariot faction would guarantee them a relatively easy victory. They did not count on the Itiwana riding on bison.

Beyond that, the Destroyers had never seen bison so large. When the Itiwana Two-Horn Riders charged forward on their bison mounts, the ground quaked. The bison ran down the Tunerak Warriors who were on foot, simultaneously scaring the rams of the Destroyer Cavalry. The rams became skittish and hard to handle when the bison stormed across the field.

The advantage of the bison gave the Itiwana momentum, and they kept it throughout the battle. The combat went on for hours and no one could say whether more Tunerak Destroyers fell from arrow wounds or from being gored and trampled by bison. Faw-Faw, who wielded a club, dispatched many foes. Tawa's Dragonfly slew half the cavalry.

The number of the Tunerak Destroyers had been whittled down by half, and they finally sounded the retreat. The remaining invaders fled the canyon, fuming from their humiliating defeat. They knew the Salt Witch would be enraged when she learned the battle had been lost but they had no choice. The Destroyers had been soundly defeated.

Tawa signaled for the Itiwana to chase the Destroyers for a while, to ensure they retreated far enough from the canyon where Shipapa-Lina sat. The Wood Man ran alongside the Itiwana. The defeated Destroyers fled the canyon and ran over a hill at the base of the Shining Rock Mountains, with the sound of bison hooves pounding close behind them. As the Itiwana reached the top of the hill, Pogum spotted something he had hoped he would never see again. He raised his hand for the Itiwana Two-Horn Riders to come to a halt.

Tawa was curious as to why Pogum had ordered a cease to the pursuit without his permission, but he then noticed something at the bottom of the hill. It looked like a simple stone statue, with a woman standing next to it. Then, however, to his astonishment, the statue moved.

"Stone coat!" Pogum cried, in alarm. "And the Salt Witch."

Tawa and the other Itiwana were amazed to see the stone creature slowly lumbering toward them. They had heard Pogum's story about the creature called Stone Coat yet seeing it was still a chilling experience. The witch behind the stone man laughed.

"Hello again, Pogum," she shouted. "How good to see you once more. I have brought a friend with me. His name is Stone Coat. Why do you not come down here and make better acquaintance of him? I promise you a unique experience. I was going to say a 'memorable one,' but the truth is, you won't live long enough to remember this day. I have never heard a dead man explain how he got so stiff. Tell me where the tree is, and perhaps I will let your tribe live."

"You've failed to kill me twice, Witch," Pogum mocked. "And your Tunerak Destroyers are currently retreating over that hill. Your threats are more impressive than your efficiency. Forgive me for not trembling. Your teacher Dagwona wasted her time on you."

The Salt Witch was stung by the insult. "Have a care, Pogum. I have it in my power to make your death either mercifully quick or slow and horrible. Which will I decide? Who can say? I advise you not to antagonize me."

Pogum laughed off the threat. "And I advise you to join your minions in their flight. You must have realized that we Itiwana do not die easily, and you have not been up to the task."

"Enough!" The Salt Witch snapped, wrathfully. "You've earned this. You will die by inches, for days and days. Stone Coat... Destroy."

The stone golem stomped with sinister intent toward the Itiwana, at its mistress' command. Tawa raised his hand to signal his warriors.

"Arrows," he shouted. Immediately, all the Two-Horn Riders fired their arrows at the creature, but the shafts had no effect. Stone Coat ignored the weapons.

"A truly monstrous foe," Tawa said to Pogum.

"Indeed," Pogum answered. "A stone feels no pain and does not die."

Tawa looked over his shoulder. "Manabazo!" he cried.

Moments later, an eagle swooped down and landed on the horn of Tawa's bison Mountain Fury. "When the *kik-mongwi* has need, I take heed," the eagle said.

"I need a way to defeat this creature, Manabazo. How do I slay a stone?"

Manabazo was quick with his answer. "A simple stone cannot move on its own. Reeds only bend low when the wind starts to blow."

Tawa understood. "Of course. We need to focus on what makes the creature move, instead of the creature itself. Thank you, Manabazo."

"I'm ever at your service, good Chief. I pray you bring this witch much grief," Manabazo said as he flew away.

Tawa had already formed a plan. "I'll distract the witch by challenging the stone monster. You settle matters in a more direct manner, Uncle."

Pogum nodded. "I know what must be done."

"Go stealthily."

"Trust in me, nephew."

Tawa left Aholi in command and prodded Mountain Fury forward. At the same time, Pogum and Walking Storm blended in with the rest of the Two-Horn Riders. He climbed from his mount and made his way covertly around the hill, while all eyes were on Tawa.

Stone Coat was halfway up the hill, moving slowly. Tawa observed his foe, as Manabazo had taught him. He noted the clumsy creature was looking a bit wobbly as it climbed the hill, because the puppet-mistress who controlled it was having trouble adjusting the balance of the rock monster on the steep slope. Tawa saw an opportunity.

Urging Mountain Fury to race down the hill, Tawa started his attack run. Moving downward at impressive speed, the huge animal built up massive momentum. At full gallop, Mountain Fury rammed Stone Coat, hitting the unbalanced stone man with incredible force.

Stone Coat was knocked backwards and rolled down the hill, too heavy and uncoordinated to stop its tumbling descent. It felt no pain but was at the mercy of gravity. It rolled all the way to the bottom of the hill before it stopped. Aholi and the other Itiwana cheered at the successful first strike. The Salt Witch hissed in frustration at the setback. This was not the way to strike fear in the hearts of the Itiwana.

"Rise. Return to your attack," she commanded. "Slay for me!"

Inflexible and extremely heavy, Stone Coat was like a turtle on its back, struggling to rise again. The Salt Witch did not suspect her creation had this weakness, because it had never been knocked off its feet before. She cursed under her breath as she utilized her powers to solve the problem. Concentrating, she began levitating the stone creature, allowing it to regain its footing.

Atop Mountain Fury, Tawa rode to the bottom of the hill and witnessed the creature floating magically back to an upright position. He knew who was causing this. Tawa raised Dragonfly over his head and tossed it at the creature, hitting it in the leg. Although the mystic properties of the Dragonfly allowed the weapon to pierce through the thick stone creature, the spear became imbedded in the rock man, coming halfway out the other side. Ignoring the spear impaling its body, Stone Coat continued its shambling progress forward.

Tawa rode nearer to Stone Coat, hoping to retrieve his Dragonfly. However, the creature had a long reach and struck faster than expected. Tawa reached for the spear, but Stone Coat swatted him off his mount. The air was knocked out of the young chieftain's body when he fell seven feet from the bison's back. While he was still stunned, Stone Coat raised a rocky, lethal fist, intending to crush Tawa's skull.

"Kill him," the Salt Witch commanded. "Squash the boy chieftain like a worm. Destroy him now."

Stone Coat swung its rock-hard fist toward the head of the stunned Tawa.

The women of the Bow Sisterhood lost sight of Tawa and his army. Having seen the enemy retreat, they were feeling positive, expecting the triumphant Two-Horn Riders to return at any moment, and the victory dance would begin.

The Shakowin stood vigil outside the chieftain's longhouse. T'Soona had a dire feeling of danger. His instincts were screaming to him that something bad was about to happen. He tried telling himself he was being foolish, but he could not push the trepidation away.

Pekwin pointed to the east because something was moving there. Everyone gazed eastward and spotted the silhouettes of numerous figures coming up the slope of the mesa. T'Soona found it strange that the returning warriors would be coming from the east when they had chased the Tunerak Destroyers to the North. He then noticed there were no bison.

"Those are not our people," he shouted. "Something's wrong."

The remaining Itiwana watched as more and more of these unidentified figures appeared on the mesa and approached Shipapa-Lina. The Shakowin and the Bow sisterhood were becoming nervous, especially when the unknown people began running in the direction of the tribe, bellowing an unfamiliar war chant. The men seemed to be carrying long, shiny objects in their hands.

The Bow Sisterhood readied their arrows. When the strangers got close enough, the bow-women fired. However, these strangers were carrying shields made of the same shiny material their weapons were composed of. The arrows bounced ineffectually off the shields and the attackers kept coming.

"Everyone fall back!" Atira commanded. "Find cover."

The Itiwana bow-women withdrew, seeking a safer place to reorganize. Bluebird was reminded of the time the Tunerak Destroyers attacked and killed the Corn Maidens. If this was them again, she intended to act, not hide.

"I'll get us help," she cried. "I go quickly to find Pogum and the other men. I'll bring them back."

"Go," T'Soona said. "Don't let them see you leave."

While Bluebird slipped away to find Tawa, Pogum and the other Two-Horn Riders, T'Soona, Atira and Grey Pekwin waited for the newcomers to arrive. As the strange men came nearer, the Itiwana were confused, having no idea who these large men were or why they were charging toward Shipapa-Lina.

The Vykans had arrived. Their long trip north had been completed and it was time to attack Shipapa-Lina in the name of their God Giwakna. Hunwulf led the assault.

"Take the village," he ordered. "Destroy any resistance. Conquer Shipapa-Lina in the name of Giwakna!"

CHAPTER TWENTY-SIX

Tawa lay on the ground, dazed from the impact of Stone Coat's rock-solid fist as well as the seven foot fall off his bison. Stone Coat stood over him, raising a heavy arm for the death blow, while the Salt Witch screamed, "Kill him! Crush him! Destroy him!"

Just as Stone Coat swung his fist for the fatal blow, the rock-creature was knocked off-balance by a strong impact from behind. To the surprise of the Salt Witch, the big bison Mountain Fury had decided to defend its master and butted Stone Coat from behind, using its considerable weight and power. This time, however, Stone Coat did not fall. The rock-creature was not unbalanced, and the bison did not have the momentum of a downhill run. Stone Coat shook momentarily from the impact but kept its footing.

The Salt Witch tossed a fireball on the ground which exploded in a plume of flame. Mountain Fury was spooked by the fiery blast and backed away nervously. The Salt Witch pointed to Tawa again.

"Kill. Crush. Destroy," she shouted. "Squash my enemies like ants."

Stone Coat swung his deadly fist at Tawa again, but Tawa had gotten enough time to recover, thanks to the distraction by Mountain Fury. The young Itiwana rolled out of the path of the blow, which missed by an inch. Stone Coat's fist made a hole in the ground. Tawa circled behind his foe and yanked Dragonfly loose. He crouched, poised for further combat.

Stone Coat stalked the young Itiwana chieftain, who backed away slowly. Tawa used his speed to hit-and-run, jabbing the stone creature with the Dragonfly. Although he could do little more than chip away at the thick stone man, Tawa did manage to cause some damage. More and more cracks were covering the walking statue.

However, he was getting tired. He was not sure how much longer he could keep this up. It would only take one direct blow by Stone Coat to kill him. *I don't know if I can destroy this monster before it gets its rocky hands on me and breaks my neck.*

The Salt Witch was getting impatient. She had not expected the battle to go on for so long or for

Tawa to do as well as he was doing. She lifted her hand and wiggled her fingers, planning to cast a spell upon the young chieftain. However, she never got the opportunity.

The Salt Witch suddenly felt a horribly agonizing pain in her back. Her whole body began to feel numb. She reached around and felt blood and something sticking out of her upper back. It felt like an arrow. She turned to see Pogum standing in the nearby shrubbery with a bow. He met her eyes with a coldly triumphant look. The Tunerak Destroyer who was meant to be guarding her rear was also dead, his throat slit by Pogum's thorny bracelet.

"You were right about one thing, Witch," Pogum said. "There had to be a reckoning between us."

The strength left the Salt Witch's stolen body, and she fell to her knees, knowing she was about to die. "I will ... be avenged. My Skinwalkers and ... my mistress Dagwona will make all the ... Itiwana suffer for this!"

"Perhaps so," Pogum replied. "But that will not help you now, will it?"

Pogum fired a second arrow. The Salt Witch opened her mouth to curse him, but her voice would not come. Her last words were a gurgle. Her world went dark, and she fell forward on the dirt. Pogum was saddened that he had to destroy the body of the Priestess of the Evening Star, but there was nothing else he could do. At least the spirit of the real Priestess of the Evening Star would be able to rest easier in the Holy Hunting Grounds.

At the same moment that the Salt Witch died, Stone Coat froze in place. Without its mystic mistress, it became nothing more than a statue. The threat of Stone Coat was over.

Tawa realized his plan had worked. "A simple stone can't move on its own."

Pogum came into view and waved reassuringly at his nephew. "Justice was indeed very swift and satisfying."

Tawa exhaled in relief. "It seemed an eternity to me. Next time, *you* fight the monster."

The Itiwana atop the hill cheered and chanted the names of Pogum and Tawa. Any remaining Tunerak Destroyers who were watching from a distance realized that the war was lost. Their leader was gone, their supposedly unbeatable weapon Stone Coat had been reduced to an ornament in a field, and there seemed to be no point in continuing this losing battle. The Tunerak Destroyers fled from the Land of Everlasting Summer, without finding the tree.

Tawa led his exhausted Two-Horn Riders back toward the canyon where the people of Shipapa-Lina would be awaiting their return. Although this day had given the Itiwana a great victory, they did not forget that there had also been casualties in the earlier battle. Also, some of the Two-Horn Riders who rode alongside Tawa were now marred with injuries from the conflict. They would be happy to get home to Shipapa-Lina where T'Soona could tend to their wounds.

While riding back, Tawa noticed someone heading in their direction. It seemed to be a female. Pogum spotted her as well. "It's my wife."

Bluebird sprinted with panicky speed toward the returning warriors. Pogum thought she was coming to greet him. He was embarrassed until Bluebird's shouts of warning resounded.

"Danger," she yelled. "Shipapa-Lina has been attacked!"

The Vykans were ransacking Shipapa-Lina. They forced their way into the adobe homes and climbed the ladders down to pit houses. They grabbed whatever they wanted, finding lots of corn and nuts to take with them. Most of the tribe were hiding inside the Sun Temple. The Vykans had not intruded into the temple yet, but the Itiwana knew they would soon be found.

T'Soona and Atira had slipped into the Chief's longhouse. T'Soona begged her to hide, fearing what these savage invaders would do to women. He worried she might be dragged off and ravaged by one of these barbarians, and so pleaded with her to find a good hiding spot.

Atira was not the type to hide when there was trouble. She was the wife and mother of *kik-mongwis*. Her brother was the War Chief. She was a member of the Shakowin. She took her duties very seriously and would absolutely not hide while Shipapa-Lina was under siege.

"I will look in the eyes of these invaders," she insisted.

Unable to change her mind, T'Soona joined her when she marched to confront the Vykans. He vowed to protect her as best he could, even though he was not much of a fighter. He hoped Bluebird would bring the warriors back soon. They stepped out of the Long House and Atira marched toward the chaos.

Grey Pekwin was standing out in the open, inexplicably calm. He stared down the invaders. The tribal elder was spotted by a Vykan named Thorfinn, who brandished his sword threateningly.

"You there," Thorfinn shouted at Pekwin. "Do not resist or I'll cleave you in twain."

"I am too old to fear death," Pekwin said. "And I have faith in mighty Awona'Wilona."

Thorfinn laughed. "I like your bravery, ancient one. It won't help you, but I like it."

Atira ran to Pekwin's assistance, followed by T'Soona. "Do not harm him!"

"Be silent and do not move, and I perhaps will allow you more days to breathe," Thorfinn said. "But the wench is a comely cow. I will take her."

"The only place I will agree to go is to see your leader," Atira said defiantly. "I represent this tribe. We are the Shakowin of the Itiwana. We demand to speak with your leader."

The amused Vykan reached out for her. "You're a spirited wench, I can't deny. I'm going to enjoy making you submissive."

T'Soona stepped between them. "You will not lay a foul, stench-ridden finger upon this woman, you buffoon."

Thorfinn swung his shield and slammed it into T'Soona's chest. The slender healer cried out and fell, clutching his sore torso.

"T'Soona!" Atira cried out, concerned.

She kneeled to tend to him, but Thorson grabbed her by the wrist and pulled her away from T'Soona. He held up his sword, preparing to chop T'Soona in three pieces as he had promised.

"Stop!" a voice yelled. "I want to deal with those two myself."

Atira knew the voice. She had heard it many times before. A moment of shock instantly gave way to anger. *Hobomok.*

Atira saw Hobomok grinning at her with the practiced arrogance that made her hate him. A large Vykan stood protectively beside him. Hobomok looked her up and down, with a smug, triumphant smirk.

"Greetings, dear Atira," he said. "So nice to see you again. Does the returning conqueror get a big kiss?"

"Hobomok. You vile..." she replied.

"Silence yourself, female," Thorfinn snapped, yanking her arm. "You speak to a close friend and ally of our lord Giwakna."

"Who in Awona'Wilona's sacred name is Giwakna, and why would he want Hobomok as a friend?" she asked.

"Curb that tongue, woman, or I'll relieve you of it," the Vykan said.

Hobomok laughed. "Just as feisty as when I left. Bring her here. The puny male, too."

The Vykan kicked T'Soona in the stomach. He gasped for air and fell over onto his side. He could not hide his pain, but he forced himself to rise. As for Atira, the Vykan slung her over his shoulder like a sack of corn and carried her to Hobomok, dropping her at his feet.

Hobomok grinned smugly at her. "I see you've finally found your place. At my feet. I like you down there."

"You needed an army to get me here," she hissed, hatefully. "You'll need one to keep me down."

Hobomok smirked at Hunwulf, who was standing beside him. "What did I tell you about her, eh?

Hunwulf chortled. "Fiery wench. She'll be fun to tame."

Atira stood tall and boldly faced the two men, meeting their gaze fearlessly. Hunwulf dwarfed her but she would not back down to anyone.

"There is no fear of you in me," she stated. "Try to break me. Fragile I am not."

T'Soona attempted to take their attention away from Atira. "So, Hobomok. This is a great moment for you. You've found someone to do your fighting for you, and you've stooped to a new level of cravenness. I congratulate you on being more putrid than we ever suspected."

Hobomok strutted in his direction. "T'Soona, old friend. I was hoping we'd meet. I've been waiting a long time to give you something."

Hobomok flattened T'Soona with a clubbing blow. T'Soona dropped like a meteor. Hobomok gave him a disdainful kick, waited, and then kicked him a second time.

"You disrespectful little cretin," Hobomok said. "Always the mocking fool. I remember clearly every jibe and insult you have ever hurled at me. I told you that I would silence that arrogant mouth one day. Let the silencing begin."

Hobomok kicked T'Soona several more times, enjoying every boot he delivered. He savored the look of pain on T'Soona's face.

"Nothing funny to say, T'Soona? No biting witticisms? Where's the little rodent who took pleasure in goading me?"

"Stop!" Atira yelled. "Please, stop it."

"Not just yet," Hobomok said. "I'm enjoying myself too much."

"You are forever a coward and a villain, Hobomok," Grey Pekwin yelled.

Hunwulf always enjoyed a good beating, but he had come here expecting a bigger battle. He yanked Atira by the hair. "Where are the warriors? Talk, women. Where are the men?"

"I'll be delighted to acquaint you with them," she said.

"Tell me where they are or...."

Hunwulf was interrupted by the feel of rumbling earth under his feet. He looked around him to locate the source of the vibration. He and Hobomok spotted the bison-riding army of Two-Horn Riders coming up the mesa where Shipapa-Lina was nestled.

"At last," T'Soona weakly mumbled.

Tawa and his army entered the city of Shipapa-Lina. He shouted, "I am Tawa, ruler of this land. I give you one chance to leave this mesa under the power of your own legs, or we will chop those legs off and drag you behind our mounts."

Hunwulf laughed at the threat. "I welcome you to come down here and make good on your insane words. Come and take your city back … if you can."

CHAPTER TWENTY-SEVEN

The Itiwana Two-Horn Riders were prepared to fight in an effort to win back their home from the Vykans who now occupied it. Tawa was worried, however. His weary warriors had only just returned from a hard-won battle. They had suffered several casualties which they had not yet had a chance to mourn as well as needing to tend to the wounds of the men who were still among them. All the Itiwana braves were tired and fatigued.

The Vykans, however, were fresh and heavily armed. Worse, they had hostages. Even if the invaders did not deliberately execute the Itiwana captives, some were likely to be injured or killed in the battle. Things were looking rather grim in

Tawa eyes. *Is there some other way to win the day besides a battle?*

The Vykans were hunkered down in Shipapa-Lina, eagerly awaiting the coming conflict. Vykans loved a good fight, whereas the Itiwana were not eager for this battle, considering their present condition. Regardless, they had to fight for their home. The Two-Horn Riders waited for Tawa to give the signal to attack. What was he waiting for? they wondered.

"Should we begin our charge?" Pogum asked, curious about the delay.

"Give me a moment," Tawa said. "I need to think."

An eagle swooped down and landed on the horns of Tawa's bison. It spoke, saying, "Waiting is wise. We need a surprise."

"Manabazo, at last," Tawa said. "I was waiting for your arrival. I need you to be very wise now. I do not think my warriors can win this battle in our current condition, and even if we do, it means destroying Shipapa-Lina and most of the hostages within. How do I get my city back?"

Manabazo, as usual, had an idea. "These are Vykans and they are very proud. They're not great thinkers, they merely talk loud. They enjoy battle, blood, and gore. You simply need to find something they want even more."

Tawa smiled and clutched the Dragonfly tightly in his hand. "Something a warrior would badly want, eh? I think I know exactly the thing to tempt these dullards. We may just salvage this wretched day yet. The rest of you remain here. Pogum, you are in charge."

Tawa rode Mountain Fury down the hill, into Shipapa-Lina. He spotted his mother in the grip of one of the invaders and it infuriated him. Hunwulf walked forward to meet him.

"Lost your nerve for a fight, boy?" Hunwulf asked. "Have you realized the insanity of your words?"

Before Tawa could come up with a defiant answer, a recognizable voice interrupted. "The whelp was always better at bravado than battle."

When Tawa caught sight of Hobomok, he burned with rage. Suddenly the reason for this whole invasion became obvious. This was Hobomok's petty little revenge.

"Matters are clearer now," Tawa said. "I see all too well how things stand. You Vykans serve a lowly coward."

"We do not serve Hobomok," Hunwulf snapped. "We serve mighty Giwakna."

"Giwak—what?" Tawa asked.

"And I am becoming irate at being called a coward," Hobomok cried.

"Accept it, Hobomok," Tawa commented. "It's who you are. Don't forget the Mudheads."

The old Hobomok would have lost his cool, but the new Coyote-Hobomok retained his composure. "You can't talk your way out of this one, child. You have no chance. I've out-planned and out-maneuvered you this time. Shipapa-Lina is mine now as it was always meant to be. All is right again in the Land of Everlasting Summer. *My* land."

Tawa focused his plan on Hunwulf. "I imagine you've come here to collect the spoils. Property, food, captives, and the like. You didn't come here just to please Hobomok, did you?"

"Of course not," the proud Hunwulf replied. "It is honorable to claim prizes of victory."

Tawa raised his spear. "Then I offer you the greatest weapon of all. The Dragonfly."

The Vykans all laughed. "That twig? You're a clownish fool, as well as a *Scraeling*."

"*Scraeling*?"

"It means a dwarf or tiny person," Hobomok explained. "It's their word for us."

Tawa smiled. "This '*Scraeling*' has a giant sting."

He spotted Thorfinn who was holding his mother roughly by the arm. He lifted Dragonfly for a toss. The Vykan chuckled, raising his metal shield. Tawa threw Dragonfly. It pierced not only the metal shield but also the Vykan himself. Thorfinn screamed his last scream as his innards tailed along behind the spear, which imbedded itself in the new stone wall.

Hunwulf was in awe. "What a magnificent weapon. I must have it for Giwakna. Our great Lord will praise me for a century if I bring him such a weapon."

Hunwulf dashed to the Dragonfly and tried pulling it free. He was mortified to find he could not dislodge it. He tried again and again but could not remove it from the cliff wall.

"I must have it," he kept muttering as he yanked.

Hobomok was becoming leery about this. *What is the boy planning?*

"You'll never pull it out," Tawa told Hunwulf. "It's enchanted. Only the owner can remove it. You'll get my spear only if I give it to you willingly."

Hunwulf ceased his efforts to pull the spear loose. "I imagine you have a bargain to make."

"Two bargains, actually," Tawa said. "The first bargain is that I fight one of you—an opponent of my choosing—if I lose, you get the spear. Should I be victorious, however, we decide the possession of Shipapa-Lina through a battle of champions ... my best warrior against yours."

Hunwulf thought over the offer. He wanted that spear very badly and was confident any of his Vykans could beat one of these *Scraelings*. "Very well. I accept. Choose your opponent."

Tawa pointed at Hobomok. "I already have."

After a moment of anger, Hobomok felt a reluctant respect for the quick-witted Tawa. *There is something different about the boy now.*

Hobomok decided this was his chance to finish the fight they had begun the previous year when victory was stolen from him by the White Buffalo Woman. Now, with the Coyote inside him, he was certain to destroy the boy.

"If there is anything I would enjoy more, it escapes my mind," Hobomok said. "I accept your challenge."

"I can't tell you how glad I am to hear that," Tawa said. "I despise leaving things unsettled, don't you?"

"We agree on that, at least," Hobomok replied. "This fight has been screaming to be fought."

As Tawa climbed down from Mountain Fury, Hobomok rubbed his hands together eagerly. When Tawa approached his opponent, the Vykans circled around them, forming a human arena for the combatants. The Vykans chanted for Hobomok while the captive Itiwana silently prayed for Tawa to prevail.

Hunwulf slapped Hobomok on the shoulder. "You're a brave *scraeling*. No wonder Giwakna thinks so well of you. Is there any message you wish me to pass on to our great Lord of Ice and Snow if you should fall?"

Hobomok dismissed the comment. "I don't think that will be necessary. I have this in hand. At any rate, I have no message for Giwakna. However, if anything should happen—unlikely as it is—promise to free the Painted White Girl."

"Done."

Tawa considered taking Dragonfly out from the wall but thought better of it because they would likely attempt to take it from him by force. It was his only bargaining advantage. He stared with loathing at Hobomok.

"You can't win, child," Hobomok said. "I very nearly had you beaten the last time we fought, and I am so much more now than I was then. I have the power of the Coyote inside me now. You may have Kachina blood, but I have a Sky God's soul. I am beyond you all."

Tawa did not have any idea what Hobomok was talking about, and it didn't matter. Tawa was a Mastop-Kachina even before Manabazo began training him. No matter what type of "soul" Hobomok now had, Tawa had also been changed by the Tree of life and by intense training.

"Whatever you think has happened to your soul, you simply don't have greatness in you," Tawa said. "As for me, I'm no longer the boy you taught to hunt years ago. But words will not prove that. Only blood will."

Hobomok clenched his fists and crouched. "Blood, you say? Yes, that's what this is about … blood and honor."

"You're about to lose both," Tawa said.

There was no "feeling-out" process, as in the previous battle. This time, Tawa and Hobomok lunged at each other with an explosion of long-constrained fury. They crashed together like two stags locking horns. Fists, elbows, feet, and knees flashed in an exchange that was an equal mix of savagery and skill. Nothing was held back. The Vykans cheered, enjoying the ferocity of the combat.

Hunwulf glanced over at Atira and T'Soona. "Am I correct that these two hate each other?"

"There are some harsh feelings," T'Soona replied.

Hobomok was surprised by how much Tawa had improved in the past year. The young *kik-mongwi* was astonishingly skillful. Whatever he had been doing over the past season, it had worked well because Hobomok was not having the easy victory he had anticipated.

Tawa had bulked-up somewhat since their last encounter. The slip of a boy who he had out-powered the previous summer was now a stocky warrior. Hobomok could not rely on having the advantage in either power or weight this time. Tawa seemed quicker and more calculated, too. Hobomok was genuinely taken aback by how formidable Tawa had become.

Tawa felt something different about Hobomok. It was not that Hobomok was significantly more skillful than he had been the year before. The improvement in fighting ability was only marginal. However, there was something different in his style. He seemed more methodical and deliberate in his approach this time. The previous year, he was like a charging bull. Now he appeared to be more patient, calculating his moves. He had a better defense. Something had definitely changed for Hobomok.

Both men had unusually high endurance because of the mystic power inside them. One was a Mastop-Kachina with the Oki-energy of Yaxche, and the other was possessed by the Coyote spirit. The fight went on very evenly for quite some time.

Finally, the stamina of youth became a factor. Despite the Coyote's energy, Hobomok was twice Tawa's age. After many, many long minutes of strenuous combat, Hobomok felt drained and exhausted. Young Tawa, however, seemed to be getting his second wind. When Tawa sensed Hobomok was slowing, he had an adrenaline surge of energy. He kicked and pounded his older opponent brutally. Hobomok found himself on the defensive. He struggled to regain control but just did not have the reserves of energy to salvage the situation.

Desperate, Hobomok decided on a change of tactics he hoped might confuse Tawa. He switched to his old, more aggressive style, thrusting himself forward with wild abandon. The tactic backfired. Tawa had been prepared by Manabazo to watch for tricks such as this one. Therefore, when Hobomok charged, Tawa met him with a spinning kick to his unprotected jaw. The blow was so hard, it knocked Hobomok off his feet.

When Hobomok fell to the ground, Tawa took advantage of the situation and leapt upon him. Tawa wriggled around behind Hobomok and locked him in a chokehold. He got a firm grip on Hobomok's throat and squeezed. Hobomok panicked, trying desperately to extricate himself from the lethal hold. He clawed and squirmed and tried with his remaining energy to save himself, but it was all for naught. Tawa was tenacious. He was not going to let go while Hobomok was alive.

Choking to death, Hobomok began to feel dizzy. His lungs were throbbing for air. His vision was going black, and he knew he was about to die. His vision waned, going black, and he knew he was about to die. The part of him that was Hobomok felt horrified at his impending death, but the Coyote part knew it still had a vessel to escape into when this body was gone.

As Hobomok's life faded from Hobomok, Tawa whispered in his ear, "It didn't have to be this way. I take no pleasure in this. I hope you find peace in the Holy Hunting Grounds."

As Hobomok succumbed to the lack of air, his body went limp. With a quick jerk, Tawa twisted his unmoving opponent's neck. It broke with a sickening snap.

You leave this world no poorer for your passing, Tawa thought.

At Nurumgard in Norumbega, the Painted White Girl was doing her chores, cleaning up Hobomok's hut, so the dwelling would be presentable when the father of her unborn child came home. She looked forward to his return. She missed him when he was away. He was the only one who treated her nicely. She anticipated his announcement that she was now Mistress of Shipapa-Lina.

A sudden sharp pain assailed her belly. It felt as if something had just pushed its way through her, entering her like an invisible object. The pain only lasted for a few moments and then passed as quickly as it had struck. She placed her hands on her belly, wondering what had happened. She hoped the baby was all right. Somehow, something told her it was now stronger than ever. She was unsure what gave her that impression.

The Painted White Girl suddenly had a feeling of dread about Hobomok. She could not escape the impression that something terrible had happened to him. She prayed she was wrong.

Please let him live to see his son. Let him be alive to take me to Shipapa-Lina.

Tawa released the lifeless form of Hobomok. Standing over his opponent, breathing heavily, he let out a victorious yawp.

"Well done, my boy," Atira said quietly, thinking about how Tawa had changed.

The Vykans were surprised at the result. They did not care much for Hobomok, but they were worried that Giwakna might be angry. Still, the fight was a fair one and Hobomok had lost.

"You fight well, *scraeling*," Hunwulf said.

"I do," Tawa replied, as he easily pulled the Dragonfly from the wall.

"You've deprived our fearsome Ice Lord of the weapon ... for the moment," Hunwulf said, embarrassed at how easily Tawa drew the spear. "Still, this is not over. I allow you to select your champion in the battle for your conquered home. Pick who will die. I am eager to see your flesh and bone ripped asunder while the Gods laugh at the fool *scraeling* who thought he could defeat a Vykan."

CHAPTER TWENTY-EIGHT

The whale swam toward the coast of Ulah-Nane, following the instructions of its passenger. The woman stood tall upon the whale's back, looking at the shore in the distance. Her loyal, obedient wolves Wind and Moon lay at her feet. She had ridden a long way over water, carried by her giant aquatic friend. She had been taken away by force and now she was finally home again.

She had no way of knowing what had happened in Ulah-Nane during her forced absence. Her reduced powers limited the scope of her Mystic Awareness. At one time, she would have known what had occurred but now only had vague sensations. She was frustrated that she could not see more.

She could tell that Hunwulf and his Vykans had made their way south and knew violence was occurring. She urged the whale to swim faster and prayed to Awona'Wilona that she arrived in time to prevent more bloodshed.

The battle of champions between the Itiwana and the Vykans was about to begin. Both leaders were choosing their respective champions. Hunwulf was furious at being deprived of that amazing spear. He burned to avenge the dishonor. He could not afford to lose the city of Shipapa-Lina as well. Giwakna would be furious. This fight had to be won.

To ensure victory, he planned to have his best warrior fight in this contest. Looking over his big, burly army of soldiers, he knew there was not a weak link among them. But for this situation, he wanted the best of the best and the most savage of the savage. His two most formidable warriors were the Berserker and the Iron Forge.

The Berserker was a towering brute of terrifying savagery. No one could swing a battle-axe the way that the Berserker could. When the bloodlust was upon him, he was a walking nightmare, slaying every foe in sight with gleeful abandon. On the other hand, no one was stronger than the Iron Forge. Not only had the Iron Forge made the weapons for the Vykans, he was a juggernaut in combat, swinging his war-hammer with frightening force. He was not quite as tall as the Berserker but was stockier and surely the strongest human being Hunwulf had ever seen. Either one was a good choice. Which should it be?

"Iron Forge," Hunwulf said. "It is you. You are the one. Come."

The brawny, barrel-chested man strode forward. He had several burn marks on his arms and torso. In his large hands he held a big hammer. "I am most honored and most eager."

The Berserker hissed and grumbled at not having been chosen for the honor of the kill. Hunwulf, however, gestured for him to be silent. "Patience, my savage friend. You may still get to hack some *scraelings* before the night arrives."

Tawa had already chosen who his champion would be. "Would you mind if I sent my mother up the hill to inform the chosen champion there is a fight waiting for him here?"

"Send the wench," Hunwulf growled. "And have her step swiftly. My impatience grows with each breath."

Tawa whispered in his mother's ear. She nodded, impressed with his plan and his performance throughout this crisis. "As you say, my *kik-mongwi*. You are wise beyond your years."

Atira ran up the hill, eager to see an end to the occupation of Shipapa-Lina. Of course, there was a chance the Vykans would not keep their word, but Tawa had a plan for that, too. *Quite a boy I've raised. He's his father's son.*

While they awaited her return, Tawa continued playing mind-games with the Vykans. "Your large friend looks somewhat over-heated."

"He can tolerate the fires of Surt's inferno if need be," Hunwulf snapped.

"As you wish," Tawa answered. "But in the interest of fairness, I should tell you there is some cool water at the reservoir across the field. Since you kept your word after my fight with Hobomok, I am obliged to give your man a fair chance."

Hunwulf thought about it for a moment. Was this some sort of trick? He could not see how it would be. And the Iron Forge could certainly use some cooling off. They were not used to this warm weather.

"Very well," Hunwulf replied. "Let us move the site of our imminent victory to your reservoir. We Vykans love to be near the water, almost as much as we love walking through a bloody battlefield and collecting the remains of our enemies to give to our dread lord as sustenance."

The Vykans laughed and cheered. Half the Vykan army followed Hunwulf, Tawa and the Iron Forge to the Deep Well and reservoir. The Berserker and the rest of the Vykans stayed behind in the heart of Shipapa-Lina, to guard the hostages. The Iron Forge splashed himself with some cold water and waited for his opponent.

Someone came up the hill from where the Itiwana were waiting. It was someone large, with a lumbering gait and long hair. Faw-Faw the Wood Man stomped towards the Vykans. The invaders from the north were taken by surprise at the size of the Itiwana's champion. They had not anticipated anyone so huge.

Hunwulf pointed at Faw-Faw. "That is no *scraeling.*"

"No, he's not," Tawa said. "Neither was Hobomok, but you didn't protest when I picked him as my opponent. But this Wood Man is an honorary member of my tribe, and I never said my champion would be an Itiwana born. Surely you Vykans don't fear anyone?"

Hunwulf felt a grudging admiration for the young Itiwana. "By Odin, I like you, boy. You're a wily cuss. What manner of schemer will you be when fully grown? It's a pity you weren't born in our homeland. I'd love to turn you loose on the Brittons."

"I don't know who the Brittons are," Tawa said. "But I would feel a great swell of pity for them if I were their enemy."

Faw-Faw the Wood Man spotted his chieftain Tawa and sought his instructions. Tawa was glad to see Faw-Faw still clutching his club. Pogum had made it for him. The handle of the club was a long, thick piece of solid oak. Fastened on the end of the handle was a big rock. It was blunt on one side. On the other, it had carved stone points, heated by fire to reshape parts of the stone into sharp edges. Backed by the superhuman power of the Wood Man, it was a deadly weapon.

Tawa pointed at the Iron Forge and said one of the words that Faw-Faw had learned. "Enemy."

Faw-Faw growled at the Iron Forge, and without hesitation, charged the Vykan. The Iron Forge was taken aback by the suddenness and speed of the assault. Faw-Faw swung his club, and the Iron Forge barely got his hammer up in time to block the blow. Despite his weapon being metal, the power behind that blow almost dislodged the hammer from his hands. Iron Forge was shocked by the strength of this giant.

In response, he swung the hammer. This time, Faw-Faw blocked it with his club. They repeated this several times, slamming their weapons with unrestrained strength. Iron Forge was getting tired, and the unaccustomed heat was draining him. Inevitably, the hammer was knocked from his sweaty hands. At the same time, however, the oak handle of Faw-Faw's hammer cracked and broke.

Both men were now unarmed. The Iron Forge stood unnerved before his larger, stronger opponent. In desperation, he leaped forward, hoping to tackle the Wood Man to the ground, but he did not have the power. The other Vykans cheered him on for support, but it did not help. As they scuffled, Faw-Faw grabbed hold of the Vykan in a vice grip. The Iron Forge was scared. He had never met anyone stronger than himself before, except mighty Giwakna. This strange being was too powerful for any mortal man to deal with.

Faw-Faw grabbed the Iron Forge's arm and snapped it. As the Iron Forge screamed, Faw-Faw picked him up and slammed him to the ground so hard, the impact broke the Iron Forge's back. Then he brought down his foot and stomped on the Vykans head. A man's skull shattered until it was nothing more than a squished clump of gunk.

The Vykans were all silent, unable to comprehend that the mighty Iron Forge had fallen so easily. The Wood Man lifted the discarded iron hammer and raised it over his head, letting out his primal victory howl. Tawa restrained a satisfied smile, although he knew this was not over yet.

Hunwulf looked down at the slain Iron Forge in disbelief. He then glared furiously at Tawa, who had outmaneuvered him yet again. He drew his sword and shouted in rage. "I may have given you my vow, but I will not see myself thrice undone by a stripling. I will not return to Giwakna with my hands holding nothing. I shall have satisfaction and blood. Spear or no spear, I will split open your head and feed that cunning little brain to my dire Lord."

Tawa was not surprised by this. He fended off Hunwulf with his spear. "Your sword is large, and your voice is loud, but as we're on the subject of brains, I am impelled to observe that yours is clearly shriveled like an old prune left out in the sun for days. Shall I tell you what you did wrong?"

Hunwulf waved his broadsword theatrically. "Still your agile tongue and face your death like the man you would have become if I had chosen to let you live."

Tawa kept up his taunting and delaying tactics. "Your mistake was getting so angry that you made unwise decisions. Too overconfident. Otherwise, you would never have let me trick you into splitting up your forces and bringing half of them here, near the water."

Tawa raised the Dragonfly. Moments later, dozens upon dozens of arrow shafts blocked out the sun and then came down upon the unsuspecting Vykans. The Vykans managed to protect themselves with their shields. However, their momentary triumph faded when they witnessed a monstrous animal rise from the reservoir. It was a mammoth-sized beaver.

Thank you, Molowia, for sending Wishpoosh, Tawa thought. *I was praying you would.*

Hunwulf realized the mistake he had made by allowing Tawa to bait him here. *Curse the Itiwana boy. I'll dismember him for this.*

As the Poshiyanki Beaver pounced upon the Vykans, smashing them with its spiked tail, Tawa hoped that the second half of his plan worked.

High in the trees on the cliff above Shipapa-Lina, various types of aerial raptors, including falcons and eagles, sat on their perches. There were hundreds of them. They had no interest in the affairs of the humans below until they were drawn into the mortal battle.

Manabazo was in his eagle form. Accompanied by Black Crow, the shape-shifting Sky God looped through the air in a circular fashion. He had gotten a message from Tawa, relayed to him by Atira. Manabazo and Black Crow continued their hypnotic swirl, accompanied by a primal caw that affected the simple brains of the birds.

Manabazo swooped down towards the city, with a loud cry. Black Crow imitated this sound exactly. The many predatory avians in the area were so caught-up in this action that they found themselves following the two birds down, without understanding why. Hundreds of them trailed Manabazo and Black Crow downward.

The Berserker and his half of the Vykan army were guarding the women, children, and elderly, as well as T'Soona, holding them as prisoners near the edge of the Hanging cliff. They were impatient for their fellow Vykans to return. The antsiest of all was the Berserker, who still wished he had been chosen to fight the Itiwana champion. He hated to miss a good fight. Or even a bad one. The Vykans could not see the reservoir from where they stood because it was blocked by some of the adobe houses, foliage and new walls that were built for defense against the Tunerak Destroyers.

They did hear the screams of their fellow Vykans, though. They could not know what had happened, but it did not take a wise sage to realize a battle had started. They were all eager for some action, especially the Berserker.

CHAPTER TWENTY-EIGHT

"Kill the hostages," the Berserker shouted. "I must kill *scraelings*."

A handful of the Vykans stayed behind, as the Berserker led the rest toward the Deep Well and reservoir. The few remaining Vykans were prepared to kill the terrified hostages, but they would not get the chance.

Manabazo and Black Crow, followed by hundreds of birds of prey, dropped from the sky and overwhelmed the remaining Vykans like a plague of locusts. The perplexed Vykans swatted at the massing birds, unable to cope with the sheer number of them. Manabazo could not participate in the battle, but Black Crow pecked at the Vykans and the other birds imitated him.

While this was happening, Pogum had made his way stealthily into Shipapa-Lina, using his familiarity with the area to his advantage. Atira had conveyed some instructions from Tawa. Pogum was part of the rescue plan. He fired an arrow and hit one of the Vykans in the heart. He continued picking off the Vykans one-by-one. The few remaining invaders ran in frantic confusion to get help from their brethren.

T'Soona, who was among the captives, beamed with relief. "Ha. That silenced their little cock-a-doodle of victory. Who's the *scraeling* now, eh?"

Pogum quickly untied T'Soona. "Free the others. I must go to aid my fellow warriors."

"Speaking for all of us, we are very much in favor of your slaying every last one of those giant-sized vermin," T'Soona said.

"Coincidentally, that is our plan exactly."

While the Vykans attempted to coordinate an attack against the mighty Wishpoosh, they heard the sound of bison hooves. The turned to see the remaining Itiwana, the ones who were uninjured from the previous battle and now rested charging toward them atop their bison herd. Led by Aholi, the riders rammed into the Vykans, trampling many of them.

As the surprised Hunwulf shouted orders, trying to regain control of the situation, an arrow flew passed his face, missing by inches. It hit one of his fellow Vykans. Hunwulf looked to the higher ground where the Bow Sisterhood had regrouped. They fired expertly at the Vykans, causing confusion and injuries.

The Itiwana and Wishpoosh had the upper hand in the battle. The tribe jabbed the Vykans with spears, while the horns of their mounts did a lot of damage, even though the Vykans carried shields. The Itiwana whittled down the Vykan forces.

Hunwulf was cussing in rage at being outmaneuvered again. He was relieved when he spotted the Berserker and the other Vykans running to his aid. *At last. Now the fires of Vykan glory will burn bright.*

However, the Vykans were unaware the Itiwana had rigged Shipapa-Lina with numerous traps, in anticipation of their battle with the Tunerak Destroyers. Tawa, Manabazo and Pogum had painstakingly set up many surprises they had not needed to employ in the earlier battle but could now be utilized. The Itiwana weavers had made a huge net to help separate the Destroyer forces. It was hidden under the dirt and dust.

Tawa shot an arrow with unerring aim and split a rope that was holding a basket of rocks in the air from a post. Once Tawa split the rope, the basket of rocks fell to the ground. A second rope connected to the falling basket was tied to the hidden net. The rope was draped over a branch. When the rock basket fell, the rope was pulled, and it raised up the concealed net.

As the Berserker and the other Vykans were rushing to help their fellow Norsemen, a big net rose up, blocking their path. The Vykans only hesitated for a moment and started hacking at the net with their swords. The woven net had been made to block the Tunerak Destroyers with their wooden weapons, but the Vykans had metal swords. They were able to cut through with relative ease.

Although the net failed to stop them, it delayed them long enough for Manabazo and Black Crow to catch up with them, leading their avian army. As they had done before, the flock of wild birds swarmed around the Vykans, causing mass confusion. While that was happening, Atira was setting in motion the next phase of Tawa's plan.

Many of the bison who were being kept for meat, instead of being used as mounts, were in a nearby pen, agitated by the sounds of battle. If it had not been for the sturdy gate, they would have stampeded already. Atira opened the gate and used her flute to draw the bison in her direction. Still nervous from the sounds of battle, the bison stampeded out of the pen.

The Vykans, already under siege from the birds, found themselves in the path of stampeding beasts. They all recoiled in alarm at the impending danger. The Vykans scattered to evade the herd but were unsuccessful. They found themselves directly in the path of destruction. The Bow Sisterhood began firing from their perch. Wishpoosh was on a rampage. The Vykans were being attacked from all sides. It was pandemonium.

Hunwulf, fighting near the reservoir, spotted the bison storming through the area, trampling his men who were coming from Shipapa-Lina, while Wishpoosh tore a bloody swath through the Norsemen. Hunwulf was overwhelmed by the chaos of it all.

This is madness, he thought. *I've never seen the like.*

Hunwulf decided to do something he had never done before and thought he would never do. He stood upon a rock and raised his sword in the air. "Brother Vykans, hear me! Withdraw! Withdraw! Return to the river. Return to the boats. Withdraw!"

The Vykans were bewildered and frustrated by the bedlam happening around them, as well as being humiliated at their inability to defeat a smaller and less well-armed foe. On some level, they were glad their leader had called the retreat. They were content to get away from these unpredictable and surprisingly formidable Itiwana.

The Vykans started their retreat, all except the Berserker, who desired to stay and fight. He remained behind, hacking and chopping at his Itiwana opponents. Hunwulf grabbed him, trying to drag the crazed warrior away. Caught up in his crazed rage, the Berserker swung his battleax at Hunwulf, who blocked it with his shield. Hunwulf was rattled by the power of the blow and very glad he got his shield up in time.

"Berserker. It's Hunwulf. Listen to me. We must go. We'll be back with Giwakna at our side, and then we'll get our revenge. For now, we must go!"

The Berserker snorted, reluctant to leave, but his loyalty to Hunwulf won out, and he allowed himself to be led from the battlefield. The Vykans fled to the river, leaving the Land of Everlasting Summer as quickly as possible.

The Itiwana were too tired to pursue. They had fought two battles this day and were in no shape for a third. Tawa was relieved the Vykans retreated when they did. The toll this day had taken on him left Tawa exhausted. He was the youngest warrior present and wondered what the older braves must be feeling. Like everyone else, he was ecstatic to see the enemy flee.

He noticed Wishpoosh lumbering back to the reservoir and sinking into the water, vanishing like a dream upon waking. *Thank you, Molowia. You saved our village. I owe you.*

At Tawa's signal, the Itiwana gathered their wounded and brought them back into Shipapa-Lina, where T'Soona the healer was aided by the women and elderly in tending to their injuries. Aholi and a party of men volunteered to collect the bodies of those fallen in the two previous battles. Tawa and Manabazo, meanwhile, took stock of the damage to Shipapa-Lina. No one was celebrating their dual victories.

Atira sat near the reservoir, playing her flute to try luring back the bison that had run off. They gradually filed back, first in small numbers and then in large groups. Most of them eventually returned, although a few were lost for good.

Despite their miraculous accomplishments of the day, no one seemed in a victorious mood. There was a great deal of mourning for the fallen. The bodies had been collected and buried in a mass grave. A ceremony was performed for the fallen, to guide their souls to the Holy Hunting Grounds.

As night fell, the exhausted Itiwana were beginning to think the trials of the terrible day were over at last. However, there was one more surprise to come.

A stranger arrived at Shipapa-Lina, who would change Tawa's life forever.

CHAPTER TWENTY-NINE

The long day of arduous battle had finally ended. The moon rose and owls flew and most of the Itiwana were either resting from the battle or mourning for their slain loved ones. The day had seen the end of the threat of the Tunerak Destroyers but introduced a newer, greater menace with metal swords and shields.

Wary of another attack in the night, Tawa ordered a lookout to stand atop the Hanging cliff. T'Soona volunteered, since he had not fought. For his protection, Tawa sent Faw-Faw the Wood Man along with him, just in case dangerous people were lurking in the darkness. Faw-Faw, however, simply wanted to sleep. T'Soona knew it was not wise to keep one of these Wood Men from their rest, and so let the big man nap while he kept watch over the now silent Shipapa-Lina.

Everything was quiet during the night except for the thunderous snoring of Faw-Faw. T'Soona mused over how this silent vista had been a battleground only hours earlier. In the nocturnal peacefulness of the moonlight, the Land of Everlasting Summer looked sublime and serene. T'Soona was saddened by the fact it would not last.

Pogum returned to the pit house where his wife Bluebird waited. Despite the exertions of the day, Pogum still felt so energized with adrenaline, he could not sleep. He had walked around for a while, patrolling the perimeter, before he finally went home. When he climbed down the ladder to his pit house, Bluebird was lying on her animal-skin bed, anxious to tell him something.

She smiled when he entered. "There you are, my brave."

Pogum sat beside her and kissed her. "I apologize for my absence. I am ... pensive."

Bluebird crawled around behind him and began rubbing his shoulders. "I have news that will take your mind from these troubles."

"It must be monumental news, indeed," he said.

"It is," she said. "I've been wanting to tell you this for some time, but emergencies made it untimely. While I have this chance, it's time to tell you of the blessing Awona'Wilona has bestowed upon us. I have visited T'Soona the medicine man, and he has verified what I already knew. I carry your child."

Pogum spun around, suddenly forgetting the Vykans. "This is certain?"

"As certain as the sunrise, my brave."

Pogum embraced her. "How quickly an accursed day turns magnificent. I'd not have walked so long had I know the cure to my trepidation was waiting here. No news could have pleased me better."

"The Sky Elders have rewarded us for enduring what we've been through," she said.

"Indeed," Pogum said. "If he is a son, I will teach him to hunt and fish and ride and fight. If she is a girl, I hope she takes after my dearest Bluebird."

"My intuition tells me it is a son," Bluebird said. "A son to be proud of. The son of my noble Pogum."

In the morning, just before the cock crowed, T'Soona was struggling not to nod off. His eyelids were weighing heavily, and he was looking forward to sleeping. His attention became focused on something moving down below, just outside Shipapa-Lina. It could have been an animal, although it seemed a decent sized one. Looking carefully, he saw two wolves appear. Strangely enough, they seemed to be white wolves. White wolves were rare in the Land of Everlasting

Summer. They were much more common in the North, which made T'Soona wonder if the Vykans were truly gone. Or perhaps they had left these fierce animals behind to vex the Itiwana.

T'Soona spotted something else. There was a human intruder approaching. Or perhaps it was just a human-like being walking along with those wolves. The animals seemed to be flanking this being on each side. The stranger had lighter hair than local people, which indicated a Vykan, because they were fairer of hair and skin than the Itiwana.

This could be the beginning of another ghastly day, T'Soona said.

T'Soona had a foghorn made from a bison horn and put to his lips. He blew a warning to the people of Shipapa-Lina, awakening Faw-Faw. After a second burst, the Itiwana people responded to the alarm. The men came carrying weapons. None of them were happy to be summoned for another emergency so soon after the wars of the previous day.

"Does it never end?" Atira whispered, as she emerged from the longhouse.

Bluebird and Pogum appeared from their pit house dwelling. "You Itiwana do not lack for excitement in your lives, do you?" Bluebird said.

"Stay here," Pogum insisted. "Our child is inside you and your task is to keep him safe."

Tawa rushed from the chieftain's longhouse and moved to the center of the gathering crowd. "Calmly now, each of you. We have no inkling yet who or what is coming. Be alert but don't be alarmed—at least not yet."

From atop the cliff, T'Soona pointed. The Itiwana focused their attention to the valley. Weapons at the ready, they waited to see what would appear. No one expected a lone woman with two white wolves. The Itiwana men lowered their weapons when the woman reached the mesa.

She was an albino, snow white in hair, skin and even eyes. She wore a silver European-style corset and cloak, which augmented her lack of pigmentation. Yet, she was not unattractive, having pleasant features and a shapely form.

She locked eyes immediately with Tawa. She had either detected he was the leader, or she sensed something special about him. Whichever the reason, she focused her colorless eyes on his and smiled a smile so enchanting, it was almost hypnotic. Tawa felt a rush of wild attraction to her. He had to force himself not to be distracted or disarmed by her obvious charms.

"Who are you?" he asked.

The albino woman continued to smile as she spoke. "This One sees that she has caused you some alarm. She apologizes to you. This One means no harm to the Itiwana. She has come to help you."

"Excellent to hear," Tawa said. "Can I assume from your strange way of speaking and unusual appearance that you are one of the Sky Gods?"

"She is such," the albino woman said. "You impress This One with your insight."

"Thank you," Tawa said. "Now, where's my other Sky Elder? Manabazo, are you here?"

A third wolf appeared abruptly from the bushes and approached the other two. The pair of white wolves began sniffing the new grey wolf. The grey wolf locked eyes with Tawa.

"Manabazo?"

"It is I, have no fears. Don't be put off by my fur and long ears."

Tawa pointed to the newly arrived woman. "Do you know her? Is she ally or enemy?"

Manabazo sniffed her. "Ah, Pinga, with the skin so fair. You've traveled far from the northern air."

"This One is pleased to see you, Manabazo," Pinga said. "She has not seen a fellow Sky Elder in far too many years."

"No surprise, dear girl. You chose to remain on this world."

"This One felt that she should," Pinga said. "She deemed it wise at the time."

Atira was out of patience with this dialogue. "Stop. We need explanations right now."

"This One will attempt to comply," Pinga said with a kind smile.

Pinga walked toward Tawa, who looked toward Manabazo for assurance. Manabazo gave him a reassuring nod, indicating she was not hostile.

Pinga touched his head. "This one senses you have touched Yaxche, the Tree of Life. The *kik-mongwi* reeks of it. He is one who knows. She can use that to Dream-Bond with you."

"Dream-Bond?" Atira asked.

Pinga touched Tawa's head, and he suddenly felt thoughts flooding into his head, like water flowing. He had not experienced anything like this since he touched Yaxche. All at once he knew things he had not known moments before. And more than that, he now felt a bond with Pinga. It was almost as if his earlier attraction to her was a premonition of this new connection they were forming. It was alarming yet he couldn't honestly say it was completely unpleasant.

Pinga poked his nose playfully and beamed affectionately at him. "The *kik-mongwi* sees now. This One knows he does. Is she correct?"

"You are," Tawa said.

"Are you all right, my son?" Atira asked.

"Quite well," Tawa said. "I am informed. Come with me to the chieftain's longhouse."

In the chieftain's longhouse, Tawa sat cross-legged in the usual Shakowin circle. With him were T'Soona, Pogum, and Pinga as well as Manabazo, now in his ocelot form.

"You're all a bit curious about our new arrival, I imagine," Tawa said. "I understand and I will now alleviate your suspense. I'm sure Manabazo and Pinga could explain this, but in the interest of brevity and clarity, I think it's best if I do it. I've always enjoyed telling stories."

"Tell us one now," Atira said.

"To the point, then," Tawa began. "Pinga chose to stay here in Ulah-Nane when the other Sky Gods returned to the clouds. She had been the advisor and protector of the northern tribes and she did not want to leave them. When she decided to stay, she had to sacrifice most of her great powers. She lived among them as a mortal, ageless but no longer powerful. Then the Vykans came. The man from across the east Blue Patowa'Kacha who called himself the Red Lord, led his Vykan warriors to a place North of Ulah-Nane, which they named Vineland. They then encountered Pinga, and she befriended them, helping them adapt to life here. She taught them the Old Speak and the common language. They saw her as an ally."

"Until the Red Lord saw This One as a bride," Pinga said. "He forcibly took me to wed."

Tawa continued. "And while the Red Lord formed his Vineland colony, he sent half his warriors to scout out the terrain of Norumbega in northern Ulah-Nane. This faction was led by Hunwulf. Or at the very least, they were until Giwakna appeared."

"Giwakna is a beast," Manabazo said. "I respect him the least."

"This One fears him," Pinga added.

"And the Vykans worship him," Tawa said. "Giwakna is one of the last of the Ice Wendigos, who were mostly destroyed in the previous war of the Sky Elders. They retreated to the frozen Northlands, but Giwakna was a rogue in exile. When he came across Hunwulf and the other

Vykans, they believed him to be a creature from their legends called Ymir the Frost Giant. They chose to serve him and built the colony Nurumgard in Norumbega. The Red Lord felt they had betrayed him and came to Nurumgard to fight. But Giwakna was fiercer than he could have guessed. The Red Lord was defeated and chose to flee back to his homeland across the other Blue Patowa'Kacha."

"Taking This One with him," Pinga said.

"Yes, the Red Lord took her away with him," Tawa explained. "She spent years as his captive in the land across the Blue Patowa'Kacha but finally escaped and found her way back atop a whale."

"Atop a whale? T'Soona asked. "Here is a woman who knows how to fish."

"This One returned because she knew there would be danger here," Pinga said. "Between Giwakna and the Vykans, she feared great danger to the people of Ulah-Nane."

"What brought you here to us?" Atira asked.

"This One still has an empathic sense," Pinga told them. "She could sense Hunwulf and his Vykans making their way south to this place, She knew violence was coming and she felt it happening. She came with the intent to stop it. She hoped to negotiate with the Vykans. This One is their former ruler's royal consort, after all. Sadly, she was too late. But perhaps she can still be of help in the future because she knows this is not over."

Manabazo agreed. "It is the truth she tells. Giwakna will not take the bad news well. Tawa slew Hobomok and thwarted the plot. Forgiving is something Giwakna is not."

"I imagine we'll have to be ready for him," Pogum said. "He and his large friends will be back."

"We'll be ready," Tawa replied. "I am plotting as we speak."

While the Itiwana prepared for future attacks, Hunwulf and the Vykans made the long trip back to Nurumgard. Hunwulf was very afraid of what Giwakna would do when he found out they had returned defeated and Hobomok was dead. Hunwulf dreaded that conversation. He hoped Giwakna would not bite his head off ... literally.

The return trip took over three weeks, and Hunwulf was not in any great hurry to get there.

Weeks later, Giwakna roared and raged upon hearing that Hobomok—his friend the Coyote—was dead. He was further infuriated that the Vykans had failed to conquer Shipapa-Lina.

"Giwakna's friend dead," the Ice Wendigo bellowed in fury. "Coyote dead. Vykans failed Giwakna."

The frightened Hunwulf kneeled humbly before his dread lord, flanked by two other nervous Vykans. "Please, great one. Hobomok chose to fight, and they had a magic spear that..."

Giwakna growled and slapped Hunwulf aside, knocking him brutally to the ground. Giwakna needed to vent his fury on someone, but he did not want to kill Hunwulf because he was still valuable as the field leader of the Vykans. Giwakna turned his rage against the other two Vykans. Hunwulf watched in fixated fear as Giwakna tore the other two apart and devoured parts of them. Blood splattered everywhere. Giwakna then turned his attention back to Hunwulf.

"You fail Giwakna," he roared. "Giwakna not happy. Giwakna should eat you too."

"Please, great one, I..." Hunwulf pleaded.

"No talk," Giwakna bellowed, gesturing wildly. "Giwakna lets you live but stupid Vykan not talk anymore. Giwakna will make Itiwana pay for killing Coyote. When air gets colder, Giwakna will go to war. Giwakna will lead Vykans to fight Itiwana. Giwakna crush them. Destroy them. Giwakna eat their hearts. Kill! Kill the Itiwana. Kill!"

CHAPTER THIRTY

Months had passed since Pinga had first arrived in Shipapa-Lina. Another summer was gone, and the nights were getting cooler. As winter approached, Tawa ordered Pogum to intensify the combat training the Two-Horn Riders were undergoing, in anticipation of another attack by the Vykans. This time it would likely be led by Giwakna himself. Pinga was familiar with the Ice Wendigo and warned Tawa that Giwakna would attack as soon as the hottest summer days were gone. Although the Yaxche made the summer endless, the winter still remained marginally cool enough for Giwakna to temporarily survive in the South.

At the moment, Tawa was sitting atop the Hanging Cliff. He was planning a strategy. Tawa knew what the Vykans were capable of. They were formidable warriors, but he had no idea what to expect from this Wendigo when they met in battle. He had a lot of thinking to do. He was glad for the advice of Manabazo and Pinga.

Tawa gazed down into the valley. He looked at the Land of Everlasting Summer and wished his home could forever remain as peaceful as it was at that moment. Ever since the Sky Elders had returned, life had been so violent and problematic. Evidence indicated the worst was yet to come.

A shadow fell over him. He was surprised someone could sneak up on him, since he was always so alert to danger. He grabbed the Dragonfly and spun around, drawing back the spear for a lethal toss.

"The *kik-mongwi* does not need to use the Spear," Pinga said. "This One is no enemy."

Tawa lowered the spear, "You may no longer have any other powers, but you still have the ability to move as silent as a shadow. Not many people can get this close without my hearing them. I suppose people who lived in the clouds must learn to tread lightly."

"This One can walk through the snow without leaving footprints," Pinga said. "She could surely take a cat unawares. Perhaps she will try it sometime."

Tawa laughed, sticking his spear into the ground. "We have different approaches. I carry a pointed stick and you walk softly."

"Clever phrasing by the *kik-mongwi*."

"Thank you," Tawa said. "Did you need something from me? I don't mean to say I am not pleased to see you. On the contrary. I've come to savor our time together. There's a lightness in my soul when I see you."

"Does the sight of This One please the *kik-mongwi*?" Pinga asked, with a lilt in her voice.

"Can't I savor beauty?"

"The *kik-mongwi* honors This One," she said.

"It is you who honor us," Tawa replied. "You make the serene grandeur of Ulah-Nane more glorious with your presence. As if you are the reason this land is here."

Amazingly, Pinga blushed. "This One does not know what to say."

"I didn't know Sky Gods could become flushed with embarrassment," he said.

She brushed away the white hairs that had blown across her face. "Perhaps it is because This One wishes to be human when you are near, *kik-mongwi*."

"It's Tawa," he said. "I'd prefer if you called me Tawa."

"She shall," Pinga said, holding out her hand. "Walk with This One, Tawa."

Tawa took her hand. "With great gladness."

Tawa and Pinga walked for a long time. Tawa had never enjoyed anyone's company more. Was this love? he wondered. Eventually, the conversation turned to more serious matters.

"This One fears what will happen when Giwakna arrives," Pinga said. "The beast will be hungry and angry. This One has seen what happens when Giwakna is hungry and angry."

Tawa tried not to be fazed by the warnings. He hoped to seem fearless in front of the woman who moved him so much.

"Every foe can be beaten," Tawa said. "My father believed that and so do I. We survived A'Chiyala and we will survive this. I simply wish I could spare my people more violence. Upon my soul, I do. They've seen enough in recent years."

Pinga began to realize how painful it was for the young ruler to see his people go through such trials. Tawa and his family had been chosen by the Sky Elders to be defenders of the Tree of Life, but each and every person among the Itiwana was paying the price for that sacred duty. She wished there were some way she could spare the Itiwana this one battle.

Pogum had spent the day drilling his men tirelessly. With the sun going down, it was time to let them rest for a few hours. Pogum could not sleep, so he hopped onto Walking Storm's back and went for a patrol around the perimeter. He knew there were already sentries stationed across the area, but it eased Pogum's mind when he personally oversaw things.

It was not long before he spotted someone moving through the darkness. He quickly put an arrow in his bow. "You are not so stealthy as you believe. Step out where you can be seen."

Pogum was surprised to see an old friend. "Nulia?"

Nulia Juk stepped into view, grinning affectionately at him. She had aged noticeably and no longer looked like a little girl. She had seen sixteen summers and was becoming a woman. Nulia was accompanied by one of the towering Wood Men.

"Hello, brave Pogum," she said. "It is most pleasant to see you again."

Pogum lowered his bow. "What in Awona'Wilona's name are you doing so far from home, lurking in the dark like an evil spirit?"

Nulia came closer and gently petted Walking Storm. "I've been wondering how you fared since last I saw you. Rumors have reached as far as the Red Sky Forest about the Tunerak Destroyers who attacked Shipapa-Lina. Few returned from that journey, I heard. I had to see for myself if the valiant Pogum was still proving himself the greatest hero in all Ulah-Nane. My large friend escorted me here for safety. His name is Joi-Joi."

"Awona'Wilona's greeting to you, Joi-Joi," Pogum said.

"Gug."

"I suspected you'd say just that," he replied.

Nulia chuckled. "Now speak truths to me, valiant hero. How many of our old foes have fallen to you?"

"A fair few," Pogum answered. "But I've no need to slay any more of them. That war is won. We have destroyed the Destroyers."

"Grand news," Nulia said. "And the witch woman?"

"Slain by my own hand."

"Truly?" Nulia squealed excitedly. "Wonderful. I've never been so pleased by any news. I could kiss you. In fact, I believe I will. Come down off that beast, you great warrior."

Pogum held up a hand. "Calm your fires, girl. Your gratitude must be limited to words."

"You disappoint me," she said. "Why? I am no longer a child."

"This heart and this soul are spoken for. I am wedded."

Nulia's joy abruptly dimmed. "The Blue Corn Maid?"

Pogum indicated she had guessed right. "She is my sun and sky. My east and my west. She has conquered my soul in a way my body has never been conquered. I welcomed the conquest."

Nulia tried not to show how sad this made her. Although she had not seen Pogum in two winters, she had thought of him frequently during that time and always hoped that when they met again, she would win his affections. That dream was now shattered.

"I see," she said, hiding her sadness. "I wish blessings on your union."

"Thank you," Pogum answered, leaning down from his mount. "Now, young Nulia, I do not wish to be a discourteous host, but this is not a safe place to be."

"But you have defeated the Tunerak Destroyers, have you not?" she asked. "Surely what remains of them will not return, except to offer apologies."

Pogum became noticeably grim when he discussed this subject. "There is a new enemy, one so fierce, the Tunerak Destroyers seem like annoying insects in comparison. These new villains love carnage like a glutton loves a meal. They are called Vykans and they serve an Ice Wendigo called Giwakna."

Nulia's jaw dropped. "Oh no."

Pogum noted her response. "You know of these foreign vermin?"

"I do," Nulia replied. "I've heard more of them than I care to from the Thrown-Aways."

"The Thrown-Aways?" Pogum queried. "Should I know what that means? I do not."

Nulia grinned slightly, knowing she was about to make herself look valuable in Pogum's eyes. He would soon see what a great prize he let get away.

"They are your natural allies," she said.

The Painted-White Girl walked alone through Norumbega, heading west. She was lost, unfamiliar with the region. Carrying a small pouch of supplies, she wandered, lonely.

At least I'm free now, she thought.

Although she had been held captive in Nurumgard for quite some time, she had not seen much of Norumbega, because slaves could not leave the colony. Not unless they were set free. She had long ago given up hope of that ever happening. But now it had.

After Hunwulf returned from his failed attempt to conquer Shipapa-Lina, he told the Painted-White Girl that Hobomok was dead, but he requested she be freed if he fell. Hunwulf kept his promise to Hobomok. He ejected the Panted White Girl from Nurumgard rather abruptly. He barely gave her enough time to grab some food for the trip.

The Painted-White Girl was experiencing some extremely mixed feelings. True, she was elated to finally be free of the Vykans, but she had expected her freedom to be under much better circumstances. Hobomok had promised to bring her to Shipapa-Lina and make her the consort of a high chieftain. She had come to care for Hobomok and the idea of standing beside him as he ruled the Itiwana had become the great hope of her life. She had come so close to that dream.

Now she had nothing. Her lover Hobomok was dead, and she wandered aimlessly across Norumbega with nothing but the clothes she wore, a pouch of food, and the baby in her stomach.

She blamed it all on this Tawa person. She knew of him from Hobomok, who described Tawa as a reviled enemy. This man had now killed the father of her child. Without ever having met him, she hated Tawa more than anyone in the world.

She remembered Hobomok once saying that his unborn son would possess special gifts and would be the instrument of his revenge if he ever fell to his enemies. Now that he had fallen, the Painted-White Girl swore to do whatever she could to ensure his son Hayoka would one day avenge his father. She knew the child inside her was special and surely had a destiny. The Painted White Girl believed his destiny was to destroy the Itiwana. She intended to encourage that destiny. She would raise him to hate.

For the moment, however, she needed to find some shelter. Next, she would need a safe place to give birth. She did not want to be lost and alone in the north lands when the baby came. No matter what, her baby must survive.

Pogum met with Tawa and introduced Nulia. He wanted her to explain about the Thrown-Aways, because the idea of gaining allies instead of new enemies was a hopeful one. They had so many enemies.

Nulia was a bit nervous to be speaking before Tawa and his Shakowin, which now included

Pinga. She was honored by having an audience of two Gods and a High Chieftain.

Tawa could tell she was nervous. "Be at peace, good lady. You are my guest, and my guests are not mocked. Speak freely. I'd know more of these Thrown-Aways."

"Yes, great chieftain," Nulia said, taking a deep breath. "I first met the Thrown-Aways last summer. I was searching for some survivors of the Corn Maidens. My search took me north, and I found a few of them living in the Earth Lodge of the north. They'd been brought there by a group of survivors from a different enemy. Numerous northern tribes had been mostly destroyed by Giwakna and the Vykans."

"Sadly, this is not a rare thing for the Vykans and their lord," Pinga said.

"Many tribes had been attacked," Nulia continued. "The best warriors were killed, the women taken as slaves, and the rest were used as food for Giwakna. A handful of children were allowed to escape, only because they were too small to be good workers. Smaller, skinnier children do not make a good meal for Giwakna."

"But it eats bigger children?" Tawa asked. "Monstrous."

"Giwakna had another reason to let a few captives go," Nulia said. "He wanted them to spread the legend of the power of Giwakna. The young survivors wandered. Somehow, many of them ended up in the Earth Lodge, under the care of the aged and respected warrior called Angakuk.

He became the leader of a new tribe composed of these young survivors. He named them the Thrown-Aways. He sent them out to look for others who were attacked. The Thrown-Aways found the surviving Corn Maidens and brought them to the Earth Lodge. Angakuk has been training them to fight Giwakna and the Vykans. As they've gotten older, they've become extremely formidable warriors and highly motivated."

"I've heard of this Angakuk," Atira said. "My beloved Yana-Luha met him long ago. They fought together against Gichi-Awas, the giant, hairless, carnivorous bear. My husband respected him highly."

"This One knows him as well," Pinga said. "She met him up north. This One knows him to be brave and honorable. She knows that Angakuk retreated to a solitary life in the Earth Lodge before the Vykans came. His has a son called the Lodge Boy."

"My father told me of Angakuk," Tawa said. "If his skills match the stories my father told, the Vykans will feel the sting of revenge when the Thrown-Aways settle matters of blood."

"We could help them," Pogum suggested. "And they us. We were born to be allies."

Atira had problems with this suggestion. "Perhaps so, but the Earth Lodge is far away, and winter is coming. Giwakna will attack when the chill is in the air. Have we the time to travel to the Earth Lodge and bring them back here to help us defend Shipapa-Lina?"

"Likely not," Tawa said. "But they are close to Nurumgard. Suppose we quickly fly to the Earth Lodge and persuade the Thrown-Aways to join us in a lightning quick attack upon the Vykans. We'll strike the vipers in their own nest."

"Ambush the Vykans in Nurumgard?" Atira asked.

"Yes," Tawa replied. "I'd considered it previously and rejected the idea. But now that we have an ally in the area, it will boost our striking power, and they know the terrain. They have studied the enemy. It seems more likely we'll succeed with their help."

"I like it," T'Soona interjected. "A wolf doesn't expect to be attacked while napping in his own den."

"And it will keep the battle far from the children of the Itiwana," Pogum added. "I give praise to your idea."

"Thank you," Tawa said. "We will see it done."

"I can help you arrange it," Nulia added. "They know Joi-Joi and me. They trust us."

"Very good," Tawa said. "I'll arrange a war party. We'll leave in the morning."

"Let me go ahead first, along with Nulia," Pogum said. "She and I will bring the sacred *chanunpa* peace-pipe and talk to Angakuk in advance. He knows the area and may be able to suggest the best attack path. This will save time. When you and the Two-Horn Riders arrive, we will be prepared to fight. Every moment is vital. We must beat Giwakna to the attack."

"It's a good suggestion," Nulia said, liking the idea of traveling alone with Pogum.

"Very well," Tawa said. "Go as soon as you are ready to travel. I will prepare our people. I pray to Awona'Wilona we'll win with few casualties."

Pogum gave a respectful nod to his chieftain and headed out of the longhouse with the peace pipe, followed by Nulia.

"Do we leave now?" she asked.

"Not so much of your youthful haste, dear girl," Pogum chided. "No urgency will prevent me from bidding goodbye to the one I hold most dear in the world. You can wait that long."

Nulia tried not to frown. "Of course. I'll be happy to wait. Go see your precious Bluebird. I'll be talking to Joi-Joi."

Pogum detected a hostile tone underneath Nulia's politeness but chose to ignore it. He strolled to his pit house chamber, where Bluebird was weaving something for their unborn child.

"It is a basket," she said. "To carry Pogum the younger in."

Pogum beamed at the sight. "It will surely be as beautiful as anything ever created by gods or men. I expect you'll have it completed by the time I return."

"Return?"

Pogum explained the current situation to his bride. He told her he would be gone for at least a month, in an effort to rid Ulah-Nane of Giwakna and the Vykans. Bluebird listened with disappointment.

"I am loath to see you go, but I suppose this is not a matter of choice," she said sadly. "You have to do what must be done. And so it goes."

Pogum stroked her hair with one hand and touched the basket with the other. "It would never be my choice to leave you. But honor and duty are stronger than our wants."

Bluebird took his hand. "Are they stronger than our love?"

Pogum embraced his wife. "Not stronger. But more urgent. We must destroy these Vykans and their monstrous master so our child can grow up unafraid of attack. I told you their leader eats children. It must be destroyed."

"Every time you leave for a battle, I fear I will never see your noble face again," she said.

"And do I not always return?" he asked with a smile.

"I do not want to lose you, husband," she softly said.

"It isn't possible for you to do so," he replied. "If I were pierced with one thousand arrows and thrown into a volcano, you still would not lose me because the spirit of Pogum will return to Shipapa-Lina to rejoin his family."

Bluebird lowered her eyes to the ground. "What should I do if you fall?"

Pogum squeezed her more tightly. "If my child is a girl, name her after the woman I love. Bluebird the Blue Corn Maid, once of the Corn Maidens and now of the Itiwana. My wife. The greatest beauty in the Land of Everlasting Summer."

"Your homage honors me."

"I speak no word that is not true from my soul," he told her.

"You'd best go now before I begin weeping," Bluebird said. "Go."

Pogum kissed her. "I will return for more of that. On my honor. Goodbye."

"Return soon, my love."

Pogum rejoined Nulia and Joi-Joi. Faw-Faw had sniffed out Joi-Joi and come to greet him. He was glad to see Nulia, too. He and Joi-Joi engaged in their head-butt ritual just as Pogum arrived.

"Faw-Faw wants to come with us," Nulia said. "You know how loyal these Wood Men are. He wants to make sure you're all right. And he hasn't spent any time with another of his kind for several seasons."

"Then I suppose he should come," Pogum said. "We can never tell what may attempt to stop us. I've come to accept that these treks are never easy."

Pogum leaped energetically upon Walking Storm. Nulia climbed onto the bison, sitting behind him. Faw-Faw and Joi-Joi walked alongside, as they usually did. Bluebird watched from a distance as they faded into the falling twilight. She wondered why she had this feeling of dread as if she would never see her husband again.

"Don't die, my brave. Don't you dare die. Never die."

CHAPTER THIRTY-ONE

Pogum, Nulia, Faw-Faw, and Joi-Joi had been traveling north for two weeks. The days were getting shorter, and fires were becoming more necessary at night to keep warm. Despite the perpetually tepid winters Ulah-Nane enjoyed due to Yaxche, the nights could still be bitingly chilly during the winter.

Pogum wished to reach his destination with haste because he knew the arrival of winter meant the air was now cool enough for Giwakna to leave the cold northern climate and make his way south to Shipapa-Lina. It worried Pogum that, for all he knew, Giwakna and his Vykans could already be on the march toward the Land of Everlasting

Summer. He hoped to beat Giwakna to the attack and allow the Itiwana to strike first.

They came across one of the nomadic Ulah-Nane tribes. Pogum planned to arrange quicker transportation up north. Surprisingly, the nomads had one of the Vykan longships in their camp. The nomad tribe had found the longships unattended while the Vykans were attacking Shipapa-Lina. The nomads stole it to use for fishing. Due to the large number of casualties Hunwulf and his men sustained in the failed invasion of Shipapa-Lina, Hunwulf did not need to look for it, having enough boats for his remaining men to return home.

The nomadic tribe decided the boat was too large to be carried from place to place in their gypsy existence. Spotting an opportunity, Pogum asked for help carrying the longship back to the river, in exchange for the promise of corn. The agreement was reached, and the longship was lugged to the Endless Agazzi river. The nomads promised to look after Walking Storm.

Pogum and his companions used the boat to sail up the river to the Earth Lodge in Norumbega. It cut down their trek time considerably. Pogum hoped Angakuk would be amenable to uniting against a common enemy, otherwise this effort would be wasted.

Faw-Faw and Joi-Joi did much of the rowing and the boat moved like a swift fish with their strength propelling it. The group finally reached the point where the Endless Agazzi River linked to the Ice Wolf River in Norumbega. Pogum guided the longship to shore and led his party into the brush.

For a time, the walk went smoothly, until Faw-Faw began looking around. He either sensed or smelled trouble. Joi-Joi joined him in watchfully studying their surroundings. Pogum's own instincts began to buzz with the feeling someone or something unseen was nearby.

"What's wrong?" Nulia asked.

"I fear we are not alone," Pogum answered, trying to detect a sound or smell that would indicate the nature of the possible danger.

The danger became evident when a volley of arrow shafts dropped from above and hit the ground all around them. Faw-Faw and Joi-Joi, alarmed by the arrows, waved their arms nervously and growled. Nulia was less fazed than the others. Pogum observed the pattern of the arrow strikes. He noted they all came extraordinarily close to four wide-open targets but hit nothing except the dirt and grass.

This is either very good or very bad shooting. His instincts told him the mysterious archers had missed on purpose. Nulia's calmness indicated she knew this as well. Pogum held up his hand, indicating the Wood Men should stay calm.

"Steady, large ones," he said loudly. "I doubt they mean to hurt us."

"They don't," Nulia said, knowingly. "Trust me."

"I do," Pogum replied. "Although they have quite an appalling way of welcoming people. I don't suppose this is their way of asking us to join their tribe and share a teepee by the ocean?"

Nulia grinned. "This is their way of saying they can kill us whenever they want, so stop trying to be humorous and treat them with the respect their arrows deserve."

"Excellent point," Pogum said, scanning the trees intently.

Ten figures came scampering down from the trees, all carrying bows and quivers of arrows. The archers kept the four strangers covered as they moved into formation. Faw-Faw and Joi-Joi roared warningly, but Pogum and Nulia calmed them down.

Pogum noted they were all quite young. None of them seemed any older than Tawa. Nine of them formed a circle around Pogum's group, while the tenth stepped forward to address the newcomers. Eight of the young men were archers and one had a sling for stone projectiles. The tenth was the oldest and clearly the leader.

"Not the warmest welcome I've had of late," Nulia said to the archers. "This can't possibly be the best greeting you can think of for me."

"This isn't the safest place to wander, Nulia," the tenth archer said. "This should not be the spot where you prefer a-going."

"Do we need to fear the Vykans or you?" Pogum interrupted.

"That is yet to be decided," the eldest archer said. "My moods change rapidly. Who are you, stranger?"

"Be at peace, my friend," Nulia said. "This is an ally of mine and an enemy of the Vykans."

"Commendable choices," the lead archer said.

Nulia gestured toward her companions. "This is Pogum of the Itiwana, and those two are of the Wood Men. They're called Faw-Faw and Joi-Joi. Pogum, this is Lodge Boy, the war chief of the Earth Lodge and eldest of the Thrown-Aways."

"An honor," Pogum said, looking at all the young archers.

"Perhaps it is," Lodge Boy said. "While I decide what sort of mood I'm in, let me introduce my brethren of the Thrown-Aways. Here are the Spring Boy, the Wild Boy, the Wolf Boy, the Turquoise Boy, the Star Boy, the Arrow Boy, Splinter-Foot Boy, Left-Handed Boy and Blood-Red Boy."

"Interesting names," Pogum commented.

"They have meanings," Lodge Boy said. "Maybe you'll find out what those are, man of the Itiwana. As for you Nulia, what in Awona'Wilona's dark mane are you doing here?"

"I hope you're in the mood to escort us to Angakuk," Nulia said. "We have something to speak with him about which could benefit us all."

Lodge Boy thought it over briefly and then signaled the other Thrown-Away archers to lower their arrows. "I'll agree to that for now. However, I may change my mind any minute and have you and your friends killed. It depends..."

"... on your mood," Nulia snapped. "We know."

Pogum and Nulia met with Angakuk. The warrior Angakuk was not a young man, but he had the build and bearing of a warrior. Stocky and adorned in furs with an antler headpiece, his presence filled the inside of the hogan where they met. Pogum knew he was in the presence of a formidable man.

"It is a privilege to meet you, honored warrior," Pogum said, holding up the pipe. "Yana-Luha spoke well of you. He was my kin by marriage."

"A fine man he was," Angakuk replied. "We fought well together. I have heard the whispers of his fate. I grieve for your loss. Such a man was rare. What brings you to me now?"

Angakuk listened in inscrutable silence as Pogum told him tales of the attack on Shipapa-Lina and laid out the plan for an alliance. He described their intention to ambush Giwakna and the Vykans.

When Pogum was done, Angakuk took the pipe and sucked in some smoke. He considered Tawa's scheme. "You have my agreement, Itiwana. It is fortuitous. I have already made a plan to attack Giwakna where he sleeps."

"I would be honored to hear your plan," Pogum said.

The next morning, Pogum and Lodge Boy led a war party to a specific spot chosen by Angakuk for an ambush of Giwakna. Along with them were Faw-Faw, Joi-Joi, and the nine young archers with colorful names. Also accompanying them was Nulia, who insisted on coming along, despite not being a warrior.

"We're here," Lodge Boy said. "Let's begin."

Pogum, Lodge Boy, Nulia, and the Left-Handed Boy—who had lost his right arm to the Vykans, which is why he used a sling—guarded the location from each direction. Arrow Boy, who was the best shot of all the boys, stood on the highest ground as a lookout. Meanwhile, the rest of the Thrown-Aways began to dig two large holes in the ground. Faw-Faw and Joi-Joi cleared away some stones.

The Spring Boy, who had a knack for finding water, had pinpointed the spots accurately. The holes went down very deep. Finally, they reached a point where hot water and steam sprang up from the bottom of the deep pits.

"Success," the Spring Boy cried. "We've found the Demon Under-Caves."

"Perfect," Lodge Boy said.

"Now cover them up," Pogum ordered.

The young Thrown-Aways covered the steam pits with thin, brittle sticks and branches. They next covered the sticks with leaves and dust. The boys did an admirable job hiding the large pits.

Pogum looked approvingly at their work. "Now we bring the foe to the slaughter."

With winter now in the air, Giwakna decided it was time to attack the Itiwana. He had waited until the air was cool enough and the nights were long enough. The Vykans had returned from pillaging many local villages. All conditions were just right and Giwakna announced it was time to make the Itiwana suffer.

Hunwulf, who had luckily escaped the Ice Wendigo's wrath after his previous failure, was preparing the Vykans for a rematch against the Itiwana. He shouted and warned them not to fail their master again or they would suffer the Wendigo's merciless fury. Hunwulf whipped them into a frenzy, and they were eager for another fight. They all loved a good fight. The Berserker was particularly anxious to swing his ax at some worthy foes.

Worthy opponents are so rare. I always miss them when they're gone, he thought.

As the Vykans shouted with savage enthusiasm and waved their weapons in the air, they suddenly found themselves assailed by arrows from the closest bushes. Several of the Vykans were hit by the shafts. Hunwulf himself was hit in the shoulder by one of the Left-Handed Boy's stones. An arrow nearly hit the Berserker but rebounded off his shield.

Giwakna was wading in the cold lake when an arrow hit the creature in the thigh. Giwakna roared a bestial, primal roar. The Ice Wendigo ripped it out roughly with his hand.

"Humans attack Giwakna," he bellowed. "Giwakna make them pay. Giwakna kill!"

In the bushes, Pogum complimented Lodge Boy on their attack. "Well done."

"Of course," Lodge Boy said, waving to his fellow Thrown-Aways. "Retreat."

"And make sure they see you," Pogum added. "They must follow us."

The Thrown-Aways raced back in the direction of the pits they had dug. Blood-Red Boy, who had scarlet hair due to some Paracas descendants, paused to show his posterior to the enemy before joining the rest in retreat. Pogum and Lodge Boy gave them cover with arrows and soon followed behind them.

Meanwhile, Giwakna was enraged, roaring "Kill humans! Kill!" over and over.

The Vykans ran after the attacking archers. Giwakna joined them, not letting the small wound in his leg stop him from joining the chase. The wound only made him more dangerous. Although the Vykans tried their best to catch the archers, the Thrown-Aways were younger and lighter than the towering Vykans, who were carrying metal weapons. Also, the Thrown-Aways knew the terrain. They ducked in and out of the bushes and easily evaded their larger foes.

Tawa was leading a group of his Two-Horn Riders, sailing to Nurumgard. He had left a full day after Pogum and his party had departed. They were slowed because they had to carry their newly built rafts all the way to the Endless Agazzi River. The whole war party was tense about the upcoming battle. They would not have the advantage of their bison mounts but were still confident they would win again, under Tawa's leadership.

Tawa hoped his uncle Pogum was all right. He was also glad Pinga had come along. She knew the north and was familiar with Giwakna and his Vykans. He felt she would be a big asset to the Itiwana.

I wish we were there already, he thought. *This trek is taking an eternity.*

Back at the Demon Under-Cave steam pits, Nulia waited with Faw-Faw and Joi-Joi, and the Splinter-Foot Boy, who had been lame since the Vykans injured his leg. He remained behind because he could not run well. It bothered him to be left behind, but he accepted it. He did not want to jeopardize his fellow Thrown-Aways. Splinter-Foot Boy sat silently with obvious agitation. Nulia paced the grass nervously.

The horn blast by the Turquoise Boy trumpeted through the region. The Turquoise Boy was named for his odd eye color and for the gem-studded horn he had salvaged when he escaped from his village. He never went anywhere without it. The other Thrown-Aways were familiar with the sound. The Splinter-Foot Boy popped to his feet, glad to hear the familiar horn blare that meant his friends were returning.

"They're back," Splinter-Foot Boy shouted.

"Thank Awona'Wilona," Nulia said.

Pogum, Lodge Boy, and the Thrown-Aways came into view, running breathlessly, having covered miles between the Vykan colony Nurumgard and the field where the underground hot spring lay.

"Is everyone all right?" Nulia asked.

"Unhurt so far," Pogum managed to say while trying to regain his breath after the long run back.

"The rest of you know what to do," Lodge Boy said to the Thrown-Aways. "Take cover and be sure to spread out."

"We want them to think we are a whole army," Pogum stated.

Most of the Thrown-Aways and Nulia dispersed and hid among the rock and bushes surrounding the field where they had dug and covered the two large pits. The strategy was to fool Giwakna into thinking he was surrounded by the Itiwana. Two of the Thrown-Aways did not want to go into hiding, however. Two brothers called the Wild Boy and the Wolf Boy were eager for combat. They had come from a warrior tribe and loved a good fight, hence their names. They preferred a face-to-face struggle over the hide-and-shoot method that Angakuk had taught them. Wild Boy was the more reckless of the two when fighting, but Wolf Boy was a more ferocious fighter and killer. He was also known to drink the blood of his kills.

"Let us stay," Wolf Boy said to Lodge Boy.

"Yes, we don't want to hide," the Wild Boy said. "We want to look into the eyes of the vermin who destroyed our tribe when we kill them."

"Adhere to the plan," Lodge Boy said. "If we deviate now, we may cause everyone to be slain. Be patient, little brothers. We'll get our revenge soon."

Pogum, Lodge Boy, Faw-Faw, and Joi-Joi stood in the middle of the field above the Demon Under-Caves, trying to block the view of the concealed pits. Pogum hoped the occasional wisps of steam escaping the covered pits did not give the plan away.

It took some time for Giwakna and the Vykans to reach the field of Earth Fire because they were bigger and slower than the young Thrown-Aways and the athletic Pogum. They arrived, tired and panting. It was hard to tell if Giwakna himself was tired because Ice Wendigos tended to breathe loudly anyway.

The creature pointed at Pogum and his companions. "Humans with arrows."

Hunwulf squinted to get a better look at them. "I think I know that big Wood Man. I believe he is the swine who killed the Iron Forge. And one of those others may be an Itiwana, I think. He resembles them. It must be the Itiwana who attacked us."

"Giwakna hate Itiwana," the Ice Wendigo roared. "Itiwana killed Coyote, so Giwakna kill them. Giwakna eat their hearts."

The creature stomped toward his enemies with his eager Vykans close behind. The Berserker was especially anxious to get his hands on a foe. Any foe, but particularly the leader.

"This is the moment," Pogum whispered to Lodge Boy. "If Angakuk's plan does not work, we will not live to see another dawn."

CHAPTER THIRTY-TWO

The Savage Giwakna led the Vykans onto the field above the Demon Under-Caves. He was too consumed with a taste for flesh and a desire to avenge Coyote to be worried about an ambush. Hunwulf, on the other hand, was curious as to why there were only four of them and why they were standing out in the open, waiting for a superior force to catch them.

Something is wrong here, he thought.

Giwakna crossed the field with his large stride, reckless in his anger and insatiable in his bloodlust. He growled menacingly. The Vykans followed behind him, fanatically devoted to the Ice Wendigo.

Lodge Boy raised a hand and signaled to his fellow Thrown-Aways. The hidden warriors fired several volleys of arrows. They picked off a few unsuspecting Vykans who were at the front of the pack. An arrow hit Giwakna in the shoulder, but he yanked it out. He and his Vykans immediately stopped their march.

"Cease and halt," Pogum yelled. "Unless you like the feel of arrows in your albino flesh, I suggest you do not move. The Itiwana have you surrounded."

Hunwulf was a bit suspicious of this situation, especially after the way Tawa had outwitted him before. Giwakna, on the other hand, was not a great thinker. Ice Wendigos were emotional creatures who cared more about eating than about reasoning.

"Giwakna hates Itiwana," the creature bellowed.

"So I understand," Pogum said. "You had your Vykan minions attacked us once, and now we're here to repay the favor. We have greater numbers and hold all the strategic positions."

Hunwulf held his shield high. "We do not fear your arrows. We have our shields."

"We defeated you before when you had the advantage of surprise," Pogum said. "What do you think will happen now that we have the advantage?"

Giwakna had had enough of talk. "Giwakna was not there before. Giwakna would have killed Itiwana then. Giwakna will kill Itiwana now."

Pogum laughed to enrage Giwakna even further. "Kill us all? Ridiculous."

Giwakna snarled and bared his fangs to intimidate his enemy. "Giwakna kill!"

Pogum pointed to Faw-Faw. "You couldn't even beat him, I'd wager."

Giwakna growled. "Wood Men weak, just like humans weak! Kill many Wood Men before. No one can beat Giwakna. Giwakna strongest!"

Hunwulf sensed a trick. "Great One. Do not let these Itiwana deceive you. They are crafty insects. They..."

"Stupid Vykan not talk," the Ice Wendigo shouted. "Giwakna is leader. You fail before. You obey or Giwakna will rip your throat out with fangs."

"Yes, Great One," Hunwulf reluctantly replied.

Pogum continued to taunt the Ice Wendigo. "I don't think you are so fierce, Girl-Wokka or whatever you call yourself. My Wood Man could kill you with ease."

Giwakna was incensed. "Giwakna can kill anyone."

"Do you dare to fight my champion?" Pogum asked.

"Giwakna fights Wood Man," the Ice Wendigo hissed. "Giwakna kill."

"Good," Pogum said. "It's agreed."

Pogum sidled over to Faw-Faw and whispered. "The pits. Remember. You must get him into one of the pits. Do you understand?"

"Gug."

"Does that mean he understands?" Lodge Boy asked.

"I certainly hope so," Pogum said.

Faw-Faw and Giwakna approached each other like feral, predatory animals. They roared at each other and postured with intimidating body language to scare the other. The psych-out test lasted no more than a minute before the two seven-foot creatures clashed with barbaric ferocity.

Giwakna made the first charge, going for Faw-Faw's throat, but the Wood Man met him with a kick to the gut. Giwakna roared but continued his attack while Faw-Faw clubbed at him with heavy fists. The two giants began to pummel each other with devastating blows while the Vykans cheered their master on and Pogum shouted encouragement to Faw-Faw.

Giwakna gained the advantage in the battle when he raked Faw-Faw in the face with his long claws. Faw-Faw backed off, hurt. Giwakna increased his wild attack.

"He's losing," Lodge Boy said, worriedly.

Pogum cupped his hands and yelled, "The plan, Faw-Faw. Remember the plan."

Pogum's voice helped the Wood Man focus. Ignoring his wound, he leaped forward, trying to push Giwakna toward the pit. They scuffled but the Wood Man could not push the Ice Wendigo back more than a step. Giwakna was incredibly powerful.

Faw-Faw tried lifting Giwakna to carry him toward the pit. However, Giwakna bit him on the arm, causing Faw-Faw to scream and lose his grip. Giwakna lashed out with his sharp claws once more, wounding Faw-Faw across the torso with deep gashes. Faw-Faw backed up again.

Giwakna took advantage of Faw-Faw's momentary backpedal by going for his throat again. Faw-Faw stopped him with a solid head-butt. The Wood Man used Giwakna's disorientation to push him closer toward the hole and managed to get his foe very close.

Giwakna focused his simple mind and pushed back with his amazing strength. He was inches from the hole, but Faw-Faw could not push him any farther. They shoved mightily, like two wild bulls.

Hunwulf watched the battle closely and noticed Faw-Faw kept pushing Giwakna in the same direction. He wondered why the Wood Man would do that. Studying the ground, he noticed a section of it seemed to be covered in leaves. Then he noticed a wisp of steam coming from the ground. Something was most definitely wrong.

"Great one, it's a trick@" Hunwulf shouted.

Pogum realized the deception was exposed. He had to act now, while Giwakna was so near the pit. If the Wendigo did not go into it now, they would never get him so close again. Pogum raised his spear and charged forward, hoping he could accomplish what he needed to do by surprise, while everyone else was confused.

Giwakna, with his limited intellect, was distracted by contemplating Hunwulf's warning and simultaneously battling Faw-Faw. This gave swift Pogum the chance to lunge at the Ice Wendigo without it seeing him. Hunwulf and the Berserker spotted Pogum and ran to intercept the Itiwana warrior. They were too late. Pogum thrust a spear into the beast's belly. Giwakna howled in agony.

Together, Pogum and Faw-Faw pushed the injured Ice Wendigo backward toward the pit. Hunwulf and the Berserker raced desperately to his rescue. They almost reached Giwakna in time to help but were cut off by volleys of arrows from the Thrown-Aways.

The bleeding Giwakna stepped back onto the brittle covering of the pit. The creature's substantial weight caused him to fall through the thin wood and plummet down into the steaming hole.

Instinctively the Ice Wendigo reached out to grab something. He managed to get his large hand on Pogum's ankle, pulling the Itiwana down into the pit with him. Faw-Faw grabbed his friend by the wrist and kept him from falling any farther. Pogum winced at the considerable weight of Giwakna hanging from his leg.

Hunwulf and the Berserker used their shields to ward off arrows as they ran to save Giwakna. They almost fell into one of the holes themselves, barely seeing the trap in time. They had to circle around, fending off arrows.

Only Giwakna's hand could be seen in the pit. The rest of him had vanished unseen into the burning-hot steam. Being sensitive to heat, Giwakna wailed in horrible pain. The Wendigo had never imagined such unendurable burning agony. Giwakna lost his strength and his sweaty grip slipped off Pogum's ankle. Giwakna fell into scalding water and steam, never to be seen again.

Faw-Faw pulled Pogum from the pit. While the Wood Man was distracted, Hunwulf and the Berserker had reached them, sword and axe raised for the kill. However, Lodge Boy and Joi-Joi appeared to guard Faw-Faw's back. Joi-Joi threw a large rock at Hunwulf, causing the experienced Vykan to turn his attention to the Wood Man. Lodge Boy fired an arrow at the Berserker, but the savage Vykan blocked it with his shield and continued his lunge at Faw-Faw.

Faw-Faw had managed to pull Pogum up but did not see the Berserker coming up behind him. Berserker raised his sword for a lethal thrust into Faw-Faw's back. Pogum was unarmed, having dropped his spear but could not let his friend be stabbed in the back. Faw-Faw had saved his life so the honorable Pogum could not let that happen.

Pogum threw himself between Berserker and Faw-Faw. The Vykan's broadsword ripped into Pogum's abdomen, tearing completely through him, splattering blood across the field.

Nulia, watching from afar, screamed, "No!"

CHAPTER THIRTY-THREE

The Berserker's sword ripped through Pogum's body, which exploded with blood. Pogum convulsed and cried out in horrible pain. He realized he had just been killed. Pogum locked eyes with the Berserker for a moment.

"This is a good death," Pogum croaked weakly.

Pogum fell face-first to the ground. Nulia screamed in horror. It took Faw-Faw a moment to absorb exactly what had happened. When he realized his good friend was fatally wounded, Faw-Faw screamed a blood-curdling howl that almost deafened Hunwulf and scared him so much that the Vykan jumped back, wisely getting some distance from the crazed Wood Man.

Roaring in uncontrollable rage, Faw-Faw charged hatefully at the Berserker who believed he could withstand Faw-Faw's immense size and power. The Vykan was wrong. Only his shield saved his life as he was toppled easily. Hunwulf ran, calling to his fellow Vykans, spurring them forward to avenge their murdered lord Giwakna.

From their concealed spots, the Thrown-Aways began to fire arrows at the Vykans, but the big foreigners used their shields to fend off the shafts. Faw-Faw and Joi-Joi were both so impressively powerful that they were able to hold off the Vykans, if only for a few minutes. Joi-Joi used a club and Faw-Faw was almost insane with rage, scaring his opponents with his palpable, seething fury. With some help from Lodge Boy, they stood their ground, but it was obvious they were doomed to defeat.

Help came in time. Tawa and the Itiwana war party burst out of the nearby greenery and charged onto the field, led by the young *kik-mongwi*. They all shouted a war-whoop.

Just where Angakuk said they'd be, Tawa thought.

The Vykans stopped the assault on the two Wood Men when they spotted their old Itiwana adversaries approaching rapidly. Hunwulf was furious at being out-strategized again.

"Cluster phalanx!" Hunwulf yelled to his men.

The Vykans formed themselves into a tight, triangle-shaped cluster. The Itiwana spread out and formed a circle around the Vykans. Tawa and his warriors had the Vykans completely sur-rounded while the Thrown-Aways targeted the Vykans with their weapons.

Tawa then spotted the bloodied, unmoving form of brave Pogum lying on the ground near the pit. He faltered at the sight.

"Uncle," he gasped in devastated shock.

Fury immediately filled his mind. His revered uncle was clearly dead, and he now wanted all these Vykans to share in his condition.

"Any last words to say, Hunwulf?" Tawa asked, containing his rage momentarily.

"You don't have your horned beasts with you this time," Hunwulf shouted in return. "And we have the superior weapons. We do not fear death and we do not fear you. Come ahead, *scraeling*. Try to kill Vykans!"

"Gladly."

Pinga, who had come with the Itiwana, was disturbed by what she saw. This battle would end in a useless slaughter for both sides. She felt they truly had nothing left to fight over. This situation had clearly been manipulated by someone else and the Itiwana would pay the price, as would the Vykans. Giwakna was gone as was Hobomok, and there was no longer a reason for this battle. She had to stop the pointless bloodshed before many lives were wasted.

Pinga rushed into the open, where the Vykans could see her. "Stop!"

The Vykans stared in befuddled shock when they witnessed their former Asa Grace Maid—the equivalent of a royal Lady—who had married their ruler the Red Lord years back. Why was she here? The last they knew of her, the Red Lord had taken her away with him when he retreated back to his homeland across the ocean. What was she doing back again? And why was she with the enemy?

"Lady Pinga?" Hunwulf asked. "What are you...?"

"Stay out of this, Pinga," Tawa ordered. "This is now about honor. We will not be wounded and fail to spill blood in return."

Pinga held her hands out, imploring him to stop. "Spilling blood will accomplish nothing, brave one. This One knows you to be a wise and compassionate ruler who would not force his people to sacrifice their lives for mere revenge. Neither you nor the Vykans has any gain or purpose in further death. We must end the violence now. She knows you would agree if you were not blinded by rage."

Tawa pointed. "That is Pogum lying there. My uncle. He was the best of us. There's not a soul among us who didn't think him a hero. And those are his killers."

"And you *scraelings* killed our dread lord," one of the Vykans yelled.

"Good," Tawa said. "Some justice has been meted out today."

"And therefore vengeance is unnecessary," Pinga said. "Blood has been spilled on both sides in a war that has no purpose."

"Our purpose now is to avenge my uncle," Tawa snapped back.

"Pogum did not believe in revenge and neither do you," Pinga argued. "Would your father have risked his people for revenge? Like him, Tawa must put his people first. You have always done so before. This One knows that to be a fact. If you attack now, there will be many deaths. That must not be. The Itiwana are needed to defend the Tree of Life from the forces of the Enemy Way. Revenge does nothing to protect Yaxche."

Hunwulf was getting annoyed by all this talk. "Are you here to fight or argue with a woman, Itiwana?"

Pinga turned and glared at Hunwulf. "This One remembers you well, Hunwulf. And she remembers the vow you made to her. Do you recall it?"

Hunwulf sneered. "Aye, I do recall."

"As does This One," Pinga stated. "This One remembers when she still had her powers, and she saved your life from the wolverine spirit Lox. Hunwulf vowed to repay This One by doing her a service one day. I have your oath. Beyond that, This One helped all of you when you first arrived in Ulah-Nane and were having trouble surviving. I am owed a debt. If you Vykans have any honor, you will repay her now."

"But they killed our dread lord Giwakna," Hunwulf yelled angrily.

Pinga gestured toward Pogum's body. "You've already slain your master's killer."

Hunwulf looked down at Pogum. "Aye, his blood is spilled, surely enough."

"Then vengeance is complete," Pinga replied. "There is no further reason to fight. This One asks you now to fulfill your debt to her and walk away from this place. Sheath your swords and return to Nurumgard."

Hunwulf hesitated, considering whether or not to withdraw. His fellow Vykans were muttering, being vocal about their various opinions. Hunwulf knew he was in charge now and had to make good decisions as the leader.

Tawa, however, was still enraged. "Pinga. You want us to just walk away?"

"She does expect you to," she cried. "This One expects you to be the *kik-mongwi* first and place the good of your people before revenge. You cannot risk losing good warriors when the forces of malevolent Malsumis are lurking, waiting to strike at the Itiwana. You must avoid this unnecessary war and preserve the lives of your people, so that the Itiwana will be at full power when the Enemy Way descends upon us."

Pogum squeezed the Dragonfly, debating whether he should toss it at Hunwulf. Should he let Pogum's killer's walk away? Should he risk these wild Vykans keeping their word and leaving the Itiwana alone? Should he try to end it now? If they did try, could they defeat the Vykans without the advantage of the bison? And even if they won, what would the losses be?

CHAPTER THIRTY-THREE

Pinga could see that both men were thinking about it.

"A fateful moment and a fateful choice, good men. Both sides have seen the loss of the best among you. Let that be the balance. Do not lose other fine warriors in a pointless war. Leaders must be sage. This One begs you both to be wise."

Tawa gave a reluctant nod. "Very well. I hate saying these words, but a chieftain should be wiser than he is prideful. Forces greater than us must be taken into consideration. Therefore, I swear by my true authority that the Vykans may walk their own way, and we will walk ours. Let this war end."

Hunwulf sheathed his sword and addressed his people. As the new leader, he had to be a better, wiser man. Aside from that, he had absolutely had his fill of Ulah-Nane and simply wished to go home. He could not predict how his men would take this, but if he was to be leader, he had to exert his authority now.

"Hear me, my brothers," Hunwulf said. "Some days, the blood hunger must go unabated, and this is one of them. The stars do not align for war and victory today. We owe Lady Pinga and we must keep our vow. Let us leave these unworthy *scraelings* to their dull life of corn crops and tedium. We will return to Vineland and drink in honor of our dread lord, who fell today. Come, my brothers. We shall walk once again upon hallowed ground, dedicated to Ymir and Odin, and watched over by the Gods of Asgard. We go."

There was quite a bit of grumbling in the ranks and the Berserker shouted his desire to continue the fight, but Hunwulf stopped his rebellion. "No power in the world will stop me from keeping my vow to Lady Pinga. You will be silent."

The Berserker pointed his axe threateningly at his leader. "No! I shall not let this stand. I must have satisfaction. I will see blood flow and I will hear the screams of dying *scraelings*. If I must slay every man among them alone, so be it!"

"Then so be it," Hunwulf said. "You stand alone. The rest of you, follow me now. We go to find a better home in a better land. The north awaits. Come."

Hunwulf led his Vykans away. Many of them were reluctant to leave the Berserker behind, wanting to avenge Giwakna, as well as their earlier defeat. However, they obeyed Hunwulf and repaid their debt to Pinga. Saluting the Berserker, they reluctantly marched away.

The Berserker stood alone in the field, glaring with loathing at his departing brethren. He spit toward them because he saw this as a great betrayal to himself and Giwakna. *Cowards.*

While the Vykans were marching for the north, Tawa ran to his bloodied uncle. Nulia had come out of hiding now that the enemies were gone. The two of them kneeled beside Pogum and looked sadly at him. Amazingly, he opened his eyes. There was a wisp of life remaining.

"He still lives!" Nulia cried, feeling some hope.

"Uncle..." Tawa began to say.

"You ... did well, nephew," Pogum whispered weakly. "You were very wise. I would not have wanted ... to be the cause of further violence. I am ... proud of you. Your father ... would be also. I am glad to have lived long enough to see ... the man you have become. I leave this world knowing the Itiwana ... are well cared for."

Tawa clasped his uncle's hand. "I learned so much from you. It was a privilege to know you. I will honor you forever."

"You are ... very welcome."

Nulia's tears dropped down onto Pogum's face. "If only we had had more time."

Pogum tried to smile at her. "We had our time. Be content."

She wiped her eyes. "I will never forget how brave you were against the Tunerak Destroyers when we met."

"I have done better since," Pogum replied. "Do not forget me."

"Never," Nulia sobbed.

Pinga stood over them. "This One wishes she had known you better, brave Pogum."

"I have ... never done better," Pogum said. "Tell my child that Pogum died bravely. And tell my Bluebird that my last thoughts ... were of her. Tell her..."

Pogum coughed up some blood, gasped his last gasp of air, and died. Everyone present lowered their heads in silent tribute to the fallen Pogum. At Tawa's signal, they raised their faces to the sun and let out a ritual chant, alerting Awona'Wilona that an Itiwana was coming to join him.

The Itiwana had almost forgotten about the Berserker. After the Vykans were gone from the battlefield, the furious Berserker raised his ax to challenge the killers of Giwakna.

"You! Boy!" the Berserker shouted to Tawa. "I challenge you. I will avenge the mighty Giwakna. If you have a man's blood in you, show some courage and fight me now. I demand my vengeance!"

"You have nothing to gain by this," Tawa replied. "Walk away."

"Not while you live," the Berserker shouted. "I will cut a bloody path through your *scraelings* to get to you."

Aholi stood in front of Tawa. "Say the word, *kik-mongwi*, and we'll carve this savage until he is nothing more than a meal for the beasts of the North."

"No," Tawa said. "I will do this for my uncle."

Tawa grabbed his spear and marched toward the gigantic Vykan, intent on avenging his uncle or dying in the attempt.

CHAPTER THIRTY-FOUR

"Y ou will die like a scrawny rodent mauled by a wildcat!" the Berserker bellowed.

Tawa stood face-to-face with the huge warrior, who was shouting in rage. The Vykan was a head taller than Tawa, with a metal shield, helmet, and axe. The Berserker had a long history of vicious bloodshed and had no other goal but to kill Tawa.

Tawa, with nothing but his Dragonfly in hand, faced the Berserker with an outer calm that belied his anger, sadness, and nervousness. His tribe chanted his name.

"Let's begin," Tawa said.

The crazed Berserker screamed an indecipherable scream as he charged Tawa. The Vykan swung his axe with all his considerable strength.

Tawa held out his spear in both hands, blocking the sword. Due to the magic quality of the Dragonfly, it withstood the impact without any damage, although the force of the blow almost caused Tawa to lose his grip.

Tawa continued moving with all his agility, blocking every swing and thrust from the Vykan axe with his spear. The Berserker became increasingly exasperated by his failure to connect with his smaller opponent. The Vykan hollered in some foreign tongue as he became more tired and angry.

Ducking under a clumsy swing by the Berserker, Tawa found an opportunity. The Itiwana chieftain thrust his mystic spear forward. The Dragonfly easily pierced through the Vykan's metal shield and into the broad chest of the Vykan. The Berserker howled in agony, dropping his axe.

The Berserker fell to his knees and stared up at Tawa in disbelief. He attempted speaking but blood spurted out of his mouth. He gurgled a sad, grotesque sound as he realized that he had just been defeated and death had come for him.

"You should have walked away," Tawa said, picking up the fallen axe. "If it gives you any comfort, you can now join your master."

Tawa used the Berserker's own axe to slice the Vykan's head off. A brief cheer of victory emanated from the Itiwana, but it was brief because they were all saddened by the death of Pogum.

Tossing the axe aside disdainfully, Tawa pulled his spear out of the Berserker and ambled back to his fellow Itiwana. He felt no joy at this victory. Pogum was still dead.

"Well done," Aholi said.

"Leave his body for the northern animals," Tawa said. "Let's bring my uncle home."

Lifting Pogum's body to their shoulders, the Itiwana carried the slain warrior back to the raft, so he could be brought home to Shipapa-Lina.

Lodge Boy put a hand on Tawa's shoulder. "My heart is broken for your loss."

"Thank you," Tawa said. "And I thank you for your help."

"I do not wish to berate you in your moment of loss, but I am disappointed," Lodge Boy said. "We had a chance to destroy the Vykans. That was the plan. But you only killed one and let the rest go. I understand your reasons, but we had an agreement. Pogum promised me."

Pinga interrupted. "Without their leader, they will no longer be the threat they were. Trust This One. Matters will be different now."

"Perhaps," Lodge Boy said. "But we here in the north are the ones who will have to suffer the consequences if they should decide to continue their pillaging. And we still want retribution. We will not rest until the Vykans are crushed under our heel."

"I am sorry," Tawa said. "I made an agreement, and as a chieftain, I cannot break it."

Lodge Boy was not interested in excuses. "Do as you will. Go back to the safety of the south and feel secure that the Thrown-Aways are guarding Ulah-Nane from the Vykans."

"And I will help you," Young Nulia said. "I shall not return to the Red Sky Woods until those who slew Pogum are destroyed. And if the Itiwana will not help, then shame upon them. And Faw-Faw will remain to help me. He loved Pogum as much as I did."

Faw-Faw grunted and moved to Nulia's side. Tawa was sorry to lose the powerful Wood Man. The huge man had been a valuable ally.

"Faw-Faw must walk his own path," Tawa said. "I am sad to see him depart. He is loyal. He is strong. He is a great fighter. Faw-Faw, you have fought valiantly for our cause. Go with our blessing and our gratitude."

Faw-Faw seemed to understand and even appeared touched by the speech. He remembered about Bluebird and Pogum's son. Faw-Faw grunted a few "Gugs" at Joi-Joi and they butted heads. Nulia was genuinely surprised.

"It seems you won't be without the assistance of a Wood Man," Nulia said. "Faw-Faw has convinced Joi-Joi to come with me to help avenge Pogum. He wants to return to guard Pogum's wife and son."

"He is gladly welcome," Tawa said. "I only wish he could be the one to tell Bluebird what happened here. I dread doing so."

Nulia pet Faw-Faw on the arm. "Good luck, my huge friend. Joi-Joi, come along."

When they were gone, Tawa gestured to Faw-Faw. "Come, mighty one. Let us return to Shipapa-Lina and Bluebird. This is a sad day and I wish to go home."

The Painted White Girl kneeled at a water hole, grateful to have found some fresh water to drink. She had been wandering for a long while and fresh water was getting harder to find.

Ever since her release from captivity, she had been living a nomadic existence. She had walked a long way to return to her tribe, only to find that her village was gone, burned to the ground and deserted. Since then, she had been walking randomly, hoping to find some trace of her lost tribe. She lived off nuts and berries. She was despondent because she had no idea if any of her people were alive. If so, where could they be?

Being several months into her pregnancy, she worried about her unborn baby. Wandering in the wild was no life for an infant. She needed to find somewhere safe to settle before she gave birth. The Painted White Girl sat on the grass near the water hole as night fell. She cried, thinking of how close she came to becoming the bride of the rightful chieftain of Shipapa-Lina, only to end up with nothing. Why did the Sky Elders always seem to be against her?

"Are you in need of help?" a voice asked.

The Painted White Girl yelped in surprise. She had not heard anyone approaching. She studied the man who stood before her. Was he dangerous?

"Can we assist you?" they asked.

Before she could answer, she spotted Nulia, Joi-Joi, and the other Thrown-Aways coming out of the greenery. She had no idea who they were and hoped they were as friendly as they seemed.

"I'm lost," she answered. "And I'm hungry."

"Where are you from?" Lodge Boy asked.

"I'm of the Northern Beothuk people," she answered. "I was taken two summers ago by the Vykans and finally got my freedom, but my village is gone. I do not know if they still live or where they may be. Now I am lost and alone and with child."

The Thrown-Aways could all sympathize with her story about the Vykans. Every one of them had lost their tribe to the savagery of the wild men from overseas.

"Our hearts go out to you and to your child," Lodge Boy said. "We surely cannot leave you here. You must come with us to the Earth Lodge. I'm sure Angakuk will approve. The Corn Maidens will help you when you are ready to give birth."

Painted White Girl felt this was too good to be true. "I ... what can I say but thank you?"

Nulia kneeled beside her. "I am Nulia. Come, walk with me. You and I will be friends."

As Nulia gently helped the Painted White Girl to her feet, Lodge Boy glanced at the Star Boy. "Which way now?"

The Star Boy, who had a natural skill in celestial navigation, looked up at the stars and pointed north. "There."

"Come," Lodge Boy said, and the rest followed. The Painted White Girl walked along with Nulia and Joi-Joi as they led her to her new home in the Earth Lodge.

EPILOGUE

Weeks later, Tawa and his Two-Horn Riders arrived back in Shipapa-Lina. They carried the body of Pogum with them. The body was wrapped in skins and furs to keep it somewhat preserved during the trip home. Members of the tribe observed a body being carried and every person in Shipapa-Lina dreaded who the slain man might turn out to be. As husbands and brothers came home, their kin were relieved. But who had died?

Bluebird was called to the chieftain's longhouse, where Tawa, Pinga, T'Soona, Manabazo, and Atira were waiting for her. Faw-Faw held the wrapped-up body in his arms. When Bluebird entered, she knew her worst fears were realized, even before anyone spoke.

"No..." she gasped.

Bluebird sank to the floor and began sobbing uncontrollably. Faw-Faw lay the body in front of her. Bluebird reached out to unwrap the face. "My love..."

Atira stopped her. "Don't look at him like this. Remember him as he was."

Bluebird withdrew her hand and closed her eyes, picturing the powerful, handsome Pogum in her mind. The thought of never seeing him again was unbearable. She could not stop weeping. Atira hugged her.

"I share your loss," Tawa said tenderly. "I have worshipped my uncle since I was knee high. When the world was cruel, he was always there to make it better. We'll see no one like him ever again."

Bluebird could barely think clearly but she forced herself to answer. "You may see his like again when I give birth to his child. I only wish the child would have a father."

"The child will have many fathers and many mothers," T'Soona said.

"He's correct," Atira said. "Every person in his village will help. If the child is a boy, he will learn to hunt and fish and fight from every man in Shipapa-Lina. If it's a girl, we'll all teach her to farm and weave and cook."

Faw-Faw made his usual "Gug" sound, but it seemed more intense and sadder than usual.

"You see, even Faw-Faw will help," T'Soona said. "I think he wants to be the protector."

"As *kik-mongwi*, I guarantee our help," Tawa said. "The child will be a child to us all, but we will make sure he knows about his real father. And we will tell the child stories of his heroic father, Pogum the War Chief of the Itiwana Two-Horn Riders."

Bluebird gave a slight nod to show her appreciation but could not stop crying. Tawa had Faw-Faw carry Pogum's body out, so that a proper death ritual could be carried out.

The following day, the ritual to honor the life and death of Pogum was held. Every person in Shipapa-Lina was there to pay tribute to the fallen hero. After the burial, drum music played and a dance ceremony was done as a celebration of Pogum's legend. His loved ones had to deal privately with the great hero's death in their own way. For several days, Tawa withdrew to the Hanging Cliff, as he usually did when he desired to be alone to think.

On the third day, Pinga joined him atop the cliff. Most people knew when Tawa wished to be alone and respected that. Pinga, however, felt he needed her now. Tawa was happy to see her.

He stood and realized he was smiling. "Of all the sights in this terrible, wonderful world, no vision could be more welcome than that of you walking in my direction."

"Tawa flatters This One," Pinga said. "Your words make her heart race."

Tawa took her hand. "Your presence does the same for me. I look forward to these moments together."

"This One feared that Tawa would be despondent."

"I was until you came," Tawa said. "And I dread the day when you will come no longer."

"This One does not have it in her heart to leave this place," Pinga answered, rubbing her hand over his heart. "Her heart is drawn to yours."

Tawa kneeled to her. "Then perhaps we should make your stay more permanent. You should become one of the tribe. And the best way to do that is to marry the chieftain."

Pinga squeezed his hand. "This One used to walk in the clouds, but she never had a more wondrous home than Shipapa-Lina, and she has never met a more wondrous man than the *kik-mongwi* of Shipapa-Lina. Being your bride would be finer than being a Sky Elder again. This one accepts your proposal."

"I will marry a woman out of legend, and I will love you with the power of the blazing sun forevermore," Tawa said. "Let us turn this sad time into a joyous one."

Tawa stood at the edge of the cliff and loudly shouted, "I am Tawa of the Itiwana, and I am horribly in love with Pinga the Sky Elder! There will never be a pairing such as ours!"

1231 AD- The Long Debi-Kway Season of the Great Turtle's Trek

Tawa and Pinga had been married since the winter. Tawa was now the age of twenty summers and had been leading the Itiwana for four years. As the harvest time came, everyone was busy tending to the corn crop. Everyone except T'Soona, who had been called to deliver a child in the village. This child was special because it was the child of the chieftain and a former Sky Elder.

Pinga was in the Star Clan longhouse. She lay on a bed of straw, skins, and feathers. Tawa stood nearby watching T'Soona deliver his child. Although it had been only six months since it was conceived, the baby was ready to be born. Pinga was not a normal, mortal woman.

Although Pinga became pregnant after Bluebird, she gave birth first. As T'Soona pulled the baby from its mother's body, he wondered about this child. Pinga was a depowered Sky Elder and Tawa was a Mastop-Katchina with Oki energy. No one was sure what to expect.

The infant had snow-white skin, like its mother, but dark hair and eyes like its father.

"Congratulations, *kik-mongwi*," T'Soona said. "You have a son."

T'Soona handed the crying child to Tawa, who beamed proudly. "Hello Pahana, my son. Welcome to Shipapa-Lina. You will be loved here. And one day, you may rule here."

Pinga stretched out her hands. "This One wants to hold her son."

Tawa gently handed her the child. She stared lovingly at the fair-skinned baby.

"Our son," she said. "Our first child. Pahana is beautiful."

"He is indeed," Tawa softly agreed.

T'Soona studied the baby. "I've brought many a child into the world, and I cannot say that I've ever seen a finer boy. I wonder if Bluebird's child will be this cute."

"My son is unique," Tawa said, trying to stop the baby's newborn cries. "Don't weep, my little Pahana. You have a destiny, my son. You will accomplish great things."

As he said those words, the baby stopped crying.

At nearly that same time—the same day and same hour—the Painted White Girl was giving birth in the Earth Lodge. Some of the surviving Corn Maidens were in attendance to help with the delivery. The Green Corn Maid was also a midwife. The Painted White Girl was exceedingly glad for so many skilled hands to help bring her child into the world.

Nulia sat beside her and held her hand. She and the Painted White Girl had become good friends in the past six months. Nulia studied the newborn carefully. The child seemed mostly normal, and yet there was something about the eyes that was not quite right. The eyes reminded her of a wild animal. They were unnerving. She told herself she was simply imagining it as the Green Corn Maiden handed the baby to the Painted White Girl.

"Hobomok has a son," the Painted White Girl said.

"What will you name him?" Nulia asked.

"Hayoka," she said. "It was his father's wish.

The Painted White Girl gazed into the baby's eyes and saw the eyes of Hobomok looking back at her. She could feel Hobomok's spirit—as if he had been reborn in his child. *You will avenge your father one day.*

Seasons passed. The children of Tawa, Pogum, and Hobomok grew. Grey Pekwin passed away of old age. Tawa ensured his people were prepared for the next battles in the war of the Sky Elders. The Itiwana continued building the cliff housing, which would be easier to defend.

With the retreat of the Vykans, the war seemed to pause. The Sky Gods were immortal and to them, years were no more than moments. They waited and plotted and left the mortals to wonder when the war would resume in earnest. The Itiwana could only wait and wonder. Except for an intermittent attack by the few remaining Tunerak Destroyers or an occasional Skin-Walker searching for the tree, life was relatively tranquil in Shipapa-Lina.

The pause in war lasted for several years. The tribe, freed of violence, lived one day at a time, focusing again on farming. This quiet period allowed them to finally complete the complicated Cliff Housing, which made their home much more defensible.

Tawa never stopped thinking about the future trials he knew must come. What horrendous trials would his people have to deal with when hostilities resumed? He had no answers. Not even Manabazo could tell him what he longed to know. He therefore remained vigilant, forever planning for what would happen in the years to come.

In time, the war would explode once again in full fury. For now, the Tree of Life was safe and there was peace. But peace never lasts.

END OF BOOK ONE

ABOUT THE AUTHOR

R.J. Young has been everything from a dog groomer, to a custodian, to a hospital worker, but his one true love has always been writing. The son of an immigrant, he's had a life-long fascination with fantasy and sci-fi stories depicting exotic and astonishing locations. The first time he saw *The Wizard of Oz* at seven years old was like a magical experience. A journalism major in college, he enjoys writing online reviews and articles. R.J. loves discussing fiction with anyone who will listen.

COMING SOON/TEASER

In the **Sky Elders: Book Two**, Tawa and his teenage son Pahana continue the fight to defend Shipapa-Lina and the Tree of Life from continued assaults by the servants of Malsumis. Their new nemesis is Dagwona, the powerful Witch of the Whirlwind.

BOOK CLUB QUESTIONS
FOR DISCUSSION

1. What does this story say about the effect colonization has upon indigenous people?

2. Were you familiar with the mythology of the indigenous people of the Americas, and did this story give you an appreciation of it?

3. What does this story say about the relationship between fathers and sons?

4. Was Molowia right in her refusal to directly help the Itiwana in the war?

5. Did Hobomok have a legitimate grievance about the hierarchal structure of the Itiwana?

6. How did Pogum's body dysmorphia affect him?

7. What meant more to Tawa: Leading his people or living up to his father's legacy?

8. Were Bluebird's feelings for Pogum organic and genuine, or a result of the traumatic events she went through?